ABOUT THE AUTHOR

Cathryn Hein is a best-selling author of rural romance and romantic adventure novels, a Romance Writers of Australia Romantic Book of the Year finalist with *Santa and the Saddler*, and a regular Australian Romance Reader Awards finalist.

A South Australian country girl by birth, Cathryn loves nothing more than a rugged rural hero who's as good with his heart as he is with his hands, which is probably why she writes them! Her romances are warm and emotional, and feature themes that don't flinch from the tougher side of life but are often happily tempered by the antics of naughty animals. Her aim is to make you smile, sigh, and perhaps sniffle a little, but most of all feel wonderful.

Cathryn lives in Newcastle, Australia, with her partner of many years, Jim. When she's not writing, she plays golf (ineptly), cooks (well), and in football season barracks (rowdily) for her beloved Sydney Swans AFL team.

To discover more about Cathryn and her books, visit cathrynhein.com

Facebook: facebook.com/cathrynhein
Twitter: @CathrynHein

Also by Cathryn Hein

Rural Romance
Eddie and the Show Queen (coming 2019)
Elsa's Stand
The Country Girl
Chrissy and the Burroughs Boy
Wayward Heart
Santa and the Saddler
April's Rainbow
Summer and the Groomsman
The Falls
Rocking Horse Hill
Heartland
Heart of the Valley
The Horseman's Promise

Romantic Adventure
The French Prize

THE *Horseman's* PROMISE

CATHRYN HEIN

First published as PROMISES 2011

This edition published by Cathryn Hein 2017

ISBN 9780648000549

Cover Art by Kellie Dennis at Book Cover by Design www.bookcoverbydesign.co.uk

For Jim

ONE

THE AIR VIBRATED. The ground trembled. Hoofs collided with sodden turf in a rhythmic thump. Excitement pounded Sophie's chest, her heart racing with the horses. She narrowed her eyes at the oncoming rush of colour, a kaleidoscope of silk, horsehair, steaming breath and flying turf. As the field hit the straight, the small crowd – a mix of dedicated punters, horsey hangers-on and bored old-timers on a day out – began the gambler's chant.

Come on, come on, come on.

Sophie leaned across the rail trying to pick out Costa Motza. He was easy to identify, and not because of the broad white blaze streaking down his nose or his four muddy white socks. The horse was coming last.

The field passed, throwing up wedges of dirt and grass. The track rating was changing rapidly from 'Dead' to 'Heavy'. More rain and it'd be a quagmire. And dangerous.

Sophie shuddered and pulled her jacket tighter around her. It was freezing, a typical April day in South Australia's south-eastern corner. A day for sitting in front of a fire reading a book, not strapping at a country race meeting and, worse, working for nothing.

Hoof beats drowned her muttered 'Come on'. Costa Motza's jockey pulled out his whip and beat it against his mount's shoulder. Thwack, two strides. Thwack, one stride. Thwack, thwack, thwack.

Sophie frowned. The jockey needed to be careful or he'd end up in front of the stewards. The horse was clearly out of contention. Overzealous use of the whip on a horse that was coming last was unacceptable, even at the Harrington races.

That didn't stop Sophie barracking, but her so-called hot tip looked more like a pantomime pony than a thoroughbred. He lolloped past the post with his neck flattened and his tail up, as though exhausted from the sprint. Last by three lengths; twenty bucks wasted on a donkey.

She screwed up her betting slip and tossed it in a nearby bin. Bloody Danny Carlyle and his sure things. She weaved through the dispersing crowd toward the mounting ring to wait for Danny and his donkey.

'You sold me a bag of glue,' she said, grabbing Costa Motza's reins. The horse was blowing hard. Too hard. She frowned and checked his nostrils. They were blood-free, but running. The horse had a cold. Poor thing.

Unrepentant, Danny grinned at her. 'Nah, this one's dog food for sure.'

Sophie stroked the horse's nose. It wasn't his fault he ran last. No one felt like running when they had a cold. She walked him back to the stalls, wishing she'd had the foresight to bring a rug to throw over his back.

'Hold up.' Aaron Laidlaw, the horse's trainer, jogged to catch up with her, a wool rug draped over his arm. Concern crinkled his blue eyes, the colour deepened by the ominous sky and the navy rain jacket he wore over the top of a dark grey suit shiny with wear. His sandy hair, normally golden with sun streaks, lay dark and flat with rain against his skull. He tossed the rug over Costa Motza's rump and then moved to inspect the animal's nostrils as Sophie had done. 'Cold, poor bugger. I didn't want to run him, but the owner insisted.' He glanced at Sophie, as though checking to see if she believed him.

She nodded, one hand on Costa Motza's damp neck. That was the trouble with racing. Any idiot could own a horse.

'What will they do with him now?'

'Knackers, I suspect,' he said, walking long-legged and tall beside her. 'It's a shame, because he's not a bad horse. He'd probably make some kid a nice showjumper.'

'Don't look at me. There's only one horse I want to buy today.'

'You've got room for two.'

'No, I don't.' Sophie had two horses in training already, and if today worked out, she'd have three. Four was getting ridiculous.

'You know it's the knackers otherwise.'

'Don't try and sway me with that, Aaron Laidlaw. Racehorses go to the knackers every day. It's a sad fact of life.'

'Lovely temperament,' said Aaron, playing with the horse's ears. 'And he has a good sire.'

'I don't care if his sire's Octagonal and his dam's Makybe Diva, the answer's still no.'

'Nice paces.'

'No.'

'I've seen him jump. He'd make a great eventer.'

'Give it a rest.' Sophie ducked her head to hide her smile. She liked Aaron when he was like this, blue eyes sparkling, humour turning up the corners of his mouth. His rangy but muscled physique and slightly weathered looks gave him a certain rural ruggedness she found alluring. Then there was the added spice of the forbidden. According to her family, they didn't come much more forbidden than Aaron Laidlaw. Although no one would satisfactorily explain why. 'Can he jump over a five-foot fence from a standing start like Rogue Explorer? No? I didn't think so. You keep him if you think he's so good. I've got bigger fish to fry.'

They reached the stalls. Sophie walked Costa Motza inside and turned him around to face the quiet action of the race yard. She

pulled his lightweight bridle off and replaced it with a halter, keeping
a gentle hold of a cheek strap until Aaron clipped the holding chains
to the rings of the halter. Not that there was any chance of Costa
Motza going anywhere. He was too exhausted to do much more than
push against Sophie, hunting for a head rub.

Aaron let out a slow breath at the approach of Costa Motza's
displeased owner, a local small businessman who owned one of
Harrington's two electrical appliance stores and who appeared even
unhappier than his horse. 'Time to face the music. See if you can't
make him comfortable.' Aaron shook his head and gave Costa Motza's
nose a light rub. 'Poor bugger.'

Sophie stroked Costa Motza's cheek, pity for the animal and
shame at the fate that awaited him a rock in her chest. She touched
his soft nose and the velvety hairs that grew there. His breathing had
eased, but mucus ran from his nostrils in a watery stream. If this were
her own horse, she would have called the vet out for a look. Just to be
safe. But Costa Motza wasn't her horse, or Aaron's, and the owner
wasn't going to fork out for a vet when the horse was destined for the
glue pot. A fact driven home as scraps of the owner's conversation
drifted toward her, heavy with words like 'useless' and 'waste
of money'.

In a futile attempt to soothe her conscience, she took her time
rubbing the horse down, trying to provide some comfort to the
doomed animal.

When Costa Motza was dry, watered and rugged up in a double
layer of blankets, she turned her attention to the real reason she was
at the track. Her reward for spending a miserable Saturday at
Harrington Racecourse strapping for Aaron Laidlaw was a chance to
buy a racehorse. But not just any galloper. A horse she saw jump
clean out of Aaron's lunging ring from a standing start. Her jaw had
dropped so wide at the sight she'd felt like one of those open mouthed
clowns in a sideshow alley.

Rogue Explorer had bent back on his hocks, the muscles of his
glossy rump bulging like those of an oiled, steroid-enhanced Mr

Universe, and launched himself over the lunging ring fence. He hung suspended like a carousel horse before landing lightly and galloping off with the lunge rope still attached to his bridle, whinnying hysterically and creating havoc throughout the stable. Aaron had released a torrent of foul language that taught even broadminded Sophie a few new words.

That was her horse. Rogue Explorer. At least, he would be if the afternoon panned out the way she hoped. All he had to do was run last in the Harrington Hardware Open Steeplechase and she'd be taking him home to start a new life as a cosseted performance horse, destined, she hoped, for a long career on the eventing circuit. That was the deal she'd struck with Aaron two weeks ago. If the horse didn't perform, she'd hand over five grand and Aaron would sign the papers. But if he did run well, she'd miss out. It was as simple as that.

Three stalls up, her prize neighed loudly. She smiled and headed over to him. Aaron said he was a rowdy sod, forever calling out across the yards like an attention-seeking four-year-old. Which, in fact, he was, but she considered four the perfect age to take a racehorse from the track and mould it into an eventer. The horse was mature and had been around a bit, but not so long that its bad habits were unalterable.

Eventers had to be more than just talented jumpers. They had to possess the temperament to go from the tightly controlled discipline of the dressage and showjumping rings to the galloping aggression and quick thinking of a cross-country jumps course. All in one day, or, in the case of a three-day event, over three days. The sport required fitness, intelligence, bravery, trust and obedience, some of which was innate, but most of which came through intense training.

Sophie knew Rogue Explorer could jump. Whether he was trainable remained to be seen.

'I'm going to rename you Rowdy Explorer,' she said, shaking the horse's halter. He bobbed his head up and down as if in agreement, but Sophie knew it was just a sign of frustration. He'd been tied up for three hours and wanted out.

'Don't worry. You'll get your chance. Just as long as you remember to go slow. No showing off, okay?' She rubbed his head with her palm, and the horse responded in ecstasy, pressing against her hand with his eyes closed.

Pushing Rowdy – as she now decided to call him – gently away, she stooped to lift his foot, pulled a pick from the back pocket of her jeans and started cleaning the muck from his offside front hoof. The horse bent his head and brushed rubbery lips over her bum as though assessing it for bite-worthiness.

'Lucky horse,' said Danny.

Though out of his silks and smoking a cigarette, the jockey still had rides to complete and should have been confined to the jockeys' room. But Danny, it appeared, was a law unto himself.

He ducked under the chain and leaned against the stall's support post, blowing smoke rings toward the warm-up area. 'Can I do that too?'

She dropped Rowdy's hoof and swapped to his offside hind one. 'Bugger off, Danny.'

'Come on, you know you want me.'

'Only in your dreams.' After a moment, Sophie let go Rowdy's hind hoof and patted his rump. Heading back to the front of the stall she tried to brush past Danny, but the jockey blocked her way.

'I could help you get the horse.'

'Don't even think about it, Danny. You pull him, and you'll be hauled up. That wouldn't look good for Aaron, would it?'

'Oh, I get it. You've got a thing for the boss.' He leaned forward to stub out his cigarette and Sophie caught a whiff of smoke and something sour and foul, like teeth turning rotten. She stepped backwards, but Danny thrust out his other arm and she was trapped at Rowdy's shoulder. Instinctively, she leaned into the horse's warm body for protection.

Danny pointed a nicotine-stained finger at her. 'Believe me, the boss isn't interested in little girls like you.'

'Well, I'm lucky then, aren't I?'

'I've seen the way you look at him.' He sniffed, then tapped his finger against the side of his nose. 'Old Danny-boy doesn't miss much.'

'You'll be missing your pay if you don't let her get on with it.' Aaron stood behind Danny with his hands on his hips and his feet apart. He stepped forward, shooting a look at Sophie before settling his gaze back on the jockey. Behind him, Costa Motza's owner stomped off without so much as a farewell pat for his horse.

Danny slowly dropped his arms. 'I was just helping.'

'Yeah, well, piss off and help somewhere else,' said Aaron, his eyes narrowed.

Giving Sophie a smile that made her skin crawl, Danny pulled a cigarette from behind his ear and a lighter from his pocket, and lit up before sauntering off.

Without looking at Aaron, she bent down and tapped Rowdy's nearside fetlock. Obediently, he lifted his foot.

'Are you all right?'

'I'm fine. You don't have to worry. I'm a big girl. I can look after myself.'

He was silent for a moment, and she cocked her head to see if he was still there. He was staring intently at her. She returned to Rowdy's hoof, carefully scraping debris from around the rubbery wedge-shaped frog.

'Be careful with him. He's bad news.'

Which was exactly what her father had said about Aaron on more than one occasion. 'Dodgy, like his old man,' he claimed. Rodger 'the Dodger' Laidlaw had been warned off the track for life. The son, people whispered, was no different, but Sophie wasn't so sure. After all, Aaron had his trainer's licence and not a black mark appeared against his name. Or maybe it was like her father insisted and he just hadn't been caught yet. Somehow, though, she doubted it. Aaron didn't seem the horse-doping type.

She dropped the hoof and moved on to the nearside hind one. 'So why do you employ him, then?'

'He's a good jockey.'

Sophie straightened. 'He gives terrible tips.'

Aaron didn't smile. 'Just be careful,' he said, before walking away.

Sophie shook Rowdy's halter and whispered to the horse. 'Do I look like a delicate little flower to you, huh? Do I? You wait til I get you over to Vanaheim, then you'll find out how tough I am.' Rowdy snorted and blew a splodge of snot into her hair.

'Gee, thanks. Just what a girl needs to look good. Snot gel.' She wiped her hair with the sleeve of her jumper, and then pressed her cheek against Rowdy's, stroking the horse's silky neck. 'You and me, buddy, are going to be champions.' She pulled back so she could look into his face. Rowdy stared back at her with deep brown eyes and a slight, horsey frown. 'All you've got to do is run last and not get hurt in the process.'

She kissed his nose and began sorting through Aaron's bag of racing tack, thinking about the forthcoming race and the danger that Rowdy faced.

Steeplechasing could be perilous, especially when the track was slippery. A horse could easily suffer any number of career-ending injuries. In recent years, the sport had been cleaned up dramatically, but jumps racing, like any other racing, still held risks. She glanced at Rowdy. The way the horse proudly held his head, the tight muscles of his body under that sleek dark coat, the solidity and strength of his conformation, made him appear indestructible. He'd be fine. Of course he would.

Sophie lined the racing tack up on the stall rail, organising the saddle, bridle and breastplate, smiling as Rowdy nudged her in the back and whickered, as if he'd already claimed her as his new mistress.

'Don't count your chickens, Rowdy. You've got to make it through today in one piece first.'

The horse jiggled as she saddled him, nervous and anxious to be out of confinement. She talked to him as she worked, muttering nonsense, telling him about Vanaheim, his new home and the pleasures that awaited him there. Her yard and its modern stabling, special tack and feed rooms, and covered wash bay, complete with hot and cold water, made her chest puff with pride. It screamed success, and a successful eventer was what she wanted to be. Her father had spent a small fortune making her equestrian set-up perfect, but then, money was nothing when it came to his little girl.

Guilt money, Sophie called it. Money to make up for never being there. Money to make up for Sophie's mother dying. Meaningless money. All she had ever wanted was for her father to tell her he was proud of her, but he never seemed to have the time or inclination. It seemed that politicians were kept far too busy running the country to worry about their own families. Sophie told herself it didn't matter. Ever since she could remember, her dream was to run Vanaheim, the family farm, and ride and train event horses. Now she was living it. But her father's indifference still hurt.

'Come on, Rowdy,' she muttered as the horse blew out his belly when she tried to tighten his girth. Not wanting to get their relationship off to a bad start, she resisted the urge to knee him in the stomach, instead waiting until he became bored with the game and relaxed.

'He's a sod for doing that,' said Aaron, walking up and tugging the horse's forelock. 'A kick in the guts usually sorts him out.'

Sophie fastened the last buckle and patted Rowdy on the neck. 'I wanted to, but I didn't want to make him grumpy before his big race. He might do something stupid.'

'Nah, not this fella.'

Aaron removed Rowdy's halter, then grabbed a blue plastic bridle from the hook where Sophie had hung it, fed the bit into Rowdy's mouth and then slipped it over his ears. The horse chewed the snaffle and tossed his head in agitation. Sophie could feel the tension in his muscles. Rowdy knew what was coming, and it excited him.

Sophie watched Aaron as he finished fastening the bridle, then checked the tiny saddle and tightened its girth another notch. He was so much more interesting than her male competitors on the eventing circuit. The expense of the sport had led to a concentration of rich hobbyists, with slick looks to match their sleek mounts and equipment. Those who were off farms were either married or had been around forever, and she knew far too much about them. Any appeal they may have once possessed had long faded, and with her days occupied on Vanaheim tending cattle and horses, or maintaining the lush pastures, equipment and amenities, opportunities to meet other men were limited.

Despite Aaron having been her neighbour all her life, Sophie didn't know him very well. Her father and aunt's indoctrination about those 'rotten to the core' Laidlaws and local whispers about the deep enmity between the two families, the cause of which people either refused to reveal or passed off with a weak excuse, had made her wary. She held vague childhood memories of Aaron and her mother chatting comfortably when they all met out on rides, but her family's hostility toward the Laidlaws made her question if those memories were real. For years now Sophie and Aaron's interactions had been pretty much limited to discussions about escaping cattle, but she had noticed how quickly his moods could alter. One minute he'd be teasing her good-naturedly and then she'd say something and he'd shut her out with terse answers and a wary expression. It always left her feeling vaguely hurt, as though he'd somehow found her wanting.

'Are you right?' he said, interrupting her thoughts.

She nodded, letting her hand trail over Rowdy's silky-soft coat as Aaron led him from the stall. He handed her the reins at the warmup ring.

'He's nervous. Try to keep him calm,' he said.

Rowdy jogged beside her, champing on his bit and tossing his head. 'Don't worry, I know.' She placed her hand on his neck, and felt the sweat already rising on his skin. The punters wouldn't like that. Sweating up was considered a bad omen.

She expected Aaron to walk away, but he stood watching her, his hands in his pockets.

A little self-conscious under his gaze, she led a twitching, jog-trot-ting Rowdy onto the sandy track that was the extent of Harrington Racecourse's warm-up area, and started on the first of many circuits.

Eventually Rowdy calmed and resigned himself to being led round and round like a show pony. His ears twitched as he listened to Sophie talk about Vanaheim and eventing, and her other horses, Prince Charles and Bucephalus – or Chuck and Buck, as they were known in the yard.

'You've done a good job,' Aaron said, coming forward to take Rowdy's reins. 'He's usually sweating like a pig by now.'

They made their way to the mounting ring. Sophie walked at the other side of Rowdy's head, her fingers digging into the horse's mane.

This was make or break time. For both of them.

'He's probably bored rigid. I've just told him my life story.'

'I doubt it's boring, Soph.'

Sophie felt a jolt of surprise and pleasure. It was the first time Aaron had ever called her that. She normally loathed having her name shortened, but from him, it sounded good, like he just touched her with the warm hand of friendship. She looked at him over the top of Rowdy's head, but he was staring expressionlessly straight ahead. 'Do you think he'll win?'

'He's got a chance. He romped home in his trials. Danny reckons he was just getting wound up when he crossed the line, but the track was good on those days.' He looked up at the sky and frowned. 'I don't know in these conditions.'

Suddenly, Sophie felt frightened. 'I don't care if he wins or loses, I just want him to get round safely.'

'He'll be fine. I told you, he's a cunning bugger. Rogue Explorer knows how to get himself out of trouble.' He stopped just inside the mounting ring and passed her the reins. 'Here, you take him, but don't let Danny give you any of his rubbish. He's just trying to pull your chain.'

As he spoke, nine brightly coloured, bow-legged jockeys walked out from their room, cracking jokes and sledging each other, each trying to gain a psychological advantage. They separated as owners and trainers took them aside to give them last-minute instructions. Rowdy started up his nervous jog-trot again.

'The going's absolute shite,' said Danny, coming over to Sophie and pulling down the stirrups. 'There's bound to be a fall.'

'It's lucky you're on such a clever horse then, isn't it?'

'Just goes to show your ignorance. If a runner turns over in front of you, even the cleverest horse won't be able to save himself. That's why the knackery buyers love jumps racing. There's always plenty of horsemeat going cheap. Isn't that right, Todd?' he yelled to a passing jockey.

Todd turned his prune-like face to Sophie and grinned evilly.

'Knacker-fest,' he said, winking at Danny.

'Told you.'

'Bugger off, Danny. You're full of it.' But fear uncoiled itself in Sophie's stomach like a snake.

'You've got your instructions, make sure you follow them.' It was Aaron, behind her. Sophie felt him touch her lightly on the back as he took Rowdy's reins.

'Ten grand would go a long way toward keeping you in a job,' he said to Danny. 'Don't screw it up.'

Danny touched his hand to his helmet. 'Yes, boss.' He stood beside Rowdy with his hands on the saddle and one leg cocked, waiting for a leg-up. Sophie obliged, wanting to lift him hard so he fell over the other side, but Danny was awake to her and sprang easily into the saddle, winking at her as he settled.

'Keep him back until the four hundred,' Aaron said.

'Yeah, yeah. You told me.'

'Don't be an idiot. I mean it.' He dropped his voice, but Sophie could still hear him. 'You screw this up, and you're out, you hear?'

The smart expression slid from Danny's face. 'Yeah, I hear.' He turned Rowdy toward the gate. The horse broke into a tight, bouncy canter, his nostrils flaring and blowing steam like a benign dragon.

'Go safely, Rowdy,' whispered Sophie as she watched him canter up the track toward the barrier, fighting for his head and trying to unseat Danny with an occasional pigroot. 'Oh, God, I hope he'll be all right.'

Aaron squeezed her shoulder. 'He'll be fine.'

They took up a place on the fence close to the finishing post. Aaron had a pair of binoculars slung around his neck. She wanted to snatch them from him so she could watch the race in close-up, but as owner and trainer, Aaron needed them more.

As if reading her mind, he held them out to her.

She shook her head. 'Thanks, but I don't know if I could bear to watch. You can tell me what's happening.'

'Right, they're all at the barrier. Rowdy – I like that name by the way, it suits him – went in no worries, but number three's playing up. Nope, he's in now. There goes number six, Ballroomblitz, that's the favourite. Danny needs to watch him. Todd Markham's on board and he's won a few jumps races in his time. Mind you, he's been suspended a few times too. They're all in. Light's on.'

Sophie held her breath, waiting for the words. Aaron's came at the same time as the tannoy squawked into life. She jumped at the sudden noise.

'They're racing. Rowdy got away well. Steady, Danny, steady. Keep him in hand like I told you . . . Approaching the first . . . Over clean.' He pulled the glasses away and smiled at her. 'He's in fourth. That's good.'

She nodded, feeling sick.

'Okay, he's clean over the second and he's dropped back to fifth. That's where I wanted him. It'll give him a chance to settle into a rhythm.'

Sophie was only half listening. She stared up at the leaden black cloud hovering over the course. A fat drop fell on her cheek. She swiped it away, but it was replaced with another. Within seconds, the pelting rain had drowned out the racecaller's voice and cut visibility across the course to almost nothing.

Aaron pulled the hood of his coat over his head, but didn't move away from the rail. He glanced at Sophie. 'Why don't you go under the stand? There's no need for both of us to get wet.'

Sophie pulled up the hood of her own coat. 'No way. I'm staying. That's my horse out there.'

'Not yet, he's not.' Aaron lifted the binoculars back to his face but then dropped them. 'I can't see a thing.'

They squinted into the distance, trying to make out the field, but the rain was too heavy. They waited, shivering by the finish, water cascading off their coats and pooling at their feet. Snatches of the call came over the tannoy, but judging from its uncharacteristic vagueness, the racecaller's high vantage point offered no respite from the downpour. Then, just as suddenly as it started, the rain stopped. They strained their ears in the silence, listening for the sound of the field until a pounding, like the slow rumble of thunder, broke the quiet.

Bold Safari in the lead, followed by Ballroomblitz, then Zanic. Bringing up fourth is Favours the Brave a half head to Rogue Explorer. Coming up to the last jump before the straight . . .

Sophie clapped her hands together and held them to her mouth as though she was praying. Rowdy was still safe.

Aaron glanced at his watch. 'They should be hitting the bend any second.' As he spoke, glimpses of colour broke the gloom. The heads of mud-splattered horses and jockeys bobbed in unison as they galloped toward the line. Sophie felt a surge of hope. Rowdy would be all right.

Ballroomblitz in the lead, a half-length to Bold Safari with Rogue Explorer only two lengths behind and making ground . . .

'He's in third,' said Aaron, grabbing her arm and bending toward her. 'He'll win it now.' He turned back to the field, now approaching the penultimate fence – a straightforward brush.

Sophie was torn between wanting Rowdy to win for Aaron's sake, and wanting him to run last for her own.

Approaching the second last with five hundred to go and Ball-

roomblitz still in front with Bold Safari, a length and a half to Rogue Explorer, followed by Zanic who's tiring fast . . .

Ballroomblitz took off, but Sophie could see he had made the leap too early. Taking its cue from the leading horse, Bold Safari followed suit, while behind them, Rowdy gathered himself to do the same. As if in slow motion, Sophie watched Ballroomblitz hit the fence and fall forward with its neck outstretched. Its jockey stood in the stirrups trying desperately to keep the horse up, but even without the sharp crack of breaking bone, Sophie knew the fall was fatal.

Bold Safari tried to swivel in the air to avoid a collision, but his early takeoff meant he hit the fence full on the chest. The horse tilted to one side, flinging the jockey out of the saddle and onto the sodden turf, before crashing to the ground.

Rowdy instinctively shifted across, but he was too close and travelling too fast to avoid the carnage in front.

'Sophie, don't look!'

There was panic in Aaron's voice, but as much as she wanted to, Sophie couldn't turn away. She watched in horror as Danny gave Rowdy a hard whack across the rump with his whip, as if that would give the horse wings to fly over the flailing animals below. Rowdy jumped, his muscles straining with the effort of leaping the danger in front.

Rogue Explorer's made the jump . . .

For a blissful moment, as Rowdy hung gracefully in the air, Sophie thought he had made it, but as Rowdy's legs stretched toward the ground, she saw the prone jockey and her heart lurched.

Rowdy saw him too. Like a cat, he twisted his body to the side, shifting his legs so that they hit the turf centimetres from the jockey's head. But as his full weight came forward, his legs collapsed underneath him and he slammed into the ground, catapulting Danny out of the saddle.

Horse and rider lay still on the mud-soaked track.

Through the appalling silence, the only thing Sophie could hear was the sound of her own choked sobs.

TWO

FROM THE STANDS rumbled the slow murmur of shocked spectators, and the sound of tearing betting slips and crumpling paper. The punters turned away, washing their hands of the human and animal cost of their wagers, while old timers tsk-tsked and shook their heads at the waste of it all.

Sophie buried her face into the comforting bulk of Aaron's chest. She couldn't remember him grabbing her, but she was grateful for it all the same.

'I'm sorry, Soph,' he said.

She let out a shuddery sigh as she pulled away from him. 'Me too.'

The fall seemed like it had happened in a dream. She needed to see if it was true. Aaron tried to shield her, but she brushed past him, grabbed at the fence rail and leaned over it, her knuckles as white as the flaking paint. He touched her shoulder and then backed off.

Ballroomblitz lay motionless on the track. As Sophie watched, his jockey staggered to his feet, reaching out his hands as though seeking purchase in the heavy air, then reeling and collapsing onto his knees. Bold Safari was up, but stood quivering on three legs, his head lowered and his sides heaving. Sophie felt her stomach turn over at the sight. She put a hand to her mouth, but the spasm passed, although revulsion kept a tight hold of her insides. At the agonised horse's feet, the jockey remained motionless, his left leg bent at a sickeningly unnatural angle. Blood smeared his face as though he'd been draped in a scarlet shroud. Sophie looked for Danny. His blue and gold mud-splattered silks caught and flapped in the wind, but Danny didn't move.

Sophie's breath caught when she saw Rowdy. She stared at him, praying, hoping he'd feel the force of her will and lift his head. Never fall in love with a racehorse. That was the golden rule, and now she was paying the price. She stared at the sodden ground and let tears chill and numb her already frigid cheeks.

'I hate this stupid sport,' she said quietly.

'Sophie.' Urgency coloured Aaron's voice.

She looked up. Despite everything, he was smiling at her. He pointed at the track.

Rowdy was sitting up, his forelegs stretched out sphinx-like in front of him. With a final heave, he stood upright and shook himself like a labrador after a swim. He turned his head from side to side, surveying the scene, then cantered off down the straight, squealing and pigrooting, swerving around the clerk of the course's grey gelding to avoid capture.

'Oh my God.' Sophie grabbed Aaron's arm, jumping up and down on the spot in excitement and grinning idiotically. 'He's okay! He's okay!'

'Yeah,' said Aaron, smiling at her. 'I told you he knew how to get himself out of trouble.' He turned back to the track and frowned. Sophie followed his gaze. Paramedics were leaning over Danny. It looked serious.

'Come on,' said Aaron. 'You go and sort out Rowdy. I'll see if there's anything I can do for Danny.'

Sophie nodded and jogged off to the mounting ring. The red-faced clerk had caught Rowdy and was leading the still whinnying animal back along the track. His placid grey calmly trotted alongside as though he'd seen it all before and didn't know what the fuss was about.

'Noisy bugger, isn't he?' the clerk said as he handed Rowdy over to Sophie.

'Yeah. He never shuts up, but at least you know he's alive.'

'Which is more than can be said for those two,' said the clerk, staring down the straight. A portable sightscreen was being erected in front of the horses. He looked back at Rowdy. 'I'd get him checked over if I were you. He took a pretty big tumble.'

'Don't worry, I will.' Rowdy let out one last high-pitched whinny as the clerk rode away before turning to Sophie, pressing his head against her chest and using her as a scratching post.

'If you don't mind,' said Sophie when his bridle caught on her breasts, but she didn't have the heart to stop him. She was too pleased to see him alive and in one piece. When he'd finished, she gave him a quick inspection, running her hands down his legs and checking to see if he flinched. Rowdy didn't move.

'Come on, then, miracle man. Let's get you undressed and sorted.'

Rowdy was rubbed down and rugged up by the time Aaron arrived, and alternating between blowing hot air on Sophie's face and trying to nip the horse in the stall next to him.

'How is he?' Without waiting for a reply, Aaron ducked under the stall chain and started running his hands over Rowdy's legs.

'He seems fine. I can't find anything wrong, but I suspect he'll be a bit stiff tomorrow. How's Danny?'

'Not good, but at least he's conscious. They're taking him to hospital now. Suspected punctured lung. Bold Safari's just been destroyed. Snapped cannon bone.'

Sophie shivered. That could have been Rowdy's fate. She reached out to stroke his nose. 'So what now?'

Aaron bent back under the chain and stood next to her, surveying Rowdy. 'You can go home, I guess.'

'But what about the rest of the horses? You won't be able to look after them on your own.'

'Sophie, I've been doing this a long time. I'm pretty sure I can manage. Anyway, don't you have an event tomorrow?'

'It's just a pony club one-day event, and I'm only taking Buck. I can stay and help.'

He looked at her with raised eyebrows. 'Aren't you a bit old for pony club?'

Sophie experienced a prickle of embarrassment. At twenty-two, she felt too old for pony club, especially on the rare occasions she arrived at a rally and ended up knee-deep in fat woolly ponies. But her membership gave her extra events to compete in, plus occasional access to some of the country's best instructors and riders, and she wasn't about to give it up.

'I can stay a member until I'm twenty-five,' she said.

'Really? I didn't know. I never got the chance to go to pony club. I always wanted to though.'

Sophie looked at him curiously. She'd never suspected he'd be interested. 'So why didn't you?'

His features turned wary, as though she had stepped over an invisible line. She felt the sting of hurt that always affected her when he looked that way. She bit her lip, and wished she'd learn to keep her mouth shut.

'As if I needed to explain.' He pushed his hands into his pockets and stared at his feet. Then, as if realising his rudeness, he straightened. 'Look, Sophie, I don't need you any more. Pony club or not, it'll still be a long day tomorrow. I can sort this lot out.'

She swallowed, feeling wretched and confused. Why did he assume she knew all about him? She knew nothing except the malicious gossip her father spouted on the rare occasions he let his politician's mask slip.

'I'm sorry,' she said. 'I didn't mean to pry.'

'I know. You don't have to apologise. It's me. Screwed-up childhood. Kinda messes with your mind.'

'Oh.' She grinned at him, trying to ease him his discomfort. 'Well, I suppose that makes two of us then.'

'Shit, I can't believe —' He stopped and swallowed, his eyes full of the pity Sophie had long grown used to seeing in people's faces when they remembered that her mother had died when Sophie was only twelve. 'Christ, Sophie. I'm so sorry.'

She shrugged. 'It's okay.'

He eyed her for a moment, his mouth tight, as though to keep himself from speaking until he'd carefully weighed his words. 'I remember her, you know.'

Sophie's heart pulsed with longing. She loved hearing about her mother. It'd been ten years since Fiona Dixon's suicide, and though Sophie tried to keep her memories vivid, time had turned them dull and fragmented. She chased any solid recollections she had through her mind, wanting to tattoo them to her brain for fear they'd be lost forever.

She tried to keep the hunger out of her voice. 'What do you remember? Did you like her?'

'Yes. She was sweet and very pretty. I didn't see her often, just sometimes in town or when we bumped into each other out riding. She always stopped to talk, though, and ask how I was. Your mum was kind and caring.' He stopped, swallowed and then continued. 'When I was young, I used to wish she was my mum.'

Sophie turned away, blinking, and fondled Rowdy's delicate muzzle. It was comforting to know someone else had been drawn to her, had wanted her for his own. Sophie always knew her mother was special.

'Your mum's suicide. Your old man keeps it quiet, doesn't he?'

Sophie felt a flutter of panic. 'You won't spread it around, will you? I think Dad worries people will blame him for it.'

'It wasn't all his fault.'

'What do you mean?'

'Nothing.' He stepped away from the post and scuffed a foot in the dirt, not looking at her. 'Forget it.'

'Aaron —'

Without warning, Rowdy sank his teeth into her hand.

'Oh, you shit!' She yanked her hand away and inspected it for damage. A neat line of teeth marks dented the ball of her thumb. Rowdy tossed his head up and down in the equivalent of an equine 'gotcha'.

She grabbed his halter, pulling his head down until she could look him in the eye. 'That's one bad habit you're going to unlearn, mister. I don't care how bored you are, my horses don't bite. Full stop. You understand?'

Rowdy stared at her dumbly.

'Listen, Soph, about Rowdy,' said Aaron.

Sophie glanced at him. There was something in his tone. 'What?'

He made as if to speak, but then shook his head. 'Nothing. It doesn't matter. Look, there's not much point you hanging around. Why don't you head off?'

Sophie hesitated and then nodded. It was getting late. She'd see Rowdy again soon enough and if all went as planned, the next time it would be as his proud new owner.

———

Six kilometres north-east from the centre of Harrington, a line of thick-trunked London plane trees marked Vanaheim's southern boundary. Past branches decorated amber and russet with autumn leaves stretched two hundred and forty undulating hectares of varying shades of green, divided by well-maintained fences and newly established windbreaks of native trees and shrubs. In the paddocks near the road, red and white Poll Hereford cows and heifers with March drop calves at their feet chomped contentedly on pasture made rich by early autumn rains and good management. Though she'd seen it countless times, it was a sight that rarely failed to lift Sophie's spirits.

At a break in the tree line, a burgundy-painted mail drum with

Vanaheim stencilled on the side in white letters signalled the entrance. Sophie indicated and turned her Range Rover into the crushed-limestone lane, smiling when Chuck's dark brown head and then Buck's lighter bay one sprang up at the sound of an approaching vehicle. She wound down the window to wave to them.

Chuck's nostrils flared as he released a welcome-home whinny. The two horses trotted toward the post-and-rail fence, heads and tails up, rugs flapping. Sophie gave them a quick once-over, checking for any lameness or change in attitude that might indicate they weren't feeling well. Both moved easily through the long ryegrass and clover of the front paddock – the smallest on the property and which, except for when she occasionally allowed a few cattle in for weed control, Sophie maintained exclusively for the horses.

Grinning at their joyous welcome, she blew them a kiss, and watched them cavort and snap playfully at one another as they followed the car down the lane.

Even bereft of leaves, the tree-lined lane was one of the things she loved most about Vanaheim. It reminded her of happy times, when she could still feel the all-encompassing love of her mother. Fiona Dixon had adored the drive as much as Sophie. In the summer, when the trees celebrated life with a spectacular display of verdancy, new growth stretched across the lane until it touched and tangled in the centre, like lovers reunited after a long, cold winter. The lane grew shadowed and cool against the hot sun and Sophie would run around the trunks playing hide and seek with her mother, laughing in the dappled light.

Sometimes, when Sophie had been good, Fiona would turn into the driveway, stop the car and look at her grinning daughter. Are you ready? she'd say, and Sophie would giggle and strain against her seatbelt, trying to reach the play button on the car's stereo.

The distinctive opening bars of Bruce Springsteen's 'Tunnel of Love' would fill Sophie's head and heart. It was a romantic song, not really one for mother and daughter, but back then, Sophie was too young to draw much from the lyrics other than their literal meaning.

Fiona would drive at ambling pace, prolonging their special time together. They'd sing to the music with smiles on their faces, Sophie convinced she had the best mother in the world.

At the lane's end, they'd emerge blinking into the bright sunshine, and Fiona would lean across to Sophie, kiss her forehead and say, 'The tunnel of love's over now, my precious.'

Sophie smiled sadly at the memory. Her mother had been right, although Sophie didn't understand that for a long time. The Tunnel of Love was over for Fiona Dixon, because at the end of that enchanted drive lay Vanaheim, and an existence consumed by a secret illness that eroded her happiness like acid until there was nothing left but a hollow, dismal shell and no hope for the future.

Vanaheim's majestic lane opened to a wide, flat expanse of crushed limestone. To the right, following the line of the lane, stood a burgundy Colorbond multi-bay equipment shed housing the farm's aging tractor and other assorted machinery, Sophie's horse float, the battered farm ute – when her aunt Tess remembered to replace it – and the farm's latest acquisition, a state of the art pasture seed drill. Beyond the shed, on a stretch of laser-levelled ground and surrounded by a white timber fence, was Sophie's all-weather riding arena. Next to it was a flat, grassy area containing a brightly coloured selection of showjumps, and a series of white, thirty-centimetre high cavaletti, over which her mother had first taught Sophie and her stubborn pony Toby to jump.

Left of the drive, where the crushed limestone gave way to neat brick paving, stood Vanaheim's pink dolomite and limestone bungalow, fronted by the pretty cottage garden Fiona Dixon had once expertly tended and Sophie less expertly tried to maintain. Opposite stood a simple stable complex, in the same steel as the equipment shed, with the three stables and concrete wash bay set back so the burgundy-painted timber half doors were sheltered by a verandah. From the eaves hung empty flower baskets. Summer would see these spilling over with pink and white impatiens, brightening the yard with happy colour.

A squat limestone building, once an exterior laundry and toilet block, took up the far side of the paved square, its wide door and two small window frames painted burgundy to match the stables and house. A heavy lock secured the door, while metal grilles covered the windows protecting the thousands of dollars worth of equestrian equipment, veterinary supplies and feed kept inside.

As Sophie drove in, her two incurably lazy Australian cattle dogs, Samson and Delilah, raised their heads for a moment before returning their chins to their paws, too comfortable on the back porch to move. A stranger wouldn't fare so well. One step toward any of the buildings and the dogs would be standing to attention. Sammy and Del might be lazy, but they were fiercely protective of their mistress and home.

Sophie reversed the Range Rover toward the float and left the engine running as she hitched it and checked the brake and taillights worked. Satisfied, she towed it into the main yard ready for loading and went to bring the horses in for the night.

Chuck and Buck were waiting for her by the gate, jostling with one another to be the first to greet her, their heavy body and neck rugs making them look like cartoon medieval chargers. She unlatched the gate and kissed Chuck's dark-brown nose, laughing as Buck bunted her back in annoyance at being ignored. Unlike Chuck, who was the sweetest-natured horse Sophie had ever encountered, Buck's temper changed like the wind. At least he seemed in a good mood.

She led them both to their stables, Chuck, as always, rubbing his muzzle against her sleeve in welcome. He was such a gentleman. Sophie didn't know what she'd do when she finally retired him. She'd miss his steady politeness and unwavering affection at events. Even when Buck was throwing one of his tantrums, Chuck always managed to cheer her, but perhaps in the future it would be Rowdy who gave her comfort.

Once the horses were settled, she loaded the float and Range Rover with all that she'd need for the following day. The process didn't take long. Most of her competition gear was already packed in sturdy, lockable trunks. It was simply a matter of lifting them into the rear of the four-wheel drive. She would place the saddles – each costing almost as much as what Rowdy was worth – in the tack compartment of the float in the morning. Even with the dogs on guard, Sophie didn't take chances with her saddles.

Although twilight was falling, she grabbed a thick coat and whistled for the dogs, and marched across the yard to the machinery shed and quad bike. With Sammy and Del perched on the back of the bike, she rode east into the dull sunset, past the old redgum stockyards, now silver with age, and her aunt Tess's limestone cottage with its constantly drawn curtains and overgrown garden, to where the cows and heifers grazed. Calving was mostly complete but a few late-joined heifers had yet to drop, and though Tess had promised to inspect the cows regularly, Sophie liked to double check.

Another heifer had given birth that afternoon. The white-faced calf hung close, eyeing Sophie from beneath its mother's belly and letting out a nervous cry. Both mother and baby looked fine, as did the remainder of the herd. She sighed and sat for a while, admiring them. Come the following January, the steers and those heifers she chose not to retain would be sent to Harrington's annual weaner sales, where Sophie was trying to build a reputation for producing quality animals. Over the last couple of years Vanaheim's weaners had brought home solid prices, but with a change to yard weaning she could earn more by producing feedlot-ready cattle. Without improvements to the old yards, however, like many ideas she had for Vanahaim, yard weaning remained something for the future.

Leaving the cattle, she motored back to the house, grinning at Sammy and Del as they leaned around her, ears pinned back, eyes squinting and jowls wobbling, enjoying the rush of wind as only dogs can.

After a last check and chat with the horses Sophie headed inside. She pulled her boots and jacket off in the laundry and placed them neatly away before padding down the bungalow's tiled hall, grimacing at the cold seeping through her socks. Out of sheer habit, she paused at the entrance to the kitchen and glanced left toward the end of the hall, where the door to the main bedroom stood open. The room appeared as it always did, with the bed made up and well-dusted photos of Fiona Dixon arranged just so on the bedside table. No overnight bag rested on the floor and no coat had been tossed on the plain white spread. Ian Dixon hadn't blessed her with one of his lightning visits – given their relationship these days that was hardly unusual.

Sophie looked quickly away, but the memories still crowded in. When she was in her early teens, he'd turn up once a fortnight and stay for a few days, sometimes even for the weekend. He'd always be busy – attending meetings, visiting businesses, talking to his constituents, dealing with those things on the farm her aunt Tess couldn't. Leaving the house early in the morning and returning late at night, after Sophie had gone to bed. Sometimes, she'd wake in the night with her skin prickling and the sense he was in her room, but when she probed the darkness he was never there. Checking his room in the mornings, she'd find the bed hardly slept in, as though he'd laid rigid all night on the surface, staring at the ceiling.

Sophie hardly saw him, but he made a point of sharing breakfast with her, and while their conversations were often interrupted or centred on banal topics such as the weather, at least she had a sense of him trying to be a father. Now, bar a visit every few months, an occasional brief phone call or abbreviated email, he didn't bother.

But she still kept the bedroom prepared. Just in case.

Her mobile phone sat on the hall table beside the house phone where she'd left it that morning. Sophie used it so rarely, most of the time she forgot its existence. As usual no one had called or texted, and the empty screen left her feeling hollow. She'd shot an email to her father's personal account last week advising him of Sunday's competition, but it seemed he'd forgotten to wish her luck again. Sometimes he called, mostly he didn't bother, and though she was unsurprised, it still hurt.

Dumping the phone, Sophie padded into the kitchen looking for something to eat. Though the house was almost a hundred years old, Fiona Dixon had set about spending a small fortune modernising it once her father-in-law's deteriorating health finally forced him into a nursing home. Where darkness once dominated, light and colour had taken over. Red and white tiles extended from the entrance to a glossy off-white kitchen with red granite benchtops and expensive stainless-steel appliances. She'd removed the wall separating the kitchen from the dining room, and divided the opened-up space with a breakfast bar. Past it, the red and white tiles gave way to lush cream carpet on which sat an oak eight-seat table with comfortable chairs upholstered in matching red fabric, and an oak sideboard filled with now rarely used white china.

Through a door on the left was the lounge, Sophie's favourite room, and where she spent most nights snuggling in her mother's old leather recliner next to a glowing gas log fire, reading horse magazines or agricultural journals, or watching television. Like every other room in the house, photographs featuring Fiona Dixon took pride of place, but the five arranged on the built-in shelves above the television were the ones Sophie loved the most. Each showed the Dixons as a family, grinning at the camera. Happy.

Sophie picked up a note from the bench. Aunt Tess wanted her to call when she came in. Given the stock and horses were fine, it could only be about her day with Aaron. She chewed at her nail, considering whether to call or not. This time of night Tess could be in any state, but avoiding her might make her angry, and Sophie was too tired to deal with that. With a sigh she put on the kettle and picked up the phone.

'Well, did you get him?' asked Tess, sounding surprisingly sober.

'Pending a vet check, yes.'

'Good. And how was your day with Aaron Laidlaw?'

Sophie thought before answering. Aaron blew so hot and cold, she wasn't sure. 'It was interesting.'

'I'd say it'd be interesting, with him. I don't suppose you caught him sticking speedballs up his horses' bums, did you?'

'I don't think he's like that, Tess.'

Her aunt sniffed. 'You ask your father about the Laidlaws.'

'What is it about Dad and the Laidlaws, anyway? Aaron looks at me like I'm the devil's daughter sometimes.'

'A long story and one I'm definitely not prepared to tell. Like I said, you'll have to ask your father.'

Sophie picked at a loose thread on her jumper. More secrets. What was it about her family and bloody secrets? Even Aunt Tess had them. She hated Vanaheim, yet here she stayed, year after year in misery, drinking herself to death. And the excuse that she was there to look after Sophie no longer washed. Sophie was twenty-two, not twelve. Besides, these days Tess was barely capable of looking after herself.

Worried her aunt would snap if she sounded too desperate, Sophie took a moment to choose her next words.

'Tess, do you know if Aaron would know anything about Mum's death?'

'Why? What did he say?'

'Nothing, I was just wondering, that's all. He mentioned in passing that he knew her.'

'Don't you listen to anything Aaron Laidlaw has to say about this family, and especially about your mother. He doesn't know anything.'

'But he knew her, Tess.'

'Don't be ridiculous. Your mother wouldn't give a Laidlaw the time of day.'

'But —'

'Oh, don't start, Sophie. If you've got issues, go and see that shrink of yours, or become an alcoholic or drug addict like a normal person. Just don't bother me with them.'

Tears pricked Sophie's eyes. She could never accustom herself to Tess's dismissive nature, so different from her mother's sensitivity. After years of counselling, she'd reconciled herself to the fact her mother committed suicide because of acute clinical depression. But

Sophie could rationalise all she liked – the niggling doubt that she was somehow to blame could never be talked away.

After her mother's death, her father and Tess had hidden the truth from Sophie, using terms such as 'tragedy' and 'accident' to describe something indescribable. And then, when the word 'suicide' somehow slipped through the web of her family's insularity, the horror of learning the truth was followed by years of thinking that her mother had committed that appalling act because of her. That she must have been a terrible child, that her mother hadn't loved her. A belief reinforced by her father's coldness and lack of affection toward his only child.

Sophie didn't blame her father for her mother's death. Fiona's illness made her do what she did, but Sophie still hadn't forgiven him for treating a confused and grieving teenager like a monster. She never would.

'Do you need a strapper tomorrow?' asked Tess in a placatory tone, as if she knew she'd overstepped the mark.

'No. I'm fine on my own. I'm only taking Buck. Will you be right to keep an eye on the heifers?'

'Of course I will. I'm not completely useless, you know.'

But given her aunt's problem, on that point, Sophie could never be too sure.

———

After the misery of Saturday's weather, Sunday dawned frosty and sparkling before turning bright with the rising sun. Knowing Buck preferred Chuck's company while travelling, Sophie unloaded the lone horse after the hour-long trip to Beachport with some trepidation, but his mood appeared as favourable as the day. To her astonishment and relief, he stood calmly next to the float and accepted her fussing with uncharacteristic equanimity.

His good mood continued through the dressage, as he pranced around the ring and completed the complex series of movements with look-at-me bounciness, leaving Sophie slapping his neck in delight and racing for the scoreboard to see how they'd fared. His performance placed them second behind long-time competitor Michelle Vickers and her talented up-and-coming mare, The Debutante. But to Sophie's surprise, The Debutante floundered on the cross-country course, running-out when Michelle attempted to take a tight apex jump over its corner, adding twenty penalties to her score, and leaving the lead open for Buck.

He didn't let Sophie down. Buck cruised around the cross-country course at speed, hurtling over the jumps as though they barely existed, and leaving Sophie ecstatic as he thundered through the finish line under time and with a penalty-free round behind him. Now all they had to do was complete the showjumping course clear and they'd win.

'Bad luck about Deb,' said Sophie as she joined Michelle while they waited for their turn in the showjumping.

Michelle shrugged her narrow shoulders, as philosophical as always. 'My fault. It was a tight fence and I should have taken more care.' She reached out a skinny arm to scratch Buck's mane. Michelle was tall and model-thin, confounding Sophie as to how she had the strength to ride. Everything about her appeared angular, from her pointed nose to her bony hips, but she possessed a good-humoured personality that belied her sharp looks, and Sophie enjoyed her company. Out of all the riders she knew, Michelle was the closest thing she had to a friend.

'Buck went well,' said Michelle with a smile.

'I know, but the day's not over yet. I just hope he doesn't do what he did to me at Naracoorte,' Sophie replied, remembering the humiliation of her last event when Buck, irritated that Sophie had gone off with Chuck and left him with an empty water bucket, had descended into an equine sulk of epic proportions. Her confidence soaring after a clean cross-country round with Chuck, who was in second place, Sophie had mounted Buck and entered the showjumping ring unaware of his foul mood. She blithely saluted the judges, gathered up the reins and then proceeded to plough through every jump. She cantered through the finish flags red-faced and furious, only to have Buck live up to his name by dumping her neatly in front of the judges' box, and then stand regarding her with a 'that'll teach you to be smug' look on his face.

For appearance's sake, Sophie had laughed it off, but inside she had seethed. If he did it to her again, she swore she'd sell him. But it was an empty threat. Vanaheim was like a horsey black hole. Once you went in, you never came out. No matter how badly her horses behaved, she couldn't bear to part with them. A fact she sometimes suspected Buck knew.

Michelle regarded her with sympathy. 'Yes, he definitely gets it over you sometimes but I can see why you stick with him. He's got talent. So are you taking them both to Lake Ackerman?' she asked, referring to a major one-day event held across the border in Victoria over the Anzac Day long weekend.

'All going well.' Sophie winced as in the ring a delicate-looking rose-grey horse skidded to a halt and brought a big oxer crashing down.

'Apparently it's Jamie Howard's twenty-first birthday that weekend and he's organised a bit of a party at the Commercial Hotel on the Saturday night. You should come.'

'I haven't been invited.'

'You don't need to be. It's automatic.' When Sophie didn't answer, Michelle added, 'They're not all monsters, you know.'

Sophie looked at her in astonishment. 'I never thought anyone was.'

'So why not join in for once?'

She swallowed. Why not? She loved the horsey scene but when it came to socialising her scars ran deep, and her habit of keeping to herself was a difficult one to break. Even after all this time she found it hard to trust people, no matter how kind they were to her.

'I'll see.'

The look on Michelle's face told her that she knew Sophie wouldn't come.

With the competitors competing in reverse order, from last to first, Sophie had to wait for all the other riders to complete their rounds before she entered the ring. Despite her rattling nerves, Buck remained calm as she warmed him up, staying nicely on the bit and listening to her leg aids. As she rode toward the judges' box she experienced a flurry of hope that her contrary horse would jump clear and win.

She saluted, gathered up the reins and eased Buck into a tight canter. 'Come on, Buck, my boy. Let's show them what you're made of.' And with that instruction she urged him through the start toward the first fence.

Buck leapt over the opening four jumps as easily as he had the cross-country course, approaching each with his ears pricked and head up. With space at a premium, the course designer had created a tight layout, with several twists and turns, requiring careful riding for the horse to keep its balance.

On landing, she let him take a stride to steady before shifting her weight and giving the aid to switch his leading leg. Eyes focused ahead, she directed him around a sharp turn and lined him up for a series of related fences running down the long side of the arena. A quick adjustment of his stride and he was placed for takeoff at the exact place she wanted, leaving him with a perfect four strides to the second spread fence and another three to the final pink and white gate. Buck cleared the first two fences without a rattle, and motored at pace toward the gate, five strides away. As soon as he landed, she gave another aid to change leg and direction before lowering her weight deep in the saddle and driving him toward a maximum height and width oxer. With a haughty shake of his head, he sailed over.

Two more simple fences followed, with neither posing a problem for Buck. Not letting her concentration lapse for a moment, Sophie held him collected through the last turn. Only a double, both elements maximum height and separated by two strides, stood between Buck, the finishing line and victory. Positioning the horse perfectly at the first upright fence was crucial. Take off too early and Buck would struggle to reach the second oxer comfortably, which would then put him at risk of a run-out or dropping a pole.

Sophie had walked the course with care, measuring strides between fences and working out where she'd need to tighten Buck or give him more rein. But as he came off the turn and saw the finish, Buck charged forward in excitement, his stride lengthening. Sophie checked him, expecting him to fight and put in at least another long stride, but to her dismay he came to hand immediately, muddling her split-second calculation. Though she tried to correct him, they approached the fence out of stride, forcing Buck to put in a little hop and take off close to the base. With a grunt he heaved himself up, Sophie urging him on with her seat and hands. He cleared the top rail and landed cleanly but came down so tight on the other side he was left no choice but to try and insert three short strides in a space designed for two.

As soon as took off, Sophie knew they were gone. They were simply too close. The front rail of the oxer fell with a clatter, the back rail falling almost immediately after. Buck cantered through the finish line snorting and tossing his head while Sophie shook her own in disappointment. In her heart, though, she couldn't help but feel elated by his performance. Buck had done his best.

Things were looking up.

Hakea Lodge was quiet when Sophie pulled in on Monday morning. She sat in the Range Rover, peering through the windscreen and wondering where to find Aaron. Rugged horses hung their heads over the rails of their yards and stared at her with curiosity. Like Vanaheim, Hakea Lodge was arranged in a quadrangle, with a wide-verandahed limestone cottage set back from the road, utility and feed rooms at right angles, and two whitewashed stables opposite. Sand-filled open yards, fitted with three-sided corrugated iron shelters and backed by aging pines, extended from the stables to the east, ending with a lunging ring dug into a sandy slope. But where Vanaheim sparkled with colour and care, Hakea Lodge, though scrupulously clean, drooped with tiredness. An effort had been made here and there – a painted horseshoe on the feed-room door, a camellia planted in an old wine barrel by the stable – but overall, the yard had the melancholy appearance of a place doing it tough.

Sophie walked up the stairs to Aaron's back door, excited at the prospect of taking Rowdy home. Before she could knock, the door opened.

'Hi,' said Aaron, stepping onto the verandah. 'I've just made a cuppa. Do you want one?'

'I'd love one, thanks. Knowing Justin, he'll be late,' she said, referring to the vet she'd booked to inspect Rowdy and make sure he was sound. She waited for Aaron to wave her inside, but he remained where he was, looking grim. Unease slithered up her spine and spread across her neck in a rash of goosebumps.

'Rowdy's all right, isn't he? Don't tell me something's happened to him? Oh, God. I knew I should've stayed.'

'No, no, it's nothing like that. Rowdy's fine.'

'Well, what then? Something's up, I can tell by your face.'

'Look, Soph, there's been a change of plan. Rowdy's not for sale.'

'*What?*'

'I'm sorry.'

Sophie couldn't believe what she was hearing. 'Is this some sort of joke?'

He shook his head.

'But you promised. You specifically said that if he ran last, I could buy him. You can't get much more last than falling.'

Aaron spoke with infuriating calm. 'He would've won if it wasn't for the fall.'

'You don't know that.'

'Come on, Sophie. You saw him. He would've bolted home. That horse proved himself talented enough to win the Springbank Cup.'

Fury made Sophie tremble. She wanted to stamp on his foot, or kick him in the shins until he was left hopping on one leg from the pain. It had never occurred to her that he would renege on the deal.

'I should've known you'd never keep your word. My father's right. You Laidlaws are nothing but cheats.' She glared at him and then stomped down the stairs and across the yard to her car, slapping her hand against the aluminium side of the horse float as she passed. At the sudden noise, the yard came alive with the snorts and clatter of startled horses.

'Sophie!'

She ignored him and climbed into the Range Rover. He banged on the driver's side window, yelling at her to open up. She started the engine, staring straight ahead, so angry her head felt like it was about to burst. Aaron opened the rear door and slid along the seat.

Sophie whipped around to glare at him. 'What do you think you're doing? Get out of my car.'

'I'm not proud of what I'm doing, Soph, but the yard needs winners to keep going. That's why I can't sell him.'

'Well, I wasn't exactly taking him for free, was I?' She pulled an envelope from her shirt pocket and waved it at him. 'Five grand's hardly nothing.'

'It's not just the money,' said Aaron softly. 'Winners attract owners and quality horses, and I need more if Hakea Lodge is going to survive. And if there's one thing I care about, it's that. If that means I have to break our deal, then I'm sorry.'

Sophie felt her anger evaporate and resignation settle in its place. She'd have to look for another horse. Rowdy's days as a steeplechaser weren't over yet. 'I just had my heart set on him, that's all.'

He gripped her shoulder. 'I know. There'll be others. You'll see.'

Sophie stared at her hands. She'd been so excited, and now she felt miserable. He was right, of course. There would be other horses, but not like Rowdy. He was special. He would have made her a champion. People would have noticed her, loved her even. Patted her on the back and told her how good she was, how talented, how *proud* they were.

'I'd better call Justin,' she said. She dug around in the console for her phone. 'How's Danny?'

'Not good. He'll be out of action for a fair while.' Aaron sighed heavily. 'I don't know what I'm going to do. I can't afford to hire another stable jockey. It'll cost a small fortune just to get one for trackwork.'

Sophie stopped scrolling through her contacts and twisted around in the seat to face him. 'I can help. I can't do trackwork, but I can do your fitness training.'

He shook his head. 'I can't afford to pay you.'

'You won't have to. We'll make a deal.'

He regarded her with suspicion. 'What sort of deal?'

'I'll help you here, but at the end of the jumps season, you sell me Rowdy for the five thousand we originally agreed on.'

He didn't say anything, just stared out over the yard.

'Come on, Aaron. It's a good deal. We both get what we want.'

He turned back to her. 'What about your horses?'

'You'll only need me in the mornings. I can work them in the afternoons. The only time you'll have to do without me is when there's a competition, and I'm turning the horses out at the end of April, so I can't see it being a problem.'

'You trust me enough to sell you Rowdy at the end?'

Sophie grinned, knowing she had her deal. 'Don't be daft. This time, I'm going to get it in writing.'

THREE

.

AARON SWORE as water shuddered through Hakea Lodge's aging pipes. He twisted off the tap and stared out of the kitchen window at his mother's overgrown and tangled vegetable garden. Ten years she'd been gone and yet some plants still survived, as though her spirit lingered, like a shadow that kept him from ever enjoying the warmth of the sun.

Pumpkin seemed to dominate everything, but thistles, marshmallow and the brown stalks of frostbitten mint were putting up a fight. Against the limestone-block fence that separated the garden from the yard and sheltered it from the prevailing wind, a warped row of tomato stakes stuck out at angles, like a giant's version of the children's game Pick Up Sticks. In the centre of the plot, slowly losing its battle against time and neglect, stood a solitary thorned Lisbon lemon tree, its fruit speckled with brown olive scale and dusted with sooty mould. An allegorical Hakea Lodge – still standing, still enduring, but crying out for attention.

Aaron tried the tap again, this time letting the water run until the air cleared the pipe. He filled the kettle and put it on the hotplate of the kitchen's combustion stove, and stood by the oven warming himself.

On the table sat Sophie's agreement. She'd worked fast, dropping the envelope around Tuesday lunchtime with a cheery smile, confident he'd sign. He'd read it twice and still didn't completely understand it. The solicitor's torturous language made his head swim. When Sophie had said she wanted the agreement in writing, he wasn't expecting a contract written in legalese.

We highly recommend you seek independent legal advice regarding this matter.

As if he could afford a solicitor. He could barely afford the vet. Or the farrier. Or the feed supplier.

The solicitor had covered everything, from how Rowdy's future winnings would be distributed to what would happen in the event Hakea Lodge became insolvent. From Aaron's understanding, ownership of Rowdy transferred to Sophie the moment he signed the contract. A peppercorn lease arrangement allowed him to race the horse and keep the majority of his winnings. If Hakea Lodge went under, he couldn't even sell Rowdy to keep the yard afloat, although Sophie's five thousand would be released from the solicitor's escrow account. Too bad if the horse was winning everything in sight. But then, if Rowdy was winning, he'd have owners knocking on his door and Hakea Lodge wouldn't be in financial difficulty.

He pinched the bridge of his nose and then dug his knuckles hard into his forehead. He should have known better than to deal with a Dixon. They had caused him and his father nothing but trouble.

But he owed Sophie. More than he hoped she would ever know.

———

At eight the following morning, Sophie's Range Rover pulled up like a sleek, expensive show pony alongside Aaron's world-weary carthorse of a Land Cruiser. Aaron stood on the verandah with a cup of tea in his hands, watching her. He'd called her Tuesday evening to say he'd signed and then spent a sleepless night worrying about her presence in the yard. Whether she could handle the horses. Whether she would be able to handle him.

He took a sip of tea, using the mug to cover his smile when he saw her outfit. Slip a black riding coat on her and she'd look set for a day's hunting in the English countryside.

'Hi,' she said, climbing the stairs to join him on the verandah. 'Thanks again for signing the contract. I was worried you wouldn't. I couldn't believe it when I saw it, but the solicitor assured me it was necessary. What did yours say?'

'I didn't consult one.'

She cocked her head at him. 'Why not?'

Aaron didn't reply.

She slapped a hand to her mouth and stared at him wide-eyed. 'Oh, I'm so stupid. I'm sorry, Aaron. I didn't think.'

She seemed genuinely remorseful and Aaron was pleased. He wanted to be able to think of Sophie as different from her father and aunt, more like the sweet-natured woman he remembered her mother to be. From his limited experience, it seemed she was, but then he reminded himself that she carried half her father's genes and he realised it would take a lot more than one show of contrition to offset over ten years of distrust and loathing.

'It doesn't matter,' he said. 'Do you want a cuppa?'

She looked at him with clear grey eyes – all youthful good health and enthusiasm that made him feel like a grizzled old man, even though he was only four years older.

'No, I'm fine, but thanks. Shall we get started?'

'If you want. You brought a helmet?'

Sophie nodded.

'Okay. Go and grab that chestnut over there. The one in the blue rug.' He pointed to one of the far yards, where a chestnut horse was attacking its timber enclosure with rodent-like vigour.

'What's his name?'

Aaron grinned. 'American Psycho.'

She cast him a look that told him she knew what he was up to, but otherwise didn't comment. Instead, she stepped down from the verandah and strode purposefully across the yard toward Psycho, only stopping to plant a kiss on Rowdy's nose as she passed his stable.

Aaron felt a stab of guilt, but he needed to test her mettle. If Sophie was hopeless, it was better to find out now, and there was no tougher test than Psycho.

———

Aaron held the front gate open for Sophie before shutting it and remounting. He had to admit she sat well, although in his opinion, her stirrups needed shortening. She was exercising a racehorse, not competing in a dressage contest.

Psycho danced and pranced and snorted beneath her, but she sat calmly, her hips absorbing every sudden movement. She didn't resort to sawing at his mouth, but her legs were firm against his sides and Aaron could tell from her intense expression that she was focusing hard on the horse.

She wore elastic-sided short boots with leather zip-up gaiters over her jodhpurs. Even on this dull day, they shone with quality and careful polishing. In the yard, she'd donned one of the new, expensive and highly unflattering helmets that had just hit the market, so huge and round it seemed like something had laid an egg on her head.

He pointed to the full body protector she'd strapped herself into, which looked tough enough to take a bullet and made her appear like something out of an American cop show. 'You're not taking any chances.'

'It's for the insurance,' she said, looking sheepish. 'I had to take out another policy to cover me while I was riding your horses.'

He nodded. That was good news. The section of the contract that dealt with personal liability had been almost unintelligible – another reason he'd spent all night tossing and turning over whether he'd just made the worst decision of his life. One fall could mean the end of Hakea Lodge.

Aaron had no doubts about the pleasure Ian Dixon would derive from suing his sorry arse, sending him broke so Hakea Lodge would have to be sold. What a day for celebration in his Canberra household that would be. No more bitter-hearted Laidlaws hanging over Vanaheim's back fence casting judgement, or watching his daughter with their guilt-ridden eyes. He'd have finally ruined them all.

'Psycho by name, psycho by nature, huh?' said Sophie as her mount shied at a plastic bag and skittered sideways into Aaron's horse.

'He's all right once he knows who's boss.'

She grinned. 'I'll just have to show him then, won't I?'

They trotted away from the gate, keeping to the roadside verge and following a track made hard by countless hoofs. In the spring, when the ground dried out a little, Aaron would take the old tractor and go over it with the harrows, just to loosen the soil and make it easier for the horses. For now, he had to make do with keeping to the grassy sides. Sophie, he noticed, did so without direction, but then she was as familiar with the track as he. It was where she worked her own horses.

They maintained a slow pace, easing the horses into their exercise and following the gravel road toward the east. After an early frost the day had risen fine and cool, but pleasant. Drops of moisture glittered on the barbed-wire fences separating the road from the paddocks lining it. Historically, this was beef cattle country, interspersed with the occasional dairy farm, but the dairy farms had long disappeared and even beef properties like Vanaheim were hard to find. The area's proximity to Harrington, combined with an exodus of traditional farming families from the land, had led to an influx of hobby farmers and cheap horse agistments.

Just last spring, the old man who'd run Simmental cattle on a few hundred hectares across the road from Aaron died, leaving the property to be split among his three children. Sensing a fat profit, they'd divided the holding and sold it off in twenty- and fifty-hectare lots. Now, on the rise opposite Hakea Lodge, a local high school teacher was constructing a double-storey cream-bricked home. He'd only owned the land since the start of December, but already his two paddocks were covered in plastic-sleeved native saplings, well rooted after being conscientiously watered over the summer to ensure their survival until the autumn rains. Then a month ago, in March, to his neighbours' amusement, the teacher introduced a small herd of black-coated Lowline cattle. Now miniature cattle grazed among miniature trees, and the landscape looked like something a child might conjure up.

As Sophie and Aaron passed, one of the Lowlines raised its head and mooed loudly. Aaron shared a smile with Sophie. The metre-high beasts might be excellent beef producers, but to old-style farmers, it was still hard to take them seriously.

Half a kilometre along, where the gravel road veered away to the right, they turned to the left and onto a sandy firebreak separating the two halves of a small radiata pine plantation. A steady incline stretched ahead. Psycho fought to be let at it, wanting to tear up the slope as if the land around Harrington were a battlefield where every hill needed to be taken at speed. Sophie held him, but Aaron could see it was hard work.

The horses were blowing when they reached the top, and Aaron eased back to a walk. Both horses were coming back from a three month spell. He didn't want to overdo it; they'd be sore enough as it was.

'I forgot to ask,' he said as Sophie drew alongside. 'How did you go on the weekend?'

A broad grin split her face, transforming her. Sophie had mousy hair, fair skin – she was really nothing out of the ordinary – but Aaron had noticed before that when she smiled, she radiated joy. He wondered where it came from. He'd drained his own reserves at sixteen.

'Fantastic! Buck was a champion. We would've won, but I put

him at the double in the showjumping wrong and he pulled a rail. I knew I was right to persevere with him. When he's bad, he's completely diabolical, but when he's good . . .' She sighed. 'You can't help but love him.'

Aaron smiled at her. She talked about the horse as though he was the most important thing in the world. 'So when's your next event?'

'I've got another pony club competition this Sunday and an unofficial showjumping day the following Saturday. Then Anzac Day weekend I'm taking Buck and Chuck to Lake Ackerman for a CNC one- and two-star event.'

'A what?'

'A one-day event,' she said, rolling her eyes at him with feigned exasperation. 'Don't you know *anything*?'

Aaron would have laughed except Psycho, noticing Sophie's inattention, put in a series of bucks even he would have had trouble sticking. Sophie was almost unseated, but with surprising strength for someone so slight she hung on, hauled Psycho's head up, and gave him a hefty kick in the guts. Psycho snorted and tried again, but she kept him reined in until he settled.

'Well done,' said Aaron. 'If that was me, I'd probably be walking home by now.'

He was fascinated to see her turn pink at the compliment and it made him wonder if it was because she rarely received them, or because he'd given it. The unrestrained delight on her face made him wish the latter.

'I'm getting better at staying on,' she said. 'Buck still catches me unawares sometimes, though. He's a bugger for dumping me when he knows it'll cause the most embarrassment. It got so bad I thought of selling him, but after Sunday, I don't think I can.'

The sand deepened at the bottom of the slope. The horses lumbered through it and then started to jog when the track firmed. Aaron's circuit never changed. Ahead of them was a long flat strip of even footing, and the horses were eager to stretch their legs. Psycho chewed his bit and broke into a tight bouncy canter.

'Keep a hold of him,' Aaron warned. 'If he gets away from you, you won't stop him.'

She nodded, her jaw tensed, and he wished he'd gone easier on her, given her a different horse. He urged his mount into a canter, but kept his eye on Sophie. She loosened Psycho's reins slightly and the horse lunged forward, thinking he was free. When he realised he wasn't, he gave a petulant pigroot.

To Aaron's surprise, she leaned forward and slapped Psycho on the neck. 'Is that the best you can do?' she asked the horse. Then she sat back and grinned at Aaron. 'Is this the worst horse in the stables, or is there another Psycho hidden away somewhere?'

'He's the worst.'

'Good, because I don't think I could manage more than one Psycho a day. My arms are killing me.'

They cantered until the next corner, Psycho still fighting for his head and throwing in the occasional pigroot, but more or less behaving. The track turned west, running parallel to the other half of the pine plantation until it gave way to the dilapidated barbed-wire fences of Hakea Lodge's rear boundary.

The paddocks were diabolical. Here and there, an aging tussock of cocksfoot fought against the encroaching bracken, but little else thrived under the carpet of fronds. Occasionally, in the spaces bracken had yet to colonise, traces of clover sprouted vivid green against the sour, yellowing pasture, saved by the legume's natural ability to fix nitrogen. No cattle grazed the land. Worried his animals would waste too much precious energy trying to keep warm – energy they couldn't replenish through grazing – and lose too much condition over the coming winter, Aaron had sent the last of his small herd to sale a few weeks ago. With no grazing stock, the paddocks looked even worse than usual.

He saw Sophie frown at the sight.

'I know it's a mess,' he said, feeling the need to justify Hakea Lodge's appalling condition. 'Trouble is, pasture renovation isn't exactly a priority at the moment. I'll get the slasher onto it in the spring. Maybe hit it with some glyphosate.'

She shook her head. 'Your soil's too sandy. The rhizome system will be enormous. Too extensive for a systemic herbicide to have a lasting effect. You're better off with a program of slashing, although you could try it in conjunction with spraying, I suppose. In which case, Brush-Off would be a cheaper option.'

She gave Psycho a warning kick as he skittered sideways and tried to wrench the reins out of her hands, then steered him back parallel to Aaron's horse. 'You need to do something. The worse it gets the harder and more expensive it'll be to fix.'

Aaron stared at her in amazement. 'Since when did you become a farmer?'

She shrugged. 'Since I realised Tess was usually too drunk to look after Vanaheim properly.'

He burst out laughing, frightening Psycho, who bounced away, nostrils flared and eyes rolling. Sophie brought him under control, and ran a soothing hand down his neck.

'I've always thought your aunt was a piece of work. Now I know why. What does your father say?'

'Nothing. I don't think he knows. Or if he does, he doesn't care. Anyway, he can't get rid of her. Who else would he get to babysit me?'

'I think you're a bit old for a babysitter.'

'Yeah, you'd think so, wouldn't you? But apparently I need someone to keep an eye on me.' She scratched at Psycho's mane. 'I can never figure out whether it's because Dad's actually worried about me, or whether he thinks I need a jailer.'

'I'm sure it's the former,' said Aaron, but now that she'd mentioned it, he started to wonder. Maybe Ian Dixon did want to keep his daughter locked away at Vanaheim. After all, he'd hardly want her spoiling all his fun in Canberra.

'Come on,' Aaron said, kicking his horse into a trot. 'We'll be all day at this rate.'

The track followed a linear path until it struck a T-intersection. Attached to a skewed post was a road sign, the black letters barely legible. Dixon Road was hardly a road, more a cutting between two properties. The difference was stark. On one side, Hakea Lodge in inglorious dishevelment, broken-fenced and sour-pastured, while opposite – verdant, fertile and lush – lay Vanaheim.

They turned to the left, toward the main road and home, the horses sensing the end and a final gallop. Psycho started up his bouncy canter and head tossing again.

'You'll really have to watch him on this bit,' said Aaron, as Psycho yanked at the reins, nearly pulling Sophie out of the saddle.

'Okay, but he seems to have settled down now. He should be all right.'

Aaron hoped so. From the way Psycho was chewing his snaffle, he didn't look settled at all. 'I'll stay close.'

There were two hills on this, the third side of the square circuit they were riding. The first was a short rise followed by a long, gentle descent and then a flat run of a hundred metres or so before the second hill began. The gradient was much steeper there and the slope didn't end until Dixon Road intersected with the main road. At its top, Aaron usually brought the horses back to a walk before turning left and riding along the verge back to Hakea Lodge's front gate.

The horses stayed neck and neck initially, but on the first descent, Psycho started living up to his name. He threw three hefty bucks that left Sophie clinging to his mane with one hand and yanking hard on the reins with the other. Realising that Psycho wasn't just testing her, but throwing a genuine temper tantrum, Aaron kicked his horse alongside and reached out to grab the left-hand rein. As his fingers touched the leather, Psycho snorted and ducked out of reach.

'It's okay,' panted Sophie, hauling on the reins to no avail. 'I've got him.'

'No, you haven't. The bastard's got his tongue over the bit,' yelled Aaron as he reached for the reins again. But Psycho had no intention of being restrained now he had control. He jerked his head forward, knowing Sophie could yank all she wanted and it wouldn't make any difference, and then bolted.

Aaron let his mount have its head and tried to keep up, but Psycho had too much of a head start. At least Sophie wasn't panicking. In fact, Aaron got the feeling she was almost egging the horse on. She leaned forward in the saddle, the reins firm but not pulling, and let Psycho run.

Aaron was glad this had happened on the home stretch and when Psycho was still unfit. In racing condition, he'd cart her all the way around the block again, but at his present fitness level, the pull up the hill would slow him down and give her back some control.

He kept on their heels but his horse was tiring fast and soon lagged behind, and he could only watch in horror as Psycho reached the top of the second hill and, still galloping, swerved sharply left. Sophie tipped to the side, and he was sure she would fall, but she stuck to the saddle and straightened. Then to his utter amazement, she kicked Psycho hard in the sides.

'What the hell are you doing?' he yelled, but his words were lost on the wind.

Psycho tore down the hill toward Hakea Lodge. As he neared the gate, he slowed, steadying himself for the sharp turn into the lane.

'Sophie, the gate!'

Unless Psycho had spent his three-month spell secretly learning to jump like Rowdy, there was going to be trouble. Big trouble.

Aaron didn't know if Sophie had heard him, but she must have remembered they'd closed the gate when they left, because she kicked Psycho onward and sat up in the saddle to pull on the right rein, using what little control she had to keep him from turning left. It worked. Psycho passed the gate at a gallop, stumbling only slightly as he crossed from grass to gravel and back to grass again. Their silhouette soon faded into the background of dark pines.

Sophie still hadn't returned by the time Aaron made it to the gate. He expected Psycho to be run out by now, but when he rode onto the road and squinted toward the corner, he couldn't see the horse. Not knowing what to do, his resolve swung between riding after her and heading back to the yard for the Land Cruiser.

Five minutes later, he still couldn't spot her. He cantered to the end of the road and then up the firebreak's first rise, his heart pounding and his throat thick. No Psycho. No Sophie. He looked into the rows of pines but the dense thatch of rotting needles remained smooth and undisturbed by hoof marks.

He considered riding to the next corner, but if she was lying injured he would then have to race all the way back to the yard to grab the four-wheel drive and call for an ambulance. And if she was seriously hurt, she might need immediate treatment and the time he might waste fetching the car could mean the difference between life and death.

Thoughts of horrific injuries, of blood and broken bones, or worse, ghostly silence, swirled through his mind. It would be his fault if something happened to her. There was no one else to blame.

Just as with her mother.

'Not again,' he whispered. His conscience wouldn't cope with the weight of another tragedy. He'd destroyed enough lives as it was.

Why had he put her on the horse in the first place? Because he'd been angry about the stupid contract. Because it had reminded him of the two people he hated most, instead of reminding him of the duty he owed to the person whose life he'd ruined.

With one selfish, pigheaded act, he'd broken the one promise he'd sworn to keep; the only penance he could pay to a twelve-year-old girl whose haunted eyes carried the guilt that should have been his to suffer alone. He was meant to look after Sophie, not hurt her.

He stared into the distance and blinked, unsure if the figure he could see was Sophie. A chestnut horse trotted around the corner and headed toward him. As it came closer, he took a deep breath and bowed his head, not wanting her to see the utter relief he felt at her reappearance.

'So,' she said, easing a sweating, blowing but much chastened

Psycho to a halt beside him. 'Did I pass?'

'*Pardon?*'

'Did I pass the test you set me?' When he didn't reply she smiled at him. 'Come on, Aaron. I know you put me on Psycho to see how I'd cope. So, how'd I go?'

He ducked his head, shaking it and smiling. 'Don't worry, you passed, but that's the last time you're riding that nutcase.'

'Why?' she asked, leaning forward to slap Psycho on his neck. 'He knows who's boss now.'

Still smiling, Aaron turned his horse and they ambled back toward Hakea Lodge. Psycho managed one last shy at a discarded Coke can, but it was cursory rather than determined, a half-hearted attempt at dominance from an already mastered animal. At the gate, they both dismounted and walked the horses up the drive.

'Tell me something,' said Aaron, looking at her. 'Why did you kick him on? You could have gotten yourself killed.'

'Mum taught me to do that, when I first learnt to ride. I had this really fat Shetland pony called Toby, and old Toby had been around the block a few times. Generally, he was bombproof, but sometimes – usually when he'd been put on one of his starvation diets and had spied food – he'd take off on me.' She grinned at him. 'I'd start screaming and crying that Toby was bolting, which was rubbish, of course. Toby's top speed was something like a slow trot. Anyway, Mum would yell at me to kick him, kick him hard. Keep him going until he's so tired he can't be bothered arguing any more and will do anything you say.'

'And it worked?'

'Nah, not with Toby.' She wiggled her eyebrows at him. 'But you'd have to say it did with Psycho.'

Aaron laughed, and decided that, despite everything, having Sophie around the yard mightn't be so bad after all.

———

They worked two more horses before heading inside for a well-deserved cuppa. Aaron leaned against the sink watching Sophie as she inspected the pictures covering his kitchen walls.

The majority were photographs of horses – horses winning races, in the mounting yard, in the winner's enclosure, carrying blue- and gold-silked jockeys to victory. Photographs from Hakea Lodge's glory days, when Rodger Laidlaw was still alive, in the aching lost time before he drowned himself in disappointment and drink. There were others too. Pictures of Aaron and his father, grinning at the camera. Young, happy. Images to remind Aaron of his penance, of what he owed the innocent.

Sophie moved slowly past them, sometimes touching their frames, as if she didn't think the images were real. They were real enough, but from another life. A parallel universe Aaron could only see through a fog of regret.

She leaned forward to read the writing on one of the largest pictures.

'Wow, a Group winner,' she said. 'I didn't know that.'

Aaron crossed his arms. 'It was a long time ago.'

She ran her eyes over the rest of the photographs as though looking for something. 'Don't you have any photos of your mum?'

He removed the whistling kettle from the stove and poured boiling water into the two mugs he'd placed on the sink. 'No.'

'She was probably always holding the camera, like mine. She moved away when you were young, didn't she?'

He put the kettle back on the stove and turned to eye her, expecting artifice or at least mischievousness. Surely she was joking? But her expression said otherwise. She smiled at him with innocent eyes and a face free from guile. Honest, sweet and almost childlike. He swallowed and turned back to the mugs, staring into one, watching the teabag stain the water.

'To Canberra,' he said. He reached for the sugar and closed his hand around the bowl, waiting for her response.

'Oh, really? I wonder if she ever bumps into Dad? Canberra's not that big. Where does she live? Dad's got an apartment in Turner, just north of the centre.'

Sophie didn't know.

Aaron wanted to put his hands against his ears to block out her voice. Instead, he looked out of the kitchen window, at Carol Laidlaw's neglected garden. Anger seethed in his head, coating his vision with a red mist, churning in his stomach like a cauldron of boiling bile.

When the horses were worked and Sophie was gone, he would plough that rotting garden back into hell where it belonged. And when that was done, when the last remnant of his mother's corruptive existence was finally removed from his sight, when he'd worked the rage out of his system and rationality was once again ordering his mind, only then would he try to figure out what to tell Sophie.

Or if he would tell her anything at all.

FOUR

SOPHIE WAS WRONG. It took less than half a day for word to
reach her father. He called, but neither Vanaheim's house phone nor
Sophie's mobile rang. Instead, Ian Dixon rang his faithful attack dog.

Sophie had just finished working Buck in the all-weather riding
arena and was walking him back to the stables when her aunt turned
up. In typical contemptuous Tess fashion, she brought her old Toyota
to a halt by disengaging the clutch and letting the ute coast into a
fencepost, as if brakes were too precious to waste on something as
pedestrian as stopping a vehicle. Sophie gritted her teeth. It was all
right for Tess, she wasn't the one who'd have to get the crowbar and
strainer out to fix the post. Sophie had a good mind to change every
fence post on the farm to concrete.

Tess picked her way across manure-strewn pasture toward her,
but stopped a few metres short. She wasn't Buck's greatest fan and
Sophie knew the feeling was mutual. Buck disliked Tess intensely,
which was probably another reason Sophie persevered with him
when deep down she suspected she and the horse weren't suited.

'My enemy's enemy is my friend, hey, Buck,' Sophie murmured,
stroking his neck as he propped and peered goggle-eyed at Tess.

Tess stood with her arms crossed over what appeared to be one of her brother's old flannelette shirts, as though she thought wearing Ian Dixon's clothes would give her authority. She needn't have bothered. Tess couldn't convey authority if she tried. Not with her baggy, bloodshot eyes and trembling hands. The wind whipped rats' tails of unbrushed grey-streaked brown hair around her head and pushed her too big shirt and ragged jeans against her gaunt frame. Although only in her forties, she looked twenty years older, and so thin one strong gust would see her tumbling end over end like an uprooted weed. There once existed a time when Sophie considered Tess good-looking, like Sophie's father, but those days had long passed. Alcohol had exacted its toll.

Sophie went on the offensive. 'I take it Dad called. Now, why aren't I surprised? What is it this time?' She held up her hand. 'No, don't answer that. Let me think for a moment. Is it because I was rude to that pig, David Williams, or is it because I bought a racehorse?'

She cocked her head at her aunt and was surprised to find Tess's eyes clearer than usual, though still full of the spite that seemed to grow worse each day. Tess had never been motherly, but she'd looked after Sophie well enough, at least until Sophie's dark years broke their relationship irreparably. Ever since, Tess had been hostile, no matter how much Sophie tried to make up for the pain she'd caused. Now, her aunt seemed to treat every encounter like a battle, and Sophie was beginning to tire of it.

Tess's cold, Dixon-grey stare told her this wasn't going to be a run of the mill telling-off. This was serious. Sophie pressed her legs into Buck's side, urging him forward and forcing Tess to follow, albeit at a safe distance from Buck's hindquarters.

Sammy and Del circled Sophie's legs when she dismounted in front of the tack room, and she reached down to give them each a pat. Despite their chronic laziness, the heelers always seemed to know when she needed comfort. She removed Buck's bridle, slipped a halter on him and tied his lead rope to a loop of bailing twine attached to a hitching rail.

Tess remained silent, but Sophie knew she was using the time to decide tactics. Emotional blackmail would be the order of the day. Either the 'think of your father and his position' argument, or, if Tess really wanted to make a point, she'd fall back on the 'your mother wouldn't have liked this' remonstrance. The latter was pulled out only rarely because it involved mentioning Fiona Dixon's name, and if there was one thing Sophie knew, it was that Tess did not like talking about her late sister-in-law.

Sophie tapped Buck's offside fetlock. Obediently, he lifted his foot so she could pull off the rubber bell boot he wore to protect his heels from overstepping. Still waiting for Tess to speak, she dropped his leg and crouched down to unzip the Velcro fastening of his boot.

'I suppose you've got some sort of crush on him,' said Tess.

Sophie blinked. That parry was unexpected. She ducked under Buck's neck to start on his other leg.

'Gigantic crush,' she said. 'He's gorgeous.'

Sophie heard Tess's sharp breath. Two could play her dirty game and Sophie had a feeling this was about to get very dirty.

Tess took a step closer, her shirt flapping in the breeze. Buck shuffled his feet.

'Sophie, I'm only telling you this for your own good. Keep away from Aaron Laidlaw. You know how fragile you are, especially when it comes to men.'

Sophie stilled. She took two long breaths and exhaled slowly. She couldn't let Tess see how much that barb had stung.

'I was referring to the horse, Tess.'

'Are you sure about that?'

Sophie carefully placed Buck's boots in a pile by the hitching post, trying to maintain her temper, but Tess had smelled blood.

'You know what happened last time you got involved with someone unsuitable. We don't want a repeat of that, do we?'

'That was seven years ago. And what would you care, anyway? You probably still wish I'd done a better job of it.'

'Oh, don't be ridiculous, Sophie. That's just the sort of reaction

I'd expect from you. Maybe you ought to go and see that shrink of yours again.'

Sophie turned her back on Tess and busied herself with running the stirrups up the leathers of Buck's saddle. Anything to stop herself from screaming, or turning on her aunt and doing something she'd regret. She was *not* screwed up. There was nothing wrong with her. She'd neither seen nor needed Dr Charlton for over five years.

'So where's this new horse of yours?'

Sophie realised Tess didn't know about Costa Motza. As far as Tess knew, the only racehorse she'd bought was Rowdy.

'He's staying at Hakea Lodge for the time being. Aaron wants him to finish the jumps season. I'll take him after that.'

'In that case, why are you hanging around that place?'

That place. Not Aaron's, not Hakea Lodge, not even 'the yard'. *That place.* Like the words were poisonous.

'Aaron's stable jockey's out of action. I'm helping exercise his gallopers.'

'I see.'

Tess poked a mottled blue and pink big toe at a piece of moss growing between the yard's pavers, and Sophie realised her aunt wasn't wearing any boots. Tess must have come straight over after hearing from her father. She tried to remember if parliament was sitting, but couldn't. She hoped it was; otherwise, unless she placated Tess now, the next visitor she received would be Ian Dixon.

Buck snorted and pulled against his lead. Sophie stroked his neck. He was becoming bored and probably cold. She lifted up the saddle flap and unbuckled the girth, then pulled the saddle off and took it into the tack room. Tess followed her.

'You don't have to worry. Aaron barely speaks to me,' said Sophie over her shoulder as she placed the saddle on a wooden horse. She picked up a bucket of brushes and turned to head back outside, but Tess guarded the door. Outside, the dogs whined.

'Excuse me,' said Sophie, trying to brush past. 'Buck's getting cold.'

Tess's eyes were hard on hers. 'Just remember he's a Laidlaw. Imagine if the press discovered the country's future Minister of Primary Industries' daughter was hanging with a criminal.'

'Aaron's not a criminal. And besides, you can't stop me. Not any more. I'm immune to your stupid games.'

'Just like your mother. Selfish. You don't care who you hurt by your actions.'

'That's not fair.'

She gave Sophie a penetrating look. 'Isn't it? I'd say you and your mother have caused enough damage to this family without adding any more.'

With her barb well and truly lodged, Tess stepped back into the yard and, giving Buck a wide berth, walked off to her ute, bare feet slapping on the pavers.

When the Toyota had disappeared down the lane Sophie sat down on the step, shaking – but not from the cold. The heelers sat at her feet staring up at her. It wasn't until Del put a paw on her knee in doggy comfort that the tears came. Maybe Tess was right. Maybe she was selfish.

But for how long would she have to keep paying for the mistakes of the past?

———

The bed was a snarl of twisted sheets when Sophie woke the next morning after a restless night, and her mood didn't improve when she ventured outside. Tess had left the gate to the hayshed paddock open. Fortunately, it was only the pasture hay the cattle had gotten into, not the lucerne hay, but that was bad enough. Tess and her father had let the paddocks degrade years before, and even with all the work Sophie had done renovating them with careful summer grazing rotations, Vanaheim, like everywhere else in the south-east, still suffered a summer and autumn feed deficit. Hay remained a valuable resource.

The last thing she needed was more grief. The eventing season was at its peak, and in just over two weeks' time, she would compete across the border at Lake Ackerman, the biggest and toughest competition of the year. It wasn't pony club, it was professional. Chuck was entered in the two-star class, while Buck, who was not quite at the same standard, was competing in the one-star. The dressage tests were demanding, the cross-country jumps huge and the showjumping course technically difficult. Winning required concentration and skill.

She reversed a box trailer up to the lucerne stack and put on a pair of leather gloves. Her breath steamed, but she left her coat off. She'd warm up soon enough.

Over a cup of tea in the warmth of Hakea Lodge's kitchen, Aaron had agreed to train Costa Motza in exchange for lucerne hay. The price of lucerne had skyrocketed because of the northern drought, and it would take little of Sophie's own stock to honour the commitment. Since she'd taken over management, Vanaheim's lucerne crop had almost doubled. Provided Tess kept the hayshed paddock gate closed, lucerne was something of which she had plenty.

Taking the hay to Hakea Lodge, she felt her spirits lift. When she pulled into the yard, Aaron appeared.

'You should have yelled. I would've come and given you a hand,' he said.

'Don't tell me you'd actually set foot on Dixon land?' said Sophie, smiling at him. The moment she'd turned in the drive her ill-temper had faded and she had been filled with anticipation. She told herself it was because she was seeing Rowdy and Costa Motza, but she knew that was a lie. She wanted to see Aaron.

He crossed one arm in front of his chest and held a finger to his mouth, feigning deep contemplation. 'Cheap lucerne's hard to come by, you know. Plus your old man's not around, and your aunt's probably still sleeping off her excesses. So, yeah, I reckon I could set foot on Dixon land.'

'Wow. Who'd have thought?'

He grinned. 'Don't be cheeky. Seriously though, Soph, I'll give you a hand next time.'

She shook her head. 'Thanks, but it's probably best if you do stay away. I don't want to risk Tess bumping into you.'

'Why? What'll she do to me?'

'Nothing. It's more a case of what she'll do to me.'

His expression hardened, and Sophie wondered what he was thinking. Probably that she was too pathetic to stand up for herself.

Aaron insisted on unloading the trailer himself and Sophie let him. Ten bales wasn't much and she wanted to see Rowdy before starting on the other horses. As she approached the stable, Rowdy whickered at her and her heart warmed.

'Hey, big fella. How are you today?' she murmured as she stroked and kissed his nose. 'Did you run fast this morning?'

Rowdy bobbed his head and she laughed. She ducked into his stable to give him the once-over. Unlike the other horses with their sand-based yards and corrugated-iron three-sided shelters, Rowdy had a warm, timber-lined stable and a floor laid down with thick straw. It reflected his importance to the yard. Only stars were given a stable.

Unable to help herself, Sophie checked the bedding, but the box had been expertly mucked out and any damp or soiled straw replaced. Unlike the rest of Hakea Lodge, Aaron kept the yards and stables immaculate.

She returned her attention to Rowdy, planting kisses on his nose and scratching at the spot behind his ears she'd discovered he adored. Rowdy rubbed his lips against her cheek, returning her kiss.

'You wouldn't be coming on to me, would you now?' she asked him in her usual horsey blather. 'I bet you are. You know who your new mistress is, don't you? You know she's a sucker for big brown eyes and long lashes.'

'I suppose that rules me out,' said Aaron, leaning over the half-door.

She smiled into Rowdy's neck. Aaron had no idea. Right now, she felt very partial to blue-eyed blonds. She turned to him with her head tilted to one side, assessing him. 'I don't think it's so much the eyes, more the lack of that lovely horse smell.'

'I dunno about that,' said Aaron, sniffing the sleeve of his jumper. 'Every woman I've known has complained about it.'

'Not me. I love it.'

'Yeah, well, I don't think there are many women in the world like you, Soph.' He pointed at Rowdy. 'If you've finished with lover-boy there, do you want to go for a ride?'

'Sure. Who do you want me to grab?'

'You can take that brown filly in the second yard, Casalinga. She'll give you a nice ride. She's one of Tony Johnstone's,' he said, referring to his main owner, 'and she's a little cracker, too. That's who Costa Motza will be up against if you decide to run him over two thousand metres.'

Sophie looked at the filly. She was gorgeous, but still under developed. 'You're having me on. That weedy little thing doesn't stand a chance against my boy.' She turned back to Aaron. 'Who are you taking?'

'Psycho.'

'But I can ride Psycho.'

Aaron shook his head. 'Nah, you look knackered enough. And you've another one-day event on Sunday.'

Under Sophie's thick jumper, goosebumps crept up her back in delicious tingles. 'You remembered.'

He gave her an amused look. 'Of course I remembered. I'm worried sick you'll fall off and I'll lose my rider.'

They rode out in the clear cold morning. Psycho snorted and chewed his snaffle, but gave Aaron a much easier ride than he'd given Sophie.

Casalinga was, as Aaron promised, a delight. She settled into a smooth trot to which Sophie barely had to rise, and although her ears swivelled as she caught the sounds of Sophie and Aaron's conversation, she remained steady.

'I didn't realise your dad was such a good trainer until I saw all the photos,' she said as they turned up into the firebreak. 'I never heard about that side of him.'

'You wouldn't,' said Aaron.

'No. All I was ever told was that he'd lost his licence for horse doping.' She paused, torn between wanting to ask and not wanting to hurt Aaron with a reminder of the past, but the words seemed to blurt out by themselves. 'But I just don't understand why he'd do that when the yard was so successful.'

Aaron kept his eyes straight in front of him, as though he couldn't bear to look at her. Sophie bit her lip.

'God, I'm sorry, Aaron. Foot in mouth disease, as usual.'

'He wasn't a horse doper.'

Sophie stared at him. Of course he was. Rodger Laidlaw had been warned off the track for life. Everyone knew that. It was public record. She didn't know how to respond.

'He never did anything, Sophie. He was a good man.'

'But . . . so why did he lose his licence?'

'He shouldn't have.'

'I don't understand.'

'You don't have to. You just need to know that Dad was a good man and a great trainer.'

Sophie stared at her hands, thinking of her mother and how, except for her suicide, Sophie still believed she could do no wrong.

Her memory had transformed her mother from sinner to saint when, rationally, she knew neither guise was the whole truth. In reality, Fiona Dixon was simply a flawed woman, an adored mum who'd given Sophie life and then taken away her own.

'You must have loved him very much,' she said.

'Not enough, Soph. Not enough.'

Sophie understood exactly what he meant.

FIVE

THE HORSES STAMPED. Rowdy pawed at the half-door of his stable and whinnied. Costa Motza hung his head over the rail of his yard and stared up the drive, the skin around his big brown eyes furrowed with worry. Psycho paced, snorting and tossing his head in agitation. Even the normally unflappable Pollyanna stood quivering at her gate, waiting.

Aaron shook his head. Since Sophie started working at Hakea Lodge two weeks ago, it was as though a spell had fallen over the yard, enchanting his horses. He stood on the verandah with his mug of tea, watching their excitement build. Rowdy called out. Loudly. Costa Motza joined in. The ears of the other horses all pointed toward the drive. A contagious shiver went around the yard and, despite his outward show of indifference, Aaron felt it too.

The Range Rover slowed to a halt and Sophie stepped out of the car wearing tight navy jodhpurs, short boots, shiny black gaiters and an old dark blue and grey polo-neck jumper. Aaron liked that jumper. It turned the smoky grey of her eyes vivid. She blew a kiss at Rowdy, waved at Aaron and walked around to the rear door of the

Range Rover. From the back, she retrieved a red plastic bucket and carried it into the feed room.

Aaron took a sip of his tea.

A few seconds later, Sophie emerged and returned to the car. Smiling her cheerful morning smile, she approached the verandah carrying a big plate.

'Anzac biscuits,' she said, waving them under Aaron's nose before disappearing into the kitchen.

He shook his head, smiling. Tuesday it had been lamingtons; on Monday, caramel slice. Tomorrow it would be some other sweet snack.

It hadn't taken Sophie long to discover that riding racehorses built a big appetite. In the beginning, Aaron had made her Vegemite sandwiches for morning tea, but one morning, when she'd asked him for jam instead, he discovered she had a major sweet tooth. He'd bought chocolate biscuits for her after that, but she'd fretted about how much he was spending on catering for her and announced that, from then on, she would bring something for them to share over morning tea.

The next day, she'd turned up with a fruitcake. Two days later, when the cake was gone, she'd bought buttery scones from the local bakery, complete with jam and cream, and soon it was Aaron's turn to worry about the trouble Sophie was going to for their morning teas.

In the end, when Sophie started waking up with the sparrows to watch Rowdy and Costa Motza's trackwork, his dilemma was easily resolved. On Tuesdays and Thursdays, Aaron invited Sophie to join him for breakfast in Hakea Lodge's kitchen. They'd drink steaming cups of sweet tea, listen to the morning news on the radio and discuss the horses' performances in between mouthfuls of sausages and eggs on toast.

It wasn't only him Sophie was spoiling. Every day, the horses were favoured with a treat. Sometimes it was a bucket of carrots she'd share out before leaving for home. Other mornings she brought apples. The week before, Aaron had caught her feeding the horses peppermints.

The horses' reactions to this unusual treat had her laughing so hard she'd had to grab at a rail to hold herself upright. Psycho kept raising his head in the air and curling his top lip like a randy ram that had just sniffed a ewe. Costa Motza was leaning so far over the top rail of his yard, his rubbery lips extended and wiggling like an elephant's nose as he tried to reach for the packet, that he was in danger of falling over. Rowdy had cocked his head to either side like a connoisseur thinking up superlatives to describe the taste, before flopping out his tongue and waggling it as if it needed airing.

Aaron had shaken his head and walked away grumbling about rotten teeth and dentist bills, but the sight of her laughing so joyously made his heart feel too big for his chest.

'You're turning my horses into a bunch of spoilt sooks,' he said.

'Is that a complaint?'

He didn't answer. He couldn't complain because the horses had never been happier, and even Costa Motza's gallops had improved, although not enough to warrant him being nominated for next month's Harrington Gold Cup. Ever-optimistic Sophie had had to admit defeat there, though her faith that the horse would one day win a race remained unwavering.

Yesterday, as they'd stood together at Harrington Racetrack, shivering in the post dawn light with grim drizzle falling around them, Sophie had promised Aaron it was only a matter of time, before going on to tell him that the dopey white-socked chestnut needed extra work to get his fitness levels up. He could probably do with more corn in his diet and she was thinking of ordering some blood tests to check for trace element deficiencies. He'd regarded her with a combination of amusement and mild exasperation, and had to bite his tongue to stop himself reminding her who held the trainer's licence. Sophie was taking Costa Motza's training very seriously. But then it appeared that for Sophie, when it came to the horses, everything was serious.

Aaron indicated Rowdy with his chin. 'You can take out the big fella this morning.'

She nodded, but her grey eyes were bright and, as she looked over at the banging, stomping horse, her cheeks bloomed a pale rose. It wasn't just excitement, it was something else. Something, for all its insanity, Aaron could only describe as infatuation.

He stared at her, irritated, and found himself resisting the urge to give her a good shake. She might think Rowdy was God's gift, but at the end of the day, he was still just a bloody horse.

————

They rode out into yet another frosty morning, the horses' bits jangling as they chewed and worked them in their mouths.

'Have you seen the dapples on Rowdy's hindquarters?' asked Sophie. 'He must be in peak condition. Funny how you don't see them on lighter coloured horses. Chuck gets them when he's feeling really well, too, but they look prettier on Rowdy because he's so dark.'

Aaron gave the horse a sour glance and said nothing.

'Remind me to bring the clippers over and I'll clean up his mane a bit.' She rubbed at Rowdy's neck. 'Can't have a handsome boy like you looking untidy now, can we?'

'He's a racehorse, not a show pony.'

'I know, but I want him to look his best.'

'For Christ's sake, Sophie, just leave him alone.'

Sophie went quiet and Aaron could tell from the quick looks she threw him that she was wondering what was wrong with him. If she asked, he wouldn't be able to tell her. He didn't know himself.

They were halfway up the firebreak before Sophie spoke. 'Aaron, have I done something wrong? You've hardly spoken to me and you keep looking at me as though I'm infected with a contagious disease.' She turned away and stared into the pine forest. 'Just tell me what I did wrong so I don't do it again.'

'You haven't done anything wrong.'

'Could have fooled me.'

'It's not you, Soph.'

She turned back to him. 'Then what is it?'

What was he meant to say? That he didn't like the way she looked at Rowdy? That he was developing an irrational dislike for a horse? She'd think he was nuts, but he had to give her some excuse for his dour mood. He shifted in the saddle. 'I'm just not used to having someone in the yard all the time.'

She blinked, as if she knew he wasn't being honest and his lie had stung. 'What about Danny?'

'Unfortunately, Danny's part of the furniture.'

She nodded but didn't look entirely convinced. Then she focused her grey eyes on his and he caught a glimpse of intense vulnerability.

'Are you sure that's all?'

Shame at his behaviour left him voiceless. He nodded, wanting to touch her.

'You'd tell me, though, wouldn't you, if I did do something that annoyed you?'

He smiled at her, needing to erase that look from her eyes. 'Soph, you're worrying about nothing. I'm just a moody sod.'

'Are you sure?'

'Positive. How can someone bearing Anzac biscuits possibly be annoying?'

———

Aaron wiped steam off the mirror and tried to concentrate on shaving, but his mind was on Sophie and the way she'd looked at him that morning.

Most of the time, she exuded either bouncy good humour or spirited determination, but occasionally he caught glimpses of a twelve-year-old girl lost in the confusion of her mother's suicide and the labyrinth of lies woven by the adults around her.

He didn't like that little girl – she was like a ghost sent to remind him of all the things he'd done wrong – but at the same time he needed her. She was his conscience. One look from her snapped him out of the fantasy world the adult Sophie sometimes wove around him, and dumped him back into cold hard reality.

He wrapped a towel around his hips and wandered into the kitchen for the clothes he'd left warming by the stove. As he pulled on his good jeans, he stared out through the window at his mother's old garden. The grass seed he'd thrown around was emerging in sickly swathes of lime and yellow, crying out for nourishment. It was unsightly, but even nutrient-deprived grass was better than the ragged reminders of his mother. He didn't need Carol Laidlaw's garden to remind him of the past; Sophie's lost and haunted little-girl face did that. Pulling on his boots, Aaron grabbed his keys and headed outside, surprised to find Sophie's Range Rover still in the yard.

He stared around, unease crawling insect-like over his skin. He'd left her playing with the horses, feeding them carrots, prattling her usual soothing nonsense to them. Had she been hurt? Kicked by one of the horses? Fallen somehow?

He looked at Rowdy's box and realised that for once, the horse was quiet. He strode over and peered in. In the far corner, Rowdy stood with his eyelids drooping and his bottom lip flopping, while lying forward on his back with her arms around his neck and her eyes closed, was Sophie. Aaron rested his arms on the top of the half-door and watched them for a moment, thinking how peaceful they looked together and how pretty Sophie's pale skin appeared against Rowdy's dark, glossy-brown coat.

'Don't you have a home to go to?' he said.

Sophie smiled but didn't open her eyes. 'Yes. And I've stock to move and a paddock to oversow and horses to work.'

'So what are you still doing here?'

'Making friends.'

'It's a horse, Sophie.'

'He's a friend, too.'

'Do you always hug your friends like that?'

'If I had them, I would.'

His smile faded. 'Come on, Soph. You must have plenty of friends.'

She let go of Rowdy's neck and sat up. Her hair was messy and a patch of dirt marked one side of her face. 'Not really. Not close ones like other people have.'

She made friendlessness sound like it was the most normal thing in the world. Giving Rowdy a slap on the neck, she slid off his back, picked up his wool rug and tossed it over his rump, and then busied herself with the front buckle.

Aaron didn't know what to say to her. He didn't want to believe it, but somehow he knew she spoke the truth. The only thing she ever talked about was horses and the events she went to. She'd told him that occasionally, when something interested her, she'd show up at one of the Department of Agriculture's farm field days to see if there was anything she could learn. But she'd said she didn't do it often. The old-timers made her uncomfortable, and no one took her seriously. They made her feel like a labourer following her father's direction, instead of Vanaheim's farm manager. Only the new agronomist at the local farm supplies place had realised that she ran the show, but she'd said even he sometimes couldn't help his ingrained sexism showing through.

Not once had Aaron heard Sophie mention going out to parties or catching up with friends at the pub, or even going to the movies. The peculiarity of this had never occurred to him. He'd simply assumed that she was like any other 22-year-old, that there was more to her existence than horses and the farm. That she had a life outside of Vanaheim he didn't know about.

He scrutinised her as she finished adjusting Rowdy's rug. Sophie was too confident not to have had men in her life, and he knew from experience she could flirt, although in his case she only did it because she knew it made him uncomfortable. That wasn't the behaviour of someone inexperienced, not from his perspective.

Unless she's faking it.

A memory of Fiona Dixon floated in his conscience, how she had used her gentle smile to mask her tormented soul. Then he recalled the way her face had folded in on itself as she heard the words he'd sobbed and yelled at her. How she'd accepted them without question. And how, when her shock had passed, she'd once more slipped the mask back into place.

How he now accepted the terrible truth of what he'd done.

He'd learnt long ago a suicide takes more than their own life. They suck those who love them into the abyss as well, and Sophie was no exception. Her reclusion was his fault. Another fallen domino in the chain he'd started ten years ago when he'd done his mother's bidding and doped his first horse.

He'd thought it had ended with the death of his father, five years before, that the burden of guilt would be his to carry alone, but he realised now the tiles had continued tumbling, catching an innocent in their wake. He had to make them stop.

For Sophie.

She patted Rowdy and kissed his nose. 'Horses are so much better than people, don't you think?'

'I don't know about that.'

'I do. They're like dogs, except bigger and not quite as demonstrative. No matter what you do, they love you.'

'They're still horses, Sophie. Not people.' The words came out harsher than he intended, but she didn't seem to notice.

'What about you? Do you have lots of friends?'

Aaron had to think on that for a moment. He had friends, yes. He was either too busy, too tired or too broke to socialise often, but that didn't make him friendless or isolated, like Sophie appeared to be.

'I've got a couple of good mates, yeah.'

She stroked Rowdy's cheek, her back still to him. 'And lots of girl-friends, I bet.'

Aaron wanted to get off this topic. It made him nervous. He needed to keep things impersonal between them.

'Not as many as I'd like,' he joked.

Her hand stilled. 'Do you have one now?'

'Nope. Are you going to let that horse get some sleep?'

'I suppose I'd better.' She spent a few seconds fussing over Rowdy before stepping out of the stable. She looked him up and down. 'You're all dressed up.'

He smiled grimly. 'Bank meeting.'

'Oh. I hope it goes okay.'

Aaron shrugged. 'It won't be any worse than usual.' And it wouldn't be. The couple of placings he'd achieved at the last race meeting were enough to keep his head above water. And Sophie's contra deal with the hay was a godsend.

Fortunately, the bank manager owned shares in a racing syndicate, and although his expensively bred, city-trained thoroughbreds were a far cry from Aaron's gallopers, he at least appreciated the fickle nature of racing and understood fortunes could turn in a heartbeat. The bank manager would do his duty, though, and nag him about the usual things. The amount Aaron forked out for the rent on Danny's flat for one. Aaron didn't want to pay for his jockey's accommodation either, but it was that or have the blackmailing little bastard living at Hakea Lodge. That wasn't going to happen again. Ever. It was hard enough getting rid of him the first time round.

Sophie nodded, told Aaron she'd see him tomorrow and headed for her car.

On impulse, as she reached for the door, he called to her. She waited until he walked over, eyeing him with curiosity.

He swallowed, suddenly feeling stupid, like a bumbling teenager trying to ask a girl out for the first time. He shoved his hands in his pockets to stop them fidgeting, and kicked at the ground, dirtying his clean boots.

She waited, her frown deepening as he struggled to get the words out.

'You do have friends, Sophie. You have me.'

'Do I?'

He nodded.

She stared at him for a second and then with a smile, she wrapped her arms around his neck and buried her face into his chest. At first he stood stiff and unsure, but as her soft body pressed against him, the awkwardness passed. He relaxed enough to pull his hands from his pockets and carefully fold his arms around her, surprised at how good it felt, like he was giving her the comfort he'd always wanted to. A tiny touch of humanity and kindness as reparation for his sins.

Friendship was good. He could cope with that.

———

The sky wept drizzle and blanketed the racecourse in granite-coloured gloom. Beside Aaron, Sophie shivered and screwed up her nose against the misty rain. Aaron knew how she felt. Mornings like this were one of the worst things about training, and there was never any respite. The horses had to be galloped regardless of the weather.

He put a hand over his mouth to smother a yawn. Christ, he was tired. With one ear constantly tuned to the yard, he was naturally a light sleeper, but the previous night every creak of the house, rustle of wind and snort of a horse had woken him. He couldn't settle, lying on his back staring at the ceiling and ruminating over Sophie's lack of friends while his body ached with the need for sleep.

'You look tired,' she said.

'Bad night's sleep.'

Although he held his binoculars to his eyes as he watched another trainer's horse gallop, he could sense her worried stare.

'Didn't it go well with the bank?'

'No worse than normal.' He dropped the binoculars. 'Don't worry about me. I'd sell myself before I'd let Hakea Lodge go under.'

She smiled a little. 'Would you?'

He nodded. 'You bet. I probably wouldn't get any takers, but it'd be worth a try.'

'I don't know about that.' She nudged him. 'I'm sure old Mrs Carpenter would love a piece of you.'

Aaron groaned. Brenda Carpenter was an extremely wealthy, highly eccentric local widow, who seemed to think the district's young men found her irresistible. Aaron had once had the dubious pleasure of being chased into the men's toilets of a local watering hole by the oversexed septuagenarian.

'I'd never be able to perform.'

Sophie grinned. 'Don't worry. I'd save you.'

'You would?'

'Of course. You're no good to me exhausted all the time. Who'd train the horses? Anyway, I may not be filthy rich like Mrs Carpenter, but I bet even I could afford your gigolo's fee.'

'Are you sure about that, Soph? A bloke like me comes pretty expensive.'

'How expensive?'

He puffed out his cheeks. 'Oh, I dunno. Twenty bucks?'

'What? An hour?'

He shook his head, grinning. 'Nah. A night.'

She burst out laughing and he had the ridiculous idea of kissing her, of putting his mouth to hers and breathing in her laughter, as if he could steal it from her and make it his own.

He waited for her to sober up. 'Do you reckon I'm over-selling myself?'

She shook her head, her eyes luminous. 'Definitely under, Aaron. Definitely under.'

And even though she was joking, Aaron felt as though she'd once again wrapped her arms around his neck and pressed her face into his chest.

———

With trackwork over and breakfast eaten in Hakea Lodge's warm kitchen, Aaron sent Sophie outside to play with Rowdy while he made a few phone calls. Though still cold, a breeze had risen, driving the worst of the early morning drizzle eastward. Between the racing clouds, scraps of sun appeared, helping to dry the yard. It wouldn't have mattered if it was still freezing. Sophie took any chance available to spend time with Rowdy and Costa Motza.

Ten minutes later, he found her leaning against the half-door chattering to the horse, arm stretched as she caressed Rowdy's neck. The flickering sunshine shot Sophie's mousy hair with pretty, pale gold highlights. Her shirt had come loose, and he caught a glimpse of white as each reach of her arm caused her snug-fitting fleecy jumper to pull up, dragging the shirt with it. Aaron crossed the yard, unable to take his eyes off that tiny patch of skin.

As he approached, Sophie didn't move, her attention focused on Rowdy. Aaron halted, his throat feeling rough as he sucked in cool air. He closed his eyes but the image of her skin stayed, like his mind had taken a photograph. He opened them again, staring at her as if he'd never seen female flesh before. Oblivious to his scrutiny and still happily chattering, Sophie reached up higher to fondle Rowdy's ears, rucking her jumper up even further.

If he waited long enough, she'd turn around, break the enchantment, but Aaron didn't want her to. Holding his breath, he took another step forward and slowly reached out, his fingers hovering over that small exposed area on her side.

Very gently, he brushed his fingertips against her skin.

She jumped and then giggled, twisting around to face him. 'That tickled!'

'I didn't know you were ticklish.'

'I'm not,' she said quickly. 'Not really. Only a little bit.'

Ticklish. The idea sent Aaron's heartbeat racing. With a grin, he snuck out his hands. Sophie's eyes widened and she shook her head.

'Don't you even think of it!'

But it was all Aaron could think of. Though Sophie jammed her arms against her sides and tried to duck away, he was too fast. He grabbed her, locking one arm around her chest and pattering the fingers of his other hand up and down the edges of her flat stomach. She squealed before breaking into uncontrollable giggles, her mouth wide and her grey eyes enormous.

Twisting and wriggling around to face him, she attempted to get him back, risking exposure of her ribs as she attacked. He wasn't ticklish – not like Sophie – but the sheer fun of playing around had him laughing with her, their voices echoing around the yard.

Laughter clutched at Aaron's belly and stole his ability to concentrate. Sensing her advantage, Sophie increased her attack. She ducked and swerved, giggling as he tickled harder. With a lunge, she threw herself at his chest and raced her hands over his sides. As he tried to push her away, their arms tangled, then their legs. Aaron reached for something to balance himself but the only thing was Sophie. He stumbled, accidentally dragging her with him, her weight causing him to overbalance. They fell, landing on their backs, chests heaving, grinning like idiots.

'Are you okay?' he asked when he could get the words out.

'Fine.' She turned her head toward him, her mouth and eyes still wide with laughter. 'Never been better.'

Hanging over the door, Rowdy peered down his long nose at them before snorting and tossing his head in disgust. Sophie raised her head to poke her tongue at him and, despite the wet ground, flopped back down again.

'God, I haven't laughed so much in ages.'

Aaron smiled at her. 'You should do it all the time.'

She slid her hand across the space between them and touched the tip of her little finger to his, causing his nerves to buzz as if they'd been electrified. 'So should you.'

He closed his eyes. He should get up. Stop this nonsense. But the moment was too perfect.

'I suppose we should do some work,' he said after too many seconds had passed. Damp was seeping through his jeans and jumper. He didn't want Sophie catching a chill, plus they still had horses to ride out and the morning was slipping away.

'I suppose we should. My bum's getting wet.' But she made no move.

Aaron propped onto his elbow and twisted to look at her. She lay on her back with her eyes closed, pale skin like porcelain, smiling at the sky.

'Thanks,' he said.

Eyelids flicking open, she frowned. 'What for?'

He shrugged, suddenly embarrassed, and looked away, heat crawling across his cheeks. 'I don't know. For making me laugh.' He swallowed and refocused on her. 'For being you.'

The frown faded and her mouth parted slightly, then a shy smile broke over face like spring sunshine. And with that single look his embarrassment disappeared, smothered by the addictive thrill of knowing that for a few too-short moments, he'd made her happy.

————

It wasn't until they were riding out that Aaron found the courage to ask the question that had been nagging him since the day before.

He'd wanted to ask her in the dim light of the track, where she wouldn't be able to see his face clearly, but his nerve had failed him. Then at breakfast, she'd been so engrossed in some farm magazine article on bloat prevention in cattle, he hadn't wanted to interrupt her reading, and at morning tea he'd been too tied up with nominations. Now he'd run out of excuses, and the tickling episode had only made his need for an answer worse.

He just had to find the guts to ask.

He looked at Sophie on Psycho and shook his head. The once lunatic gelding now behaved like a besotted donkey whenever she was on board. When he'd asked her what she'd done to his horse she'd laughed and said she wished she knew, because Buck certainly wasn't under the same spell.

Pollyester Girl, the horse he was riding, was another of Tony Johnstone's gallopers – the half-sister to Pollyanna he had wanted for himself but couldn't afford to buy when she came up for sale. An injury had interrupted her autumn preparation and though Aaron felt a spell would be better for the horse, Tony insisted she finish her campaign. He should have given her to Sophie to ride, but he'd wanted an excuse to trail behind the much fitter Psycho if things became awkward.

'Sophie, can I ask you something?'

She smiled at him. 'Of course.'

'Have you ever had a boyfriend?'

The smile slipped. She blushed, and turned to look at Vanaheim's lush pasture. Aaron wished he had kept his mouth shut. When she finally spoke, she did so without looking at him.

'Not for a very long time.'

He couldn't help himself. He had to know. 'How long?'

They'd reached the bottom of the first hill. Psycho jog-trotted and champed at his bit, gearing himself for the run up the final hill. Catching the tension, Pollyester Girl fought for her head. Aaron held her tight, his eyes on Sophie's face.

'What's the date today?' she asked.

Aaron couldn't see what that had to do with anything. 'The twenty-first.'

As she spoke, Sophie kicked Psycho into a canter. Her words blew back to Aaron, ragged and sad.

'Seven years, two months and nine days.'

Although Pollyester Girl nearly pulled his arms out of their sockets, he didn't let her go. The horse pigrooted and yanked at the reins, but she could have performed the Macarena and Aaron wouldn't have noticed.

Sophie Dixon hadn't had a boyfriend since she was fifteen years old.

And to Aaron's utter shame, the revelation pleased him.

SIX

THE BUNTING SURROUNDING the warm-up area at Lake Ackerman in Victoria's far western corner vibrated and hummed in the increasing wind. Normally well-behaved horses shied at the flapping coloured triangles and riders swore under their breaths as their mounts refused to come to hand. Every now and then, a few drops of rain would fall and then stop, as though nature had conducted a quick test run. Then the clouds would part and sunlight would appear for just long enough to give the riders hope it wouldn't pour, before the sun ducked behind a dark cloud once again.

Sophie stood on a bucket plaiting Chuck's mane and twisting it into tiny rosettes. She kept half an eye on the three dressage rings in operation, watching for Buck's main rivals in the one-star event. Not that there was much point. Buck's test had been atrocious. He definitely hadn't appreciated being woken so early in the morning, or travelling for two hours in the float. Sophie wished he'd find some other way to express his resentment than by playing up in the dressage ring. She was getting sick of being made to look a fool. One of these days, when the thought of giving up didn't seem like such an anathema, she'd find the strength to sell him on.

She cocked her head at the old-fashioned radio sitting on the float's wheel arch. Aaron had given her some tips, and in a rush of blood, Sophie had opened a betting account. Though busier in the spring and autumn when the major metropolitan carnivals were on, the country racing calendar continued through the colder months and trainers willing to travel could race at least once a fortnight, often more. Today's meeting was closer to home, north of Harrington at Penola, a small town at the bottom end of the Coonawarra wine-growing district. Aaron had promised her Pollyanna was a certainty, and likely to be underpriced. Sophie figured it couldn't hurt to place a bet if the odds were right. Twenty-five dollars each way wouldn't ruin her, and if Pollyanna came home, she might shout herself a trip to the hairdresser. God knows she needed it.

Turning to Penola. Weather is showery, track is good. Race one and two, all clear. Race three, take out five, Gold Stargazer. Eight, Jump Start. Nine, Bobbydazzler. Repeat. Five, eight, nine. Race four . .
.

Sophie sighed. She found the racing preview incredibly boring. Even though the announcer changed inflection and tried to inject some excitement into the broadcast, it still came across in a soporific drone. At least Pollyanna wasn't on the list of scratchings.

Her mind drifted to Aaron, a place it had constantly wandered to these last few days. Every thought of him did something wobbly to her insides. Last night, instead of resting as she should, she lay in bed going over all their conversations, trying to interpret his words, hunting for any indication he might have feelings for her. Because if there was one thing of which Sophie was sure, it was her feelings for Aaron.

She smiled at the memory of him tickling her. The laughter they'd shared. The way he'd leaned on his elbow and looked at her, blue eyes full of something indefinable. The way he'd thanked her for being herself.

Simple words that left her overflowing with happiness.

She sighed again, this time with longing, then smiled as Chuck nudged her.

'I know, I'm being silly.' But she wasn't. Aaron turned her inside out and it wasn't just his good looks that did it, but the way he made her feel, like she was someone special and important. How special and important, she couldn't figure out.

She twisted a plait into a rosette and secured it with a rubber band, taking care to keep the knot loose so it wouldn't pull at Chuck's neck. She moved on to his forelock. Chuck lowered his head to make it easier for her to reach, and Sophie felt tears prick her eyes as she realised this could be the last time. Chuck was getting on, the poor old fella, and ready for retirement, but Sophie wanted one final victory.

She loved Chuck with a passion she found impossible to articulate. He wasn't just her horse, he was her memory. On a day she would never forget, her mother had returned from the local horse sales, unloaded a handsome, placid-looking, dark-brown horse from the float and handed its lead to Sophie. 'We're going to train him together,' she'd said. And they had.

From that time on, her feelings for the horse she had called Prince Charles, because of his noble bearing, became intrinsically linked with her love for her mother. With gentle patience, they started him on the flat, teaching Chuck the basics of dressage, developing his muscles and teaching him to respond to his rider's aids. Then came jumping, and hours spent drilling him over poles and small fences under Fiona Dixon's expert tutelage. Gradually, they introduced him to pony club and then shows, competing in the junior classes and building both Sophie's and Chuck's confidence until they worked in perfect accord. Until, after years of dedication, they finally reached the heights they were at today.

As long as Chuck lived, so did a little bit of Fiona Dixon.

If they won this weekend, she'd put him out into the front paddock and watch him eat himself into contentment. He'd been a superstar for long enough. He deserved a rest.

In race three, Jack Cooper likes number four, Wombling, from one, Opaque, to seven, Sosume, and eleven, Chairman of the Board. That's four, one, seven and eleven. Race four . . .

Sophie placed her hands on Chuck's cheeks and planted a kiss in the middle of his nose, then pulled her phone out of her pocket.

'Did you hear that, Chuck?' she said, swiping the screen. 'No Pollyanna. That means we'll get her at good odds. I could be rich.'

———

The morning's dressage results were up when Sophie passed the scorers' tent on the way to walk the cross-country course. As she'd expected, Buck was well down the list. For a moment she contemplated withdrawing him altogether, but decided to give him a chance to redeem himself. In a few hours, when it came to tackling the showjumping course, he might be in a better mood.

As there were so many competitors, the one-day event had to be spread over two days, with all of the dressage and some of the showjumping held on the Saturday, and the cross-country and the remainder of the showjumping on the Sunday. Sophie wished it were the other way around. The weather forecast for Sunday wasn't good. At least she'd have two phases out of the way once Chuck completed his dressage and showjumping later in the afternoon. The horses would be tired enough after galloping over three kilometres and jumping thirty-plus obstacles without having to showjump as well.

Rugged up and rubber-booted in preparation for her walk of the cross-country course, Sophie paused at the Range Rover and, in the faint hope her father might have called, pulled her phone from the glovebox. To her surprise the screen showed someone had left a message.

'Sophie, it's your father. Tess informed me you have a major event this weekend and I wanted to wish you all the best. I'm sure you'll do very well.' He paused to clear his throat. 'And I need to speak with you about Aaron Laidlaw. He's not . . .' He cleared his throat again. 'I'm worried about you, that's all. But we'll talk another time. Good luck with your event and take care.'

Sophie stabbed the disconnect button and frowned at the screen. She didn't know whether to feel pleased he'd called or annoyed about the cryptic Aaron comment. After he'd ignored her last two emails advising him of her competition schedule, she hadn't bothered to let him know about Lake Ackerman. She didn't even know if that account was still active but given the emails hadn't bounced and he was the one who had told her to use that address, she assumed it was. His lack of response could only be because he was too busy to reply or simply didn't care. Their long-deteriorating relationship made her suspect the latter. Yet in this call, the concern in his voice was unmistakable. The question was where that concern was directed – at her or at her association with Aaron.

But contemplation of such matters was for another time. Today, Sophie had a competition to win.

The course swarmed with riders stepping out distances and measuring heights, and dogs with their noses down in the grass sniffing out rabbits. Sophie nodded at a few people she knew, but tried to keep her mind on the jumps. Competition in Chuck's class was stiff. She'd already seen two former Olympians and there were plenty more famous names listed on the scoreboard. It was hard not to feel intimidated.

She was stepping out the distance between two jumps when the father of one of her competitors approached.

The hackles on her neck rose. Nico Di Stasio had never been one of her favourite people. Not only was he one of her father's local political allies, she had once overheard him describe her mother as an albatross Ian Dixon was well rid of.

'What's this I hear about you working for Aaron Laidlaw,' he said after an interminable period of chitchat in which Sophie barely participated.

'I'm just helping out,' she said, continuing with her count.

'You want to be careful.'

She turned and retraced her steps. She was right on the first count. Four long strides or five short ones. She pulled a notebook from her coat pocket and made a note in it. How she rode these fences would depend on how well Chuck was placed. If he was in contention after the dressage and showjumping, she'd tackle the course with as much aggression as she could, but if he was way down the list, there was no point in going fast. She'd only tire Chuck unnecessarily and put him at risk of an injury.

She walked on, but Di Stasio followed.

'The Laidlaws don't have the best of reputations,' he said.

'Oh, so you think hanging around Hakea Lodge will turn me into a horse doper, do you?'

Di Stasio stopped walking and Sophie hid a smile, amused by his shock at her small rebellion. He was used to the old polite Sophie, not the lippy one.

'Of course not,' he spluttered. 'It's more a case of what people think.'

'People like you, you mean?'

'Your father certainly wouldn't like it.'

'Well, that's for him and I to discuss then, isn't it? Now if you don't mind, I need to concentrate.'

Leaving Di Stasio open-mouthed, Sophie stalked on, her mood blackening with every step. How dare people talk about Aaron as if he were some sort of criminal? They didn't know him like she did. He'd never in a million years hurt one of his horses. And then there was his assertion that Rodger Laidlaw was innocent. She was positive he wouldn't say that without reason. But why was it so important that she keep away from Aaron? Had he done something terrible she didn't know about?

She hoped not, but the more she thought about it, the more confused she became. Aaron's eyes told her he was hiding something, but what?

———

'Sophie Dixon. It's been a while.'

'Not long enough,' said Sophie. She kept walking, automatically pulling at the sleeves of her jumper so they stretched over her wrists.

'Don't be like that, Soph.'

Sophie's overworked hackles rose once more. 'Soph' was Aaron's name for her, not Michael Fenton's. Ignoring him, she pulled a tape measure from her pocket. She couldn't believe the size of the fence in front of her. The oxer had to be over regulation.

'I see you've brought Prince Charles and Bucephalus. You want to hope you don't fall off. The trans-Tasman selectors are here.'

'I won't fall off.' Sophie read the figures on the yellow tape in disbelief. The height was right on the limit. She let the tape go. Michael leaned against the jump's front rail, regarding her with a smile she had once thought sexy. Now, his mouth seemed too wide, his hazel eyes too sleepy. Even the long-legged and lean-hipped body she'd once admired for its sinewy athleticism was too scrawny for her liking.

'So. Did you miss me?'

Michael had spent the last year in England working for one of the world's leading eventers – a position Sophie would have applied for if she hadn't had Vanaheim to worry about.

'Not even a little bit.' Sophie handed him the end of the tape. 'Here, make yourself useful and hold this so I can measure the width.'

He held the tape against the jump's creosote-treated pine upright while she jumped the deep ditch the fence was built over and pulled the tape to the other side.

'It's Jamie's twenty-first party tonight. Michelle said she told you about it but reckons you'll do your usual thing and hide in your hotel room. Why don't you come? Be sociable for once.'

'No thanks. You can let go now.'

Michael released the tape and stepped over the ditch to stand in front of her. 'Are you always going to be like this?'

'When it comes to you, yes.'

'Oh, come on, Sophie. I can't believe you're still hanging on to that. It was years ago.'

She gave him a filthy look and stepped around him, wanting to get on with walking the course.

'No wonder you have no friends, when you won't go anywhere or see anyone, even just to be friendly.'

Sophie turned around, stalked back to him and poked a finger hard into his chest. 'The reason I have no friends, Michael, is because of you.'

'That's bullshit. No one gives a toss what happened at that camp. They probably don't even remember.'

Sophie blinked. Was he being serious? When Sophie was fifteen, Michael Fenton had not only persuaded her to sleep with him in the back seat of a car – an act she certainly wasn't ready for – he'd then collected twenty dollars from each of his sniggering mates and branded her a slut in front of the whole camp. She'd had to endure the sneers of the other ponyclubbers for two more endless days – during which Michael totally ignored her – before Tess came to pick her up.

She did try to talk to Tess, but her aunt wasn't interested in a fifteen-year-old's private hell. One day after arriving home, Sophie decided that if suicide was good enough for her mother, then it was damn well good enough for her. No one cared anyway. Now, standing in front of Michael, she flinched away from the memory of sitting in a crimson-stained bath, waiting to die, while Tess stared bleary-eyed at the television in another room.

Michael Fenton didn't know what she'd done. No one except Tess, her father, Dr Charlton and some paid-off medical workers knew.

Sophie sighed. 'Maybe you're right.'

'So you'll come for drinks?'

'No. I don't think so.' She turned away, suddenly overwhelmed with tiredness. She needed to get this course walked and head back to the float. Buck might have pulled himself loose and be running around causing chaos.

Michael reached out and pulled her to a stop. She stared at his handsome face and then down at his hand, holding hers. He let her go.

'I really am sorry about what happened between us. We were both too young to know what we were doing.'

She nodded, unable to speak.

'Listen, why don't we go out sometime, just the two of us? Dinner or a drink or whatever you like. Somewhere quiet where we could, you know, just talk.'

Sophie stared at him. 'Are you asking me out on a date?'

'Yeah, I guess I am.'

She shook her head, amazed by life's strange twists. Then, without answering, she turned and walked away.

SEVEN

OLD PUNTERS in checked trilbies and worn suits leaned over the fence of Penola Racing Club's mounting yard. Their leathery faces crinkled as they squinted and studied the thoroughbreds walking and jogging past. Some made notes in their race books, others scratched chins or sucked at their teeth before turning away and heading toward their favourite bookmakers. Aaron watched them as Pollyanna pranced and snorted beside him.

He knew all the serious punters and most of the part-timers. In the days when his father trained, the less informed would sidle up to Rodger Laidlaw and ask about the runners. The truly dedicated ones – the ones who crawled out of bed every morning to stand in the freezing pre-dawn watching trackwork – didn't bother. They already knew everything there was to know, and if they did have questions, they'd rely on their network of contacts for information.

As he walked Pollyanna along the fence, the punters nodded politely before their gazes slid away onto the more favoured horses. Pollyanna's dapple-grey coat was dark with sweat and Aaron had yet to prove himself equal to his father. But he would. One day.

Two young women in fancy hats and long wool coats used their youth and good looks to manoeuvre through the older men to the front of the rail. As Aaron passed, they giggled behind their hands. The prettier – a tall, long-haired brunette – gave him the look. The one that said, 'Come and talk to me later'.

A month ago, he would have sought her out. Asked her to watch the race with him, maybe invited her out for a drink. And if he was lucky, she'd stick around for few weeks, pretend the early mornings and constant equine distraction didn't bother her. Play at being his girlfriend for a while until the appeal wore off. Never anything more. No matter how well he treated the women in his life, they never stayed. Horseracing was glamorous only from the outside.

Aaron placed a hand on the filly's hot neck and wished Sophie was there to help. The horses seemed to find her chitchat calming and he missed her cheeriness, the blind faith she had in each horse's ability to win – even a no-hoper like Costa Motza.

He hadn't stopped thinking about her since he'd waved her off on Friday. He'd bent to kiss her, just to wish her luck at Lake Ackerman, but she'd turned her face and he'd caught the edge of her mouth with his lips. He'd jerked away, mumbling apologies, but she'd stood there in the yard staring at him with a dopey smile and flushed cheeks, and even though he knew it was completely insane, all he'd wanted to do was kiss her properly.

He sighed and looked toward the jockeys' room, wishing they'd hurry up, but there was no sign of them. The stewards were probably still having a word. Rough riding and interference had marred race two. They wouldn't want a repeat.

His mind drifted back to Sophie. Cheerful, clever, tough, spirited, determined, talented. That was the Sophie he'd come to know, and she filled him with emotions he hadn't felt for years. Emotions he liked far more than he wanted to admit. But he had to keep perspective.

She could be many things, but she was still Sophie Dixon, the living, breathing reminder of all the lives he'd damaged.

The jockeys emerged from their room. Todd Markham's prune

face was soon looking up at Aaron, waiting for instructions. Aaron didn't like Todd, but he'd booked him because he was a good rider and Pollyanna needed an experienced jockey on her back to get her across the line.

'Keep her close to the front,' he instructed. 'She's got a hell of a burst of speed, but I think it'll be a few weeks before she's at peak fitness. She might tire if you go too early.'

Todd nodded. 'Sure thing, boss.'

Aaron gave him a leg-up, keeping hold of Pollyanna as Todd sorted himself out and found the stirrups. When the jockey was set, Aaron gave Pollyanna's nose a rub and let her go. She tossed her head and followed the horse in front out onto the track, breaking into a canter as she passed the judges' box. Aaron shoved her lead in the jacket pocket of his race-day suit and headed toward the finishing post.

The brunette was leaning against the rail chatting to her friend and posing, as if this were Royal Ascot instead of Penola. Aaron stopped and studied her. She was pretty, in an over-made-up way, with perfectly manicured fingernails, expensive clothes and shoes so high she had to keep her weight on her toes to prevent the heels sinking into the grass. He could imagine her picking her way daintily through manure with her lips pursed, complaining about the smell, the horsehair on her coat, the muck on her shoes. And what was he supposed to talk to her about? Racing? She'd be bored to tears in ten minutes.

The brunette's companion noticed him staring and nudged her friend, but when the brunette turned and smiled, he shook his head and walked away.

———

As the sun set over Hakea Lodge, Aaron took a can of beer from the fridge and walked out to the verandah to watch its descent and ponder the day. Chilly air bit his cheeks but he had grown up in the cold, and he barely noticed the sting. Rowdy whickered at him from the warmth of his stable, no doubt hoping for a scratch or a treat.

When he realised Aaron wasn't about to spoil him like Sophie, the horse turned away in a sulk.

Aaron sat on the step with his beer beside him and his phone in his hand, idly scrolling through his contacts until Sophie's name appeared on the screen. He stared at it, and before he could stop himself, hit the green button.

The call went straight through to her voice mail.

'Hey, Sophie. It's Aaron.' He stopped. What the hell was he calling her for anyway? 'I'll talk to you Monday,' he said, and then quickly hung up. He took a gulp of beer, his face burning.

Thirty seconds later, the phone rang. Sophie's name flashed at him. He stared at it, his stomach somersaulting, and thought about not answering, but the lure of hearing her voice was too much.

'Hey, Soph.'

'Are you all right? Is Rowdy okay? Costa Motza?' She sounded breathless.

'Everything's fine. Costa Motza's alive and well and I'm looking at Rowdy right now. Well, I'm looking at his backside. He's sulking because I'm not giving him any attention. So it's situation normal here. I just thought I'd call to let you know Pollyanna won.'

'I know! I listened to the race on the radio. She was wonderful. You must be so proud, but you know the best thing?'

He smiled. 'What?'

'I just checked my betting account and I'm three hundred and seventy-two dollars and thirty-five cents richer!'

He laughed. 'That's great, Soph. But I reckon I can beat that. Pollyanna made three grand and I scored a case of the sponsor's wine, so I was thinking maybe you and I could grab a couple of steaks and try a bottle one night.' The words tumbled out of his mouth unbidden. He closed his eyes and banged his head softly against the verandah post. What was he thinking?

There was a long pause, and when she spoke, he could picture the shy smile behind her words. 'I'd really like that, Aaron. Thanks.'

The pleasure in her voice sent his heart hiccupping. 'So what about your day?'

'Up and down.' She sighed. 'I don't know what I'm going to do about Buck. He hates me. His dressage test was terrible and he knocked up a cricket score in the showjumping. I don't want to sell him, but I don't know what else to do.'

'He'll come good, you'll see,' he said, trying to cheer her up. 'What about Chuck?'

'Oh, he was wonderful. It's almost like he knows this could be his last event. You should have seen him in the dressage. He was amazing. Even his counter canter was brilliant and that's always been his worst movement, and then in the showjumping, he just bounced around like the jumps weren't there. He's such a superstar.'

'So where does that put you?'

'In the lead, but only by two and a half penalties. We can't afford to put a foot wrong tomorrow in the cross-country. We have to go clear, and we have to go fast, but the weather isn't looking too good. I don't know how we'll go if it gets slippery.'

'I'm sure you'll do great.'

'I hope so. I really want him to win. I just wish Mum was here to see it.'

Aaron's heart constricted, gripped by an invisible clawed hand. It was like nothing he'd ever felt before. Every breath sent the talons deeper into his chest.

I'm sorry, I'm sorry, I'm sorry.

'Aaron?'

He squeezed his eyes shut and leaned forward, his hand tight around the phone's shell, his breath held to stop his gasps. This is what he'd left her with. An aching hollow that would never be filled.

'Aaron, are you there?'

He pulled the phone away from his ear and pressed it hard against his side, then exhaled in a shuddering heave. He forced himself to take a couple of deep, long breaths. It was half a minute before he felt able to speak.

'I'm sorry, Sophie. Something's come up,' he said, straining to keep his voice even. 'I'll catch you later.'

'Aar—'

He hung up.

As the sun slid away and the yard dissolved into darkness, Aaron stayed on the verandah staring at nothing. Cold seeped in through the cheap fabric of his race-day suit, but still he didn't move. It wasn't until he started shivering uncontrollably that he forced himself into the warmth of the house. The barely touched can of beer stayed on the verandah, slowly turning flat.

———

Aaron's skin turned red under the heat of the shower and he cursed himself for being stupid enough to sit in the freezing cold, brooding over something he couldn't change. Who'd look after the horses if he became sick? Who'd train them? Race them? Feed them? Hakea Lodge would be broke within a month.

Stepping from the shower and wrapping a towel around his waist, he headed for the kitchen where his jeans and an old rugby jumper were warming by the combustion stove.

He was halfway across the room when he saw her. She'd made herself at home. A tumbler full of red wine sat on the table in front of her, a half-drunk bottle alongside. He glanced at the label. Redgrove Estate, the race sponsor's brand. The wine he'd asked Sophie to share with him. The box sat on the kitchen bench where he'd left it, except now the cardboard flaps gaped where they'd been torn open.

'Well, well, well,' said Tess. 'Haven't you grown up?'

Aaron glared at her. 'What are you doing here?'

Tess picked up her glass and downed the contents in three gulps. She nodded her approval before reaching for the bottle. With one hand holding the towel around his waist, Aaron used the other to snatch it away from her. She shrugged and sat back, smiling.

'I've come to talk about Sophie.'

He placed the bottle on the sink and under cover of the towel pulled on his jeans and quickly tugged the jumper over his head.

'What about Sophie?'

Tess casually walked over to the sink, picked up the wine and carried it back to her seat. She eyed him as she topped up her glass.

'Her father and I are very concerned about her.'

Aaron snorted. No doubt they were concerned. He knew every secret rattling around in the Dixon family closet. Secrets no one had ever bothered to tell Sophie.

'Are you worried about what I might tell her?'

Tess took a sip of wine and eyed him. 'Possibly.'

'I suppose Ian's shit-scared I'll tell her about him and my mother. Why is it such a bloody big secret anyway? They've been together for ten years.'

'To protect Sophie, of course. She's very . . .' Tess clicked her tongue and raised her eyes as if searching for the right word. 'Sensitive.'

'She's twenty-two. I'm sure she can handle it.'

He reached for the bottle, wanting to wrap his lips around the neck and pour wine down his gullet like his father had once done. Something about Sophie's aunt made his skin crawl. It wasn't that she was ugly. When she put in the effort you could almost call her handsome. Tonight, she'd styled her hair into a loose but neat bun at the back of her head and attempted to cover her worst of her reddened skin with makeup. But her hair looked dull and brittle, and though she'd used eyeliner and mascara to highlight eyes as startlingly grey as Sophie's, they bore none of her sweetness. Her clothes looked clean, but they hung off her thin frame, and the hand she held around her glass seemed more birdlike than human. If Tess's aim was to appear normal, she'd failed. Aaron recognised her demon too well.

Tess sighed. 'Oh dear. She obviously hasn't told you about her illness. Poor thing. Such a disturbed child.'

Aaron stared at her, his heart beating hard. 'What are you on about?'

'Just like her mother. It does make you wonder if this sort of thing isn't genetic.' She shook her head. 'I'm sure you can understand our concern.'

Aaron wanted to choke the words out of her. 'What are you talking about?'

Tess smiled and patted the seat next to her as though this was her house and not his. 'Pour yourself a drink and sit down, and I'll tell you all about it.'

'I'll stand, thanks,' he said, upending the bottle he still held into an old Vegemite glass. He moved toward the stove but then thought better of it. It'd only make him hotter and angrier than he already felt. 'Spit it out,' he said. 'I don't have all night.'

'But, Aaron, I think you do. When it comes to our Sophie, I think you have all the time in the world.'

'Get on with it, Tess, or get out. I'm not in the mood for games.'

'I'm ashamed to say that Sophie suffers from severe depression. Her illness is acute, suicidally acute. The first time she tried to kill herself, she came very close to succeeding. If I hadn't found her when I did, she'd be dead.'

Unable to look at Tess, Aaron stared into the deep burgundy depths of his wine. He wanted her to stop, but he also had to know. The more he heard, the more he suffered. And suffering was what he deserved.

His throat felt raw. 'When was this?'

'The first time? When she was fifteen.'

Fifteen. The age when she'd last had a boyfriend.

'What do you mean, "the first time"? How many times are we talking about?'

Tess shifted her eyes from his. 'Quite a few.'

He swallowed. 'Why?'

She held out her glass. 'Confession is such thirsty work.'

Aaron felt like he had no choice but to top it up.

Tess smiled her thanks. 'The first time it was over some totally unsuitable boy she had a crush on. She was going through this rebellious stage. Attention-seeking, of course.'

'Are you talking about her rebelling or her suicide attempt?'

'Both, I should imagine.'

'But you said she almost succeeded. It sounds like she meant it.'

Tess shrugged. 'Maybe she did. You'd have to ask her about that.'

Aaron intended to. 'And what about the other times?'

'No idea,' said Tess, inspecting the sleeve of her jumper.

Aaron watched her closely. Was Tess lying?

She plucked at a tiny ball of matted wool and dropped it on the floor. 'Probably something to do with her father. Who knows? Maybe she just wants to follow in her mother's footsteps, so to speak.'

Tess's flippancy made Aaron sick. This was Sophie they were talking about. The smiling girl who made him laugh, who bought useless horses from knackers for him to train, who was willing to work for nothing because she'd fallen in love with a steeplechaser. The girl Tess described bore no resemblance to the Sophie he knew. Although sometimes full of self-doubt, his Sophie was determined, resilient and tough. Tess was talking about a stranger.

Or was she? Aaron had seen that twelve-year-old girl Sophie kept so expertly hidden, but did that make her as damaged as her aunt alleged? He wanted to call her, to ask if it was true, but first he had to deal with Tess.

'So what's all this got to do with me?'

Tess leaned forward. 'There's to be a shake-up in the ministry in the next few weeks. Ian's tipped to take over Primary Industries.'

'And you're frightened Sophie might cause a scandal?'

Tess nodded.

'Get out.'

'Pardon?' said Tess, blinking at him.

Aaron pointed to the door. 'I said get out.'

'I haven't finished.'

Two strides and he was in front of her. He yanked the glass from her hand and threw it in the sink. It shattered on impact. Tess jumped. Aaron grabbed her by the jumper, stretching it as he forced her to stand.

He let her go. 'I'm giving you ten seconds to get out that door. One. Two. Three.'

'Oh, for God's sake, calm down.'

'Four.'

Tess stared at him, and he saw the fear in her eyes. Good. She should be scared, because right now he could strangle her with his bare hands.

'Five.'

She took a step backwards, and stood with her palms held up to him. 'Just listen for a minute. Sophie's sick. She's been under the care of a doctor for years. Anything could set her off.'

Aaron ignored her. 'Six.'

Suddenly, Tess's demeanour changed. Fright morphed into guile and she started to laugh. 'Oh my God. You've fallen for her, haven't you? You're in love with the daughter of the man you hate. The irony!'

Aaron kept his face blank. He wanted this monster out of Hakea Lodge. He needed her out, before the seal on his rage melted and spewed his hatred throughout his house.

'Seven.'

Tess poked a finger toward his chest. 'You don't frighten me, Aaron Laidlaw. You're nothing. The son of a horse-doping drunk and a whore.'

His hands clenched into fists. 'Eight.'

'I should have left Sophie bleeding in that bath,' she spat. 'At least I'd have escaped this place.'

Aaron breathed in deeply through his nose, trying to keep calm. 'Nine,' he said, but his voice was cracking. What sort of monster had Sophie had to endure all these years?

They stared at each other, their mutual loathing curdling the air. Then Tess's bravado failed and she wilted as though poisoned by her own bile. With a turned-down mouth, she regarded Aaron with defeat in her eyes.

'You of all people should know when Ian sets his sights on something nothing stands in his way. Don't fight him. You won't win. Trust me, I know.'

He didn't need to count the last number. With that warning Tess left, a different woman, but Aaron felt no pity. Whatever her issue was, he had no time for it. He waited for her car to fade into the night before dragging out a chair and slumping into it. He pressed his forehead hard into his hands, trying to erase what he'd heard.

How much of it was true? If any? Tess could be bullshitting about Sophie for all he knew.

Despite any rumours you might hear and all appearances to the contrary, I'm actually not screwed up. At least, not any more.

Sophie had told him she was fine, but what if she was lying? What if she wasn't fine at all?

The only thing he'd managed to determine from the whole miserable mess was that Tess hated her brother just as much as she hated Sophie. All Ian Dixon cared about was his career, all Tess cared about was herself, and no one, it seemed, cared about Sophie. No one.

Except for him.

Tess was right. The irony of it was unbelievable.

EIGHT

TEN, nine, eight, seven, six . . .

Sophie kept her breathing steady as the timer droned the countdown for the cross-country. Beneath her, Chuck trembled, ready to burst out of the starting box and take the first jump at a gallop. As the numbers dropped, her fingers twitched and curled around the reins. This meant everything to her. Not only could this be her first two-star win, it would do much to repair the confidence Buck's behaviour was slowly destroying.

Five, four, three, two, one. Good luck.

Chuck leapt forward, his ears pointed straight ahead at the first fence, a big but inviting jump made of large timber logs bound together with rope. A tough fence designed to test the riders and give the horses a taste of what was coming. Like the old pro he was, Chuck gathered himself and cleared it easily.

They cleared the next few fences without mishap, and Chuck settled into the long, comfortable stride that had given Sophie no end of pleasure over the years. But this was no pleasure ride. In just under six minutes they had to cover over three kilometres of sometimes difficult terrain and clear thirty-two obstacles, each requiring intense concentration and more than a bit of courage. Eventing was not a sport for the faint of heart.

With her mouth set in a determined line, she steered Chuck through every aggressive option and galloped every section possible. She'd woken that morning wanting this win so badly her chest had ached, but now she was out on course, all she could think about was Chuck and the jumps. Her focus was absolute.

Over the Fallen Log, the Brush, the Flowerbed, the Arrows. Over Langford's Leap, Malcolm's Maze, the Bull Fight, the Old Quarry. Over jumps named because of their construction, the course builder, the sponsor, or after some person or event in local history. High fences, wide fences, colourful fences, natural fences, banks, drops, ditches, mounds – Chuck faced and conquered them all without a moment's hesitation, his faith in her complete.

Only two jumps had given her real pause during her course walks. Fence fifteen was one of them. The fence was made up of two brush jumps on either side of a wide gully. After leaping over the first fence, the horses descended into the gully via a giant staircase, popping down off each step until they reached the bottom before cantering up a steep incline and jumping the other brush.

Individually, the obstacles posed no problem, but together and in slippery conditions, the fence doubled in difficulty. The first brush was large enough to warrant an approach with some speed, but the bounce down the steps required tight control. The horse would need to be well checked, making the subsequent scramble out of the gully and jump over the second brush harder than it appeared.

As soon as they cleared fence fourteen, Sophie switched her mind to fifteen. There was an easier alternative – she could take a smaller jump into the gully and then wind her way over two more jumps along the bottom, but that route was circuitous and would cost her time. And in this competition, time was her enemy. For every second she went over the set limit, point four of a penalty was added to her score. Any more than six seconds over, and she could lose the lead.

Chuck threw up wedges of mud as he galloped toward the fence, and although he was now halfway around the course, he showed no sign of tiring. They passed through an open gate and into yet another cypress-ringed paddock. Chuck tossed his head when Sophie eased him back, as though annoyed they were slowing down.

'Steady, boy,' she muttered, her eyes on the first brush.

She steered Chuck toward the fence, checking him until he coiled like a spring. She measured the distance in her mind, calculating the stride length needed to pitch their take-off perfectly, and then relaxed her hold on the reins. Chuck sprang forward, and in two strides he was up and over the first brush and then bouncing down the steps and across the base of the gully.

She sat deep in the saddle and drove him onward with her hips and legs, urging him up the steep slope. She could feel the power in his muscles as he used all his strength to haul himself up, but his great effort had put them closer to the second jump than she had anticipated. They took off right at the base of the fence and she was sure Chuck would leave a leg behind, but although his hoofs struck timber and his knees scratched through the stiff brush, they were over and galloping on before she could even think to grin.

Mud-splattered, sweaty and steaming, they barrelled on. They jumped the water combination with such panache, the crowd that had gathered around in anticipation of carnage, cheered.

Now the oxer she'd measured with Michael Fenton's help loomed. One and a half metres high, the fence straddled a narrow but deep ditch that left the horses staring into blackness. It was a big fence anyway, but coming toward the end of the course, when the horses were lagging and looking for home, it was enormous.

As the oxer came into Chuck's view, Sophie felt his stride falter. She leaned forward and placed an encouraging hand on his neck.

'You can do it, boy. I know you can.'

Chuck gathered himself, and with a shake of his head that said, 'Let me at it', he charged forward.

'Steady on, big fella,' she cautioned as she checked him. They needed a good speed to get over, but attacking an obstacle that big at a full gallop was asking for trouble.

The fence reared up in front of them. Sophie assessed the distance and then kicked Chuck on as she realised he needed to lengthen his stride. He accelerated like a Ferrari.

Four strides to go. Three strides. Two strides.

'Come on, boy. You can do it.'

Chuck leaned back, and with his front legs curled up under him, leapt into the air and sailed over the fence as though it were a tiny cavaletti built for ponies.

But as they came down, his off foreleg buckled slightly and he stumbled. To help him balance, she kept the reins tight, but as she felt him lurch forward, she hauled on them, desperately trying to keep his head up. Chuck's nose almost touched the ground, but he kept going, using every ounce of muscle to stay upright. Two, then three strides and he was back in balance and galloping on.

Sophie touched his neck, thanking him. Her superstar.

The rest of the course passed in a mud-caked rush. At the final fence, she glanced at her watch and then eased back to let Chuck take it in his stride. They were under time and without a single penalty. He had given her his all, and now it was over. No one could catch them. They'd won.

Sophie crossed the line with tears running down her cheeks and her spirit soaring. As she slowed Chuck to a walk, she leaned forward and hugged him. When she finally sat up and wiped away her tears, someone had hold of his reins.

Sophie blinked, and then blinked some more.

It was Aaron.

The course vet approached to give Chuck the once-over. Sophie barely noticed him. Not taking her eyes off Aaron, she slid out of the saddle and stood by Chuck's shoulder, tangling her fingers in his mane, unsure of what to say or do. Her already pounding heart hammered even harder.

'Hey, Soph,' said Aaron.

Sophie opened her mouth but the vet butted in with questions about Chuck. Were there any on-course incidents, had he knocked himself, had he shown any signs of distress, was she worried about him in any way? She answered in monosyllables while staring at Aaron in amazement. She couldn't have been more stunned if it was her father standing in front of her. Finally, the vet gave her the all clear and she was allowed to leave.

'Aaron, what are you doing here?'

He grinned at her, his eyes bright under the broad brim of his battered felt hat. Sophie's stomach somersaulted.

'Thought I'd come and see first-hand what you did.' He shook his head. 'And you reckon steeplechasing's dangerous.'

'Eventing isn't dangerous. It's fun!' She winked at him, feeling even more on top of the world now he was here. 'Especially when you win.'

'You won?'

She nodded, almost bursting with pride. 'It's not official yet but yes, I think so.'

Aaron's smile broadened in delight, then, without warning, he bear-hugged her, oblivious that he was crushing her body protector into her ribs and the stiff band of her helmet into her cheek. 'You are one amazing girl, Sophie Dixon.'

Given his habitual standoffishness, Sophie was shocked at the fervour of his embrace, but the euphoria of his words and her win washed it aside.

He was still grinning when he let her go. He looked so sexy with his wide smile and sparkling eyes, Sophie nearly threw herself back into his arms, but Chuck was blowing hard and needed attention. Sweat stained his dark-brown coat almost black, and steam rose off him in waves. Thunder rumbled in the distance. She needed to get him dry and rugged up before the rain hit, and by the sound of the sky, she needed to be quick.

Sophie dragged her helmet from her head and wiped her face on the sleeve of her top. 'Come on,' she said, taking the reins from Aaron. 'The sooner we get the big hero sorted, the sooner I can bore you senseless with a jump-by-jump description of our round.'

He followed alongside as they walked to the float. 'You don't have to tell me. I saw it.'

She nudged him. 'Yeah, but it's different when you're on board.'

'What? Scarier?'

'No! More exciting.'

'I'm not sure I'd call what I just witnessed exciting. Try petrifying. I thought you and Chuck were goners at that big fence.'

'Nah,' she said, lovingly rubbing Chuck's cheek. 'The superstar here would never let me down.' Tears stung her eyes. 'It's funny. I so desperately wanted to win, but now I know we have, I can't help feeling sad. I know he'll always be with me at home, but competitions won't be the same without him. It's like I'm losing the love of my life.'

He gave her a sharp look. 'You've got Buck.'

Sophie made a noise. 'Not for much longer. I'm advertising him on *Horse Deals* next week.'

Aaron frowned. 'What did he do this time?'

'Refused to jump the first fence. Three times! We were eliminated before we even started. He hates me.'

'He doesn't hate you. He's just a bit spoilt. All he needs is a good kick up the bum. You never let Psycho get on top of you and he's the biggest lunatic there is, so Buck should be a breeze.'

'I've tried. He just ignores me.'

Aaron draped an arm around her shoulder and squeezed. 'Don't give up, Soph. You'll sort him out. You're a great rider.'

She wanted him to leave his arm where it was, but he'd dropped it back to his side. She glanced at his hand, wondering what he'd do if she took it, held it as they walked. As if reading her thoughts, he slid his hands into his pockets.

They reached the float. Buck stood complacently snatching at his hay net as though butter wouldn't melt in his mouth. Sophie glared at him.

'How did you go?' yelled a female competitor as she rode past.

'Clear,' Sophie called back.

The rider nodded. 'Well done.' Then she pulled her horse to a halt and stared at Aaron with raised eyebrows and a predatory expression. Sophie pointedly ignored her until she moved on.

Michael Fenton approached, a wicked smile creasing his handsome face. Flicking Aaron a look, he flung his arms around Sophie and pulled her tight against his chest.

'Congratulations,' he said, planting a lingering kiss close to her mouth. 'Great ride.'

Sophie tried to push him away, but he hung on.

'So that's why you won't go out with me,' he whispered into her ear. 'Come on, Soph. You can do better than that.'

'Bugger off, Michael,' hissed Sophie, not wanting to make a scene in front of Aaron. 'And don't call me Soph.'

With a grin and a wink, Michael let her go.

'Who was that?' asked Aaron when he'd sauntered off.

'No one.'

'Must have been someone. He kissed you.'

She busied herself with Chuck's saddle. 'Just another competitor.'

Aaron took the saddle from her. 'Looked like he knew you pretty well.'

She shrugged. She didn't want to talk about Michael Fenton, especially with Aaron.

'Have you two got a thing going on?'

Sophie stared at him. He was joking, surely. She'd already told him there was no one.

Aaron's eyes swept over her face as though searching for something he was afraid to find. Was he jealous? She almost laughed. She never thought she'd have anything to thank Michael Fenton for, but it seemed that now she had.

'Not jealous, are you?' she asked. She said it like it was a joke, but it wasn't.

He didn't reply immediately, intent on fiddling with the buckle of Chuck's breastplate, but then the words came out, leaving Sophie wishing she hadn't asked.

'Of course not. I couldn't care less who you went out with. He just looked like a tosser, that's all.'

Despondency settled over her like a heavy wet blanket, but she refused to let it show. Instead, she concentrated on Chuck. With two of them working on him, it took no time to wash off the sweat and dry him down with towels. Once he was rugged and settled, she sent Aaron off to buy coffee while she changed out of her muddy clothes in the back of the float.

She was sitting on the Range Rover's tailgate, alternating between sticking her tongue out at Buck and blowing kisses at Chuck, when Aaron returned. He handed her a foam cup and sat down next to her.

'I checked the scoreboard for you. There's a big E by Buck's name but Chuck's score looks the same as before.'

She nodded. 'Thanks.'

An awkward silence fell between them. They drank coffee, looked at the horses, watched other riders go by. Anything except look at each other. Sophie picked at the edges of her cup until the rim was a jagged mess and the surface of the coffee sprinkled with tiny white balls. Aaron took it out of her hands and tossed the contents. He jammed the cup onto the base of his own empty one.

'Do you want me to go?'

She looked at her watch. 'I suppose you'd better. Even if you leave now you'll still be late with the feeds.'

'The yard's sorted. My mate Josh is looking after it for me.'

'Oh.' Sophie gnawed at a fingernail, unsure what that implied. It sounded like he intended to hang around for the rest of the day, but why? Only one of them was suffering a pathetic crush and he'd made it quite plain it wasn't him.

'Well, if you want to watch the three-star competition you'd better head back,' she said. 'There aren't that many competitors.'

'I'm not interested in the three-star.'

So what was he interested in? Buck? Chuck? The horse float? Her annoyance grew with every silent minute, but just as she was about to ask him why he was sitting looking like a stunned mullet, the sky opened up. Rain dropped in fat heavy globules, splattering the float and Range Rover with such intensity it sounded like hail.

The horses snorted and pranced, turning their backsides in the direction of the weather. Sophie jumped down from their perch. Aaron slammed the boot shut and helped her gather the few items that were yet to be packed away. As the rain intensified, they ducked into the side door of the float to wait it out.

She peered out the window at Buck. Chuck, ever the stoic, would stay where he was, but Buck was likely to pull back and take off. His ears lay flat against his neck, but despite his mulish expression, he seemed content to stay where he was. Sophie let out her breath in relief.

The aluminium sides of the float vibrated as thunder rumbled overhead. She gave Buck another glance, but he appeared fine. She turned back to Aaron. He leaned stiffly against the right-hand chest bar with his hat in his hands, watching her.

'I suppose we'll just have to wait,' she said.

'It'll blow over soon enough. In ten minutes the sun will probably start shining.'

'Yep. Typical western districts weather. Four seasons in one day.'

With the ramp and top rear doors closed and little light penetrating the tinted windows, it was strangely intimate inside the float. The comforting, familiar smell of leather, hay and horse hung in the still air. The spacious float seemed cramped and small, and unable to accommodate two people at once.

Despite the cold, Sophie's skin flushed in the close confines.

Aaron's eyes seemed anchored to hers, but not in a way she wanted. He was scrutinising her, in the same way a child would observe an insect, as though she were something alien and scary, but awesome and fascinating at the same time.

'I wonder if they'll cancel the presentation,' she said.

He didn't answer.

'You should probably leave.'

'I want to stay.'

'Oh.' She took a deep breath, trying to summon up the courage to ask why. He said something but she couldn't hear him through the rain. 'Sorry, what did you say?'

'Do you wish I hadn't come?'

'No. I'm glad you're here.' She took a step toward him. His Adam's apple bobbed as he swallowed. She took his hand and held it with both of hers. 'It means a lot.'

He swallowed again and gave her a tight smile. 'I'm glad,' he said, and then, very gently, he removed his hand from her grip.

———

Cold seeped through Sophie's socks as she stood in her kitchen staring at the phone she'd placed onto the sparkling surface of the granite breakfast bar. The old house's thick stone walls kept it insulated from the worst of the cold but the tiled floor seemed to suck the chill from the ground.

She thought about making a cup of tea but didn't fill the kettle. Instead, she drummed her fingers on the benchtop, thinking. Suddenly, she snatched up the phone and hit dial. The call went through to a message bank.

'Hi, Dad. It's me, Sophie. I just thought I'd let you know Chuck and I won the two-star at Lake Ackerman today. It's the first two star I've ever won, you know, so it's pretty exciting. And I've decided to retire Chuck.' She stopped and took a shuddering breath as her throat choked up. 'Mum would've been so proud of him today.' She took another breath. 'I guess I'll talk to you later. Bye.'

She hung up and stood staring at the phone, immediately wishing she could erase the message. She shouldn't have mentioned her mother. She should have left the call until the morning when she was feeling less emotional. He'd only punish her for her neediness by not calling. He'd done it before. Like that memorable Christmas three years ago, when yet again he'd chosen to stay in Canberra. She'd left a long drunken message on his home phone late at night, asking why he didn't love her. He'd never returned the call, never mentioned its existence. And when she'd finally enquired if he'd received it, he denied all knowledge and then asked if it wasn't time she went back to seeing her doctor. She'd mumbled she was fine, but the hurt had lasted for weeks.

The gas fire was barely winning its battle against the cold when, after a long shower, she padded into the lounge in her pyjamas. She turned it up to flat out before sinking into her favourite armchair and flicking on the television, hoping to distract herself.

God knows how many pay TV and free-to-air channels, and there was still nothing on. She stared at the fake logs and dancing flames of the gas fire and let tears flood her eyes. This time, her tears weren't over her father, but for another man she didn't understand. Another man who didn't want her love.

They'd been trapped in the float together for fifteen long, embarrassing minutes. After his gentle rebuff, Sophie had found she couldn't bear to look at Aaron. She'd turned her back and stood at the window looking out at Buck and actually wishing he would do something obliging for once and run off so she'd have to chase him.

It wasn't until the rain had eased that Aaron spoke. He held his hat in his hands, rolling and unrolling the edges of the brim like an obsessed milliner.

'You scared the crap out of me today,' he'd said.

She'd turned to look at him. Holding hands with her had scared him?

'I watched some of the others. None of them went as fast as you or took the hard options like you did. Why?'

'I guess they just didn't want to win as much as me.'

'Is that the only reason?' His eyes were fixed on hers.

She'd shrugged, not understanding what he was getting at. 'I can't think of any other.'

'Are you sure?'

'Yes,' she said slowly, staring at him and wondering if this was some weird joke. 'I'm sure.'

'Good.'

Apparently satisfied, he'd donned his hat and walked toward the door. He held it open for her but as she'd brushed past he'd put his mouth close to her ear and spoken again. 'You holding my hand scared the crap out of me too.'

When she'd looked at him, he'd shaken his head as if he couldn't believe what he'd just said and nudged her out the door.

She'd wandered around in a fog of lust the rest of the afternoon, trying her hardest to engineer another close encounter, but Aaron had kept his distance. Even after the presentation, when she'd sidled up to him and asked if he wanted to kiss the winner, his kiss was brief to the point of rudeness. And if that wasn't bad enough, he'd then ruffled her hair like she was his ten-year-old sister.

Tess and the others had been right, though for the wrong reasons. She should have stayed well away from Aaron Laidlaw.

And now it was too late.

NINE

AARON STILLED and cocked his head. The distinctive knock-knock of the Range Rover filtered in through the door of Hakea Lodge's feed room. He smiled and allowed himself a moment's mild fantasy before shutting down his thoughts. Making it through the morning without touching Sophie would be hard enough.

But it was a day for optimism. The storm had blown through, leaving clear skies and a landscape scrubbed clean. Earlier, he'd sat on the verandah steps watching the sun rise and the horses snort and stamp as the first rays of light drifted across the yards.

He'd thought about Sophie, and dreamed of how it could have been between them – but never would be. At sixteen, he hadn't understood that mothers were capable of selfish exploitation. Or that fathers could die of shame. They were lessons he'd learnt too late, just as he'd learnt too late that pity and compassion could turn into something else. Something they shouldn't.

The combined thrill and terror of watching Sophie ride cross-country like some equestrian kamikaze still lingered, plucking at his conscience the way Tess's words did. Little pecks of doubt, eating away at his perception of Sophie, making him question her fortitude and query his own judgement.

Yet the memory of her expression when she had looked up from Chuck's sweating neck and saw him eclipsed everything.

Mud-splattered, wearing that stupid egg on her head and that equally stupid body protector, she'd gazed at him with huge grey eyes full of tears and amazement, as if seeing him was the best thing that had ever happened to her.

No one had looked at him like that before. Ever.

He'd known straightaway he was in trouble. That something had shifted between them. If he'd had any doubts about his feelings, they'd been dashed the moment he'd seen that weedy wanker kiss her. Jealousy had clotted his bloodstream and he'd wanted to yell at her for making him feel things he didn't want to feel. But he couldn't. So he'd hurt her instead by saying he didn't care, and realised too late when he saw her face that he'd hurt himself too.

But what was he supposed to do? A relationship between them was impossible. He could fantasise about her all he liked but that's where it had to end. Love required openness and honesty, yet he could offer neither. The truth was too destructive.

Although that didn't stop him dreaming.

'Hi.' Sophie stood leaning against the doorframe with her arms crossed, silhouetted against the light.

'Hey, Soph.'

She came into the room and sat on an unopened sack of oats. Aaron went back to measuring out feeds, but could sense her scrutiny. From his stable, Rowdy let out yet another whinny. He'd been at it non-stop since six-thirty. Aaron suspected he was calling out for Sophie, and knew exactly how the horse felt.

'Rowdy's living up to his name,' she said.

He glanced at her. She was looking at his arms. He shot a look at them, self-conscious. The sleeves of his flannelette shirt were rolled up almost to the shoulders. Oaten dust had turned his blond hairs white, but otherwise they looked like they always did – a bit more muscular than average from working with horses, but overall the arms of a normal male. Maybe she preferred men with darker hair.

'I think he missed you over the weekend,' Aaron said, wishing she'd stop staring. It was making him paranoid.

'Mmm.'

He stopped measuring feeds and eyed her. 'Are you all right?'

She blinked. 'Fine, fine. Sorry, I was miles away.'

'Still daydreaming about your big win?'

She shook her head. 'No. Just daydreaming.'

He went back to work, digging oats out of a hessian sack with a large galvanised iron dipper and dropping them into the buckets he'd lined up across the room. The feed room was dusty and smelt of chaff and the unmistakable odour of mice.

'There's a thumping great snake in here somewhere,' he said.

'Carpet python?'

'Yeah.'

'Vanaheim's got one too. They're the best rat-catchers.' She smiled. 'Are you trying to scare me?'

He was. He wanted her to stop eyeing him that way. It didn't help that she looked morning gorgeous. Ruddy-cheeked from the cold, scrubbed and fresh, with her hair pulled back and the pearly skin of her neck teasing him with its smoothness. Even her mouth was conspiring against him with its inviting soft smile.

He was definitely trying to scare her. He wanted her away from him before he did something stupid. Like kiss her.

'I thought girls were supposed to be scared of snakes.'

She shrugged. 'It's a carpet python. It's harmless. Who are we taking out this morning?'

'Costa Motza and Pollyanna to start with.'

She stood up. 'I'll go fetch my horse then. It's about time I showed you how it was done.'

'How what was done?'

'Slow training.'

His jaw dropped open. 'You're joking, aren't you?'

'No,' she said, but her mouth twitched.

It took him a few seconds to realise she was pulling his leg. He blamed it on the way her lips quirked as she tried not to laugh, but she could have been poking her tongue out and he still wouldn't have twigged. He was too busy thinking about things he shouldn't.

'Are you sure you wouldn't prefer to ride a real racehorse, like Pollyanna?'

She crossed her arms. 'Costa Motza is a real racehorse.'

'You keep telling yourself that, Soph.'

'*He is.*'

'Yeah, yeah.'

She glared at him, then picked up a handful of oats and threw it at him. 'Is.'

A single grain caught in his collar and slipped down into his shirt. He dropped the dipper and pulled his shirttails out of his jeans, shaking the fabric until the oat fell out. 'You don't want to start something you can't finish, Sophie.'

She threw some more at him.

'I'm not warning you again.'

'Take it back,' she said.

'Take what back?'

'What you said about Costa Motza.'

It was bad form for a trainer to criticise one of his charges, but she looked so deliciously outraged he couldn't help but tease, just to see how far she'd go.

'I told you before, Costa Motza's not a racehorse's backside.'

Another handful of oats landed against his chest.

'Isn't.'

'No more oats, Sophie. This is your last chance.'

As she dug into the sack, he pounced. He pulled her against his chest, pinning her arms to her sides with one arm. With his free hand, he scooped a handful of oats from the sack.

She tilted her head back to look at him. 'Don't you *dare.*'

He grinned. He would dare. He'd dare a lot. Holding her firmly, he squirreled his hand down the back of her jumper. Her skin felt warm and smooth, and as he tunnelled further into that snug burrow her breath shortened into sexy little pants. Slowly, his gaze locked on hers, he released the oats. Her eyes widened as the scratchy little seeds tumbled down her back. She wriggled, her mouth parting in a shocked 'O'. A whimper escaped her lips as she writhed against him. The sound turned his heartbeat arrhythmic and sent his groin hard.

He let her go.

She arched her back and dug one hand down the neck of her jumper and the other up the bottom. He glanced at her chest, at the breasts pushing toward him, and swallowed. Unbidden, an image of her naked and sprawled over the bags of oats, waiting for him, panting those little breaths as her nipples hardened with desire, invaded his mind.

His hands twitched as he fantasised about what he'd do to her, the pleasure she'd feel, the sensations he'd arouse. He'd take it slow, very slow, making the moment unforgettable. He'd scatter kisses on her stomach and ease his way up her chest, blessing each of her perfect rib bones with his mouth. And as he touched her, she'd make that same whimper before gasping his name as his hot mouth closed over the nub of her breast.

With a grimace, she tossed the few grains she'd managed to retrieve at him. 'That's not fair!'

He dusted off his hand, driving the fantasy from his head while hoping like hell she wouldn't notice his hard-on. 'You started it.'

'I didn't put any down your back, though.' She squirmed and he knew the itch must be near unbearable. Oats were terrible, but by wriggling, she was only making it worse.

He regarded her, trying not to laugh as she started picking at the seat of her pants, jigging comically as she tried to shake out the oats.

'Itchy?'

Her bottom lip stuck out, sulky and adorable. He wanted to suck on it.

'They're in my underpants.'

He drew air between his teeth, feigning sympathy. 'That's gotta hurt.'

'There's probably mouse wee on those oats.'

'A little bit of mouse wee never hurt anyone.'

'Says who?'

Suddenly, the yearning to touch, to feel, overwhelmed him. He reached out and ran his thumb over that deliciously pouty lip, his bursting heart free and in control. 'Says me.'

The atmosphere changed, as though all the dust motes were rubbing against one another, electrifying the air with their friction. Sophie stopped wriggling and gazed at him, and then her lips parted and her pink tongue darted out to wet their soft surface. He couldn't stop looking at them, hungering to know what they tasted like. Sweet, he decided. They'd taste sweet, like her.

She touched his face with warm fingertips and slipped her hand around his neck to draw him close, so close he could feel her breath on his skin. He breathed it in. It smelt of toothpaste. He closed his eyes and nuzzled at her cheek, inhaling the aroma of her skin as if it were the last oxygen on earth.

She pressed her mouth against his ear and he felt her smile against his cheek. Electricity jolted down his spine.

'Kiss me.' Her voice sounded husky, full of need, like him.

She pressed against him, and he groaned at the pressure on his erection. He cupped her face, studying those wonderful grey eyes, searching for reservations. There were none. Only pure desire for him.

'Sophie.' It was all he could say. Just her name. Just her beautiful, perfect name.

Very slowly, he kissed her smooth forehead, then her fluttering, delicate eyelids. He kissed the infinitely soft skin beneath her eyes and felt the tickle of her lashes against his nose. He heard her shallow, excited breaths. He felt anticipation engulf her body as he moved inexorably down the contours of her face until his mouth rested at the very edge of her quivering, parted lips.

And in that long ecstatic moment, he felt every tiny thing about her and knew he was lost forever.

Rowdy whinnied.

His eyes flicked open. The odour of grain and chaff penetrated his nostrils, waking his love-sodden brain. He jerked his mouth away and stared at Sophie's bliss-filled face, then dropped his hands and took a hasty step backwards, his chest heaving. What the hell had he been thinking? This was Sophie, for Christ's sake. The Sophie whose mother he'd as good as killed. The little Sophie who'd screamed at her mother's funeral as though it was her being buried. The same Sophie he'd vowed to protect and then never had.

The Sophie to whom his guilty heart owed everything except *this*.

'I'm sorry.' He grabbed at his hair with his hands, horrified at how close he'd come to wounding her in a way that would never heal. 'I shouldn't have done that.'

She crossed her arms and cocked her head at him. 'Done what? Put oats down my back or nearly kiss me?'

'Both.'

Her head dropped for a moment. 'Thanks. Nice to know you find me so attractive.'

He opened his mouth to tell her he thought she was beautiful and then realised it would only make things worse. She raised her head, grey eyes limpid, and they stared at each other through the dusty air of the feed room. Two people starving but only one knowing the food they wanted was poisonous.

Sophie was the first to move. She reached for his hand and took it in both of hers. 'It's not scary,' she said, but he knew she was wrong. What was happening between them wasn't just frightening, it was impossible – but he couldn't tell her that without admitting what he'd done. And he could never do that. Not now.

For the second time in two days, he pulled his hand from hers and endured her face crumpling with hurt. He looked away, hating himself.

'You can use the bathroom to shake out your clothes while I go get the horses ready.'

She touched his sleeve. 'Aaron.'

'Don't, Soph. It's no good.' With his hands deep in his pockets, he left her alone in the feed room.

TEN

THE WEEK PROGRESSED with painful slowness. Sophie's red-rimmed eyes seemed to worsen with every day and Aaron felt guilt tear at his heart every time he looked at her. He knew he didn't look much better. Sleep refused to give him respite from the long nights of worry.

He knew he was driving Sophie insane, but he couldn't stop himself from calling her every evening, needing to hear her voice, sad but unmistakably alive. And every morning, as he waited for her to pull into the yard, anxiety yanked and pulled at his insides and ugly words circled his head, reminding him who would be to blame if she didn't come.

The memory of Fiona Dixon haunted him. The way her face had morphed from horror to a strange serenity with every word he'd flung. She'd been so calm, taking him in her arms and comforting him the way his mother never had, stroking his head and promising him it would be all right, giving him hope when all the time she knew she had none.

Suicides lied. He wouldn't be misled again.

On Thursday night, he'd rung Sophie only to have her snap at him that, no, she wasn't all right. Her rotten father hadn't called, Tess had left the hayshed paddock gate open again and Buck had dumped her twice that afternoon. He'd panicked, racing around to Vanaheim and banging on her door like a lunatic. He gave Sophie credit for being more polite than if he'd been in her shoes, but her intention was clear.

Piss off and leave me alone. You've hurt me enough.

The situation couldn't last. They were both going crazy.

'Are you going to tell me what the hell's going on with you, or do I have to guess?' asked Sophie on Friday morning, to Aaron's relief. Since she'd booted him off Vanaheim the previous night, he'd been mulling over how to bring it up. They were sitting on the verandah step – him at one end, Sophie at the other, and at least a metre of empty space between them – drinking tea and soaking up rays of autumn sunshine.

He took a sip of tea to collect himself, wondering where he should begin.

Sophie filled in the silence for him. 'Why do you call me every night?'

That question was easy to answer. 'To see if you're okay.'

'Why wouldn't I be okay?'

That one was harder. 'I don't know.'

She sighed. 'You ring me every night to see if I'm okay and yet you won't come within breathing distance of me. I'm starting to think I smell or something.'

'You don't smell, except of horses.' And wonderful Sophie things like toothpaste and soap.

'Are you scared of me?'

'No.'

Sophie tossed the contents of her cup out into the yard and stood. 'If you aren't going to talk to me, Aaron, then there's no point having this conversation. Who are we taking out next?'

He glanced at her. Her cheeks were red and her grey eyes dark.

She was angry. He looked away, knowing that what he was going to say was likely to turn that anger into pain.

'I'm not scared *of* you, Soph. I'm scared *for* you.'

'Why?'

He closed his eyes, his heart aching, and tried to find the words to ask what he needed to hear. The words wouldn't come, but they didn't need to. From the moment he looked at her again, he knew she'd already figured it out.

She gasped and took a step back, her eyes full of disbelief. She tugged at the sleeves of her jumper, stretching the woollen fabric over her hands. It was done so quickly, he knew it was automatic, like an animal hiding its wounds from a predator.

'Oh, God. Tess came to see you, didn't she?'

He nodded and stood. She looked so pale he thought she'd collapse. He took a step toward her, but she held up her hand, warning him away.

'Give me a minute.' She turned and stumbled across the yard to Rowdy's stable and disappeared inside. Aaron stood helpless, not knowing what to do. Wanting to comfort her, but fearing it would only make things worse.

He sat back on the step and put his head in his hands. Once again, he'd failed. He'd made her miserable when all he wanted was to see her happy, to see her living a life filled with joy and love and laughter.

There could be no forgiveness for what he'd done, but he could at least watch over her and keep her from harm. How was he supposed to do that, though, when the very thing he needed to protect her from was himself? But he had to be strong. The time had come to pay for Fiona Dixon and Rodger Laidlaw's deaths.

And he knew now the price was Sophie.

She came out of Rowdy's box with her shoulders squared and her stride steady, and he admired her for her composure. She sat down next to him on the step. There were no tears, just the same determined look he'd seen on her face before she took off out of the starter's box on Sunday.

'What did she tell you?' she said.

He swallowed. 'That you'd tried to kill yourself.'

She nodded. 'I did. When I was fifteen.'

'Did you mean it?'

She laughed but bitterness tinged its edges. 'Oh, yeah. I meant it all right.'

Oh, shit.

'Why?'

'I was upset over a boy, among other things.' She looked at him and then sighed. 'Go on. Ask away. I can see you're dying to. You want all the gory details? I'll tell you, every single last horrible moment of it if you want. Just get it over with so we can go back to being whatever it was we were before.'

But what were they before? Two people pretending to be friends? Real friendship required honesty, and he could never be honest with her. Almost lovers? That was a joke. The only sex he could ever have with Sophie was in his head. So what were they? Romeo and frigging Juliet, that's what. Destined never to be anything except fated because he'd once been stupid and naive and unforgivably cruel.

He rubbed his hand over his face, overwhelmed by bleakness and sickened by his own pessimism. Sophie sat beside him clench-jawed and rigid, drawing on a strength he wished he shared.

'Who was he?'

'No one important.'

'He must have been important to you.'

She turned to look at him. 'Why do you need to know?'

He needed to know so he could hunt the bastard down and beat the shit out of him, but Sophie didn't need to hear that.

He shrugged. 'Curiosity, I guess.'

She looked away. 'It was just someone from pony club I had a teenage crush on.'

He took her hand. It felt cold. 'What happened?'

When she spoke, her voice was unemotional, robotic, as though she'd repeated the explanation a hundred times and was now bored with it.

'He asked me out. There was no one to stop me, so I went. I was fifteen. He was eighteen. He acted like he really cared about me and, like the stupid little fool I was, I fell for it. Two weeks later, I lost my virginity to him on the back seat of his car at a pony club camp. Afterwards, I found out he'd done it for a bet. Slashing my wrists seemed a good idea at the time. Happy now?'

No. He wasn't happy. His gut burned with anger and his heart ached with sorrow and guilt. But as he'd discovered over these past weeks, when it came to Sophie, his guilt was like a hungry animal that fed on her suffering. It needed more.

'And the other times?'

'What other times?'

'Tess said you've tried a number of times.'

'Tess is full of shit.'

He scanned her face, trying to work out if she was telling the truth.

'I don't lie, Aaron. I hate lies, just like I hate secrets. Ask me anything and I'll give you a truthful answer, even if it hurts.'

'Are you okay now?'

'Yeah. Two years of Dr Charlton and lots of drugs put paid to that. Now I'm just your average 22-year-old going through another rebellious phase. The difference being that I'm older and a bit smarter this time.' She smiled, this time genuinely. 'And I have no intention of having sex on the back seat of anyone's car, including yours.'

'I don't blame you. Given the springs have gone in the Land Cruiser's, it'd be bloody uncomfortable.'

She laughed. 'I'll remember that.'

He squeezed her fingers, serious again. 'Promise me you'll tell me if you ever feel like that again.'

'What, like having sex on the back seat of a car?'

'No, I meant the other.'

'I know you meant the other.'

He touched her face. Her skin was soft and cold from the frigid morning air. He wanted to kiss it. She closed her eyes and pressed against his fingers as though his touch was the loveliest thing she'd ever felt. His stomach flipped over.

'Promise me you'll tell me.'

She opened her eyes and shook her head. 'I don't need to. It won't happen again. And that, I can promise you.' She turned her face from his hand and stood. 'Come on, let's get back to work.'

Aaron didn't want the moment to end. He wanted to stay on the step talking to her. 'It can wait a bit longer. We'll have another cuppa.'

She shook her head, her mouth narrowed and her eyes focused on the distance. 'Nope, let's get this over and done with.'

'Why?'

'Because the sooner I leave here, the sooner I can get back to Vanaheim and murder my aunt.'

ELEVEN

THE COTTAGE STANK of unwashed clothes and stale alcohol. Sophie stepped over an empty wine bottle and yanked on the kitchen curtains. Light exposed the squalor in which her aunt lived.

'Tess!'

A grunt issued from somewhere in the next room.

'Oh, for God's sake,' muttered Sophie, kicking another bottle out of the way and stomping into the lounge. Tess lay on a fully extended recliner wearing yet another of her brother's old work shirts, scarlet lace underpants and football socks. A balled-up pile of denim sat on the carpet in front of the television. Sophie assumed it was Tess's discarded jeans.

She jerked open another set of curtains. Blissful sunlight streamed in. Outside, in contrast to the cottage's dust and grime, ryegrass and clover pasture swayed glossy and vibrant green in the breeze. Against the boundary, Vanaheim's plane trees stood solid and strong. Whatever her aunt threw at her, Sophie knew she had to do the same. She turned back to Tess.

'You're a disgrace.'

Tess shrugged, reached down for the bottle sitting beside her chair and drank straight from it.

Sophie crossed her arms and leaned against the wall. Tess had her moments, but Sophie had never seen her this degenerate. She wondered what had happened. Dumped by a lover? It was hard to imagine her aunt having one.

'What do you want?' The words came out slurred and Sophie realised that even though it was barely lunchtime, Tess was incredibly drunk.

'What do I want? Now, let me see.' Sophie put a finger to her mouth as though thinking hard. 'I want Buck to stop being horrible, I want Costa Motza to win races and make me rich, and I quite fancy the idea of sleeping with Aaron Laidlaw. Um, what else is there?'

Tess's flaccid mouth turned up in a shiraz-stained smile. 'Told you.'

Sophie ignored her. 'Oh, yeah. I wouldn't mind knowing why my father dislikes me so much, and you, for that matter. But what I'd really like – no, what I want and will do my utmost to achieve, is you off Vanaheim.'

The smile fell from Tess's lips. She narrowed bleary eyes at Sophie. 'Can't make me.'

'I'm going to apply to the trustees to take my inheritance early. I've proven I can look after the farm. I think they'll take that into consideration.'

'Bitch.'

Sophie pushed off the wall and snatched the bottle, holding it out of Tess's grasping reach. 'What is your problem?'

'You!'

Sophie stared at her, heart hammering. Tess may have been drunk but the loathing in her eyes was unmistakable.

'What have I ever done to make you hate me so much?'

'Exist.' Tess flicked a lever and the recliner's footrest snapped down. She stood, wobbly but upright, facing off her niece. 'It's your fault I'm stuck here in this miserable hole. Yours and your selfish bitch of a mother's.'

A slap would have been better than hearing those words. At least Sophie could have hit back and felt justified. But words had always been Tess's greatest weapon. Her victims bled slowly from their wounds. She liked to watch their suffering.

'You can leave whenever you want.'

'No I can't!' Tess fell back into the chair.

'Why not?'

'Your fucking father, that's why not.'

Sophie stared at her in confusion. 'What are you talking about?'

Tess surveyed Sophie through narrowed eyes. 'Why didn't you do it properly when you had the chance?'

There it was, a reference to Sophie's suicide attempt. Tess always brought it out when she really wanted to hurt. Sophie glanced at the trees again and straightened her shoulders. She could endure this.

'Because unlike you, I have some strength of will. I'm tougher than you think, Tess. I always was. It just took me a while to realise it.'

Tess grunted.

'Why can't you leave?'

Her aunt wrapped her arms around her bare legs and hugged them to her chest. 'Do you know what I was doing before I came here?'

'Not really. I thought you were working in a hotel or something.'

Tess made a noise of disgust. 'Is that what Ian told you?'

Sophie couldn't remember. She thought it was Tess who'd told her, but perhaps it was her father. It was all too long ago and she'd been too young and too distraught to care. And they'd never had the sort of relationship where it was normal to share such things.

'It wasn't a hotel. It was a guesthouse called Braeburn, over-looking Corio Bay. A grand old house built in the '20s as a seaside getaway by a wealthy Melbourne family, which was converted in the '50s to holiday accommodation. And it was once your grandmother's.'

'My grandmother's? Why haven't I heard about this?'

Tess gave her a 'don't be so stupid' look before staring sulkily at her socks. 'It was my house. And your father took it.' A tear slid from her eye. She swiped it away and reached for the bottle, but it remained in Sophie's grip. Tess glared at her. 'Give me my drink.'

'Not until you tell me what's going on.'

'Won't make any difference.'

'Why don't you let me be the judge of that?'

Tess said nothing. She stared at her feet, mouth tight, fingers digging into her legs as she held them curled up tight to her chest. Sophie waited. She wasn't leaving until she had the truth.

'Braeburn was meant to be mine. She promised it to me.' She regarded Sophie, red eyes watering. 'We visited each summer, in a room set aside especially for us. Just Mum and me, and for two weeks of the year *I* was the most important thing in the world, not Ian. It was our special place, where we were both happy. Then she died and Dad claimed it.' Her mouth tightened even further, as though she was trying to hold herself in. 'He said I didn't deserve it.'

Sophie took a breath. As a child she'd picked up hints of a rift between her grandfather and Tess. On the rare occasions Sophie was naughty in his presence, he'd shake a finger and tell her to watch it she didn't turn out like her aunt. And more than once she heard Wally Dixon tell his son how glad he was to see that Sophie took after him and not Tess. But like everything else, when she'd asked for details, everyone clammed up. Even her mother.

'Is that why you left Vanaheim?'

Tess snorted. 'Hardly. I left because the only thing Dad cared about was Ian. No matter how well I did at school or sport, or how hard I worked on the farm, Ian did it ten times better. So I stopped trying. Decided to have fun instead.' She smiled a little, lost in a memory. 'The old boy didn't like that much, but belting me only made me worse.' She sobered, bit her lip and stared out the window. 'I hate this place.'

If what Tess said was true, then Sophie couldn't blame her. 'Then what happened?'

'I got pregnant.'

'And the baby?'

'Miscarriage.'

'I'm sorry.'

Tess sneered. 'No, you're not.'

Sophie did feel sorry for Tess but wasn't going to waste her breath convincing her aunt otherwise. 'So why come back here if you hated it so much? Dad could have found someone else to look after me.'

Her aunt eyed the bottle. 'I need a drink.'

'You've had enough.'

'Just give me the bottle,' said Tess wearily. 'Or you can forget about me telling you anything else.'

Sophie twisted the bottle in her hands, considering; then, with a sigh, she handed it over. Tess snatched it from her fingers, pressed the neck to her mouth and drank in gulps. Disgusted, Sophie looked away.

'Your father promised me Braeburn. He knew how much I loved that place. He'd arranged a job for me there when things were bad, and kept it secret from Dad. I thought once the old boy died he'd pass it on, but Ian kept telling me I wasn't ready.' A tear leaked from her eye. 'I was. I'd worked hard, stayed clean. I deserved what my mother promised me, but he wouldn't budge. Then your mother killed herself and he came up with an offer he knew I wouldn't be able to refuse.' Tess's voice choked as the tears fell harder.

Sophie reached for the wall, her stomach clogging with guilt and despair, and slowly slid down its length.

'Six years with you was all I had to do. I told myself I could manage, that the sacrifice was worth it, but this place eats at you.' She pointed a shaky finger at Sophie. 'Then you had to go and ruin it all by slitting your fucking wrists!'

The bottle smashed against the wall above Sophie's head. Glass and red wine sprayed over her in brown and burgundy drops. The tough base of the bottle struck her shoulder and fell to the carpet with a dull thud. Sophie started to shake.

Tess rose and advanced across the room, red-stained teeth bared, eyes glowing like a rabid animal. She stood over Sophie. 'Do you know what he did?'

Unable to speak, Sophie shook her head.

Tess crouched in front of her, grabbed her jumper and yanked on it. 'He kept Braeburn. Your bastard father punished me for your weakness. I've got to stay in this place with you until you turn twenty-five.' She let go and fell backwards onto the glass-covered carpet. 'I hate you,' she said to the ceiling.

And at last Sophie understood why.

She crawled to her aunt's side. 'I'll get you help.'

Tess shook her head. 'Just do one thing for me.'

'What?'

'Don't do anything to upset your father.'

Sophie closed her eyes, knowing she meant Aaron. 'I can't, Tess. I think I'm in love.'

'Then we're both fucked.'

———

'I pity her,' Sophie said to Aaron as they rode out on Monday morning.

The sky leaked wintry drizzle, as if nature understood the futility of Sophie's plight. She'd spent the weekend cleaning the cottage and trying to think of a way to help her aunt. Burdened by guilt and feeling she owed Tess, Sophie had invited her to move back into her old room, but it didn't last a single night. Tess could be a nasty drunk, but sober and surrounded by Vanaheim's memory-laden walls, she was diabolical. The only solution Sophie could come up with was to speak to her father, but Tess was adamant that she keep out of it. If she upset him, Ian could take Braeburn from her forever, and then everything would be lost.

'She doesn't deserve your pity,' said Aaron. 'Not after all the things she's done to you.'

'I still feel sorry for her. We're both the victims of my father.'

'We're all victims of your father, Soph.'

Sophie looked at him. 'What do you mean?'

He shook his head. 'Nothing.'

They rode on. Sophie's mind circled his words, trying to work out what they could mean. Nothing made sense. She'd tried to ask Tess about Aaron, but after her initial confession, her aunt had clammed up.

'We should get drunk together one night,' Sophie said to Aaron as they walked the horses along the firebreak. The pines seemed menacing today, as if bad things hovered in the forest's dark depths. She wished she could shake off her despondent mood, but today seemed a day for unhappiness.

'Why?'

'Because then for once you might tell me what's going on in that handsome head of yours. It worked for Tess.'

'Some things aren't worth knowing.'

'Everything about you is worth knowing.'

'Stop it, Sophie,' said Aaron quietly. 'You're only making it worse.'

She wanted to keep pushing but Aaron had that shuttered look, like he was keeping himself from the world. His jawline was rigid and his hands were tight on the reins. What was he hiding that was so bad he thought she wouldn't love him any more if she found out?

'Can I ask you something?'

He gave her a guarded look, and nodded.

'What happened in the feed room . . . did I dream that or was it real?'

He glanced away into the trees. 'It was real but it should never have happened.' Suddenly, he reached out, grabbed her hand and clutched it tight, blue eyes concentrated on hers. 'Sophie, listen to me. You're gorgeous and sexy and funny and strong, and I care about you more than I can say, but you have to understand, I can't be what you want. Not now, not ever.'

A lump formed in her throat. She tried to swallow it away but it wouldn't move. 'I thought —' She stopped, finding she couldn't go on.

'I know. I'm sorry.'

'But you wanted to kiss me. You —'

You said my name like you loved me.

He squeezed her fingers, eyes filled with sympathy and something her ever-hopeful heart thought might be regret. 'Friends, Soph. Let us have that.'

'It's not enough.' It would never be enough. Not for her.

He let her go. 'It'll have to be.'

———

Aaron said he just wanted to be friends, but the evening phone calls kept coming. It was as though he'd developed a habit he couldn't drop. Sophie felt torn between wanting to tell him to stop and the rising hope that there was a chance for them.

The calls were never about anything in particular. Mostly, he asked how she was, how her afternoon had gone and then hung up, but occasionally they'd get talking and wouldn't stop for an hour. Some nights Sophie took the phone to bed and cuddled up under the blankets while they chatted. If she closed her eyes, it was almost like having him beside her.

It amazed her that he could maintain his distance in the yard, when on the phone they'd be whispering their dreams and aspirations to one another. It was as if he lived in two different worlds. In the mornings, they worked the horses together, drank tea in Hakea Lodge's kitchen, and talked about nothing but horses. Trainer and owner, pretending that's all they were. In the evenings, Aaron let down his guard.

'Did you always want to be a trainer?' she asked him one night.

'Not always. When I was six, I wanted to be a fireman.'

She smiled, imagining a blond, blue-eyed little boy running around in a yellow raincoat and a red fireman's helmet.

'And when you were older?'

'A trainer.'

'Didn't it put you off training when your dad was warned off?'

'No. It made me want it more.'

'Why?'

'I had to set things right.'

'What things?'

'Nothing. It's late. I have to go.'

And so it went on. Some subjects remained off-limits, but as long as they were talking, she hoped that one day he'd give away enough so that she could work out his problem for herself – and then solve it.

Aaron did his fair share of probing too, she noticed. He seemed to like hearing how bad things had been for her, as if knowing what she'd gone through helped strengthen his resolve to keep his distance. If she hadn't such a pathological aversion to lies, she would have made stories up to confound him. But she could only tell the truth, no matter how much she fretted that it was the truth of what she'd been through that was keeping him from loving her.

'Soph,' he said one night. 'Can I ask you something?'

'You can ask me anything.'

'Anything?' He sounded amused.

'Anything.'

'All right. What colour underpants are you wearing?' He was laughing when he asked, as if it was a big joke, but he soon stopped when she replied that she wasn't wearing any.

The silence lasted for ten long seconds.

'Aaron?'

'I wish you hadn't told me that.'

'Why?' He didn't answer.

'Aaron?'

'Yeah.'

'What were you really going to ask me?'

His relief could be heard over the line. 'I was going to ask about your friends.'

Now it was her turn for silence.

'Soph?'

'I told you, I don't have any.'

'Why not?'

'At school, when everyone else was making life-long friends, I —' She took a deep breath, hating the memory and the pain it evoked. She could still recall the agony of alienation. Teenagers could be unbelievably cruel, especially girls. 'I found it hard to talk to people. I wasn't . . . I was very screwed up after Mum died.' She gave a small laugh. 'No one wants to hang with the freaky girl, and believe me, I was pretty weird.'

'Did you really think you were weird?'

'No. I thought I'd gone mad. In a way, I did in the end. Slitting your wrists isn't a sane thing to do, but you know what? When I did it, it felt good. Like everything was all over at last.'

'Jesus, Soph.'

'You asked.'

'I wish I could have made you happy then.'

'You can make me happy now.'

'No. I can't. I've got to go. I'll see you tomorrow.'

The following morning she caught him checking out her bum when she bent over to pick up a bucket. He quickly turned away.

'Don't worry, I've got some on,' she yelled across the yard. 'They're white.'

Aaron stared at her before hastily backing into the feed room.

She smiled and strode toward him. Crossing her legs and arms, she leaned against the doorjamb to watch him work, loving the way his long, solid body moved, the concentration on his face as he tried to ignore her, the way his gaze kept sliding to the door and down her body. Why, when what they felt was so huge and undeniable, did he believe anything between them was impossible?

'Are we going to keep playing this game forever?'

He stopped scooping and looked at her. 'What game?'

'The game where you keep telling me that you only want to be friends and then perve at my bum when you think I'm not looking.'

'I wasn't perving.'

'No?'

'No.'

'Just checking to see if I was wearing underpants then?'

He didn't answer.

She pushed off the wall and stepped forward until she was standing in front of him. 'You nearly kissed me in this room.'

'It was a mistake.'

'I don't think so. You wanted to. I wanted to. You shouldn't have stopped.'

'I had to.'

'Why?'

He looked at her with eyes turned down with sadness. 'If I tell you, you'll hate me.'

She took his hand. 'I'll never hate you.'

'We've got friendship, Soph. Be grateful for that.' Then, in a replay of their last feed room encounter, he walked out.

TWELVE

SOPHIE REACHED over the tailgate of the float and smacked Buck on the rump.

'Cut it out. You don't know what frustration is.' Sophie did, and it went by the name of Aaron.

Buck twisted his head around to look at her, as if to say 'Up yours', and then carried on stamping and kicking his annoyance. Sophie wished she hadn't bothered wrapping his legs in protective floating boots. He might stop kicking if it actually hurt. She gave him another whack before stepping down.

In the faint hope that a change of scenery might freshen him up, she'd taken him out to the pony club grounds that afternoon for a run around the cross-country course. The moment she unloaded and tied him to the float, she knew it was a mistake. His expression turned mulish, his ears turned back and his tail flicked back and forth in annoyance, but in desperation she'd persevered. She saddled him, fixed boots to stamping legs, mounted, and worked him quietly on the flat, trying to use the discipline of dressage to coax out his bad temper before attempting to jump. For thirty minutes he behaved, but as soon as she faced him at a jump, he threw a tantrum. Sophie ended up flat on her back with Buck careering around the grounds bucking and squealing like a bronco.

She'd cried the whole time it took to catch him, but knew her tears weren't just for the horse. Frustration with Aaron, anger at Tess and irritation with herself all played their part. A fortnight ago, she'd celebrated her greatest victory. She'd felt strong and ready to take on anyone. Now, she just felt bruised, inside and out.

Back at Vanaheim, she peered into the old drench drum that posed as the roadside mail drop. The only delivery was a newsletter from the South East Showjumping Club, advertising its coming winter showjumping series, which would conclude with a heavily sponsored three-day carnival in August. A glut of magazines had arrived the previous week but they lay on the kitchen bench still in their plastic wrappers. Usually they were dog-eared and tatty within a week, but Sophie was too distracted to concentrate on articles about equine nutrition or the latest clover varieties.

Chuck looked up from his grazing and whickered. He'd only been retired for two weeks and already his coat was thickening and his belly expanding. She still brought him in from the front paddock every night to the warmth of his stable, but when the spring arrived, she'd turn him out permanently.

Ignoring Buck's increasingly hysteric kicking, Sophie climbed through the rails and wandered through the long grass toward her best friend.

'Hey, superstar,' she said, kissing Chuck on the nose. 'Are you enjoying your retirement?'

Chuck bunted his head against Sophie's arm and let her rest her cheek against his for a while. She played with his ears and tickled his chin, thinking how much she missed having him in work. He was a horse, but like the dogs, he seemed to know her moods better than herself and was always willing to offer comfort.

She ran her hands under his rugs, checking to see if he was warm, and then circled him, keeping a look-out for any cuts or bumps. She leaned against his shoulder, stroking his neck, half watching the float as it rocked under Buck's assault. He needed to learn some manners, but Sophie wasn't the one to teach him. The decision had been made that afternoon. He was going. She'd given up.

'Listen to that silly bugger,' she said to Chuck. 'Anyone would think he's the centre of the universe. If only he was like you, hey?' She sighed and kissed Chuck's cheek. 'Mum would have known what to do, wouldn't she, boy?'

Sophie hadn't thought much about her mother lately. Her mind had been too full of Aaron and, to a lesser extent, Tess, but for once, she didn't feel guilty. Fiona Dixon had chosen to leave this world. She'd chosen herself over a daughter who needed her, and left confusion, anger and heartache in her wake.

It wasn't just Sophie's life affected, it was Tess's too, and, she supposed, her father's. He hadn't always been so distant. He'd once loved her, or at least acted as though he had, but her mother's death had damaged their relationship beyond repair. It wasn't so bad at the start. He'd tried, in his clumsy way, to be there when she was young and overflowing with hurt and confusion. But the older she grew the less she saw of him, and when he did visit, he struggled to even look at her. Not until she was older did she ask herself the question of who he saw when he looked at her face. She'd resigned herself to never knowing the answer.

'I'll take you for a walk later,' she promised Chuck, then let him get back to grazing. Buck slammed his hoofs into the rubber-lined tailgate of the float. Sophie shook her head in defeat. The horse had to go. She wasn't strong enough for him. What control she'd once had over the animal was now gone. He'd lost all respect for her.

An unfamiliar silver four-wheel drive sat in Vanaheim's yard. Sophie's jaw clenched at the sight. The last thing she needed was a visitor. At that moment, all she really wanted was to wallow in a black fug as she composed an ad for *Horse Deals*.

'Damn,' she muttered when she saw the rental car company sticker and realised who it could be. Immediately, her thoughts darted to Tess. It wouldn't do her cause any good if her father found out what sort of state Tess was in, but perhaps it also wouldn't hurt for him to see what he'd condemned Tess to.

She pulled the Range Rover to a halt and opened the door. Sammy and Del sat side by side nearby looking up at her. They started to whine.

'I know, I know,' she told them. From the float, as though sensing her nerves, Buck began yet another hoof-beat tattoo.

By the time she'd completed her chores, her father still hadn't appeared and her stomach had almost turned itself inside out with worry. He had to be with Tess. Either that, or he was deliberately unsettling her with his continuing absence.

A blast of hot air hit her in the face when she pushed open the door of the cottage. The rarely used central heating had been cranked up to maximum. She'd always thought it a waste of energy and made do with the gas log fire, but her father preferred the temperature tropical, as though the tropics was where he really wanted to be. She pulled off her boots and glanced down the hall. Sitting at the breakfast bar, with a laptop in front of him and a mobile phone pressed to his ear, was her father.

Irritation had her clenching her fists. How dare he waltz in unannounced after weeks of no contact, as if this was a hotel instead of her home?

'Send me the details and I'll look at it and then talk it over with Gerry,' he said to whoever was on the phone. Despite herself, Sophie smiled. Ever since she could remember, she'd loved her father's deep, mellifluous voice.

She padded into the kitchen, trying to keep her nerves at bay, knowing that the ensuing conversation would be difficult. She had to stand up to him. She was twenty-two years old, not fifteen, and she was strong now. She couldn't let him make her feel pathetic again. She wouldn't let him make her beg for his approval.

'Yes. Email is best. CC it to Gerry as well. That will save time.' He hung up and glanced at her before looking back down at his mobile and dialling another number. 'Sophie, I won't be a minute.' He smiled. 'Politics.'

Sophie blinked and then let out a breath. She leaned against the sink, watching him. Ian Dixon was a tall, craggily handsome man with dark hair turning an attractive salt and pepper and eyes the same grey as her own. Despite the years he'd spent in Canberra, his farmer's body remained trim and fit, free of the flabby paunches of his contemporaries. His looks and good health appealed to his rural electorate, though that would have little bearing on the outcome of an election. The district was blue-ribbon conservative. Ian Dixon's seat was as safe as they came, but Sophie knew there were some in the branch who would do almost anything to usurp his position and destroy his dream of a cabinet position. A good reason, in her father's mind, to keep any family skeletons firmly in the closet. Politics was, after all, a filthy game.

'Nathan says he'll email the report through to you. If you can look at it and then let me know your opinion —' Ian paused, and then went on. 'I am aware of that, but this is a major export industry. I don't want to be the one to have to tell the PM that we lost a 220-million-dollar contract because of bureaucratic chest beating . . . Exactly. Read it and let me know.' He snapped the phone shut and smiled at Sophie.

'Hi, Dad.'

He surprised her by walking over to kiss her lightly on the cheek.

'You smell like horse, as usual.'

'I've been riding,' she said lamely, watching him as he returned to his seat. 'Have you seen Tess?'

He nodded. 'She's in bed with the flu.'

'Mmm. She hasn't been well. Do you want a cup of tea?'

'Thank you. I could do with one.'

She switched the kettle on, grabbed two mugs from the cupboard and dangled a teabag in each. Her father was reading something on his laptop, something that obviously mattered more than his daughter.

'Tess tells me you won the Lake Ackerman event,' he said without looking at her. 'You should have told me.'

'I did.'

He eyed her. 'I don't think so.'

'I left a message on your machine.'

An odd look flitted across his face. 'I should have realised,' he muttered, then looked directly at her. 'I'm sorry. It must have been accidentally deleted.'

Prevarication and lies. How typical of him. And today of all days, when she felt angry and fragile, and when heaping blame for all that was wrong was hard to resist.

'Why do you lie to me all the time, Dad? I don't deserve it.'

'I don't lie to you.'

She smiled sadly. 'You do. You've been doing it for years. Starting with Mum.'

He sighed, and pressed a finger against his right eyebrow, closing his eyes as though suffering a severe headache. 'I apologise for not telling you the truth about your mother's death. It was wrong of me. I should have explained what happened.'

She leaned across the bench. 'But what did happen, Dad? Mum just didn't kill herself for no reason. Something must have happened to push her to do it.'

'She was very depressed.'

'I'm aware of that, but you're forgetting that I've been there. I know what it's like. Something must have happened. She loved me. I know she did, and I know she would never have left me alone like that without reason.' She grabbed his forearm and squeezed it. 'Tell me. Tell me why someone as beautiful as Mum took her life. Please.'

He snatched his arm out of her grip. 'Your mother was not a saint, Sophie!' He looked away, as though disgusted by his outburst before turning back to her and softening his voice. 'She was a very difficult woman.'

'Why didn't you get a divorce, then?'

His mouth compressed into a grim line. 'Because she wouldn't let me. She wanted you to grow up in a normal family, but we were never a normal family.' His eyes sharpened. 'Or have you forgotten that? Think, Sophie. Think back to what it was like.'

Sophie dug into her memory, probing it for signs that what her father said was true. Her parents had argued. She knew that. Slamming doors, the harsh whispers of a couple trying to hide their altercation from their child, her mother's puffy eyes and blotched skin. She remembered those things but they were hazy, faded, like gauze curtains that had seen too much sun. As soon as she touched them, they broke into a thousand threads and were gone.

She frowned. 'I remember arguments. Is that why she did it? Because you'd had a fight?'

He looked tired, his face collapsing as her words touched him. 'She threatened to kill herself all the time, Sophie. I couldn't stay and I couldn't leave. She had me trapped.'

Her question remained unanswered, but then she hadn't expected him to give an honest response. Evading the truth was a Dixon speciality.

'Did you love her?' She watched her father's face closely. 'The truth, Dad.'

'If it's truth you want so badly, then I'll give it to you. Yes, I loved your mother, but she wore me down. In the end, I hated her. It's not something I'm proud of, but that's what happened.'

The implication of his words hit her like a blow. In his eyes she was no different to her mother. Unstable, depressed, needy and attention-seeking.

'Is that what I did to you? Wore you down until you learned to hate me?'

He stared at her as though she were mad. 'For God's sake, Sophie. I don't hate you.'

'But you don't like me.'

He shook his head, his eyes closing momentarily as if he couldn't believe what he was hearing. 'That's just not true.'

Anger gave her breath. 'Oh, come off it, Dad. You resent me. You have since Mum died. You might have tried to be a father at the start but that didn't last long. First chance you had you escaped to Canberra to tend your all-important career. I was left to grieve on my own and I didn't know how. No wonder I was screwed up. As for now, I may as well not exist. I had the biggest win of my career and you didn't even ring to congratulate me.'

'I told you, I didn't receive your message.'

'Don't lie to me! I'm sick of it. I'm not one of your cronies, I'm your daughter!'

Her father's palms slapped down on the granite bench. 'And I'm a father who loves you!' He sat back, and Sophie could see the effort he was taking to calm himself, to put the politician's mask back where it belonged. 'I'm worried about you. So is Tess.'

She gave a derisive sniff. 'The only thing you care about is your career.'

'That's not true. I do care a great deal about my career, but believe it or not, I also care a great deal about you.'

Sophie closed her eyes as tiredness overwhelmed her. She was so sick of this. A tear slipped from her eye. She wiped it away with her hand. 'Then why don't you ever show it?'

His mobile rang. He looked at the screen and then back to her. 'I must take this.'

She looked at the ceiling, her eyes watering and her throat aching. After a pause, he picked up the phone and began speaking quietly to the caller.

For something to do, she switched on the kettle again and stared at the teabags still hanging dryly in the mugs.

Your mother was not a saint.

Of course she wasn't, but she was very sweet and very loving. Everyone knew that. Even Aaron had said so. Aaron. They hadn't even started on him and Sophie was positive Aaron was the very reason her father was sitting in her kitchen.

The kettle boiled. She poured the water and waited.

Her father ended the call, closed the lid of his laptop and started shoving it into its bag.

'You made it quite clear how you felt about me when you were fifteen,' he said. 'Your suicide note said it all. I have only complied with your wishes and kept out of your way, but I'm very sorry that you haven't recognised the actions of a loving father.' He zipped the laptop bag closed and began walking to the door. 'I'll leave you in peace.'

'Don't you want to talk to me about Aaron? After all, it's what you're here for.'

He stopped, caught her gaze for a moment and shook his head. 'No. I can see now that whatever I say won't make any difference. You'll have to learn from your own mistakes.'

'He's a good man.'

'No, Sophie, he's not. He'll hurt you, and you're going to let him. And to my shame, there's not a damn thing I can do to prevent it.'

———

Sophie worked her way through the marble and granite graves dominating the upper tiers of the old section of Harrington cemetery, where only descendants of the pioneering families still owned plots. She didn't need to count the headstones or orient herself with a crumbling angel or towering monument. She'd trodden this path hundreds of times, although this was her first visit in weeks.

For Harrington's dead, the town's forefathers had, with unrealised irony, selected a resting place with a panorama the interred would never appreciate. The cemetery lay to the south of the town on the slope of a north-facing hill and sported magnificent views over the township and landscape beyond. In the late afternoon sun, the vista glowed, but Sophie didn't notice. She was on a mission.

Toward the end of a long row of neglected graves, next to her paternal grandparents' ostentatious black and gold double plot, she stopped, crossed her arms, and studied her mother's memorial. Though in better condition than those around it, the normally polished white marble appeared dirty, dull and unloved. Pine needles and small cones from the trees lining the cemetery perimeter littered the surface, and dust and sap had sunk into the headstone's deeply carved gold letters, blunting their lustre. On an adjacent slab, someone had left a posy of white paper daisies and Sophie realised that, for the first time she could remember, she hadn't brought flowers from Vanaheim's garden. The realisation roused no guilt. Her mother didn't deserve them.

She scraped away the needles and sat on the slab, letting its cold hardness seep into her bones. She needed it to cool her anger. Fiona Dixon had deserted her and now, when Sophie desperately needed her guidance, she hated her for it.

Her mouth thin, she swivelled away from her mother's name and focused on the view. To the north, past the town, sprawled a patchwork quilt of paddocks. Dark pine forests broke the vibrant greens and browns of pasture, and several new plantations of bluegums added a hazy grey to the landscape. As her gaze swept to the east, Sophie picked out Vanaheim, easily discernible by the majestic plane trees lining the front boundary.

She couldn't remember the funeral – grief or horror had somehow razed it from memory – but the day afterward remained clear in Sophie's mind. In the last act of kindness she could recall from him, Ian Dixon had taken his distraught daughter's hand, walked her out into Vanaheim's highest paddock and pointed to the south. 'See, Sophie? She might be gone but she'll always look over you.'

The idea had given her comfort but now she wasn't so sure. Her father knew how unhappy his wife was at Vanaheim, so why bury her where she could see it?

Sophie shook her head. What did it matter? Her mother was dead. She couldn't see anything. Not Vanaheim, not her daughter.

She lowered her eyes to the cemetery, gazing at the weeping stone angels, crosses and towering obelisks. This was a peaceful place, yet Sophie felt restless. No matter how she tried to shed them her father's words clung.

Your mother was not a saint.

No, but in Sophie's mind she was kind and gentle, not difficult, and certainly not the sort of person you could end up hating. She tried to remember the parental fights she knew were locked in her memory but couldn't – not the details, only fragments. Her mother turning away to hide her tears, the bitter words she sometimes uttered about her husband, the look on her face when Vanaheim's enchanted tunnel of love ended and she pulled into the yard. Sophie remembered these things, but they seemed incongruous to the woman she knew and loved.

And it wasn't just her mother she didn't understand. Today she'd learned her father wasn't the man she thought either. She'd written terrible things in her suicide note. How much she hated him, how she wished he'd died instead of her mother. Afterwards, when her pain seemed incurable and he distanced himself even further, she'd deemed him cold and unloving, and herself as unlovable. Yet all he'd done was follow her wishes.

Even Tess, who she'd thought had no aim but to make Sophie's life difficult, was driven by a need so desperate she was willing to suffer for years in a place she hated.

Then there was Aaron, a man she thought she knew. A man she thought might love her, who'd once said her name like it was precious, but who held a secret he believed was so terrible that its revelation would result in her hating him.

She spread her fingers across the cold stone slab, tired and overwhelmed with doubt. 'Have I judged everybody wrong?'

But Fiona Dixon's grave remained mute. Though she strained, Sophie heard only the breeze through the pines. Nothing called, no icy fingers caressed her skin, no presence whispered from the beyond. The dead, as always, refused to speak.

Her mission had failed. She'd just have to muddle through on her own.

THIRTEEN

AARON EYED SOPHIE from the safety of the verandah as she said farewell to Rowdy. The urge to cross the yard and gather her to his chest was huge. Since her father's visit, Sophie had been distant and quiet, and he didn't know what that meant. She hadn't even admitted to seeing Ian, which worried him even more. Her father could have told her any number of lies.

She still arrived each morning with a smile and laughed when the horses did something funny, but it lacked the joy he adored. And several times he'd caught her looking at him with a frown, as though she was trying to work out what was in his head.

But after his talk with Ian Dixon, there wasn't a chance in hell he'd reveal that.

Aaron had been sitting on the verandah step with a cup of tea and the local paper, warming himself in the fading Tuesday afternoon sun, when Ian pulled in the drive. He'd stepped out and looked around with an expression that made Aaron ball his fists. Finally, when he'd made his disdain clear, Ian approached the house. Aaron placed his mug down carefully and stood.

'What do you want?'

'Your mother sends her love,' replied Ian.

'She wouldn't know the meaning of it.'

Ian's mouth thinned. 'Still like your father, I see.'

Aaron said nothing, but he reached for the verandah post and wrapped his hand around the timber. Even after all this time, his loathing for Ian Dixon hadn't faded.

'I'm worried about Sophie,' said Ian.

'That'd be a first.'

Ian's grey eyes, so like Sophie's, narrowed. 'I didn't come here to argue. I came here to talk about my daughter.'

'She's fine.'

'No, she's not.' He looked toward Vanaheim and shook his head, and to Aaron's surprise he caught a glimpse of genuine worry on Ian's face. 'You have no idea how vulnerable she is. If she finds out about me and Carol . . .'

The sentence hung. Instinctively, Aaron followed Ian's gaze to the west even though all they could see of Vanaheim from Hakea Lodge was a flush of green. Christ, he hoped Sophie was all right.

'Look,' he said, 'if you're worried about me telling her, forget it. Believe me, I'm not in any hurry to spill that dirty little secret, but you won't be able to keep it from her forever. Better she hears it from you than anyone else.'

'She won't cope. It'll be like before.'

'Then you don't know your daughter very well.'

Ian threw him a sharp glance. 'And I suppose you think you do.'

'I know her a damn sight better than you do.'

For a long moment, they regarded one another, anger festering. The yard moved with restless horses, attuned to the tension. In his box, Rowdy snorted and stomped. Psycho let out a whinny.

Ian opened his coat and reached into his jacket pocket. 'I understand you and Sophie made some sort of a deal about a horse.'

'Not that it's any of your business.'

Ian swiped at his phone, tapped a few times and looked up. 'I'll pay you double whatever the horse is worth, with the funds transferred in seconds.'

'In exchange for what?'

'In exchange for keeping away from Sophie.'

Though they burned, Aaron managed to say the words he didn't mean. 'Save your money. I'm not interested in Sophie.'

'That's not what Tess says.'

'Tess is a drunk.'

Ian kept his finger poised over the screen, eyeing him.

'Put it away, Ian. I'm not for sale. I made a deal with Sophie and I'll keep it. As soon as Danny's back I'll have no need of her.' Aaron held his gaze. 'And that's where this will end.'

Though Ian's face betrayed his disbelief, he'd been left no choice but to retreat.

Yet now, as Aaron watched Sophie fondly tugging Rowdy's ears, his heart aching, he wondered if it would ever end. Since Ian's visit he'd stopped calling her at night, unable to kid himself any longer that he did it for altruistic reasons. When she asked, he made the excuse it was because he needed sleep, but without her comforting voice he found sleep near impossible. Instead, he lay awake in the darkness, racked with over-tiredness and torturing himself with visions of Sophie, of them together, enjoying a life where the past never existed.

Shoulders low, he walked back into the house. He'd get over it. He had to. For Sophie's sake.

———

As if Aaron didn't have enough to worry about, the following day the Land Cruiser chugged to a standstill and no amount of swearing, kicking or tinkering would make it go again. The timing was appalling. Not only did he have a pile of overdue bills sitting on the kitchen table, but Saturday was the Harrington Gold Cup. He had three runners in the lead-up races, including Costa Motza, and he desperately wanted to make Sophie's first race as an owner special. To make matters worse, Rowdy, who'd been due to race in a hurdle the following week with good prospects of winning, had picked up a stone bruise during morning exercise and was likely to be out of work for several days.

The mechanic let out a whistle. 'Expensive, mate.'

Aaron's heart sank. 'How expensive?'

Leaning against the front fender, the mechanic pulled a packet of cigarettes from his shirt pocket, shook one out and lit it, sucking smoke into his lungs. 'A fair bit. Transmission's gone.'

Aaron stared at Rowdy. The horse was hanging over the half door of the stable, his tongue dangling out like the village idiot. So much centred on him. Rowdy was good enough to win the major steeple-chase of the season, the Springbank Cup, held every year in the first week of August and worth two hundred and fifty thousand dollars in prize money. Quarter of a million dollars would wipe out Hakea Lodge's debts and allow him to make the improvements owners expected in a successful yard. But Rowdy winning was a dream, and dreams didn't solve real-life problems.

The Land Cruiser would have to stay dead. He'd call in some favours, tap some of the old-timers who had known and loved his father, ring anyone who could lend him a suitable vehicle. He'd even phone his mother if it came to that. Pride could take second place. The yard had to keep going. The memory of his father demanded it.

'Leave it,' he said to the puffing mechanic. 'I'll make do without.'

'Yup, you can always use horsepower.'

The mechanic was still chuckling when he stepped into his van. Aaron wanted to punch the laughter straight back down his throat.

As the van left, Sophie pulled into the yard. He cast her a grim smile, then slammed the Land Cruiser's bonnet down and leaned on it.

'What's the problem?' she said, coming to stand next to him.

'Apparently the transmission's buggered.'

'Oh. Anything I can do?'

'No, it's okay. I'll work something out. You go and saddle up Costa Motza.'

She placed a warm hand over his and rubbed her thumb over his knuckles, grey eyes wide with concern. The gesture was so intimate, so loving, that he wanted to bury his face in her neck and cry hot tears of self-reproach.

'Aaron, I know things are tough. I can help.'

He stared at their hands – hers fine and clean, his large and dirty with grease – and wished he could tangle them together forever.

Gently, he slid his fingers from beneath hers and, crossing his arms, turned to prop his backside against the car. Out of the corner of his eye, he caught Sophie's hurt expression before she quickly hid it. He jammed his hands hard into his armpits to stop himself from touching her.

'You can borrow the farm ute,' she said, and though she tried to sound normal the hollowness in her voice was unmistakable. 'It's not great, but it goes and it'll pull your float no worries. I can drop it off this afternoon.'

He stared at his worn boots, the frayed cuffs of his jeans. He knew she was only being kind but all her offer reminded him of was Ian and his dirty money offer. 'I'm not a charity case,' he said quietly.

'It's not charity, Aaron. It's friendship. Just like you wanted. Anyway, you'll be doing me a favour.'

His eyebrows rose. 'Oh, yeah? How?'

She smiled, delighting him with a bit of her old Sophie spark. 'By keeping it out of Tess's reach. She nearly drove it through the back of the shed yesterday. Trust me, it'll be much safer here than at Vanaheim.'

———

Harrington Racecourse sat adjacent to the showgrounds, three blocks off the main street, surrounded by a ring of aging pines that every year the council threatened to cut down yet never seemed to find the budget to do. The close proximity to the town meant that, unlike so many other provincial race clubs located on the outer edges or even further out of the townships, the club was positioned at the centre of Harrington social life. Even autumn and winter meetings attracted good crowds, who were well cared for with gas heaters to warm them against the cold, an undercover bookies' ring and on course tote, and, most importantly, a well-stocked bar.

Harrington Gold Cup day dawned glorious. May days in South Australia's south-east didn't come much better. The sun saturated the landscape with cheerful warmth, and a mild breeze from the north replaced the usual southerly, drying the soggy ground and bringing hope of a benign winter. The sunshine brought out the locals, especially those of the younger generation, who preferred a day dressed up at the races to football, and by the second race the lawns in front of the grandstand milled with people enjoying the party atmosphere.

The runners for the race were lining up for the barriers but still Sophie hadn't arrived. Aaron stood by the winning post playing with a lead rope, clicking the spring clip with his thumb. He'd last seen Sophie the day before when she'd dropped the ute off and refused his offer of a lift home, saying instead she'd cut through the paddocks. Although Costa Motza's race was over two hours away, this was her first race as an owner and Aaron expected her to arrive early, overflowing with excitement for her horse's big day.

Trying to ignore his unease at her continued absence, he raised his binoculars and focused once more on Casalinga.

'Hello, Aaron.'

'Thank Christ,' he said, hearing Sophie's voice at last. 'I was starting to think you weren't com—' He couldn't continue. In front of him stood Sophie, but not the Sophie he'd grown to adore. This was a Sophie he'd never seen before.

She gave him that same shy half smile he remembered from her first days at the yard, just a slight quirk of her mouth that made him want to kiss all her lipstick away and get to the pink flesh underneath. She tucked a strand of newly styled hair behind her ear but it immediately fell loose, as though with a life of its own.

She'd transformed from mousy, grey-eyed, borderline prettiness to blond-streaked, made-up, classy gorgeousness – and he hated it.

'You look nice,' he said, grudgingly.

The tannoy crackled as the caller readied himself. Aaron turned back to the track and lifted the binoculars to his eyes, but her disappointment wafted over him like the scent of her expensive perfume. He hated that too. He hated everything. All the things he wanted but couldn't have, standing beside him in a clingy grey woollen dress and long black leather boots, radiating a beauty that dulled the day and made his insides curl with panic at the thought of losing her to someone else. Someone deserving.

All in . . . light's on . . . and they're racing.

'Did the ute go okay?'

He nodded, keeping his eyes on the field.

'How's Costa Motza?'

'Dopey as usual.'

'And Pollyanna?'

'Fighting fit.'

At the eight hundred and Casalinga is starting to move on the outside. Torvina still in the lead followed by Grey Nurse, then a length to Passionpop with Casalinga close behind . . .

'Push on, Todd,' he muttered.

'Will you need any help?'

'Nope.'

Turning into the straight and we have Torvina and Grey Nurse neck and neck and Casalinga a length away. Passionpop is fading fast . . .

He dropped his binoculars. 'Come on, Todd.'

The crowd chanted. The fall of hoofbeats sounded like thunder.

The racecaller's voice rose to a crescendo. Aaron beat his hand against the fence rail.

'Go, Casa. Go, girl.'

And Casalinga and Grey Nurse are fighting for the lead . . .

'Come on, Casa. Come on, girl.'

And it's Grey Nurse to Casalinga, followed by Tittletattle, then two lengths to Torvino . . .

'Shit!' He slapped the rail. Casalinga should have won. He turned to ask Sophie what she'd thought of Todd's ride, but she was gone. He stared into the crowd under the grandstand but couldn't pick her out amongst the punters milling around the bookmakers' stands. He didn't have time to go chasing after her. Tony Johnstone, Casalinga's owner, would need placating and Pollyanna had to be readied for her race.

'What happened?' he asked Todd in the mounting yard.

The jockey shrugged. 'Ran out of legs, boss.'

That was rubbish and Todd knew it, but Aaron wasn't about to argue with him when Tony was standing by his side. Casalinga was as fit as she could be. Todd hadn't ridden her hard enough.

Tony slapped Aaron on the back. 'She won't lose next time.'

Aaron heard it for the warning it was. The message was clear. Next time Casalinga raced, Tony expected her to win. If not, it'd be goodbye owner. He couldn't afford to lose Tony's business even though the man was an obnoxious prick.

He stroked Casalinga's nose, scrutinising the crowd while he waited for the all clear. He caught a glimpse of Sophie's newly blond hair before it disappeared behind a pillar. She deserved an apology, but what could he say to defend himself? Sophie, I'm sorry but I can't stand you looking so beautiful? Sophie, I'm scared someone better than me will fall in love with you? Sophie, I don't want you to love anyone but me, even though I can't love you back? Better he said nothing. Let her fall for someone else and find the happiness she so deserved.

At the stewards' okay, he led Casalinga to the stalls and settled her next to Costa Motza. The white-socked chestnut whickered at him and Aaron stopped to give him a quick scratch.

'So, are you going to win for your mistress today?'

He smiled. Costa Motza didn't stand a chance in hell. Not only had Sophie insisted on nominating the horse for a two-thousand-metre race, she'd hired some unknown apprentice to ride him. Aaron had argued that she was wasting her time and money, but Sophie had stubbornly told him that Costa Motza was her horse, and she'd do what she liked. He'd almost told her to find another trainer but he needed the lucerne hay contra deal. And if Tony Johnstone walked, he'd need it even more.

As soon as Casalinga was settled, he started on Pollyanna. The filly was in fine form. She'd run brilliant times during her morning gallops and although the field was strong, Aaron knew Pollyanna had more class than the other runners. This was a step up from the race she'd won at Penola, but, given her form, he had to take the chance. And ten thousand dollars in prize money wasn't to be sniffed at.

Pollyanna danced at his side as he led her around the warm-up ring. A light sweat darkened her dapple-grey coat and Aaron wished he had Sophie's ability to chat incessantly about nothing. The soothing monotony of her ramblings calmed the horses, or, as Sophie said, bored them into relaxation. He smiled and ruffled Pollyanna's mane.

'She's one of a kind, our Soph, isn't she, Polly?'

As he turned Pollyanna down the far side of the track, he saw her. She stood in front of Costa Motza stroking his nose, the soft woollen dress clinging to her hips, swinging as she moved. Aaron found it mesmerising.

She turned suddenly, and smiled. Limping toward her, wearing neat jeans over long, muscled legs, a blue-striped shirt open at the neck, and a navy jacket that made his broad shoulders appear even wider, was a dark-haired man possessing the sort of sculpted face normally seen in men's shaver ads. He smiled back at her and pointed at Costa Motza with an eyebrow raised. Sophie nodded, and then laughed when the man said something. Aaron felt sick.

Ben Moore was the new agronomist at Harrington Rural Traders – the man Sophie had said was one of the few who realised she ran Vanaheim single-handed. Tall, good-looking and, until a hamstring injury put him out for the season, touted as a certainty for the local football league's best and fairest medal. Worst of all, he had a reputation as a genuinely nice guy. Ben Moore was everything Aaron wasn't.

Seeing Sophie and Ben together was like watching his own heart break.

She blew a kiss to Costa Motza before leaving the stall. Ben placed a hand on the small of her back as they walked toward the grandstand. Aaron's fist clenched around Pollyanna's reins. Sophie glanced in his direction, said something to Ben and left him to walk to the warm-up ring. She waited by the post-and-rail fence until Aaron brought Pollyanna to a halt in front of her.

'I'm sorry Casalinga didn't win,' she said.

He shrugged.

Sophie picked at the rail with her bitten-down fingernails. 'I just wanted to say good luck in the next race. I hope Pollyanna wins. And not just because I've got money on her either. I hope she wins for you.'

'So do I. I'll be able to get the Land Cruiser, fixed amongst other things.' Aaron indicated Ben with his chin. 'What's Ben want?'

Sophie glanced at Ben and then back at him, her cheeks turning pink. 'I think he likes me.'

'Anyone would like you in that dress.'

She smoothed the wool over her stomach. 'So you approve, then?'

'It's all right.'

'Only all right?' For a brief moment her eyes swam with disappointment, then she took a deep breath and quirked her mouth into a wry smile. 'Not quite the reaction I was hoping for. Anyway, I'll see you.'

He watched her return to Ben's side, feeling like a complete shit. He yanked on Pollyanna's reins, but Pollyanna kept staring at Sophie, probably wondering why she hadn't been given a kiss or a scratch like usual.

'Sorry, Polly. My fault. Maybe one of these days I'll learn not to put my big foot in it.'

But when it came to Sophie, somehow he doubted that was possible.

———

Aaron took his usual position by the finish post. Behind him, a group of delighted picnickers sat on the grass in front of the grandstand soaking up the rare sunshine, drinking beer out of plastic cups and digging cracker biscuits into a tub of French onion dip. They laughed among themselves – friends enjoying an autumn day at the races, couples comfortable in the company of others, unconcerned with rivalry, unaffected by the crippling jealousy that scratched Aaron's soul with tiger's claws.

The skin on the back of his neck kept prickling as though Sophie's eyes were boring holes into it, but he didn't turn around. He lifted the binoculars and watched Pollyanna circling behind the barrier. Behind him, the picnickers laughed as they compared bets. They'd all gone for long shots, hoping for easy money.

Like him.

An attendant took Pollyanna's reins and led her into her barrier. The gates closed behind her. Aaron transferred his focus to the front of the barriers, waiting for the jump. Ten grand. The figure ran round in his mind, allocating itself to overdue bills, settling on the most important. Spent before it was won.

Ben Moore leaned on the fence beside him, Sophie with him. 'Sophie tells me your horse is a sure thing.'

Aaron's stomach burned. He nodded, keeping the binoculars up but looking at Sophie out of the corner of his eye. She held a glass of red wine in one hand and a race book in the other. Her cheeks were flushed as though she'd been standing too close to a fire, and he had the irrational conviction that Ben had been touching her up in the top tier of the grandstand like a randy teenager. His jaw ached from clenching it. He made a concerted effort to relax but couldn't, not with Ben beside him.

Another burst of laughter erupted from the picnickers and Aaron felt like it was directed at him. The lovesick fool who could do nothing but stand by as the girl he loved was seduced in front of him. He put a hand on the rail to steady himself. He could see Sophie watching him, alert to his mood but uncertain.

Lights on. They're racing. Mister Magic jumped well followed by Pollyanna and Shindig, Rainbow Warrior, then Havabeerortwo . .
.

'She jumped well,' said Sophie.

He smiled. 'Yeah, she did.'

As they go towards the twelve-hundred-metre marker and still in the lead is Mister Magic from Shindig then a couple back to Pollyanna . . .

The crowd hushed, concentrating on the field as they galloped the turn. Aaron held his binoculars to his eyes, watching Pollyanna as she hung steady in third. The pace was slower than he'd expected but that didn't trouble him. It would leave Pollyanna with more in her tank when she hit the straight.

Approaching the six-hundred-metre marker now and no change . .
.

'Steady, Todd. Not yet. Not yet,' he muttered.

As they sprint for home three hundred metres out and it's still Mister Magic with Pollyanna challenging hard on the outside, half a length to Shindig . . .

The crowd chanted, the picnickers stood up, Sophie and Ben leaned across the rail, the horses flew down the straight, necks stretched out, manes flying, jockeys' silks flapping, whips flailing. Excitement surged and rolled like a breaker through the crowd, the thrill of a close finish bringing them to their feet. The sport of kings glorious in the glowing, autumn, sun-drenched heart of Harrington.

'Go, Polly. Go!'

A hundred to go and it's neck and neck . . .

'Come on, Polly,' screamed Sophie.

Please, prayed Aaron. Please, Polly.

Pollyanna, Mister Magic . . . and Pollyanna wins, a half head to Mister Magic, a length to Havabeerortwo . . .

Without thinking, Aaron grabbed Sophie and hugged her, holding her to his chest and burying his face into her neck.

'She did it, Soph.'

'Oh, God, Aaron. I'm so happy for you.'

When he let her go, Ben was watching them with a frown on his face, but Sophie's smiling eyes remained focused on his. She looked so delighted all he wanted to do was kiss her. He took a step back, afraid he'd give into the urge.

'Congratulations,' said Ben, holding out his hand.

Aaron took it and had his fingers crushed. 'Thanks.' He glanced at Sophie. 'Hopefully Pollyanna will give Costa Motza some tips.' He looked toward the returning field, Pollyanna leading and cantering alongside the clerk of the course's grey with flared nostrils and a coat made steel by sweat. If she kept this form up, Rowdy would find himself booted out of his stable and back in the yards.

'I'd better go grab her,' he said, and left them to it.

As he jogged toward the mounting ring, he wondered if Sophie realised the strength of Ben's attraction. His handshake had said it all. Had their meeting been a chance occurrence or had Ben Moore been looking for a way to meet up with Sophie away from work? Opportunities to do so were rare – besides pony club and eventing competitions, the only places she regularly frequented were the local saddlery, her feed supplier and Harrington Rural Traders. Ben was unlikely to bump into her in the pub.

He glanced back at them and found his answer. Ben and Sophie were leaning on the rail studying Sophie's race book together, but

Ben's hand was on the small of her back and his thumb was running circles in the soft fabric of her dress.

Aaron swallowed and looked away.

———

Ignoring Aaron's protest, Sophie insisted on walking Costa Motza before his race. He might be the trainer, she told him, but Costa Motza was her horse, and she'd do what she damn well wanted.

With a sigh, Aaron handed over the reins. 'You'll wreck your boots.'

'I'll buy a new pair with the winnings,' she replied.

For something to do, he retreated to the stalls to fuss over Pollyanna and Casalinga. He wasn't surprised when Ben came to join him. He would have done the same in his shoes.

Ben didn't beat around the bush. 'Look, I reckon Sophie's a great girl but I don't want to tread on any toes, so if there's something going on between you two . . .'

'There's nothing between me and Soph.'

Ben's eyebrows shot up. 'Soph? You want to watch she doesn't catch you calling her that. She hates being called Soph.'

Aaron blinked. Did she? She'd never said.

Ben scratched at his chin, assessing him. 'You two looked pretty close before.'

'We're just friends.'

'Good, because I'm hoping to become more than friends with Sophie.'

Aaron concentrated on stroking Pollyanna's cheek while he took deep, even breaths. The conversation was killing him.

'Just don't hurt her,' he said, when he'd calmed himself enough to speak.

'Sophie? Not a chance.' He looked toward the warm-up ring. 'I'm more worried she'll hurt me.' He fixed brown eyes back on Aaron. 'Don't worry, I'll look after her.'

When Ben had limped away, Aaron pressed his head against Polly's and squeezed his eyes shut, overwhelmed with sadness. He'd always hoped that, over time, he'd be able to atone for the ruin he'd brought his father, for his cruelty to Sophie's mother, for the lives he'd so blindly destroyed. That if he worked hard enough, if he made the yard a success, somehow he'd make the world right again. But now he realised there would never be atonement, only punishment.

And right now he was gaining an idea of just how bad that punishment could be.

He sighed and gave Polly's ears a final scratch. No point stressing over it. He had a race day to get through.

Sophie was waiting for him by the fence, alone with Costa Motza. Ben must have headed back to the betting ring.

'Are you okay?' she asked when he approached.

'Why didn't you tell me you hated being called Soph?'

She shrugged. 'Because it's different when you do it.'

Delight snaked up his back as though Sophie had just run her bare fingers up his spine. Her response showed how much Ben knew. He looked at her but she wouldn't meet his eye.

'You better not tell your new boyfriend that.'

That got her attention. 'Is that what he called himself?'

He shook his head. 'No, but he wants to be.'

'And what do you think, Aaron? Do you think he'd make a good boyfriend?'

'You're asking the wrong person, Soph.'

'Yes,' she said with a slight smile. 'I suppose I am. Maybe I'll just have to find out for myself.'

Aaron had to look away.

As they approached the mounting yard, Sophie stopped. 'Aaron?'

'Yeah?'

'Will you do something for me?'

'Depends what it is.'

She rolled her eyes. 'Just say yes.'

'Not until I find out what it is.'

'*Aaron.*'

'*Sophie.*' He nudged her, loving having her back to normal. Loving her teasing, loving the look she was giving him, loving her with every pathetic, agonised bit of his heart.

She nudged him back. 'Say yes.'

'Okay. Yes.'

Her grin told him he'd just been trapped.

'If Costa Motza wins, will you kiss me?'

FOURTEEN

RUNNING through the back straight toward the eight-fifty and we have Palliser three lengths to Boundly, followed by Turning Turtle, Urban Delight, and Finlanda . . .

Aaron wished he had his binoculars, but he'd handed them over to Sophie. Costa Motza was where he expected him to be – running last – but not as far behind as he'd anticipated. The pace was moderate, and only five lengths separated first from last. Costa Motza was still in the hunt.

Sophie had ordered him away when she'd given her apprentice jockey his instructions. He didn't know how she'd directed him to ride, but from her calm demeanour, the jockey was riding to orders. He bent down to whisper in her ear. He saw Ben's set face, but didn't care. Ben Moore could take a running jump.

'I don't know what you promised that apprentice but it must have been good.'

She said nothing, responding only with a complacent smile.

Coming up to the five hundred and it's still tight with Boundly and Palliser neck and neck, a length to Turning Turtle, Finlanda a half length from Costa Motza and Urban Delight on the outside . . .

Aaron stared at the field, his ear on the call.

Inside the three hundred and Palliser to Boundly, a length to Turning Turtle, Costa Motza and Urban Delight . . .

'Holy shit,' said Aaron.

Sophie dropped the binoculars and leaned across the rail.

It's Palliser and Boundly fighting it out, but Costa Motza's coming hard . . .

'Go, Costa!' Sophie punched the air in front of her. 'Go, boy, go!'

It's a three-horse race between Palliser, Boundly, and the surprise contender Costa Motza . . .

Aaron couldn't believe it. Beside him, Sophie jumped up and down, screaming in excitement, her grey eyes wide with hope.

Palliser, Boundly, Costa Motza . . . and Boundly puts its nose in front . . . Boundly and a photo between Palliser and Costa Motza – who would have paid a motza if he'd got up – a length to Turning Turtle and the favourite Urban Delight . . .

'Damn, damn, damn,' said Sophie, banging her race book against the rail.

He grabbed her by the shoulders. 'Tell me that's not the same horse.'

She grinned. 'That's Costa Motza all right, and don't worry, I didn't slip him anything.'

He narrowed his eyes. 'Are you sure?'

'Of course I'm sure. I hate horse dopers. As far as I'm concerned they should be all taken out and shot.'

He let her go and stared at the returning horses with eyes that felt too big for their sockets. Why did he have to bring that up? It brought everything crashing back. Any joy he'd felt had evaporated with those words. And it served him right.

As if there weren't already enough reasons for Sophie to hate him, now she'd have another. Not that she knew. No one did except for that conniving little bastard, Danny, and, of course, his mother. She was the one who'd manipulated Aaron into doping his father's horses in the first place.

Costa Motza could win a thousand races, and he still wouldn't touch her. He'd contaminated her life enough.

Sophie fingered his arm. 'I'm sorry. Your dad. I didn't think.'

'I told you, my father didn't nobble anything.'

'Wasn't he banned or something?' asked Ben.

Aaron glared at him and then pushed off the rail, walking away before he gave into impulse and rammed his fist into Ben's face.

'What's his problem?' he heard Ben say to Sophie. He didn't catch Sophie's reply and was grateful. He didn't know if he'd like what he heard.

Everything. That was his problem. He was under threat of losing an owner he couldn't afford to see walk, was in love with the one person he couldn't have, and was so racked with jealousy and anger his head felt about to burst. A walking, talking, steaming, human pressure cooker. Knowing his luck, he'd probably have a stroke.

'Hey, boss.'

He looked up to find Danny Carlyle standing in front of him, cigarette dangling from the fingers of his right hand, beer in his left.

Aaron shook his head and pointed to the cigarette. 'I don't think your doctor would be too thrilled to see you with that.' Not that he cared. If his stable jockey dropped dead tomorrow he'd probably cheer at the news.

Danny grinned, exposing yellow-stained teeth. 'What he don't know won't hurt him.' He nodded to the incoming horses. 'You give him a speedball or something?'

'Bloody looks like it, doesn't it?'

Danny took a drag on his cigarette. 'Stewards might want a chat.'

'Yeah, but in this case, they'd be better off grilling his new owner.' He tipped his head toward Sophie and Ben. 'She's calling the shots with the horse.'

Danny squinted. 'Sophie Dixon? Who let her own a racehorse?' He looked back at Aaron. 'Doc reckons I'll be riding again shortly.'

Aaron nodded, thinking about the implications of Danny's return to the yard. At least Ian Dixon would be happy. 'Whatever he says.'

'I'd be back tomorrow if he'd give me the okay. I'm bored rigid at home.'

'Count yourself lucky. If I weren't enjoying the peace and quiet so much I'd have you back shovelling shit in heartbeat.' Ignoring Danny's black look he started toward the mounting ring.

The race caller announced the placegetters over the tannoy. Costa Motza had come second and paid an enormous dividend on the tote. Sophie had probably made a killing.

'You might've won if you'd used your whip,' he said to the diminutive apprentice.

The apprentice regarded him with scared eyes, yet to learn the prevarication of jockey-speak when it came to defending his riding. 'Miss Dixon said I wasn't to use it, boss. She said it only frightened the horse. I should have used the stick, shouldn't I? It won't happen again, boss. I promise.'

Aaron suppressed a smile. 'Miss Dixon spoils her horses rotten, but you were right not to use the whip. Those were your instructions and you stuck with them. Well done.'

The jockey grinned his relief.

'You're turning my horses into big sooks,' he said to Sophie as she stood at Costa Motza's head planting kisses all over his white blaze. 'What's this about not using the whip?'

'He's frightened of it.'

'Says who?'

'Says me.'

'God help me, I've a horse whisperer for an owner.' But he knew Sophie was right. Costa Motza's performance had proved it. 'Are you staying for the rest of the races?'

She shook her head. 'No. I'll follow you back and help with the horses.'

'Your new boyfriend won't like that.'

Sophie chucked him under the chin, her grey eyes sparkling. 'Careful, Aaron. A girl might start thinking you're jealous.'

———

The horses were unloaded and in their yards by the time Sophie arrived at Hakea Lodge. Aaron was determined to keep his mouth shut, even though he was sure Ben was responsible for her delayed appearance.

'Sorry,' she said, leaning on the rail of Costa Motza's yard as Aaron adjusted the horse's rug. 'I was held up.'

Costa Motza wandered over to snuffle his nose through Sophie's new hairdo. She batted him away but not before the horse had made a mess of her streaked blond bob. Aaron felt ridiculously pleased. The perfection of the style had been irritating him all afternoon.

He lounged against a post, surreptitiously studying her as he pretended to inspect a stain on the cuff of his race-day suit. Since she arrived, she'd worn the same excited expression, as though her insides were bubbling like newly popped champagne. He had a fair idea where it came from.

She gave Costa Motza a last kiss and pushed him away before sliding along the rail and stopping near him. She rested her cheek on her arms, looking at him sideways.

'Ben asked me out.'

He shrugged. 'Good for him.'

'Don't you want to know what I said?'

'Not particularly.'

She smiled and slid closer. 'Are you sure?'

'You can go out with whoever you like.' He stared at Costa Motza's white legs, almost luminous in the half-light of the fading day. He knew what she was doing, but it wouldn't work. Not today. Not ever.

'I said I'd think about it.'

'Ben's a good bloke. You should have said yes.'

'I might yet. He's coming to Vanaheim on Thursday afternoon to look at the new lucerne stand. I might tell him yes then.'

Aaron shook his head and looked at the sky. He needed to walk away, do the feeds, anything to escape her test of his resolve.

'Do you wish Costa Motza had won?'

'Of course. I could have used my cut of the winnings.'

'What about our wager?'

He swallowed. He had to stop thinking about that. 'I don't remember saying yes to any bet.'

'But you didn't say no.'

'I didn't think I needed to. Costa Motza had no chance.'

'Ahh, but he did.'

'So I discovered.' He glanced at his watch. 'I need to do the feeds and you need to go home.'

'I thought I might stay. Take you up on that steak and red wine dinner you promised.'

'I don't think I've got any steaks.'

Sophie grinned, her teeth bright in the approaching sunset. 'But I have. You didn't think I was late because I was hooking up with Ben, did you?'

———

The yard was hushed and the horses sleeping when Aaron finally walked Sophie to her car. To his combined relief and disappointment, the evening had passed without Sophie trying anything. Not that she needed to. Everything she did made him churn with longing.

If she smiled, he wanted to kiss her. If she raised an eyebrow or rolled her eyes or laughed or turned serious, he wanted to kiss her. As the night progressed, his obsession with her mouth had spread to every part of her, until he hadn't known where he wanted to look the most.

And when she'd turned from the stove after checking his cooking, pink-cheeked and with tiny drops of moisture speckling her brow like glitter, the urge to take her hand and drag her to his bedroom had been almost primitive in its ferocity.

He opened the car door for her but she didn't step in. Instead, she leaned against the rear passenger door looking up the stars, her neck pearly in the moonlight. He stared at it, overcome with the need to run his tongue up and down her delicate skin and feel her shiver with pleasure.

She smiled and looked at him, grey eyes shiny with amusement. 'I can almost hear what you're thinking.'

He smiled back. 'I hope not.'

She poked a finger at his chest. 'You have a very dirty mind.'

'I wasn't thinking dirty things.'

'You weren't? What were you thinking then?'

'I was thinking it's about time you went home and put your horses to bed.'

She shook her head. 'You know what, Aaron? You're a terrible liar.'

They were silent for a moment, the quiet interrupted only by the snort of a restless horse and the cry of a night bird. She looked at him expectantly but he made no move toward her. With a sigh and a crooked smile, she climbed into the car and wound down the window. 'Thanks for dinner.'

'You're welcome.'

The Range Rover was halfway across the yard when he realised he wanted to tell her something. Something important. He ran after it and banged on her window.

She wound it down, smiling. 'What?'

His mouth went dry.

'Aaron?' Her moonlit expression shone open and hopeful.

'I just wanted to say I thought you looked beautiful today.'

As she registered his words, her face transformed, glowing with unrestrained delight and sending his heart into orbit. She looked as luminous as the moonlight that bathed her, and far more lovely than his inadequate words could ever express.

But then her smile faded and her eyes clouded, and he saw the vulnerability she kept so well hidden. The twelve-year-old girl that haunted Sophie, and who Aaron could never banish from his memory.

'Yes,' she said sadly, turning from him as her eyes filled. 'But apparently not beautiful enough.'

FIFTEEN

THE BRILLIANT SUNSHINE of the weekend gave over to several days of heavy rain that never seemed to ease. To prevent damage to the soils and pastures of Vanaheim's lower paddocks, Sophie moved the cows and calves to the lighter ground on the western side, choosing the larger paddocks with the best windbreaks so the cattle could spread out but still have protection from the cold. She did the same for Chuck and Buck, changing their day paddock from the front of the house to the paddock between the stockyards and Tess's cottage. With pasture growth once more slowed, all the animals needed extra feed to keep warm, especially the horses, who were still growing back their winter coats.

Though she tried to maintain a sunny outlook, the long days looking after Vanaheim, dealing with a severely rattled Tess, battling an increasingly recalcitrant Buck, who she'd yet again decided to give a second chance, and helping out at Hakea Lodge left Sophie even more tired than usual. Worst of all was the disappointment that her effort on Saturday to grab Aaron's attention with a makeover had failed.

By Thursday, fatigue had shortened her temper, but it was nothing compared to Aaron's.

He'd been sullen all that morning, barking at the horses and grumping at Sophie during trackwork when neither Costa Motza nor Rowdy galloped good times. The track was a quagmire. No horse was running well, but Aaron didn't want to hear that.

Back at Hakea Lodge, he barely spoke as they worked the other horses. She asked him several times what the matter was, but he'd only growled back that he was fine and she should concentrate on riding. At first, she'd been hurt to the point of tears. By the end of the morning, her hurt had turned to anger and they were snapping at one another and bickering over nothing.

'I'm going to give Costa another scoop,' she said as she pulled the lid off a plastic bucket of mineral supplement.

'He only needs one.'

'Two won't hurt him.'

'I said he only needs one.'

'Well, I'm giving him two.'

Aaron pulled the bucket out of her hands. 'I'm the bloody trainer. If I say he only needs one, then that's all he's getting.'

She tried to wrench the bucket back, but he was too strong. 'Yeah, and I'm his owner, and if I say he gets two scoops then that's what he'll be given.'

Aaron let the bucket go. The sudden release sent her sprawling backwards onto a sack of oats. The crystalline mineral supplement puffed up and spilled down her jumper, covering her in glittery sparkles.

'If you think you know it all,' he said, taking the bucket from her and hauling her to her feet, 'then why don't you apply for a licence and train the frigging horse yourself?'

She glared at him as she swiped the front of her jumper. 'I just might. It'd be a hell of a lot better than hanging around with you!'

She walked out, fuming. She flung open the door of the Range

Rover, stepped in and slammed it shut, scowling through the windscreen as he stood in the doorway of the feed room. His arms were spread, his hands bracing the jamb as though he needed to keep the doorway from collapsing. With a last filthy glance, she started the engine, spun the wheel hard and sped out of the yard, showering gravel behind her.

———

Back at Vanaheim, Sophie picked up a brightly painted timber showjumping pole and slotted one end into the metal cup she'd hooked onto the jump wing. She walked to the other wing, counted holes and readjusted the height of the other cup, before lifting up the other end of the pole and dropping it into place.

She counted out three strides, and made a mark with her boot into the soft soil. She didn't know why she was bothering. She wasn't in the right humour for any of Buck's shenanigans and he'd probably only make her angrier by refusing to jump anyway. With the local eventing program in hiatus until the spring, he wasn't even supposed to be in work. He should be lazing about with Chuck, getting fat and woolly, but after studying the program for the Showjumping Club's winter series, she'd kept him in, hoping the extra work might improve his behaviour. It hadn't.

The thought that she'd failed with him wrestled with her once unshakable belief in her riding ability, sapping her confidence and making her worry whether Rowdy would be any different. The beautiful, dark thoroughbred was fine in the yard and on the exercise track, but how would he behave away from Hakea Lodge? Would he turn into another Buck? The thought made her shoulders sag.

'Don't tell me you forgot?'

Sophie spun around to see who had spoken. Leaning over the gate and grinning, almost irresistibly handsome in his moleskin jeans, blue and white checked shirt and navy wool jumper with the sleeves pushed up, stood Ben Moore. He pulled off his hat.

'Remember me? Ben Moore. Local agronomist. Man of your dreams.'

Suddenly she understood. She might have forgotten all about Ben's appointment, but Aaron hadn't. She closed her eyes, cursing herself for her idiocy.

'Ben,' she said, walking toward him. 'I'm sorry. I did forget.'

'Nice to know I made such a big impression.' He undid the latch and opened the gate for her. 'Are you still right to look at the lucerne? I can always come back another time.'

'Now's no problem. I was just setting up a few jumps for later.'

They walked slowly toward Ben's ute, his limp pronounced on the uneven ground of the paddock.

'It must be hard going with your injury,' she said.

'It's okay.' He smiled at her. 'But there won't be any dancing on Saturday night, I'm afraid. Just dinner. Assuming I can convince you to come.'

She looked at the ground and gnawed her thumbnail. Her aunt would laugh if she found out Sophie had captured an admirer, and laugh even harder if she discovered it was the wrong one. Tess had marched into Vanaheim the week before, looked Sophie up and down and announced it was no bloody wonder Aaron wasn't interested in her. Wreck didn't begin to describe the mess Sophie had made of herself.

She had snapped back that Tess was hardly one to talk, but the insult had taken effect. As soon as Tess marched off with another bottle of purloined red wine, she'd walked into the bathroom and stared at herself in the mirror, trying to see herself through Aaron's eyes. A puffy-eyed, mousy-haired disaster looked back at her. The girl Aaron had once called pretty had turned ugly.

So she'd drawn on her fortitude and done something about it. But now it appeared her attempt to make herself attractive had not only failed, it had backfired.

Ben's hand settled lightly on the small of her back, sending her nerves buzzing like wires in a high wind. She could see him looking

at her, a teasing smile on his lips as though he thought her discomfort
was an act. She whistled for Sammy and Del. The heelers wandered
out from behind the stables and, seeing someone touching their
mistress, trotted to Sophie's side. She gave them each a pat. Ben's
hand fell away.

She peered at the cluttered interior of Ben's car. The passenger
seat was piled with plastic bags of soil, rural newspapers and fertiliser
brochures. 'Maybe we'd better take the Range Rover.'

Sophie deliberately kept the radio up as she drove Ben out to the
lucerne paddock. She wanted this over and done with as quickly as
possible so she could go back to Aaron's and apologise. Sammy and
Del sat panting in the rear, fogging up the windows with their doggy
breath. She smiled. Ben wouldn't try anything while the two dogs
were protecting her. Blue heelers weren't renowned for their genial
nature and although her dogs were lazy, they were also ferociously
loyal.

Ben raised his voice over the radio. 'I had a good time on Saturday. It was a pity you had to go.'

She kept her eyes on the muddy track. 'Horses take up a lot of
time, I'm afraid.'

'There's more to life than horses, Sophie.'

'Not in my world.'

She concentrated on driving. The track was hard from years of
vehicles compressing the soil, but it was still slippery, and although
she wasn't interested in Ben romantically, she wanted his respect.
Sliding off the track and bogging the Range Rover would make her
seem amateurish, like the spoilt, rich-kid-playing-farmer many
thought she was.

They pulled up at the gate. Stretching east over the hill toward
Dixon Road lay ten hectares of vibrant green lucerne. There were
other stands at Vanaheim, but they were older, and this was one
Sophie had planned and planted herself.

Twelve months' hard work had gone into preparing the paddock.
Dull days spent on the tractor spraying weeds, applying lime and

fertiliser, cultivating the soil to get the seed bed perfect. She'd spent hours talking to seed company representatives, the Department of Agriculture's district agronomist, and local lucerne growers, who'd indulged her interrogation with bemused expressions.

She'd immersed herself in brochures and research papers and management books until she was so stuffed with knowledge about lucerne she dreamed about it. Then came the actual planting and the watching and waiting as it emerged from the soil and unfurled its tiny leaves into the cool autumn. Fourteen months on, and it was magnificent – a testament to a life that revolved around nothing but Vanaheim and horses.

A life before Aaron.

She unlatched the gate and wandered out into the stand, picking at leaves and studying them. The heelers took off with their noses down, following rabbit and mice trails. Ben lagged behind, slowed by his football injury.

She waited for him to catch up and handed him a stalk. 'Phosphorus?'

He took it from her fingers and inspected the sprig's small, purplish leaves. 'Shouldn't be, not after the preparation you did. Are there any others?'

Sophie crouched down and went through the plants at her feet. 'Can't see any.'

'It's probably just an isolated patch, but if you're worried we'll do another soil test at the end of winter.' He looked around. 'It's looking great. With good management, you'll get ten years out of this. You should be proud.'

She smiled her thanks and stood up, staring into the distance toward Hakea Lodge, wondering if her suspicion about Aaron was right. That it was Ben's visit that had made him so fractious.

'You've done all this on your own, plus you're a successful eventer and now a place-winning racehorse owner.' He smiled and fixed her with soft brown eyes. 'You're one special girl, Sophie.'

She crossed her arms and contemplated her feet, puzzled as to why someone as good-looking as Ben was bothering with her. He'd been out to the farm enough times to know she wasn't really that girl he'd seemed so interested in on Saturday. She didn't usually wear dresses or make-up or perfume. She wore jeans and jodhpurs, and smelt of horses and hay, and kept herself deliberately isolated because for so long she hadn't been strong enough to face the world. But now she was, and the world was proving more complicated than she ever imagined.

'You make it hard for a bloke. Saturday was the first time I've seen you anywhere out.'

'I don't go out much.'

He took a step closer. Sammy and Del bounced towards her, tongues lolling. Without instruction, they took position either side of their mistress, heads cocked as they regarded Ben.

'Maybe you should. Ever been to Chez Nicolette?'

Sophie shook her head. Chez Nicolette was Harrington's poshest restaurant, though in a town whose dining experiences barely extended beyond pub food, Chinese and a solitary Thai restaurant, that didn't mean all that much.

'I'd like to take you there for dinner on Saturday night.'

'It's sweet of you to ask, Ben, but I'll have to say no.'

He brushed his boot through a lucerne plant. 'You seemed pretty keen last Saturday.'

'I know. I'm sorry.' She wanted to leave. This was becoming awkward.

'I don't like being used, Sophie,' he said quietly.

She didn't know how to respond. He was right. She had used him to get at Aaron and now he was hurt. She felt dismayed by her immaturity. She was twenty-two. It was about time she grew up. With the dogs at her heels, she began walking hunch-shouldered back to the car. Ben hesitated, then limped to follow.

She drove him back to his ute, fingers curled hard around the wheel. When she pulled up, they both stared through the windscreen in heavy silence, trying to find something to say. After several long seconds he hooked his fingers in the door handle and pushed it open.

He was halfway to the ute when she lowered her window and called his name. Turning back, he leaned an arm against the car and fixed her with a hopeful expression.

'I'm sorry.'

He shrugged and smiled. 'It's okay. My mum always says all's fair in love and war. But if you change your mind, the offer still stands.' His expression turned serious. 'I just hope that horse trainer of yours realises how lucky he is.'

———

The moment Sophie turned Buck into Hakea Lodge's drive the horse seemed to gather himself. Instead of the head-tossing, snorting and skittering he'd performed at home, he held steady, neck arched, ears pricked and prancing like an Olympic dressage horse. It was as though he knew competition awaited, and wanted to show the others exactly who was the star around here.

'You think you're so cool, don't you, Buck?' she said, scruffing his mane. 'But you wait until Aaron gets on your back. Then we'll see how cool you are.'

Arrogant as ever, Buck simply broke into a canter so round and elevated, he seemed to bounce down the drive.

After Ben's departure she'd stayed in the car, gnawing on a finger nail and thinking. When taken in context with Ben's visit, the reason behind Aaron's conduct that morning seemed plain, but she was hardly in good form when it came to interpreting people's behaviour. Someone like Ben was easy. He made it clear what he wanted, through words and actions. Aaron, on the other hand, said one thing and then looked at her in a way that belied those words. While her heart told her the truth lay in his eyes, her head remained cautious. And her father's assertion always echoed through her mind.

He'll hurt you, and you're going to let him.

One thing she'd decided was that she wasn't prepared to embarrass herself by rushing around and interrogating him. She needed an excuse to return, and none came better than Buck.

Aaron was sitting on the verandah step with a heavy canvas rug over his knees and a needle threaded with waxed cotton in his hand when she clip-clopped into the yard. He glanced up, frowning at the sight of her on Buck. Noticing an intruder, the other horses came to life, calling out and stomping. Nostrils flared, Rowdy glared at Buck from his stable before snorting and tossing his head, and whirling around to present his rump.

As Sophie dismounted, a ray of sun broke through the heavy sky and covered the quadrangle in a golden glow. Puddles and water drops sparkled with reflected colour. The wind, which had been absent and kept the weather front over the district, began at last to rise, shuffling the trees and shifting the clouds. She sucked in a breath, hoping it was a sign.

She led Buck to the step and sat down beside Aaron. 'I'm sorry about this morning.'

He sighed and rubbed a hand down his face. 'Me too.'

They both stared at Buck, standing stock-still with his muscles quivering, haughty head held high. Only the twitch of his tail and the swivel of his ears betrayed his mood.

'Was it because of Ben?'

'I'm just tired, Sophie, and worried about the yard. I took it out on you and I shouldn't have. I'm sorry.'

She twisted Buck's reins in her fingers, doubt circling again. Each time she thought she'd worked out where his heart lay, he acted in a way that made her question what she'd determined. Maybe he spoke the truth. Maybe she'd misread all he'd said and done, just as she had her father.

She looked at the feed room, remembering. Aaron's touch so gentle, the desire burning in his eyes, the way he'd said her name. The way he'd rejected her and continued to do so. She bit her lip.

He lifted his chin toward Buck. 'Please tell me you're not hoping to retrain him as a racehorse.'

'No. I was hoping you might teach him some manners.'

'You can do that yourself.'

Sensing he was the topic of discussion, Buck lowered his head toward them. Aaron held out his fingers to be sniffed before scratching Buck's nose. The horse took a step closer so Aaron could reach his ears, and closed his eyes. Sophie regarded Buck sourly.

'Believe me, I've tried. Please, will you ride him? You're twice my size and a lot harder to get off.'

'He'll probably kill me.'

'No he won't.' Waylaying any further protest, she grabbed his hand and slapped the reins onto his palm. 'Think of it as a return favour for the ute.'

Aaron said nothing for a moment, eyeing Buck with scepticism. The horse blinked innocently back at him. He sighed, set the canvas rug he was repairing aside and stood. 'All right. But I'm putting him in the stock saddle, just in case.'

Fifteen minutes later, Sophie stood in the centre of Aaron's lunging ring with her hands on her hips, looking sulkily at Aaron as he circled around her. The lunging ring was a large, fenced circle filled with deep sand, which served a dual purpose – a way for Aaron to work the horses on his own, and as a sand pit in which they could roll and scratch after exercise. Wary of Buck, Aaron had suggested they work him there first, but from the way the horse plodded around, a portrait of equine docility, the precaution proved unnecessary.

'I hate you,' she announced.

'Come on, Soph,' replied Aaron, blue eyes twinkling. 'I thought we were friends.'

'We were until today. How the hell do you do it?'

Aaron couldn't stop laughing at her and now, as if her humiliation wasn't complete, he sat sideways in the saddle, one leg hooked around the stock saddle's knee pad, the other dangling free of the stirrup. He'd even let go of the reins, but Buck, the rotten traitor, continued plodding along like a cart horse.

'Don't you know? It's my manly touch.'

She stomped toward them. 'Right. Get off.'

Aaron slid from the saddle and grinned at her. 'I don't know what you're on about, Soph. Old Buck here seems fine to me.'

She poked her tongue out at him and mounted, determined to show Buck's behaviour had nothing to do with Aaron. The horse was simply in a benign mood for once, perhaps made obliging by the breaking sunshine. The moment she landed in the saddle, Buck perked up, his ears swivelling like periscopes. Recognising the signs of developing discontent, she kept her concentration, feeling with her foot for the other stirrup in case he started up.

'See? He's fine,' said Aaron from the centre of the ring.

Sophie cast him a dirty look before gathering up the reins and urging Buck into a trot. As they circled, she marvelled at the mighty effort it must have taken Rowdy to jump over the fence from a standing start. The sand was deep, the enclosing fence high. She doubted Buck could manage it, or even Chuck, and they were trained to jump enormous fences under difficult conditions. If Rowdy could be trained, there'd be no stopping him. She just hoped she was up to it.

Though tenser than he had been with Aaron, Buck kept his temper, and Sophie's flagging faith in her ability and her horse began to rise. She eased him back to a walk and asked him to collect himself. Romping around the ring was one thing, but like all the racehorses watching the scene with interest from their yards, Buck wasn't a pleasure horse, he was a performance horse. She needed him to behave like one.

Using her legs and weight, she brought him to hand, feeling him elevate and lighten, as though all his muscles had tightened into a ball of controlled power.

'Looking good,' said Aaron, and from the tone of his voice he seemed genuinely impressed.

She gave the aid to trot, and Buck responded, bouncing along through the sand as though his hoofs were made of springs. Her spirits soared. He hadn't performed like this for months. With each circle, her confidence ballooned. She directed him to canter, and the change came like clockwork. A grin broke across her face. She looked at Aaron.

'I don't know what you did but I can't thank you enough.'

'I told you, it was just my manly touch.'

'I think you horse-whispered him.'

He laughed. 'That's your style, Soph, not mine. Anyway, Buck's not as gullible as Costa Motza.'

'Costa Motza is not gullible. He's a champion.'

'Hardly.'

'Oh, yeah? And who was the one who described him as not a racehorse's backside, huh? Had to eat your words on Saturday, didn't you?'

'Saturday was a fluke.'

Sophie turned Buck into the centre of the ring. 'Was not.'

Aaron stared at the sky, shaking his head in feigned exasperation, the dark gold stubble on his chin glittering, his mouth quirked. Though his jeans were faded and tatty, his wool jumper full of pulls, they only made him appear more rugged and leg-jellying handsome. Ben Moore might possess chiselled movie-star looks, but it was Aaron who made Sophie's insides melt.

'Go on. Admit it. Even you were impressed by his performance.'

He eyed her through long blond eyelashes in a way that made her tingle all over. 'Maybe a little.'

Grinning, Sophie cupped a hand to her ear. 'What was that? I couldn't quite hear you.'

'Bugger off.'

As she reached out to pull his hat off, Buck dropped his shoulder and skidded sideways, neatly depositing a caught-out Sophie onto the sand at Aaron's feet. The horse trotted around the ring, stirrups flopping, reins flapping and his head held disdainfully in the air as though delighted to at last be rid of the woman on his back.

Aaron crouched on one knee beside her, blue eyes crinkled with concern. 'Are you all right?'

Sophie sat up, rubbing her left shoulder and biting her lip to stop from sobbing in frustration. How dare Buck humiliate her in front of Aaron?

'No.'

'Are we talking pride or an actual injury?'

'Both.' She rolled her shoulder and though it gave a bit of a twinge, she decided it was fine.

He pressed gentle fingers against her collarbone. 'Sore?'

She shrugged. 'A little.'

'This might help.' Kneading carefully, he worked his way to the base of her scapula and back again. His touch was tender and sure and made her nerves buzz. As he massaged her shoulder, his breath brushed her neck, shooting goosebumps down her back. She felt his gaze on her cheek, sensed it drifting toward her mouth. She swallowed, thinking again of how he'd caressed her in the feed room, how he'd looked at her, breathed her name. The feel of his mouth so close to hers. How she yearned to experience that just one more time.

Unable to help herself, she pressed back into him and closed her eyes.

The kneading ceased. She thought she heard him swallow hard but when she opened her eyes he was focused intently on her shoulder, not her mouth. And his own mouth was held in a resolute line.

'That should do it,' he said, letting her go.

He stood, dusted sand off his knee, and held out a hand for her to grab. She searched his face for insight to his feelings, but his expression remained shuttered, his gaze not quite on hers. Only his eyes had darkened, though it was likely an illusion caused by the shadow of his hat.

She stared at the sand, blinking away her pointless longing.

'Come on, Soph, you know the rules. Time to get back in the saddle.'

Buck had stopped gallivanting and was patiently waiting for someone to pay him attention. When Sophie was upright, Aaron strode over to him and grabbed the reins. After dusting herself down, Sophie joined him, and though she knew she needed to remount, her heart wasn't in it. If today had taught her one thing, it was that Aaron had told the truth. Friendship was all he wanted.

After another half an hour in the ring, during which Buck infuriated her even more by behaving once again impeccably, she thanked Aaron for his help and left. That evening, she called Ben and apologised for being contrary, but if the invitation to dinner was still open, she'd love to accept.

After all, she had lots of life to catch up on.

SIXTEEN

AARON WANDERED into the pub and held his hand up in greeting when he saw Josh. They'd been friends since high school, both horse-mad, although in different ways. Josh was seduced by the thrill of the punt, but he also knew his way around a horse and could be relied on to help out in the yard when needed. Aaron valued his friendship, but it was hard for them to find time to see each other. Josh worked for a local logging contractor and his mornings started as early as Aaron's.

Aaron mimed taking a drink and Josh nodded. He leaned against the bar and looked around as he waited for his order.

It'd been weeks since he'd been out but nothing had changed. The pokies room was filled with the local addicts. In the main area, men like Josh were staring at rows of screens, checking the fields for the dogs or the trots, drinking beer and sitting on bar stools. At the other end of the bar, half a dozen people of various ages, a family Aaron supposed, ate counter meals while watching football on yet another television.

No one seemed to be talking. He couldn't blame Sophie for keeping away. There was no comfort here.

He paid for the beers and carried them over to the tall table Josh had commandeered in front of the big screen. They tilted their glasses at one another and then drank. Josh's eyes returned to the race he was following. Aaron wasn't interested, but it was better to be out than moping around Hakea Lodge thinking about Sophie.

He'd had a good day. Two placings had put some much needed cash in his pocket. He would have liked to celebrate with Sophie over another steak and red wine dinner, but that was only asking for trouble.

'So how's things?' asked Josh when the race had finished.

'Not bad. Couple of placings today.'

'Yeah, I saw. How's Sophie?'

Aaron shrugged. He wished he'd never mentioned Sophie but he had to say something when he'd asked Josh to look after the horses while he rushed off to Lake Ackerman. Josh had taken one look at him, shaken his head and announced, 'Mate, you've got it bad.' Aaron hadn't believed him then, but he did now.

'She's fine.'

Josh looked up from sorting his betting slips. 'So it's going crap.'

'We're just friends.'

Josh gave him a 'yeah, you keep telling yourself that' look, but didn't say anything more. He checked his form guide and rose to place another bet. Aaron picked up his slips and went through them. The amounts he wagered were staggering, but then Josh had always gambled big. Aaron sometimes wondered if he was at the wrong end of the business. Josh invariably had money, whereas Aaron was always broke.

He took another gulp of beer. Josh sat back down, a peculiar look on his face.

'You're not going to like this,' he said.

'Like what?'

Josh used his head to indicate the public entrance to the front bar. 'Sophie's sitting in there with Ben Moore.'

A jealous burn scorched Aaron's insides. He shrugged, trying to show he didn't care, but his eyes darted toward the doorway. The angle was wrong. He could only see a table at which a middle-aged couple were drinking small glasses of beer and picking at a packet of nuts. He feigned interest in the dogs and trots for a while, chatting to Josh about the yard until he'd finished his beer.

'You want another?'

'My shout,' said Josh.

'Doesn't matter. I'll get it.'

Josh threw him a look and went back to staring at the screens.

He walked slowly up to the bar, the burn growing worse with every step.

Sophie sat alone at a table, fiddling with the strap of a small evening bag and staring out of the window to the street. Her fingers worked incessantly, twisting the strap into a knot and then untying it again, the agitation of her hands belying her calm expression. She was made up and combed to perfection, and wearing an expensive-looking dress made of stretchy blue fabric. It clung to her breasts, showing off their perfect, round softness. The sight of her, so exquisitely gorgeous, filled Aaron with hunger and despair.

The pub's all-knowing bar lady stepped in front of him. 'She's out of your league, sonny.'

'I know.'

She patted his hand. 'Not to worry. Good-looking sort like you will never be short of offers.'

But Aaron only wanted Sophie. The one person he couldn't touch.

With another sympathetic pat, the bar lady moved away to pull the beers, returning Sophie to Aaron's view.

She was now gnawing at a thumbnail, but her expression remained unfathomable. Aaron wondered where Ben had disappeared to, and then he was there, handing Sophie a glass of white wine and sitting down close to her. She smiled at him, and Ben leaned forward and whispered something, his eyes lingering on her mouth. Aaron's gut clenched. The urge to leap the bar and drag

Sophie to safety had him gripping the edge of the counter with curled fingers.

Then his view was blocked once more. He ignored the bar lady's look and paid, catching a last glimpse of Sophie in the moment before he walked away. She was still smiling, but it wasn't a polite smile – it was the same shy one he'd fallen in love with, and Ben was looking at her in a way he recognised only too well.

He stayed for another beer, talking racing with Josh and trying not to look as though he cared, but he drank quickly, eager to be out of there and back at Hakea Lodge, where he could lick his wounds in private.

He left via the front bar, but when he checked Ben and Sophie were gone.

———

Aaron sat slumped on his threadbare sofa. An almost empty bottle of red wine sat on the coffee table, an empty glass beside it. In his right hand, he held his phone. Sophie's name glowed bright on the screen, but he didn't press the button.

He needed to keep control. He needed to remember what he'd told Ian. Remember that this was for her own good, just as it had been in the lunging ring, when she'd fallen and he'd rubbed her shoulder. When she'd pressed back against him with her lips parted, and the sight of her trembling mouth had threatened his carefully constructed resolve.

Friends, that's all. Yet the thought of her with Ben ate and ate and ate.

At midnight, drunk on red wine and his gnawing, ravenous jealousy, he crumbled and called, closing his eyes as he heard her sleepy hello. He didn't reply, intent on listening, needing to know if she was with Ben.

Through the earpiece came the shuffle of sheets, the phone moving then an intake of breath.

'Aaron?' She sounded more awake. 'Aaron, what's wrong? Are you okay?'

'I saw you with Ben.'

'I thought you didn't care about him.'

He wanted to say he didn't but it'd only be a lie. He rubbed his hand over his face. His head swam with alcohol and longing. Why had he called her? It was stupid and selfish. He couldn't think straight. And he ached.

Christ, he ached.

'Aaron, can I come over?'

He almost groaned with his need to say yes. 'That's not a good idea.'

'We can talk.'

'There's nothing to talk about.' Except this burning, pointless jealousy he'd brought on himself.

'There's plenty.'

He gripped the phone, knowing he should hang up, unable to.

The quiet stretched. He could hear her shallow breaths as she waited for him to speak. Delicate little Sophie breaths like the ones she'd panted on his lips in the feed room in that magic, doomed moment so long ago. Breaths he couldn't stop dreaming about.

Breaths he wanted to suck into his lungs and never breathe out.

'Did you kiss him?' The words were out before he could catch them and bury them back in his aching heart where they belonged.

'Aaron, please.' She sounded upset.

'Did you?'

Her reply came very soft. 'Yes.'

He pressed his palm hard against his right eye, wanting to cry with sorrow and pain. She'd kissed him. Shared what should have been his, experienced a pleasure that he should have given.

'Why?'

'Aaron, don't.'

'Why, Sophie?'

He could hear her tears as she spoke.

'Because I wanted to pretend it was you.' She let out a sob that twisted his heart. 'You have to understand, it's been years. I can't even remember what it was like to have someone touch me.'

He closed his eyes.

'Aaron?'

'What?'

'I'm coming over.'

'Sophie, don't.' But she'd hung up.

He stood, intending to lock the kitchen door to prevent her coming in, but instead he flopped back onto the sofa and put his head in his hands. He had to resist. He had to remember who she was.

Because I wanted to pretend it was you.

Her words had sent his sludge-filled blood racing.

But she would have to go on pretending, because it would never be him. No matter how much he wanted it. He was a horse doper and destroyer of lives. And that could never be pretended away.

Or forgiven.

After a few minutes, he managed to pull himself together enough to make it to the kitchen. The kettle had only just gone on the hob when he heard her car. He stood shivering by the combustion stove, waiting. Wanting her desperately while praying for strength he wasn't sure he had.

The door opened and shut. He looked up. Sophie stood with her back against the door in work boots and baggy, striped flannelette pyjamas, her hair flat on one side and tangled in knots on the other. She looked utterly adorable. He turned away.

'You shouldn't have come.'

He heard her cross the room. A warm hand slipped into his cold one.

'I had to.'

He gazed at her shyly smiling face and grey eyes filled with something he wished wasn't there, and broke. His arms went around her, wrapping her to him and as he marvelled in the feel of her soft, pliant body against his. Although his face was buried in the hollow of her neck and he was inhaling her like a drug, he made sure he didn't let his lips touch her skin. He simply felt her, and grew warm on her tender touch.

He let her go. She stared up at him with glistening eyes, her lips parted and moist in expectation. So infinitely, sweetly kissable. He looked away, then took an oven mitt and wrapped it around the kettle's handle and removed it from the hottest hob to the back of the stove.

'You want a cup of tea?'

'Only if you're having one.'

He stared at the kettle. He didn't want tea. He wanted to take Sophie to bed. He wanted to lay her naked on the sheet and nestle his head against her chest while listening to every precious breath she took and every exquisite beat of her huge, beautiful heart. And then he'd sleep and dream of a parallel universe where the ugly past had never existed. A place where she'd always be safe and happy and cherished.

A place where he could tell her he loved her.

With his jaw clenched, he grabbed mugs from the cupboard, spooned sugar into them and dropped a teabag in each. Sophie watched him in silence, waiting for him to crack and kiss her. But he wouldn't. Not tonight. Not ever.

He poured water into the mugs and carried them to the kitchen table. He sat down, reached for the biscuit tin and wrenched off the lid, waiting for her to join him.

She didn't. From behind, her hand touched his neck, her fingers as light and fluttery as butterfly wings as they brushed across his skin and under his ear, then traced a line to his mouth.

'Sophie.'

'Shh.'

Her lips were on his neck, planting delicate, feathery kisses across his skin. His flesh broke out in goosebumps and his cock hardened as her tongue twirled lightly down the nape of his neck. Christ, he wanted her. Right there in the kitchen. Except he wouldn't do what she wanted. Not straightaway. He'd make love to her but he had a thousand kisses to bestow on her first, a thousand tiny pleasures to grant before that happened.

Her hand slipped down his front, reaching for the buttons of his shirt. He grabbed it.

'Don't.'

She responded by kissing her way up his neck and sucking on his earlobe. She had to stop. He had to make her stop before he ruined her with his despicable past.

Abruptly, he stood, bumping the table so the mugs slopped tea.

He turned around to face her, the chair between them.

'I can't do this,' he said.

'But you want to.'

He swallowed and looked toward the window at the darkness that enveloped what was once his mother's garden.

If they followed this path, if he gave into her, the past would never stay hidden. Now, more than ever, he couldn't risk its exposure. He had to protect her from the horror it would bring. The reality of knowing he'd hurled accusations in Fiona Dixon's face like acid and then walked away, cloaked in her hope and comfort, while she was left with nothing but despair and a life drained of its future.

He closed his eyes. The room swam. 'Go home, Sophie.'

'No. I want to stay. With you.'

She tried to tuck her hand in his. He yanked it away, angry with her, but even more furious with himself. 'You don't. And you know why you don't? Because when you find out what I did, you won't be able to scrub hard enough to clean yourself of me, that's why.' He grabbed her face and stared into it, trying to make her understand. 'I don't want to do that to you, Soph. I don't want to hurt you any more than I already have.'

'Nothing can be that bad, Aaron. Nothing.'

But it was.

He dropped his hands and retreated to the other side of the table, out of harm's way. 'Please, you have to leave.'

She looked at him for a long time, hurt swimming through her wide eyes. Finally, she sighed. 'Fine. If that's what you want, I'll leave.'

Her boots thudded dully as she walked to the door. Cold air swirled into the kitchen as she held it open. His throat felt like it was seared shut with regret. Then she turned around and smiled so gently it filled his chest to bursting.

'One day you'll see that the past no longer matters. That no matter what you've done, I'll still love you. I'm strong enough to face anything, Aaron. Even your demons.'

It was what she believed, but he knew she was wrong.

SEVENTEEN

ON SUNDAY, after lunch, Sophie wandered up the track toward Tess's cottage, Sammy and Del trailing along, her mind on Aaron. He'd called that morning to apologise, his voice hoarse but quiet, his embarrassment palpable. He'd told her it would never happen again, but she wondered who he was trying to convince. It *would* happen again, and it would keep happening until he gave in to his feelings and acknowledged the bond between them.

Why did he believe she'd stop loving him? He wasn't a bank robber or murderer or child molester. He wasn't cruel or indifferent, or a drug addict or alcoholic. He was simply Aaron, the man she loved. The man who made her insides flip-flop with a single crinkly blue-eyed smile. Who shot excitement buzzing through her veins with a touch of his hand. Who looked at her with pride and faith and longing. And who sometimes, in unguarded moments like last night, allowed his true feelings to show, and then scared himself with how big they were.

She sighed, earning curious looks from the heelers.

'Can't help it,' she said to them apologetically, 'I'm in love.' But they were already off chasing trails in the grass, tails wagging.

Ben had also called, asking her if she'd slept well, teasing her that she probably would have slept even better if he'd been allowed to stay. Her stomach had curled and twisted as she tried to find the words to tell him he was wasting his time with her. Nothing sounded right, and then to her frustration, he'd hung up before she could explain.

Her aunt was watching the Sunday football when Sophie knocked and then, as there was no answer, walked in. Tess lay on her recliner, a glass of red wine dangling from the fingers of one hand.

'You're killing yourself. You know that, don't you?' said Sophie, standing in the doorway. Despite Sophie's clean-up, Tess had quickly returned to her slovenly ways and the cottage was a mess.

'Maybe that's the point.'

Sophie crossed the room and removed an empty bottle from what was once a pretty, pink chintz sofa, and sat down.

'Tess, I know what you're going through. I've been there.'

Tess didn't take her eyes off the television. 'You know nothing about nothing.'

She sighed. 'You need help. Antidepressants. Rehab.'

'What I need is to get off this miserable place and away from you.'

'I am not your enemy!' She took two long breaths, straining to keep herself under control. 'I want to help. I'll talk to Dad. Get you an appointment with Dr Charlton.'

Tess pointed a finger at her. It shook. 'Don't you dare tell your father. Don't you dare.'

Sophie raised her hands in defeat, then stood and went to the kitchen. She wasn't a psychologist or a doctor. Tess didn't know what was best for Tess except that her aunt was right. She needed to get the hell away from Vanaheim and the memories it held.

Sophie picked a glass out of the myriad piled in the sink and carried it back into the lounge. Picking up the half-drunk bottle at Tess's feet, she poured herself half a glass, paused, then filled it to the brim.

Tess narrowed her eyes at her. 'What do you want, anyway?'

Sophie sat down, took a mouthful of wine and leaned back with her eyes closed. 'Believe it or not, I want your advice.'

Tess laughed. 'You want advice from me?'

'I don't have anyone else to talk to. Not about this.'

'Try that boyfriend of yours,' Tess said in a bored voice.

'It's him I want to talk about. Dad seems to think he's going to hurt me.'

Tess snorted and took a slug of wine. 'He'd have the inside running on that.'

Sophie sat forward. 'What do you mean?'

Her aunt's eyes swam back into focus. 'Nothing.'

Frustration mushroomed in Sophie's mind like an atomic blast. She was so sick of everyone keeping secrets. She dumped her glass on the floor, then grabbed Tess by the shoulders and shook her. Red wine slopped over Tess's T-shirt and stained it burgundy. 'Tell me what you know!'

Tess rolled her eyes. 'The teenage horror rises again. Are you going to make a decent job of killing yourself this time?'

'Screw you,' said Sophie, backing away.

'My, my. Don't tell me your boyfriend's been teaching you bad language. What *would* your father say?'

'Why are you like this?'

'I've told you why.'

'And I've told you I can help, although God knows you don't deserve it. I don't want you at Vanaheim any more than you want to stay here. Let me talk to Dad. If I tell him what it's like for you he might listen. You could get back Braeburn. Make a proper life for yourself.'

'Don't be so naïve. You think that bitch is going to let Ian give me what I want after all the grief I caused him? She hates me nearly as much as she hates you and your mother.'

Sophie's heart almost stopped. 'What bitch? Who are you talking about?'

'No one. Get out and leave me alone.'

'Who, Tess?'

Tess reached for the wine bottle and drank straight from it, then snatched up the television remote and turned up the volume until the commentator's voice became so loud the furniture vibrated.

'Please, Tess. *Tell me.*'

'Ask your bloody father. Now piss off and leave me alone.'

As she walked slowly home, Sophie reflected that not only did she still not know what to do about Aaron, she had also added another mystery to her growing collection. She and her father needed to talk, and this time, he wasn't walking away until she had the truth.

With her eyes narrowed and her mouth stretched in a determined line, she pulled her phone from her pocket and began dialling.

A fat slice was missing from the chocolate cake Sophie had left on Aaron's kitchen table when she and Aaron walked in the next morning. A half-drunk mug of tea sat there too, surrounded by cake crumbs. A crystal-crusted spoon sat in the sugar bowl where someone had put it back wet. Her favourite horse magazine lay open, its glossy pages covered in drink rings. From the lounge came the sounds of morning television. In the air, faint but discernible, hung the smell of cigarettes.

'Have you been burgled?' she asked Aaron, staring at the mess before heading to the sink for a sponge and some kitchen spray.

Aaron stomped down the hall without answering. The door to the lounge slammed shut and an argument ensued. Sophie cocked her head to listen but the words were too muffled. The row was brief and Hakea Lodge quickly settled back into creaking serenity. Aaron returned to the kitchen, his face thunderous. Behind him, grinning like a nicotine-stained Cheshire Cat, trailed Danny.

'Nice cake,' he said, giving Sophie a wink and sitting down at the table.

'Nice mess,' she replied, keeping watch on Aaron as she rinsed out the sponge.

Aaron glanced at her, his expression unreadable. She raised her eyebrows, but he ignored her unspoken question and returned to putting the kettle on to boil.

She sat down, picked up her magazine and flicked through it, looking for the article she'd been reading about equine flu. No one spoke. The atmosphere curdled with Danny's pervading body odour and tension.

'Well, I guess I'll be off then, boss,' said Danny, scraping his chair back. 'Leave you to enjoy your last day with young Sophie here.'

Sophie's head jerked up. What did he mean, her last day? Aaron kept his back to her. Giving Sophie a smarmy look, Danny sauntered out of the kitchen, leaving his verbal grenade ticking its countdown.

She waited until the scrape of spinning tyres on gravel and the ning-ning of Danny's trail bike had faded before she spoke.

'What did he mean?'

Aaron poured the hot water for their tea. He placed the mug in front of her and then sat down. He didn't look at her, but he'd barely made eye contact all morning. The events of Saturday night still hung between them, a curtain of embarrassment that Aaron refused to draw.

'He comes back to work tomorrow.'

She stared at her mug. Their days of intimacy were over. She'd miss them.

'It means I won't need you any more.'

She looked up, blinking. 'Of course you will.'

He shook his head and fingered the sugar spoon. 'Danny and I can work the horses.'

Her breath failed. She took a gulp of air, but that panicked, drowning sensation remained. 'But what about Rowdy and Costa Motza? Danny can't ride them. They'll be upset with him on their backs.' She knew her words were irrational, but she couldn't stop. 'And what about the others? Who's going to talk to them when they're bored and feed them carrots to make them happy and brush the dirt off their legs and comb their manes and tails and kiss them when they've been good?'

She took slow, careful breaths through her nose. Still her lungs burned. 'I can't stay away. Not from the horses. Not from you.'

'This was never a permanent arrangement, Sophie. You knew that.'

She shook her head. 'You can't make me go.'

'I know, but I'm asking you to.' He looked at her, his blue eyes imploring. 'I don't want you near Danny. I might not always be around to protect you if he tries anything.'

She peeled his fingers from the mug and held them. 'I can look after myself.'

'I'm asking you to stay away, Sophie. Not for my sake, for yours. He's not to be trusted.'

'So get rid of him.'

'I can't.'

'Why not?'

He laughed but it held no humour. 'Like everything to do with this place, it's a long story.'

She sat back and let his fingers fall from her grip. 'And one you won't tell me.'

'Yeah,' he said. 'It's another one of those.'

————

When Sophie arrived home that afternoon, she found a message on her home phone. Her father had called, but then, he could hardly ignore her this time. The trail of messages ran from his electoral office all the way to Canberra via numerous mobile phones and through every political contact she could find.

At least this was good news. No matter how much she had pleaded, Aaron wouldn't budge. She was no longer welcome in the yard. The pain was almost unbearable.

Her father's beautifully articulate voice filled her with yearning for her childhood. The time before the dark days descended, when he'd taken her hands and twirled her around, and laughed with his giggling daughter. A normal father with a happy, loving family. She wanted the comfort of that time, the love of a father to help ease her shattered heart.

'Sophie, I received your messages and I agree. We need to talk. As it happens, I'll be in Ballarat tomorrow, so I've made time to be with you. I have a meeting in the afternoon, but I'll drive to Harrington afterwards and should arrive around seven. Do you wish to talk at home or somewhere neutral?'

There was a pause, as if he had forgotten he was talking to a machine and expected her to answer, but then he continued, his voice lowered and gentle.

'Sophie, what I have to tell you will come as a shock, and for that I apologise. This has been far too long coming, but that's my fault, not yours. Leave a message on my mobile with your decision.'

Sophie stared the machine, elation and worry warring within her. Her father was going to tell her the truth about her mother. She might not like it, but at least one void in her life would be filled. The message bank switched to the next message. It was Ben.

'Hey, Sophie. I've been trying to reach you but your mobile keeps going straight through to voicemail. What're you up to tonight? I thought I might call in after work. If you want, I can grab a pizza or something on the way and we can have dinner together. What do you think? Call me.'

Sophie sighed. She had to sort that out, and fast. She picked up the phone and, after leaving a message for her father that she'd see him at Vanaheim, rang Ben.

'The man of your dreams at your service.'

Sophie smiled. If it wasn't for Aaron, she'd probably be half in love with Ben. Sex appeal and charm made an intoxicating combination.

'How did you know it was me?'

'I have a secret Sophie antenna. So, are you up for tonight?'

Sophie took a deep breath. 'I'm sorry. You're lovely, but I don't think this is going to work out.'

For a few seconds he was quiet. 'It's Aaron Laidlaw, isn't it?'

'I can't help the way I feel, Ben.'

'Neither can I.' He sighed. 'I guess I should have realised when you changed your mind the first time.'

'I'm sorry.'

'Yeah, I know, but that doesn't help much right now. Look, I'd better go. Work and stuff to do. I'll catch you around.'

She began to lower the phone, her finger on the disconnect button, saddened by the hurt she'd caused.

'Sophie?'

She pressed the phone back against her ear. 'Yes?'

'Take care. And if you need me – for anything – just ring.'

This time, after he said goodbye, he cut the call.

Sophie carefully returned the handset to its stand and stood looking at it. One day, when his disappointment wasn't so palpable, she'd apologise again, but that time would have to wait.

Right now, she had greater worries.

EIGHTEEN

FOR THE THIRD TIME, Sophie checked the place settings and inspected the knives and forks for dirty spots. Finished, she stood back and surveyed the table, then decided that she preferred the wine glasses in line with the soup spoons rather than the knives, the way she'd arranged them the first time. Only when they were aligned to her satisfaction did she head back to the kitchen to stir the soup and check on the roast.

She hoped her father liked pumpkin soup. She knew he liked roast beef. That much she could remember from their family meals. Roast beef, roast vegetables, peas, carrots and corn, all smothered in rich, thick gravy made from the pan drippings. Her father had loved it. Once.

She dropped the soup ladle in the sink and stared out the window. She should have made something else. Something that wasn't so homely, so reminiscent of Vanaheim when her mother was alive.

Before both her parents left her, one in body, one in spirit.

A metallic-grey Mercedes pulled into the yard. After a few minutes, her father stepped out. He looked tired, soul-weary. Sammy sniffed a rear wheel and then cocked his leg against it before moving on to check the other tyres. Ian Dixon didn't appear to notice.

He opened the boot and pulled a small suitcase from it, but as he reached up to close the lid, he stopped, staring at the bag at his feet. Del snuffled at its rollers. He shooed her away, then picked up the suitcase, tossed it back in the boot and, after slamming the lid closed, trudged toward the house, the heelers trailing behind.

Sophie swallowed her disappointment. Her father wouldn't be staying.

'Hi,' she said, standing on tiptoe to kiss his cheek. 'You look tired.'

He smiled, but Sophie could see it was forced. 'It's been a long day.'

'Do you want a drink?'

He nodded and followed her into the kitchen.

Sophie poured two glasses of red wine and handed him one. 'I hope you like pumpkin soup.'

'I do.'

They sipped their wine.

'This is nice,' he said.

'Yes.'

He nodded at the oven. 'Dinner smells good.'

'Thanks.'

They drank some more. Her father walked toward the window and peered out. 'How are things with the farm?'

'Okay. We had a good calving and the renovated pastures have made a big difference to dry-matter yield, but the older paddocks aren't coping as well.'

'Understandable. They haven't been touched for quite a while, but the Bureau's forecasting a mild winter, so that will help.'

'Yes, it should.' Sophie took another sip of wine. 'And the ministry. How are you finding it?'

'Very challenging. Very busy. There are never enough hours in the day.'

'Yes. I can imagine.' Sophie put down her glass, picked up the ladle and stirred the soup. This was horrible. They were like strangers. 'Are you hungry?'

'Not particularly, but if you want to eat, then go ahead and serve.'

She put down the ladle and turned off the gas. 'No. It can wait. Let's go into the lounge. It's warmer there.'

Sophie sat on the edge of the recliner, her hands around her wine glass. Her father sat at right angles to her, on the long, darkly tanned leather sofa his wife had bought so many years ago. Silence crept its way into the room and turned the atmosphere frigid and fragile, as if Vanaheim was holding its breath. Every noise they made became uncomfortably loud. The sound of wine carefully sipped, the creak of leather as bodies shifted, breaths drawn and exhaled in quiet sighs – all reverberated in the awkward stillness.

Her father placed his wine glass on the coffee table and then stood. 'I think we should have dinner after all.'

'Yes, let's get that out of the way.'

————

The roasting pan lay soaking on the sink. On the bench, commemorating a meal no one could eat, sat dogs' bowls full to overflowing. Sophie stared out the window waiting for the kettle to boil.

Dinner had been a disaster of untouched plates and murmured apologies. She would have been better off bunging a frozen pizza in the oven. After all, her father hadn't come to Vanaheim to play happy families. He was here to talk, although given his uncharacteristic reserve Sophie wasn't sure how much she would get out of him.

All she wanted was the truth about her mother, and to know why he'd abandoned his daughter when she needed him most. She'd choke it out of him if she had to. If nothing else, he owed her that.

The kettle clicked off. Sophie poured hot water into a coffee plunger, then carried a tray with cups, sugar and milk into the lounge.

Her father stood with his back to her inspecting the photographs

she had arranged on the shelf above the television. He pointed to one
of Chuck. 'Which horse is this?'

'That's Chuck – Prince Charles – at Lake Ackerman.'

'It's a very big jump.'

She smiled, remembering. 'It was enormous.'

He turned back to her. 'That was the event you won?'

She nodded, not wanting to speak in case she snapped, and
busied herself pouring coffee. He would have known the answer to
that question if he'd bothered to listen to her message. The one he
claimed had been mysteriously deleted. But she didn't want to fight.
Not tonight.

She handed him the mug and perched, like before, on the edge of
her seat. Not knowing where to start, she waited for him to speak.

Without sitting down, he took a sip of coffee and then placed the
mug back on the tray. 'This is very difficult, Sophie. I've let this go for
far too long. At the time, I believed I had reason to keep things from
you, but now I realise it was a mistake.'

He stopped, and she could see him inhaling deeply. The air
stilled. In the hush, her breathing sounded loud and asthmatic. She
held her breath, waiting.

He locked his eyes on hers. They were creased and brimming
with what she could only describe as shame. Her heartbeat
accelerated.

'Your mother was depressed, had been for years, but I never
believed for one moment . . .' He took a shaky breath. 'Sophie, your
mother killed herself after she found out I was having an affair with
Carol Laidlaw.'

The cup spilled from Sophie's hands. Coffee soaked the carpet
by her feet, but she couldn't see it. A mist had crept into the room,
swirling around her like a ghost, clawing her with icy fingers, trying
to drag her into the void. She heard her father's voice, but it seemed
to come from outside, as if he were yelling at her from behind a door.
Her head felt strange, like someone was popping air bubbles
inside it.

A hand pressed into her back, pushing her forward until her head dropped between her knees.

'Take a deep breath, Sophie.'

She tried, but it seemed she could only draw shallow ones.

'And another. That's it.'

The popping stopped.

'Keep breathing. Good girl. You're all right. I have you.'

Slowly, the mist began to clear. The pressure on her back eased, and she could sit up.

Her father knelt beside her. He brushed a hand over her hair, easing it away from her face. 'Are you okay?'

She shook her head, tears stinging her eyes.

'It was a shock, I know.'

She began to cry, and, as he had once done, so many years ago, her father held her and stroked her hair, and whispered soothing sounds into her ear. When the tears had worn themselves down to hiccups, she pulled away, staring at him in disbelief.

'Go and wash your face,' he said gently. 'You'll feel better. Afterwards, I promise we'll talk properly.'

Knowing he was right, Sophie did as she was told.

She stared at the blotchy-skinned person reflected in the bathroom mirror and wondered if she had changed. So much had been revealed in that single statement – the lies, the secrets, the obfuscation – but it wasn't enough to reverse ten years of confusion, and certainly not enough to allow her to shed the guilt that had been her companion since she was twelve years old.

And then there was Aaron.

He had known this all along. He had known it had been kept from her. The shame of what his mother had done – what both their parents had done – must have boiled inside him, but it wasn't his fault. He wasn't his mother, just as she wasn't her father. This guilt wasn't his to carry.

But he'd wanted to protect her from pain. He didn't want to see her hurt. He wanted to hide what he knew because he loved her.

And she only loved him more for it.

As for her father, redemption was still a long way off.

The carpet was damp where she'd spilled her coffee, but her father had mopped up the worst of the stain. The tray was gone, and in its place sat an open bottle and two glasses filled with red wine. He handed her one.

'I thought this would be better.'

'Yes.' She took a sip, holding the wine in her mouth for a moment before swallowing. 'But next time I suggest you warn me if you're going to drop another bombshell like that.'

'That was the worst of it. I apologise for not being more tactful.'

'I don't think it would have helped.'

'No. I suppose not.'

She put the glass down. 'Tell me from the start what happened.'

He sighed and picked up a photograph of the woman who was once his wife. He traced a finger down her face. The gesture seemed almost loving, but Sophie knew it wasn't.

'She was very beautiful, your mother. You look a lot like her.' The frame went back on the shelf. 'As I explained to you last time I was here, your mother was a very ill woman, but she refused to take any medication to control her depression. Dealing with her became exhausting.' He smiled sadly. 'You won't remember, perhaps.'

'Not definite things, just impressions.'

'Yes. You were young and far too busy with school and your horses.'

She stood and joined him. Just as she had so many times before, she stared at Fiona Dixon's photograph, but this time she saw a woman she didn't quite recognise.

'Riding is the only thing I remember us doing together,' she said. 'That and the tunnel of love.'

'The tunnel of love?'

Sophie shook her head. The tunnel of love was her secret memory. It wasn't for sharing. Not even with her father. 'It doesn't matter.'

'She wanted to be a professional showjumper. Did you know that?'

Sophie didn't, but she wasn't surprised. Her mother had been a gifted horsewoman.

'Her dream never came true, unfortunately. She met me and then she had you, and then her illness kept her incapacitated, but she had high hopes for you.' He touched her cheek, the motion tender, paternal. 'I think she would be very proud of you now, Sophie. As I am.'

Her eyes welled up. 'You've never told me that before.'

'I know. I've been a very bad father to you.'

She didn't correct him. She didn't mean to be cruel, but it would take more than this to make amends.

His hand dropped. 'Yes. You have every right to be angry.'

'I do, but my anger isn't important right now. I want to know about Mum.'

'Of course.' He took a mouthful of wine. 'Living with her became intolerable. I asked for a divorce. She refused. She said she didn't want her daughter growing up in a dysfunctional family.'

'Ironic, considering what she did,' said Sophie.

Her father smiled. 'Yes. It is rather.' The smile faded. 'I won't bore you with details, but during this time, Carol Laidlaw – Aaron's mother – and I became lovers.'

'How nice for you.'

His expression hardened. 'Be careful, Sophie. It's not wise to pass judgement too hastily. One day you'll learn that the world doesn't operate in absolutes.'

'There are some absolutes, Dad. Husbands shouldn't cheat on their wives, mothers shouldn't kill themselves and fathers should love their daughters.'

'I do love you. I always have.'

She wanted to believe him, but it was hard after all this time. His actions, or lack of them, over the years, surely revealed his true feelings, and it was difficult to summon sympathy for a man who had shown her so little.

'It's just that when I look at you . . .'

'You don't see me, you see her.' She took a shuddery breath, understanding now. 'And the older I got the worse it became.'

His face collapsed. He blinked rapidly, and Sophie caught a glimpse of a man she didn't know. A man tortured by his wife's death, by blame and failure. She put her hand on his forearm but it was as if he couldn't feel it. With his empty glass in his hand, he crossed the room and sat down heavily on the sofa. He reached for the bottle and refilled his glass, and Sophie realised how very, very hard this must be for him.

'I'm sorry.'

'It's not your fault, Sophie. It's never been your fault. You should be proud to be like her. She was fragile, yes, but when she smiled . . .' He shook his head, as though no words could ever describe what Fiona Dixon radiated. 'She just didn't smile enough.'

'I'm not fragile any more, Dad.'

'Yes, I can see that.'

'So tell me the rest of it.'

He sighed. 'Carol wanted to leave Rodger. Fiona was still refusing me a divorce, but Carol said it didn't matter. She would move to Canberra. I was spending most of my time there anyway. In the end, I agreed.'

'Were things so bad at Hakea Lodge?'

He nodded. 'Rodger used to hit her.'

Sophie began pacing the room. This went completely against Aaron's memory of his father. 'Are you sure?'

'That's what Carol told me. I have no reason to disbelieve her.'

'Is that why you don't like Aaron? Because of what his father did to his mother?'

Her father's face turned rigid. 'He never defended his mother, never once stood up to his father. Carol said he used to hide in the corner with his hands over his ears. He's a coward.'

Sophie slumped back into her chair, staring at the ceiling, her mind working overtime. Aaron a coward? She didn't believe it. Aaron was no coward. There was something fishy about this story. She turned to her father. 'Dad, are you absolutely positive Carol is telling you the truth?'

'Why on earth would she lie about something like that?'

'For sympathy? So you'd protect her? Stay on her side?' Suddenly, her brain chugged over and she finally understood. 'It's her, isn't it? She's kept you away from me. That's who Tess was talking about when she said "she" hates me more than my mother. It was Carol.'

She sat up. It was all becoming clearer. 'Did you tell her I was working with Aaron?' Ian nodded.

'And is that when she told you Aaron never protected her?'

'I know where you're heading with this, Sophie, but you're wrong.'

'Am I?'

Her father didn't answer. He didn't have to. Sophie saw the truth. Tess knew too, so did Aaron. Carol Laidlaw had played Ian Dixon for a fool. Aaron had said she was never happy unless she was the centre of attention, and there was no greater threat to a relationship than a needy daughter. And for years, Sophie had been as needy as they came.

But as she now realised, love was a funny thing, and criticising Carol Laidlaw wasn't the way to make her father see reason. If she was honest with herself, she wasn't even sure she wanted him to. No matter what his excuses, he'd made his bed and he could damn well lie in it.

'Tell me something,' she said. 'Do you love her?'

It took a while for her father to answer. 'Yes. More than I loved your mother, much to my eternal shame.' He shifted, and Sophie saw how uncomfortable the subject made him. 'I broke it off after your mother died. I couldn't live with what we'd done, but then I found I couldn't live without Carol, either. It only made the hollowness worse. Carol has her faults, I admit, but she came to my rescue at a time when I was beginning to question my own sanity. Your mother had a way of making me feel worthless. Carol made me feel like a man again.'

'But why keep it a secret for all these years? Surely no one would care now?'

'I thought it was best for you. You were so young, you wouldn't have understood. I thought I would just wait until you were older to explain, but then you started having problems.' He spread out his palms and stared at them. 'I didn't want another Fiona on my hands. And you have to realise how impossible it seemed at the time. First there was the scandal with Rodger and if that wasn't bad enough, your mother went and killed herself. Carol was terri-fied of being blamed for both. The way she acts sometimes, I think she still is.' He looked at Sophie, pleading for understanding. 'I loved her and I loved you and I was desperate to protect you both. So we kept it all a secret. But I can see it was a mistake. Perhaps if I'd told you the truth from the start none of this would have happened.'

Sophie held herself back from pointing out that none of this would have happened if he'd managed to stay faithful to his wife, but they'd fought enough for one night and, as she was so fond of telling Aaron, the past was over. It was time to stop the blame and move on. Besides, there were other things to discuss.

'I know about Braeburn, Dad.'

Immediately, his eyes narrowed. 'Tess told you, did she?'

'I had to force it out of her, but yes. She told me.' She leaned forward. 'Vanaheim's killing her. There are too many bad memories here. She needs to escape and get her life back in order. She needs Braeburn.'

'No. She must stay her time.'

Sophie blinked. 'Why?'

'Your aunt had only one job to do, and that was look after you. She failed. She can stay here and rot for all I care.'

A whirlwind of fury overtook her. How dare he? Of all the selfish rotten things he had done, this was right up near the worst of them.

With deliberate care, she lowered her glass before she threw it at him. Then she let him have it.

'And what about me, huh? You're condemning me to a life of looking after a drunk. Gee, Dad, thanks very much. On top of everything else, that really goes to show how much you care about your daughter, doesn't it? You don't love me. You never have.'

'That's not true! I do love you, but I cannot forgive your aunt for what she did. She let my daughter slit her wrists in the bathtub while she sat drunk in this very lounge! Do you have any idea how close you were to dying? Well, do you? They pulled you from the tub unconscious and barely breathing. Tess couldn't even bring herself to do that. She just babbled incoherently into the phone until an ambulance arrived. I will never forgive her, Sophie. Never.'

'For God's sake, Dad. Can't you see you're only making things worse? You say you care about me, but then you go and do this. How do you think it makes me feel knowing Tess is suffering because of something I did when I was fifteen? If you want to blame someone, blame yourself. You were the one who was never here. You as good as abandoned me when Mum died. I didn't understand anything. I was twelve years old. All I knew was that both my parents had left me and somehow I was to blame.'

His eyes were huge. 'But you weren't to blame.'

'How was I to know that? I was twelve! Mum was dead and you wouldn't even look at me. And don't even get me started on Tess.'

'I'm sorry,' he said, his voice like gravel, and Sophie was shocked to see tears in his eyes.

Her anger died, exhausted by a fight that served no purpose but to hurt. She sat down and put her head in her hands. How many lives had been ruined by Fiona Dixon's suicide? Surely, after ten years, they'd all suffered enough?

'Dad, listen to me. This has to end. It's been ten years. We need to move on. All of us need to, including Tess. Give her Braeburn and let her go.'

'She doesn't deserve it.'

'Perhaps not, but when you punish her you punish me and that's not fair. Let her go. And if you won't do it for her sake, then at least do it for mine.'

It took a long time, but in the end, she talked her father around.

Tess finally had her freedom. And so, Sophie hoped, did she.

———

The following day, for the first time in his parliamentary career, her father called in sick. The night before had taken its toll on them both. They faced each other over breakfast weary-eyed and yawning, but also, Sophie felt, with a new perspective on each other's life.

Conversation was stilted at first, but gradually eased into something more relaxed. They talked about the farm, about Sophie's hopes for it. She told him about Buck and Rowdy and her dreams of competing on them at three-star level, of maybe one day reaching even greater heights. Emboldened, she even told him about Costa Motza and how he'd improved, what a thrill it was to watch him race, and how she hoped he might prove everyone a fool and win.

Too wary of spoiling their rapport, she didn't speak of Aaron, though the absence of his name only made the issue of her relationship with him more palpable. Several times she observed her father taking a long breath, as though fortifying himself to broach a difficult subject. Each time, his mouth thinned instead of opened, keeping whatever he wanted to say trapped inside. He was right to avoid it. Aaron could wait for another time. This morning belonged to family.

After breakfast, surrounded by sweet morning air and weak, late-autumn sunshine, they walked down the track to Tess's cottage. Sophie hesitated at the door, nervous of the confrontation to come, then tightened her jaw and knocked. She'd faced her father, she could damn well face Tess.

As usual, there was no answer, but as Sophie went to push inside, Ian held her back.

'Maybe it's best if I deal with Tess alone.'

'I should be there too, Dad.'

He shook his head. 'No. There are things we need to sort out between the two of us. I don't want you getting caught in the crossfire.'

Sophie bit her lip, uncertain. Tess might need her. 'I'll wait here.'

'Don't you have work to do?'

'Yes, but —'

'No buts.' He smiled and brushed his hand over her hair in a paternal gesture that made her spirit swell. 'Don't worry. I'll yell if I need help.'

He waited until she'd reached the old stockyards, halfway back to the house, before entering. Sophie halted and regarded the cottage for a moment, then perched on one of the weathered redgum rails, biting a thumbnail.

Vanaheim remained quiet, undisturbed except by the warble of magpies and the occasional lowing of cattle, and a light breeze whispering through the plane trees. To distract herself from what was occurring in the cottage, Sophie constructed plans for the future, when the property would be at last hers.

First on the agenda were new stockyards. Solidly built, the old ones still served their purpose, but they lacked modern innovations, like a sheltered work area where she could set up her laptop and have shade from the elements, rounded races that made stock handling easier, and extra space and troughs for weaners. The more she researched, the more she realised yard weaning was the future. Though a lot of extra work, the animals were less stressed and showed increased weight gain over those paddock-weaned, which meant higher prices at the saleyards. Vanaheim's profitability was solid, but that didn't mean it couldn't be better.

Shouts from the cottage broke her contemplation. Tess's shrill voice sliced through the air. Cattle grazing the lower pastures raised their heads and stared. From the front paddock, Chuck let out a whinny. Sophie considered going to the rescue but the escalating argument, so vicious and filled with long pent-up blame and bitter-ness, held her in place.

She tensed, torn over whether to interfere. Abruptly, the yells stopped. She slid off the rail and took a few steps toward the cottage. Her father appeared at the door. He caught sight of Sophie and then looked back inside. Sophie took another two steps, but he held up his hand, signalling for her to stop. Sophie saw his mouth work as he spoke once again with Tess. Then he closed the door and cut through the grass toward her.

'Is she okay?' she asked when he'd reached the yards.

'She will be.' He held her gaze. 'I said she could have Braeburn.'

As Sophie went to smile he held up his hand. 'But she has to go to rehab first. She's in no state to take it over. As soon as I can arrange a place somewhere you'll be free of her. You'll have everything you want.'

This time she let her smile break. At last, it was over. Buoyant with relief, she leaned into her father and hugged him.

'Not everything, Dad. But close.'

———

Ian Dixon had barely turned out of Vanaheim's lane toward the late afternoon sun before Sophie was in the Range Rover, heading for Hakea Lodge. The moment she pulled into the drive, the horses started calling to her. Rowdy banged his front hoofs against his half-door and whinnied, but when Sophie approached to give him a kiss, he tossed his head away in a grump. For once, she ignored him. Aaron was more important.

She found him sitting on a bag of corn staring at the made-up evening feeds. He didn't move when she walked in.

She sat opposite him, leaning forward and letting her hands dangle between her legs in a mirror of his pose.

'Dad came last night,' she said.

He nodded. 'I saw the car.'

She swallowed, wondering where to start. 'We talked. A lot. About Mum. About me.' She paused. 'About your mother.'

He glanced at her and quickly looked away, his expression unsurprised. He looked like he'd barely slept. The skin under his eyes was bruised and puffy, as if he'd been in a fight and come out the loser. It made his blue eyes appear dark, sad. Sophie wanted to wrap her arms around him.

'Why didn't you tell me, Aaron?'

He pressed his thumbs into the corner of his eyes. 'I guess I was scared.'

'Of what?'

'That you'd be upset. That you'd do something stupid. Your father warned me not to tell you. He said you wouldn't cope. Tess said the same. I thought they were wrong, but I couldn't take the chance.'

She looked at her hands, at the fingers that had once held a razor blade. She remembered gouging her flesh in an orgy of blood-letting. It had felt so good at the time, like floating in salty water with the summer sun blazing down while the tide dragged her to peace. She sighed at the damage she'd done: to herself, to others.

Like mother, like daughter. But no longer.

'I don't care about your mother or my father, Aaron. I only care about you.'

He stood and, as if he hadn't heard, began to snatch at bucket handles.

'Your mother says your father hit her.'

Aaron dropped back down, staring at the buckets, his eyes unfocused.

'Nothing's safe from her, is it? She'll try anything, say anything. Just as long as the world stays revolving around her.' He shook his head. 'Christ, I hate her.'

'I don't blame you. But she and my father aren't important any more. Only you and I are.'

'There is no you and I,' he said flatly. 'There never will be.'

Sophie swallowed her rising panic. 'Why?'

He resumed picking up the buckets. 'I've told you why.'

'And I told you that I don't care.' She rose and grabbed at his arm. 'I know the truth now. You don't have to feel guilty about your mother.'

'I never felt guilty about my mother.'

'Then what is it?'

He didn't answer.

'Aaron, talk to me!'

'I can't.'

'You can!'

Chaff and oats went flying as he threw the buckets across the room. He turned and gripped her shoulders.

'Don't you get it? It's you, Sophie. That's what I feel guilty about. For what I did to you!' He let go, snatched up a tattered straw broom and with aggressive sweeps began cleaning up the mess he'd made.

Sophie blinked through the rising dust. 'I don't understand. You never did anything to me.'

He dropped the broom and reached out to touch her face, his fingers cold on her skin. 'I did, and I'm sorrier than you can ever imagine.' His hand fell. He turned his back and resumed his sweeping. 'Go home. There's nothing for you here.'

All her hopes slithered from the room like nest of hatched snakes. She sat down heavily on a bag of oats, and gazed at the dusty timber floorboards.

'I love you,' she said softly. 'Doesn't that mean anything?'

He stilled, his knuckles tight on the broom handle. 'It means everything.' He looked at her with an aching compassion that made her throat burn. 'But it's pointless.'

'Because you think I'll stop loving you the moment I find out what you did?'

He nodded.

'But isn't that what you want, for me to stop loving you?'

He looked away.

'So tell me. Get it over and done with. Tell me your big secret, so I can do what you want. Tell me so I can start hating you.'

The feed room filled with the echo of her demand, reverberating off the ceiling, bouncing off the walls, multiplying. Growing louder, until it reached a shriek so high it could only be heard in their heads.

'But you can't, can you, Aaron?' she whispered. 'Because you don't want me to stop loving you. Because you love me back.'

Without saying a word, Aaron dropped the broom and walked out.

But Sophie knew she had hit her mark.

NINETEEN

AARON COCKED HIS HEAD. It didn't take much to work out Sophie had arrived in the yard. If it wasn't for the sound of her car, the reactions of the horses would be indication enough.

Although he'd never say it to her, he was glad she'd defied his ban, that their fight in the feed room a week ago hadn't stopped her from coming to see the horses each afternoon.

He still missed her morning presence acutely. He missed her laughter, her kindness, the way she made his stomach lurch when she smiled that beautiful, gut-twisting shy smile, her intelligence and humour, the easy, confident way she rode, her unconscious sexiness, her vulnerability, the way she made him feel protective and desperate to keep her from harm.

He missed every perfect and imperfect bit of her.

Why couldn't he just tell her? Everything would be resolved then. All he had to do was sit her down and say the words and it would be over. But Sophie had been right. He couldn't, because he loved her and didn't want to lose her.

He was as selfish now as he was then. Time had cured nothing.

He stared at the bills spread out over the table. Several had 'Final

Notice' stamped across them in red ink. Both Rowdy and Pollyanna were racing this weekend, and if they won, the red ink would be gone. He'd still have the heavy weight of Hakea Lodge's mortgage on his back, but he didn't care so much about the bank – it held the title deeds as surety and would never be out of pocket if he went under. The local businesses he owed money to, small operators like himself, people he'd known for years, weren't so lucky. They could only rely on his honesty and the hope he'd come good. He couldn't let them down.

He packed the invoices and statements into a pile, keeping the most urgent on top. It still looked bad, but the tide had started to turn. Proving his previous performance wasn't a fluke, Costa Motza had run another second, beaten by a very short-priced favourite against a strong field. The other horses had gained some much needed placings, and last weekend, Rowdy had taken out the Mount Campbell Steeplechase, which injected forty thousand dollars into Aaron's overdraft. Word of his latest winning streak had spread and the phone hadn't stopped ringing. Creditors, knowing he had money, demanded their cut before it went to someone else.

He left the bills on the table where he knew Danny would see them. It never hurt to remind the jockey that his position, not to mention his extorted free accommodation, was only secure as long as Hakea Lodge remained afloat. Aaron mightn't be able to sack him, but a bank would have no qualms. He'd love to see the look on Danny's face when that happened. All the secrets in the world wouldn't save him then.

Aaron fingered the top bill. It would never come to that because he wouldn't let it. Hakea Lodge would survive no matter what, and if that meant putting up with Danny, then he would endure his presence regardless of how much the little bastard made his skin crawl.

To his surprise, when he went outside, he found Sophie sitting on the verandah step, her head leaning against the post and her eyes half-closed. The sun was shining, beaming warmth onto the yard, teasing them that, though it was now the first day of June, winter hadn't really arrived.

'Sophie?' He crouched down next to her. 'Is everything okay?'

'Tess is gone,' she said flatly. 'She left for rehab this morning.'

'That's good, isn't it?'

She nodded. 'She's stuck in a pretty bad place but at least she has hope now, and knowing she'll have Braeburn at the end makes all the difference. She even gave me a hug and thanked me for talking to Dad.'

He gently brushed hair away from her face, wondering why she looked so sad. 'So, what's the matter?'

'I don't know.' She raised her head to look at him. 'I guess I'll miss her.'

'Tess? After all she's done to you?'

'I know it sounds stupid, but yes.' She wrapped her arms around her legs, staring across the yard at Rowdy with her chin resting on her knees. 'Tess could be horrible but at least she was always there.' She frowned as if she didn't like the way that sounded. 'I don't know. I feel like something's ended. Like I've been cut free at last.'

'And that's a bad thing?'

'No, it's not. But I think it might take a while to get used to.' She let go of her knees and stood up, looking back down at him. 'Dad's going to talk to the trustees. He can't see any reason why they wouldn't let me come into my inheritance early.'

'That's great, Sophie. It's what you wanted.'

'Yeah,' she said, squinting toward the horizon. 'I have almost everything I wanted. So why do I feel so empty?'

Aaron knew the answer, but what was the point in saying it?

Suddenly, she smiled. 'Still, I can't complain *too* much. I have loads to be grateful for. Besides, if I get really desperate for someone to talk to, there's always Sammy and Del. And unlike Tess, they don't answer back.'

Relief bathed him with warmth that far outdid any morning

sunshine. Sophie was back smiling, her gloomy thoughts forgotten. He grinned at her. 'And Buck and Chuck. Don't forget them.'

'Never.'

'And cattle. You have lots of fat Herefords to keep you company.'

'They burp and fart a lot though.'

'True.' He laughed. 'But then so do I.'

'Do you?'

'No. Not really.' He eyed her sheepishly. 'Well, a bit.' He stood and gripped her shoulders. 'I'm a bloke, Sophie. It happens.'

She rolled her eyes. 'No wonder I prefer horses.'

'Oh, and you don't burp and fart?'

'No. Not much.' She paused. 'Well, a little.'

They stared at one another and then burst out laughing. Aaron gave her a hug, wanting to feel her giggling against him, wanting so much of what he couldn't have. He let her go, smiling at her shining eyes and tucking her hair behind her ears so he could see her face properly. He wanted to tell her that he loved her, that she'd always have him to talk to, but kept the words buried where they belonged.

'You'll be fine, Soph. It'll just take a bit of getting used to.'

'Yeah, I know.' She sighed. 'Anyway, I'll be too busy to think about being lonely.'

'Why?'

'You should see the state of the cottage. It'll take me a week just to get rid of the bottles.'

———

Aaron stared into the distance. A ute was parked at the gate of Sophie's lucerne paddock, its occupants having wandered into the centre of the stand. Aaron recognised the unmistakably solid form of Ben Moore. He stood with a long-lensed camera in his hands and his face turned to Sophie as she, oblivious to his scrutiny, knelt in the dirt, busily inspecting plants.

She'd warned him Ben was coming to take some photographs for the Harrington Rural Traders newsletter, that it was purely a professional arrangement, but the sight of them together was still a horse-kick in the stomach. He turned away.

Danny drew Psycho alongside Rowdy. 'That's Sophie with that bloke from the farm place, isn't it?'

Like the rat he was, Danny had sensed something was up. More than once he'd brought up with Aaron the rumour that Sophie had had a one-night stand with Ben Moore, just to provoke a reaction. It had taken every scrap of willpower Aaron had to stay impassive. He knew exactly what had happened that night and it still haunted him.

He ignored Danny's question and they rode on, Aaron restraining himself from galloping Rowdy at the barbed-wire fence separating him from Sophie and jumping it like some deranged medieval knight ready to defend his maiden's honour.

As they reached the corner, Sophie rose and turned to watch. Ben stood with her and Aaron found he couldn't take his eyes off him. But Ben wasn't interested in him. Aaron may as well have not existed. Ben was looking only at Sophie, at her watching Aaron with an unwavering gaze.

Rowdy called out to his mistress and baulked as Aaron urged him on. The horse kept whinnying and staring back at Sophie, and Aaron had the weird feeling Rowdy had read his mind and was only doing what he would do if he had the guts.

'She's coming to the fence, boss,' said Danny. 'You want to stop?'

'No.'

'She's waving.'

Aaron kicked Rowdy hard. The horse pigrooted and was rewarded with another kick. 'I don't give a toss if she's cartwheeling. Keep going.'

Danny smiled, exposing yellow teeth that reminded Aaron of a rabid dog. 'You've got the hots for her, I reckon.'

Aaron was too angry with himself to speak.

'Yep, you've got it bad for young Sophie. She'd be a good catch, too, with that farm of hers and her old man being so rich and powerful. Marry her and you'd be set. Probably forget all about old Danny-boy.' Danny let out an exaggerated sigh. 'Lucky she doesn't know about that other business. Imagine what she'll say when she finds out what you did.'

'Shut up.'

Danny's eyes narrowed. 'She'll find out one day. Word can get around, if you know what I mean.'

Aaron grabbed Danny by the front of his jumper, almost dragging him off Psycho. 'If anyone's telling her anything, it'll be me, you hear?' He shook him. 'You hear?'

'Yeah, boss. I hear.'

Aaron let him go, furious with himself for exposing his temper. He pushed Rowdy into a canter and then let him have his head, galloping up the two hills toward home and allowing the wind to whip away his anger until he was left with only sorrow and the haunt of Danny's threat.

TWENTY

'I DON'T WANT you to run him,' said Sophie, reaching out to stroke Rowdy's nose. 'It's too dangerous.'

It had been over a month since she had spoken properly to Aaron, since she had confessed her fear of loneliness and he had responded by holding her in his comforting, secure embrace. Just as she told Aaron she would, she'd ignored his ban from the yard, paying it the lip service it deserved. Every afternoon at three o'clock, when she knew Danny had gone for the day, she drove in and parked in her usual place. She wanted to see the horses, *her* horses. If he wanted to stop her, he'd have to lock the gate.

Her visits also served as a way to remind him of her presence, that no matter how pointless he claimed her love was, she wasn't about to give up and leave his life. Each time she left Vanaheim for Hakea Lodge, she clung to the hope that today would be the day Aaron caved in and told her his secret, and finally freed himself from the past. That she would take his hand and, with her forgiveness, walk him into the future. A future together, where they laughed and touched and kissed and loved. Where her terrible yearning for him would at last be assuaged.

Mostly he avoided her, hiding in the house, or in the feed or tack rooms, but today he'd actively sought her out. It was early July. The Springbank Cup was just four weeks away and Aaron needed to organise Rowdy's work schedule so he was in peak fitness for the race. But as stipulated in their agreement, he had to first ask Sophie's permission, something she wasn't inclined to grant.

'Quarter of a million dollars, Sophie. Have you any idea what that could do? It could turn this place around. I could build more yards, take on more horses, renovate the pastures and have spelling paddocks, agist, make hay like you do.'

'Yeah, and Rowdy could be dead.'

He raised his eyes skywards. 'Don't be so melodramatic.'

She glared at him. 'You're not running him.'

He leaned his back against Rowdy's half-door with his arms crossed and his head down. His voice was quiet when he spoke, but she could hear the passion behind it.

'This is my chance, Soph. I only have one shot at it. The Springbank Cup would save this place.' He looked at her, his eyes intense. 'I have things I need to do, to make up for the mistakes I made. This is one of them. Don't take it from me.'

Sophie looked at Rowdy, at his big brown eyes and white star and floppy lips, and then back at Aaron. There was no contest.

She sighed. 'Danny's not to ride him.'

He straightened, reached out for her hand and briefly clasped it. 'Thank you.'

She shrugged. 'You've made it pretty hard for me to say no.'

'But he's your horse.'

'Yes, but you're much better looking.'

Aaron turned away from her, a cute blush creeping up his neck, then he mumbled something about organising feeds and walked quickly away. For a moment, she wanted to give chase and kiss every embarrassed bit of him. But then Rowdy snuffled his nose in her hair and her heart sank as she remembered what she'd just agreed to.

She stepped into the stable and pressed her face against Rowdy's warm neck, stroking his shiny coat. He'd been so brave this last month – fighting for the lead in some tough races. Aaron had been right from the start. Rowdy had enormous potential. Although he'd only won once, he had yet to finish a race out of the money. It was logical to enter him in the biggest race of the season.

The Springbank Cup. The name rattled with the weight of its past and its history of tragic accidents. The race was infamous not for its length – at five thousand metres one of the longest in the country – but for the sheer number of obstacles the horses had to negotiate. No other steeplechase in the world had that many fences. The Springbank Cup was unique, treacherous, and terrifying.

And now her beloved Rowdy was going to run in it.

'Knowing you, you'll probably win,' she said, tickling him under the chin. Sophie knew there hadn't been a death of either horse or jockey during the Cup for over five years. The jumps, although still numerous, had been altered and made safer, and the steeplechase track redesigned to provide better footing for the horses. She understood this, but the knowledge didn't stop her panicking at the thought of Rowdy competing.

———

Two more weeks passed. Winter shrouded the south-east in its dull coat. To Sophie and other graziers' relief, the Bureau's forecast remained correct. The weather, though cold and wet, was mild in comparison to the previous few years, with days of sunshine followed by overnight rain.

Through careful paddock rotation Sophie had ensured this year's calves were spoilt with feed, and they gained weight at an impressive pace. Sophie had lost only one older cow to grass tetany, and daily feeds of magnesium oxide-treated hay had helped prevent further occurrences. The new bull she'd purchased during the district's Beef Week back in February had taken to his task with enthusiasm, and she'd repainted and tidied Tess's cottage to the point where she could now consider putting it up for rent. Yet instead of contentment, Sophie felt restless, plagued by a vague illness she couldn't identify. No matter what she did, her mind was constantly drawn to Hakea Lodge and Aaron.

On top of that, there was Rowdy. Magnificent, beautiful Rowdy. When she wasn't dreaming of Aaron, her nights were filled with images of Rowdy's muscled brown body lying still and silent on the track, of eyes filled with agony as he tried not to put weight on a broken leg. Of screams as his forelegs thrashed the ground in front of him while his hind legs remained unmoving, the result of a broken back.

To keep herself from brooding, she slogged away at Buck, determined, this time, to get him right. The extended time in work hadn't improved his temper, but then her disposition wasn't the sunniest either. Two weeks into July, during one of their training sessions, Sophie decided she'd had enough.

The first time he tried to dump her he succeeded, although his victory was short-lived. Leaving him running around the arena squealing and pigrooting in glee, Sophie stomped to the tack room for a long, leather-handled riding crop. She batted it against her leg. The loop of leather at its end made a satisfying crack as it hit. Grim-faced, she shoved it down the side of her gaiter until only the handle stuck out, and then went back to fetch him.

The second time Buck tried to throw her, Sophie let him have it. With an almighty whack, she brought the crop down on his rump and dug her spurs hard into his side. Buck stopped in shock, goggle-eyed, and with all four feet splayed out like a cartoon character. Sophie had never hit him with a whip before. He twisted his head to look at her, blinking in equine surprise, and for the rest of the session, he grudgingly behaved.

He tried it on a few more times, but Sophie had his measure. Workouts became a pleasure instead of a chore, and Sophie's flagging confidence received a welcome boost.

Sometimes, when she took Buck out for a stretch around the

roads, she ran into Aaron and Danny and would join them as they trotted and cantered around the block. Aaron always rode in the centre. He'd barely glance at her, and his face would be set and angry. Danny tried to engage her in conversation, but each time Aaron would turn to him, and although she couldn't see the look he gave, it was enough to make Danny shut up. The three of them would continue in awkward silence until, with a mask of cheeriness to cover her discomfort, she made an excuse and cantered off.

When she asked Aaron about it during her visit to the yard, he simply reiterated that he didn't want her anywhere near Danny and would prefer it if she stayed away. But avoidance was not an option for Sophie. Wherever Aaron was, she wanted to be there too.

Not all of her life was so unsettled. Succour came from welcome if unlikely quarters, providing her with brief moments of peace, and easing parts of her conscience she was unaware were troubled.

She hadn't realised that she was even worried about Tess until a card from her arrived in the mail. As she stood at the head of the lane reading, sheer relief had her reaching for the Range Rover's bonnet to steady herself. Tess had completed her recovery and was now at Braeburn. From the tone of her writing, she sounded happy and optimistic, but what warmed Sophie the most was Tess's invitation to stay once she was more settled. Tess couldn't guarantee they'd get on, but given her age and the unlikelihood Tess would ever have children, one day Braeburn would be Sophie's. It was time she became acquainted with her legacy.

The other bright light in her life was her father. He now phoned at least once a week to see how she was and to keep her updated on any progress being made with the trustees. Unfortunately he never had much to report on that score. Her grandfather had made his wishes clear. Sophie would not inherit until she turned twenty-five.

To her surprise, Sophie found she didn't care. There was no reason to. She was running Vanaheim exactly the way she wanted. More importantly, the bridge of love between father and daughter that she'd thought long collapsed was slowly being rebuilt. Their relationship would never be perfect. They'd been disconnected for far too long, and as much as she tried to forget, residual bitterness at being abandoned by him remained. But the phone calls were something, and meant far more to her than the wads of money that had once been his contemptible substitute for love.

But still the Springbank Cup came closer and with it, the possible end of her fragile relationship with Aaron.

———

Sophie stood by the kitchen window hastily swallowing a ham and cheese sandwich, and wondering what Aaron was doing. Knowing him, he was either brooding over his bills or sorting through his nominations and acceptances, but she ignored that image in favour of a mild fantasy and pictured him instead sitting at his kitchen table with his sleeves rolled up. A slowly cooling mug of tea sat in front of him, the edges of a barely touched sandwich curling on a plate beside it. He was staring at his walls of photographs but he wasn't seeing horses and jockeys, or his father. His mind was filled only with her. The woman he loved.

She shook her head and chuckled at herself. Pathetic, that's what she was. Pathetic. No matter how benign, she had no time for fantasies. The Bureau had issued a storm warning for that evening, and she wanted to get out and move the cattle to the more sheltered paddocks before it hit.

A trail bike revved and then stopped. Sophie cocked her head, listening. The bike sounded close. She waited and sure enough, the engine restarted and the ning-ninging grew louder, the noise channelling through the tunnel made by Vanaheim's plane trees.

The bike skidded to a halt in front of the stables, leaving a dark streak on the pavers. The rider kicked down the stand and paused to inspect Sammy and Del as they circled and sniffed at the wheels. When Sammy did nothing more than cock his leg, the rider removed his helmet, pulled a cigarette from the top pocket of his jacket, lit it and looked around.

Sophie stood on the back doorstep with the half-eaten sandwich in her hand and called for the heelers. Their ears pricked at her tone, and immediately the sniffing and urinating stopped. Sammy and Del trotted to her side and took up sentry duty at her feet, their eyes intent on Danny.

'What do you want, Danny?'

He dismounted, hooked his helmet over the bike's handlebars, and, cigarette dangling from his lips as though he was out on a Sunday stroll, wandered over to peer into one of the stables.

'Always wanted to have a look at this place,' he said, turning back to her.

'Well, now you've seen it.'

'Don't be like that, Soph.'

'Don't call me Soph.'

'Why not? The boss does. I've seen you and the boss on race days. He likes to talk to you up real close, doesn't he, Soph? Even likes to touch you sometimes when he thinks old Danny-boy won't see.' He smiled in a way that made her break out in goosebumps. Del whined and licked her hand. 'But then, I think we all know the boss has a real thing for you.'

Sophie stayed silent. There was something malevolent about Danny, something evil in his sparkling eyes, a malicious glow cautioning her against danger. She bent slightly and stroked each heeler on the head, but kept her focus on him.

He walked toward her. Sammy growled, but Danny didn't appear bothered. He stopped at the garden gate and leaned over it, his eyes hard on hers.

'You know, me and the boss, we've been through a lot together.' He held up a pair of crossed fingers. 'Like brothers, him and me.'

Sophie blinked. What was Danny on about? Aaron loathed him.

'Yep. Hakea Lodge's like my second home. The old man took me on as an apprentice when I was fifteen and I've never worked anywhere else. Don't intend to either.' He took a drag on his cigarette. Smoke curled around his head in tendrils. 'Been through a few ups and downs, I'll admit, maybe seen a few things I shouldn't have, but even when the old man was losing it and things were going to shit old Danny-boy stuck it out. Loyalty, that's what that is. Loyalty. I stick by the boss, and the boss sticks by me.'

'Is that why you're here? To give me a lecture about loyalty?'

'Nah. Just wanted a friendly chat. Maybe pass on a bit of advice.'

'I think I can do without your advice, Danny.'

'Maybe, maybe not, but I'm gunna give it anyway. The boss . . .' He shook his head as if incredulous. 'The boss, well, let's just say he's a good bloke and all but he's no saint. He's done some bad things. Real bad things. Things a young girl like you wouldn't like.'

Her heart hammered but she maintained her bravado. 'Oh yeah? Like what?'

Danny tapped his nose and then waggled his finger at her. 'Old Danny-boy would never rat on a mate. I told you that. But take it from a bloke who knows, you should steer clear of him. After all,' he said, tossing the cigarette on the ground and crushing it with his boot, 'we wouldn't want to see you getting hurt now, would we?'

Sophie took a step forward, the dogs alert at her side. 'Are you threatening me?'

Danny held up his hands, his face a veneer of pained innocence. 'Who, me? Nah. Old Danny-boy wouldn't hurt a fly. I'm just trying to help. Reckon you'd be better off with that Ben bloke than the boss. Someone who isn't so heartless.'

'Right. And since when have you been so interested in my wellbeing?'

He winked at her. 'I've always been interested in you, young Sophie. You oughta know that.'

'Yeah, well, I'm sure not interested in you. So if you don't mind, I've got work to do.'

'You don't know what you're missing,' he said over his shoulder as he sauntered toward his motorbike.

Sophie watched him as he donned his helmet and kick-started the bike. He circled the yard twice, waving at her on the final lap before leaning forward, revving the engine, and accelerating up the drive in a spray of stones and dirt.

She looked at the sandwich in her hand. Her hunger had passed, replaced with a sense of nausea, like she'd just eaten something unsavoury. She tore the sandwich in half, tossed the pieces to Sammy and Del and wiped her palms on her thighs, but still her hands felt dirty, like Lady Macbeth with her damned spot.

She shook her head and sighed. She didn't have time to stand around thinking about Danny. The cattle needed to be moved and there would be opportunity enough to mull things over on the quad bike.

With another rub of her hands against her jeans, she headed for the shed.

She finished moving the stock and took a side trip to measure pasture growth in the paddock she'd renovated in April; it wasn't until she was done that Sophie worked it out. She could have smacked herself for failing to unravel the mystery earlier, but she'd been distracted by the sight of Aaron out in one of his paddocks, attacking a small stand of variegated thistle with a hoe. She'd noticed the plants a few days ago and had advised him to eradicate them immediately before they spread. Hakea Lodge had enough to contend with without adding a dangerous plant to the list.

She'd squatted down next to the quad bike pretending to look at ryegrass and clover plants while her real focus remained on him. He'd rolled his shirt sleeves up and, although she was too far away to see, she knew the muscles on his forearms would be bulging.

Since that day in the feed room, when he'd almost kissed her, she'd harboured an infatuation for his arms. It was crazy, given so many other parts of him were just as appealing, but his forearms in particular continued to enchant her, and it wasn't until he'd wandered off that she could turn her mind to other matters.

That Aaron was gone when she worked it out was probably just as well. She would have run across the paddock to yell sense into him if he'd still been there.

Danny knew what Aaron had done and was blackmailing him with it, which made Sophie a threat Danny couldn't tolerate. She had the power to convince Aaron the past no longer mattered, that he was safe from whatever haunted him. And if that happened, Danny's hold would be broken. The jockey could squeal all he liked but it would cost him the one thing his festering black heart held dear: Hakea Lodge.

Aaron might end up short a stable jockey, but at least he would be free, and Danny would finally discover that true loyalty didn't come with conditions.

TWENTY-ONE

SOPHIE STROKED Costa Motza's cheek. The horse had his head in her lap, dozing in the sunshine. The rain that had drenched the district for almost a week had passed, leaving behind a lightly clouded sky and, out of the wind, patches of sleepy warmth. The other horses leaned across their fences, watching her through half closed eyes, digesting the carrots she'd treated them to. Sophie's eyes drooped too, seduced by the yard's peace and its rain-washed shabby beauty.

'He needs a break,' said Aaron, leaning relaxed against the rail, as though the change in weather soothed him in a way Sophie could not. He'd wandered out of the house ten minutes before and joined her in soaking up the sun at Costa Motza's yard.

'He's tired, Soph. It's been a long season for him.'

'I know.' She traced her finger around Costa Motza's eye, admiring the length of his lashes. She turned to Aaron. 'Can I take him to Vanaheim? With Buck still in work Chuck could do with the company.'

He shrugged. 'I can't see why not.'

'You can come and visit him if you like.'

Aaron frowned. 'Why would I want to do that?'

'Because he's such a superstar.'

'Only in his dreams.'

Her attention returned to Costa Motza. Her leg had gone dead under his weight but she didn't push him off.

'What do you think horses dream about?' she said.

'I dunno. Buckets of oats. Paddocks full of lucerne. Mints.'

'Sex?'

'Costa Motza's a gelding. I'm pretty sure he's lost the urge.'

'Is that what's happened to you?'

He made a choked sound, as if he couldn't believe his ears. 'What makes you think I've lost it?'

She looked at him. His blue eyes were bright, but they were also wary. He didn't like the way the conversation was going. He'd walk away soon. Turn his back on her as had become his habit the moment their rare conversations turned personal. Hide in the feed room or the house until she'd gone.

'You hardly look at me any more.'

'I'm looking at you now.'

'That's not what I meant.'

They stared at each other until Aaron glanced away.

'I'm trying to do the right thing,' he said.

'It's okay. However misguided, I know you are.' Sophie traced her finger up the edge of Costa Motza's left ear before turning her attention back to Aaron. 'I'll walk down tomorrow to pick him up.'

'If you want.'

They went back to what they were doing – enjoying the sunshine. Puddles of water speckled the yards where the past week's rain had yet to evaporate or soak away. Horses like Psycho took sanctuary under their shelters where the sand was dry, while the mudlarks, or the plain stupid, as Aaron called Costa Motza, slushed around, treading in their droppings and making the pens impossible to clean. When they dried out, Sophie had offered to help Aaron remove the soiled sand and lay down fresh fill but he'd refused. Shovelling shit was Danny's job, he'd said. Sophie couldn't have agreed more.

She'd contemplated telling Aaron about Danny's visit but had decided against it. Aaron already had enough on his plate. The previous week, Pollyester Girl had crossed the line first but, much to Tony Johnstone's disgust, had been beaten on protest. Pollyanna, tired after a long season, was still racing, but only because Aaron desperately needed the money. The bills, Sophie knew, were once again piling up, taking Aaron's anxiety levels up with them.

'I love you,' she said quietly after several minutes had passed.

'You're wasting your time, Soph. I don't think he can answer.'

'I wasn't talking to Costa Motza.'

'You sure about that?' He pointed at the horse's head, still resting on Sophie's lap. 'I mean, look at you two. You're like a pair of soppy teenagers.'

'You can take his place if you want.'

'Nah, I dribble in my sleep.'

She smiled. 'Do you?'

'Yeah, all the time. And I snore.'

'You're not putting me off, you know.'

They lapsed back into dozy silence. A bird flew down and perched on the edge of Costa Motza's feed trough. It spent a moment cocking its head and scrutinising the yard for danger before hopping down inside. Its beak sounded a gentle pock-pock as it picked at left-over feed. Psycho wandered out from his shelter, his feet squelching in the puddled yard, and hung over the fence hoping for attention. No one paid him any.

'Aaron?'

'Mmm?'

'Can we make another bet?'

'Depends on what it is.'

'Don't worry. It won't be for a kiss this time.'

'Good.' He straightened and turned, leaning his back against the top rail and crossing his arms, suddenly mesmerised by the mud at his feet.

Sophie pushed Costa Motza's head off her lap, slid from the fence and walked toward him. He eyed her warily. She leaned against the rail, copying his stance.

'This time I want you to promise me something.'

'I'm not very good at keeping promises.'

'This is one I'll think you'll keep.'

He kicked at a clod of mud and sighed. 'Sometimes, Sophie, you're so transparent.'

'I'd have thought that was a good thing. If you can see through me, at least you know I'm not trying to blackmail you.'

He gave her a sharp look, his eyes wandering over her face. She kept her expression innocent.

'A bet, Aaron. You could win, or you could lose. Simple.'

He squinted into the sun. 'I'll lose whatever happens.'

'You don't know what the bet is yet.'

'You're wrong. I do. If Rowdy wins, you want me to tell you everything.'

She nodded. 'But he could lose.'

He faced her again. 'And what happens then, Sophie?'

'I take him home and —' She closed her eyes as she realised what he meant. 'God, how could I be so stupid.' She opened them again, staring at him in disbelief. 'You don't need my bet, do you? You've already made a deal with yourself.'

He nodded.

'So let me see if I've got this straight. Rowdy wins, you tell me your big secret, and I hate you and never want to see you again. Yes?'

'Yes.'

'Okay. And if Rowdy loses, our contract ends, I take him home, and then that's it. You cut me off, refuse to see me, keep the gate locked so I can't come in. No more Sophie and Aaron. No more of this. No more of anything. Am I right?'

'Something like that.'

She shook her head, feeling the sting of hot tears and the choking grasp of her throat closing over, but under this, in her chest, anger stewed and steamed like a geyser.

'You bastard,' she whispered, and then in a lash of fury, she rounded on him. Her hands pushed hard into his chest. 'You absolute bastard!'

'Sophie —'

She pushed him again. 'I've done nothing to deserve this. Nothing!'

He grabbed her wrists. 'Stop it.'

She wrenched them free and tried to push him again but he caught her in his arms and held her trapped. She squirmed and writhed but his arms were strong and hard.

His mouth pressed close to her ear, murmuring, 'Don't, Soph. Please don't. It's bad enough as it is. Hate me, but don't fight with me. It's the only way, you'll see.'

She shook her head, sobbing. 'No.'

'It'll be okay, I promise. You'll be all right. You'll get over it, and in a few months, you'll think back and laugh and wonder what the hell got into you.'

'I won't.'

'You will. You're strong. You can cope with anything.'

She pressed her face into his chest and breathed in the scent of him – washing powder, horse, chaff and something unidentifiable, the essence of Aaron – and shuddered. He didn't understand how she felt, the force if it. This wasn't a crush. She'd had those, experienced that squirming longing for someone she barely knew, someone whose only appeal seemed to stem from extreme attractiveness or the ability to charm.

This wasn't that. This was love. Aaron might have his secrets, but she didn't care. She loved every bit of him, from his handsome, rough exterior to his gentle, flawed core. Nothing would change that. Nothing.

She tilted her head back to look at him. His mouth was turned down, as if weighted by the unbearable sadness of what he was going to put them through. She felt a tear dribble down the side of her face and wanted to wipe it away, but his grasp was too tight. It slid toward her chin.

'I love you,' she said.

He stroked her hair. 'I know.'

'I won't hate you, no matter what you tell me. You're a good man, I know you are.'

'No, I'm not.'

'But you are.'

Gently, he traced the journey of her tear with his finger and then cupped her face with his hand. 'No, Sophie. If I was, I would never have let it go this far.'

'But it *has* gone this far.'

'Yes,' he said, letting her go. 'But come Saturday week, one way or another, I'm going to make sure it ends.'

TWENTY-TWO

AN EXPECTANT HUSH fell over the Millicent Showgrounds as Sophie rode into the ring. Several competitors ceased their warm-ups and rode closer to watch. Others made their way ringside, murmuring among themselves. This wasn't one of the premier classes – they weren't scheduled until the weekend – but competitors in the South East Showjumping Club's three-day Winter Championship carnival took even the most minor classes seriously. Despite their outward friendliness, inside, competitiveness reigned. Sophie was no different.

The buzzer went. A large digital clock began its forty-five-second countdown. With her weight on her knees, Sophie leaned forward and slid her hand down Buck's sweaty neck. He tossed his head, snatching at the bit, wanting to get on with it.

They cantered a circle, Buck's gait collected, bouncy, his neck arched. A fleck of white froth flew from his mouth and landed on Sophie's shiny black boot. She didn't notice, her mind focused on the first jump. Nine competitors had made it through to the jump- off, serious showjumpers chasing prize money and grading points. If she and Buck were to win, they had to go clear and fast.

They approached the start flags. Sophie sat back, and with her backside and legs driving him forward, faced Buck at the first fence. With a snort and a shake of his head, he crossed between the flags and charged at it.

In this showjumping event, the jump-off was a shortened and heightened version of the course they had all jumped in the first round. The winner would be determined by whoever made it around in the fastest time with the least number of faults. In the more advanced classes like Buck's, where dropped rails, refusals, run-outs and falls were few and far between, it was speed that counted.

They cleared the first – a simple parallel bar – at an angle and raced for the second. They jumped the brush and rails almost on the diagonal, and then turned sharp left to take a formidable white gate. It rattled loudly, but Sophie didn't look behind to see if it fell. She'd count faults when it was over. With a shift of her weight, Buck changed his leading leg and spun right toward a green and gold painted double. In his excitement, he launched half a stride too early and although he cleared the fence, on landing, he found himself in trouble. Only one stride separated the first and second elements of the double, and it was a long one. Sophie rode him hard, trying to give him the impulsion he would need to make that stride and clear the wide parallel of the second fence.

Buck grunted with the effort, but it wasn't enough. He'd taken off too far away from the second fence, and as they came down, his hind legs caught the last bar. Sophie knew from the rattle and thump that it had fallen, but she pushed him on over the remaining jumps anyway. Never look back, her mother had taught her, and she never did.

They scooted through the finish flags and pulled up with a skid, Buck huffing and shaking his head as they jogged out of the arena. Four faults. Five horse-and-rider combinations had already gone through clear. They were out of the money.

'Bad luck,' said Michael Fenton, grinning at her from the back of an enormous grey. 'You were making pretty good time until the double.'

She shrugged and slapped Buck's neck. 'He gets a bit excited sometimes.'

Michael winked. 'So do I.'

'Give it a rest,' said Sophie, rolling her eyes.

'Not until you agree to have a drink with me.'

'Not a chance.'

'Dinner?'

'Nope. As of right now, I'm out of here.' She kicked Buck into a canter.

'A quickie in my trailer then?'

Sophie smiled and kept going.

'Come on, Soph. Give a bloke a break.'

His voice faded as she wove through the cars, horse trailers and goosenecks scattered across the showgrounds. Most would be staying for the weekend and the even bigger events, but Sophie wouldn't be there. Come this time Saturday, she'd be leaning over the rail at Springbank praying for Rowdy and swallowing her fears over Aaron.

Michael was nothing if not persistent. From the moment she'd arrived early that morning, he'd been hanging around, lounging nonchalantly against her float, regaling her with stories from his time in England.

'You're looking good these days, Soph,' he kept telling her, unaware she was immune to his pick-up lines. 'Damn good.'

Michael had been friendly, funny and oh-so-charming, but Sophie knew from experience it was an act. Even if she weren't in love with Aaron, she could never see Michael as anything other than the man whose cruel teenage prank had almost caused her to self-destruct. She might have forgiven him, but forgetting was another matter.

For the sake of politeness she'd accepted an invitation to join him and a few other riders for coffee in the kitchenette of his massive horse trailer. But ten minutes in, when still no one else had shown up, and after having removed Michael's hand from yet another part of her anatomy, she'd had to leave.

'Come on, Soph,' he'd complained. 'We'll be great together. Just like before.'

She'd stared at him in disbelief and then shook her head at the weirdness of life.

She'd always believed she was unattractive, a dull version of her mother, but over the last four months, it appeared that she'd blossomed. Many times, she'd looked at herself in the mirror and studied her face, puzzling over what had changed to make her attractive to men like Ben and Michael, when they once wouldn't have given her a second glance. All she could see was that her hair was different. She still had the same boring grey eyes, the same pale skin, the same undramatic looks of the chronically plain.

Yet Aaron had once called her beautiful, and for one brief ecstatic moment, she had felt it, like a flush of happiness warming her from the inside as if a bulb had been switched on.

Maybe that's what love did, made people radiant. There was no other explanation, because if there was one thing she knew for certain, her newfound allure wasn't due to pregnancy.

———

The car rocked as Buck kicked at the tailgate and stomped on the floor of the float. It never ceased to amaze Sophie that the horses knew they were nearing home. Chuck had been no different, and even Aaron's horses became agitated as they approached Hakea Lodge.

She turned into Vanaheim's drive and stopped at the gate to check the mail, smiling as Costa Motza looked up and whinnied, then goofily trotted over to say hello. Chuck followed close on his heels, his neck snaking and his teeth bared as he tried to nip his rival.

From the day she'd let Costa Motza into the paddock, the two horses had become friends. At first, they'd squealed and sniped, but soon settled down to the business of grazing. Only Sophie's presence caused a breach in their domestic harmony. Jealousy, it appeared, was not just a human emotion.

She leaned over the rail to give them both a scratch. Costa Motza looked put out that Chuck received his first, but he'd have to get used to coming second at Vanaheim. As much as she adored the gangly chestnut, Chuck would always be her favourite.

After kissing both horses and checking the mail, she returned to the Range Rover. It would be dark soon, and there were too many things that needed to be done around the place to spend any more time playing with Chuck and Costa Motza.

It was after nine by the time she made it back into the house. She sat in front of the television with her dinner of microwaved leftovers perched on her knees, listlessly picking at it while watching the late news. A suicide bomber had killed seventeen people in Pakistan. In eastern Europe, unexpected heavy rain had caused flash flooding and landslides. In America, a gunman had opened fire in a crowded shopping mall, killing five, two of them small children. But Sophie hardly registered the barrage of grim tidings. Her mind, as always, had drifted to Aaron.

She wondered what he was doing, how he was feeling. More nervous than her, she imagined. Tomorrow, if Rowdy won, Hakea Lodge's future would be secure. He'd have what he wanted, and so, she supposed, would she. She'd have Rowdy, the horse she'd fallen in love with all those months ago. Life could go back to normal.

Except it wouldn't. It never could.

She stared at her half-eaten casserole, and then walked to the kitchen and scraped it into the dogs' bowls. She rinsed her plate and gazed at her reflection in the window. He loved her. He hadn't said it, but she knew it, and where there was love, there had to be hope.

———

No light came from Hakea Lodge. Despite the hour, Sophie had assumed Aaron would be up, pacing, thinking, worrying like her, but he must have gone to bed. It was a stupid idea anyway. If he wouldn't let her comfort him before, he'd hardly allow her to now.

Her breath foggy in the night cold, she dug her hands in her coat pockets, fingering the apples she'd placed there, and continued walking up the drive. She wanted to spend a few minutes alone with Rowdy, anyway. Not that she could be sure of his reception either. Work at Vanaheim, preparations and the showjumping competition itself had kept her away for the last two days. Rowdy normally descended into a sulk if she was absent for even one.

The yard was silent, the horses asleep, the only noise a light breeze rustling through the trees and skipping fallen leaves and twigs around the quadrangle. Quietly, she unlatched the door to Rowdy's stable and slipped inside, softly talking to him. He whickered and buried his soft muzzle into her hand. Sophie pressed her face against his warm nose and stroked his neck.

'Tomorrow's a big day for all of us,' she whispered. 'You have to win for Aaron's sake and you have to stay safe for mine. You think you can do that?'

Rowdy breathed hot air onto her chest. She scratched at the spot around his ears she knew he loved, smiling as he tilted his head into her fingers, demanding more. When she deemed he'd had enough, she pulled an apple from her pocket and held it out to him. The crunch of his teeth sounded unnaturally loud in the confines of the stable.

When the apple was gone, he bunted her for more, snuffling around her coat and slobbering apple juice. She pulled the other apple from her pocket and hid it behind her back, but he could smell it. He pushed at her with his nose, demanding she produce the fruit, and then curled his head around her side, his lips rubbery on her hand as they reached toward the smell.

She let the game last a little longer, finding it strangely comforting, before giving in and holding out the apple. In the dim light, she saw Rowdy's eyes close in equine ecstasy as he sucked and crunched. She kissed him fondly.

A hollow bang, like someone kicking a drum, made her jerk upright. A horse snorted and moved in the night. She stilled, cocking her head and straining her ears. The skin of her scalp prickled, but she heard only the breeze and Rowdy's blissful chewing.

She stepped toward the door, cursing inwardly at the sound of her boots catching on the straw, and looked out into the yard. The house remained in darkness. Nothing moved on the verandah, no one sat waiting for her on the step. The door to the kitchen remained closed.

She opened the half-door and stepped out, squinting toward the yards. Something drifted on the air, a faint, sickly-sweet smell, like rotting compost or bad body odour, and then it was gone. She frowned, unsure if she was imagining things. She turned back to kiss Rowdy's nose, then closed the stable door and slipped the bolt, unable to shake her creeping unease. Rowdy hung his head over the door. She stroked it absently, looking at the yards.

A horse snorted again. Sophie could see moonlight reflected off its faded canvas rug as it shuffled around its yard. Sophie let her shoulders drop. It was nothing, just an insomniac galloper knocking at its feed bin. She shivered and drew her coat around her and, after checking the stable bolt once more, headed off across the yard. It was time she was home in bed. Tomorrow would be long and stressful enough without adding sleep deprivation to the mix.

Halfway down the lane she stopped to look back, disturbed by the goosebumps creeping up her neck and the unshakable feeling that someone was watching. The wind dropped, leaving the yard eerily quiet. She swallowed, wanting to call out, but afraid of waking Aaron. She waited, senses sharp, her heart beating hard, but still there was nothing.

Shaking her head at her paranoia, she broke into a jog and slipped away into the night.

TWENTY-THREE

WITH A STEAMING mug in his hands, Aaron wandered out onto the verandah to inspect the yard. He yawned and stretched, careful not to spill the hot tea, and leaned against a post. The sun was just rising, casting muted peach-coloured light through the pines and gracing Hakea Lodge with an incongruous beauty, as though nature was indulging in a touch of soft-focus photography. A pair of magpies serenaded the new day with a warble from the feed-room roof, and a rabbit peered wide-eyed at Aaron from beside the tractor shed before turning its fluffy white tail and darting back into the bracken.

Aaron stared absently at Rowdy's stable, thinking of Sophie. No matter what happened today, tonight, once the yard was settled, he'd tell her everything, the whole sordid, sorry mess. Then, when she'd gone, he was going to ring Josh, go into town and drink until he could no longer remember the look on her face. Until the alcohol washed the bitterness from his mouth and numbed the aching core of his body.

He sighed, knowing it wouldn't work, knowing nothing could ease the torment of losing her, and of causing her suffering yet again.

He took a sip of tea, and tried to think of the good things in his life. He had the yard, and after last night, regardless of whether Rowdy won or lost, it was safe for a little longer.

He'd had a call from a man offering him a couple of horses to train. The man – a local farmer and a highly respected racehorse owner named Colin Dickinson – had known and admired Rodger Laidlaw, but mostly he'd been impressed with Aaron's record over the last few months, especially with horses the so-called experts considered no-hopers.

Aaron had wanted to tell him that it wasn't him, it was Sophie, but Colin had ploughed on. Aaron would start with two gallopers, and if he did well, they'd look at doubling that number. Aaron's gratitude was so profound that, had Colin been standing in front of him, he'd have cried in his arms like a baby.

He smiled at the memory and took another sip of tea, then frowned. Something about the yard wasn't right. The horses were restless, pacing, tossing their heads, and the air seemed close, heavy, as though laden with fear.

Pollyester Girl circled her yard, snorting, and suddenly it dawned on Aaron. For the first time in memory, there was no Rowdy hanging over the half-door yelling for his breakfast.

'Oh, Christ,' he said, dropping the mug and sprinting across the yard.

He yanked at the stable bolt, cursing as it caught in his bumbling fingers, and threw the door open. The stable's air was thick with the stench of fetid manure, stale sweat, and the indescribable, indelible smell of an animal in pain.

Rowdy stood in the corner of the box with his head down, his sides heaving as he took shallow, jerky breaths. He lifted a foreleg as though to move towards Aaron, but then dropped it back down, as if the effort were too much. His woollen rug was dark and soaked with sweat. His hind legs were dull, his once shiny coat stained stiff with dried excrement where he'd scoured during the night.

'Hey, hey,' Aaron soothed, carefully approaching. Wet straw stuck to his boots and legs, the smell worsening with each step. 'It's okay, boy. It's okay.'

He touched the horse's neck. It was wet but not over-hot. He pressed two fingers below Rowdy's ear to his jawline and felt his pulse, and let out his breath when the beat was regular, albeit fast.

Murmuring calming words, he unbuckled the rug and slid it slowly off Rowdy's back. Rowdy's stomach was tucked up, like a dog straining to defecate. Aaron pressed his ear to the belly and listened. It sounded normal, and he began to hope that whatever it was that had caused Rowdy to scour had been purged.

He walked round the horse, checking for any injuries he might have given himself fighting off the pain. Rowdy's right knee was swollen and a light scab had formed on a graze where he'd probably knocked it, but that appeared to be the only damage.

Aaron checked the water bucket. It was almost empty. He carried it toward the horse and let him drink, stroking his neck as he sucked down the last of the water. Dehydration was a risk, but Rowdy was drinking, and it appeared the real danger had already passed. The horse would need to be carefully nursed, but if Aaron was correct in his diagnosis, a vet wasn't necessary. Thankfully. A vet would ask questions.

As he walked to the tack room to fetch Rowdy's halter and lead, his mood darkened. He mightn't know exactly what had been used, but he knew Rowdy had been dosed with something. All he could do was pray it had been something mild, a mineral oil like paraffin or perhaps an off-the-shelf laxative. Something from which Rowdy would recover quickly.

He burned with anger. A doping scandal was the last thing he needed. If word got out, it could mean the end of everything he'd worked so hard for. Goodbye new owner, goodbye trainer's licence, goodbye Hakea Lodge. He'd have to lie when he phoned in the scratching. Tell them Rowdy had come down with colic, or hadn't shaken the cold he'd had all week. Anything to avoid an enquiry. Hakea Lodge had seen enough of those.

And then he'd have to deal with Sophie.

———

Rowdy was so miserable he accepted Aaron's ministrations without protest. He stood forlornly at the foot of Hakea Lodge's back steps while Aaron washed his hind legs and tail with warm, soapy water. He didn't even move when Aaron stuck a thermometer up his backside. The reading, much to Aaron's relief, was normal. The worst was over.

He was rubbing Rowdy down with towels when Danny turned up. The jockey sauntered over with his hands in his pockets and a raised eyebrow.

'What's up?' he said, putting his hand on the horse's rump. Rowdy's head went up, and he shuffled nervously until Danny took his hand away.

Aaron glanced at him, and went back to his rubbing. 'He's been doped.'

Danny whistled. 'How do you know?'

'I just know.'

'Yeah,' said Danny. 'You would.'

Aaron clenched his jaw and breathed through his nose, trying to keep his boiling temper from exploding.

Danny lit a cigarette. 'He all right?'

'He won't be racing, if that's what you mean.'

Smoke curled around Danny's head in spirals. 'Shame.' He picked a piece of tobacco off his tongue and inspected it. 'I'm sorry, boss, but I got to tell you something. Don't think you're going to like it, but.'

Aaron eyed him, but remained silent. He threw the towel on the step and picked up a soft-bristled body brush.

'I heard word around the traps that someone might have a go at the big fella here, so I thought it best to hang around last night. You know, guard him.'

'Didn't do much of a job then, did you?'

Danny shrugged. 'Couldn't help it. Fell asleep on the job. But I got to tell you, young Sophie was here.'

Aaron stared at him.

'Yep. She turned up about midnight. Saw her go into the big fella's box. Fed him something by the sound of it.'

Aaron's jaw began to ache from the pressure he was putting on it. With an effort, he forced himself to relax, breathing slowly through his mouth. It didn't help.

'She never wanted him to run, did she?' said Danny.

Aaron continued brushing.

'Too afraid he'd get hurt. Mind you, Springbank has a shit reputation. Can't blame her, I guess.' Danny flicked his butt into the yard. 'I didn't hear nothing else after she left.'

Aaron ran the brush through Rowdy's tail. 'The feeds are made up. I haven't had a chance to get them out. When you've done that, you can start on the yards.'

Danny looked at him, his hands in his pockets, his lips pursed, but then he nodded and wandered off. When he'd disappeared into the feed room, Aaron pressed his forehead against Rowdy's rump.

'I'm sorry, Rowdy,' he whispered. 'I should have known.'

———

In the end, he was glad when Sophie arrived early. He didn't think he could stand another second of Danny's smug company. At least Rowdy looked a little better, a bit more alive.

The horse lifted his head and whickered at Sophie when she got out of the car. She had a puzzled look on her face, as if she knew something was wrong but couldn't quite fathom what.

Then her mouth parted and her eyes widened, and she strode

over to Rowdy and held his head between her hands, tears turning her eyes bright.

Aaron leaned on the rake and watched her from the stable door. She kept stroking Rowdy's face, her lips moving as she spoke softly to him, her eyes scanning his coat. It was clean, but the shine that had made him seem so powerful, so magnificent, was gone.

Aaron dropped the rake onto the pile of soiled bedding and walked over to her. She gazed at him with huge liquid eyes and he felt sick with what he was about to do.

'Have you called the vet?' she asked, her voice cracked with worry.

'No.'

'Why not? He's sick. Can't you see that?'

He ignored the question. 'Did you come here last night?'

She looked at him as though he'd gone mad. 'What?'

'Did you come here last night?'

'Yes, but what's that got to do with anything?'

'Did you give him anything?'

Her brow scrunched in bafflement. 'Huh?'

'It's a simple question, Sophie. When you were here last night, did you feed Rowdy anything?'

'Some apples but —' She stopped, staring at him.

Aaron looked toward the yards. Danny had a wire pooper-scooper in his hand and was eyeing them from behind Pollyester Girl's fence. He dropped the scoop, ducked under the rail and began walking toward them. Aaron turned back to Sophie.

'Go home,' he said. 'Rowdy won't be racing. He's been scratched.'

Sophie peered at Danny, frowned, and then looked back at Aaron. 'What's going on?'

'Just do as I say and go home.'

'No! Not until you tell me what's going on.'

Rowdy lifted his head at the shrillness in her voice, pulling at his lead.

'What's it look like?' yelled Danny. 'He's been doped, hasn't he? But you already knew that.'

'*What?*'

Aaron closed his eyes and prayed for strength.

Not far from Sophie, Danny halted. He glanced at Aaron, as if checking whether he was too close. Apparently satisfied, he crossed his arms. 'You heard me. Old Danny-boy's not a fool. You were here last night, I saw you. What did you give him?'

Sophie turned her pale face toward Aaron. 'Oh, my God, Aaron. You can't think . . . you can't possibly believe . . .' She grabbed his sleeve and tugged at it. 'I wouldn't, you know I wouldn't.'

Danny pulled a packet of cigarettes from his shirt pocket and flipped the top. 'You never wanted him to run. Scared he'd fall, weren't you?' He extracted a cigarette, put it in his mouth and dug around in his pocket for a lighter.

Sophie snatched the cigarette from his mouth and ground it into the dirt. 'Now you listen to me, you piece of —'

Pressing his palm to her back, Aaron tried to guide her toward the Range Rover. 'I said *leave.*'

Sophie jerked away and stared at him in shock, and then her face crumbled. She tilted her head, her mouth wobbling. Tears welled, spilling over her eyelids and sliding down her face.

'Can't you see what he's doing?' She pointed at Danny. Aaron didn't need to look at him to know that he was smirking. '*He* did it. He poisoned Rowdy. He was here last night. I could smell him. He did it!'

Ducking around him, she ran at Danny. Aaron swore and grabbed her from behind, pinning her arms to her side. She kicked and spat, wrenching against his hold. She was so strong he was afraid he'd hurt her with his grip, but he had to stop her from attacking Danny. The jockey wouldn't think twice about fighting back.

Frightened by the commotion, Rowdy pulled back on his lead, his eyes rolling. The clip attaching the rope to his halter snapped. He cantered off toward the lunging ring.

'Christ! Go get the bloody horse while I deal with her,' snarled Aaron.

Danny tapped out a fresh cigarette and coolly lit it before wandering off to do as he was told. Sophie continued to strain against Aaron's grasp.

'Don't you touch him, you bastard!'

'Sophie, listen to me.'

'Let me go!'

'For once in your life, please, just bloody well listen!'

She stopped struggling. Aaron kept hold of her, afraid to let her go. He could feel her heaving as she drew in gulps of air. He let her settle for a second, then released her, prepared to grab her again if he needed to.

'You need to go home. Right now. No more arguing. Just go.'

She turned to face him. Her cheeks and neck were wet and flushed, her big grey eyes wide and tear-filled. She looked at him with heartbreaking hurt.

'I was wrong. Seems I'm always wrong about people. I've been wrong all my life. You don't love me at all.'

Out of the corner of his eye, Aaron could see Danny leading Rowdy back towards them. 'Go,' he ordered.

Suddenly, her hunched shoulders straightened and she turned to him, her eyes narrowed and her mouth hard. It had started, the metamorphosis of love into hate, but there'd be plenty of time to mourn its loss later.

Her voice shook, but it was full of fight, full of the tough, strong Sophie he loved. 'I'm going home to get the float and then I'm coming back for my horse.'

'I don't care what you do,' he said, glancing at Danny again, 'just as long as you get the hell out of here now.'

She gave him one last look and opened the car door. Aaron watched her buckle herself in and start the engine. As she reached for the gearstick, she stopped and wound down the window.

'I hope you're happy, Aaron. You've got what you wanted.'

He waited until the Range Rover swung on to the road before turning back to Danny. He eyed him, but decided he could wait a moment longer. He took hold of Rowdy and led him to Costa Motza's empty yard. The horse kept looking up the lane as though wondering why Sophie had left him so soon. Aaron locked him in the yard and then walked back to the stable. Danny was lounging against the wall.

'Are all the feeds done?'

'Yes, boss.'

'The yards?'

Danny shrugged. 'Not quite, but I'll get there.' He indicated the drive with his chin. 'Sneaky, just like her old man, hey? Who'd have thought young Sophie had it in her.' He shook his head. 'Still, you never could trust a Dixon, could you?'

Aaron glanced up the drive to satisfy himself Sophie hadn't decided to turn around and come back, and then let his carefully controlled temper explode. He grabbed Danny by the throat and slammed him against the stable wall. The jockey's head cracked against the timber and he cried out. Aaron wouldn't have heard him even if he was listening. All he could hear was the whoosh of his rage as it burst.

He slammed him against the wall again. 'You bastard! You dirty little fucked-up piece of shit!'

Danny gasped for air.

Aaron squeezed harder. 'I ought to strangle you, you prick. How fucking dare you!'

Danny's eyes widened. From his open mouth came a choked gurgle.

'How dare you try to lay the blame on Sophie. It was you all along, you filthy bastard.'

Danny's legs hammered against the wall, his fingers scrabbled at the hand Aaron held around his throat. He let out a strangled cry, his nails tearing into Aaron's skin.

Aaron blinked and let go. Danny fell to the ground. He crawled on his hands and knees, gasping and trying to get away. Aaron watched him as though he were a particularly nasty insect he wanted to squash.

'What did you give him?'

Danny coughed, but didn't answer. Aaron kicked him in the stomach, not hard, but hard enough to give him a fright and flip him over. 'I asked you a question.'

'Milk of magnesia,' Danny spluttered, turning back onto his knees and trying to stand.

Aaron flipped him over again so he could look at him. He wanted to kick him, but didn't trust himself enough to pull it this time. Instead, he put his boot on Danny's face and pressed. Danny yelled and wriggled. He pushed down a little harder, wondering how much more pressure it would take until he heard the satisfying crack of Danny's nose breaking.

This confrontation had been so long coming he was almost revelling in it. This is what he hadn't wanted Sophie to see, the animal in him, the black void of his festering resentment, his ugly, primal need for revenge. He'd had to hurt her to get her away, but he felt as though he'd had no choice. He needed to know she was safe, that Danny couldn't retaliate by attacking her.

But most of all, he didn't want Sophie to see the truth. That he could beat a man half his size, half his weight. Kick him while he lay helpless, and *enjoy* it.

He pulled his boot away from Danny's face. 'Just in case you're too thick to figure it out for yourself, you're fired. I want you out of the flat by tomorrow night. And don't even think about testing my patience, Danny, because I'm in no mood to show restraint.'

Danny rubbed at his nose and then inspected the streak of blood smeared across the back of his hand. 'You broke my nose.'

'It's not broken.'

'Bloody is!'

'Trust me, if I'd have wanted to break it, I would have. Get up.'

Danny looked at him warily then slowly stood, sniffing at the trickle of blood dribbling from his left nostril. 'You can't sack me.'

'I just did.'

Danny pointed at Rowdy. 'And how're you going to explain him to the stewards?'

Aaron recycled the excuse he'd used when he'd phoned in the scratching. 'Nothing to explain. Horse looks fine, except his knee's a bit sore where he knocked it yesterday in the float.' He slid a look at Danny. 'Such a pity it didn't come good in time for the race.' Danny glared at him. Aaron shrugged and headed for the house. He needed a drink, something – anything – to wash the foul taste of self-disgust from his mouth.

But Danny wasn't finished.

'You want to play dirty? Well, I know all about how to do that. How 'bout I start with young Sophie?'

Aaron stopped.

'Yeah, thought that might get your attention.'

'You so much as breathe near her and the next time you feel my hand around your throat will be the last time you feel anything.'

Danny smiled. 'Oh, I wouldn't hurt a hair on her pretty little head. Nope, not a hair. I don't hurt women, you know that. But I sure like to talk to them. And I bet Sophie would just love to hear all about what you got up to when you were a lad. I'm sure she'd be very interested in the time you gave —' He snapped his fingers, trying to remember. 'Damn, what was that horse's name again? No, don't tell me, it'll come. Golddust, that's it. Yeah, the time you gave Golddust a good old dose of Danthron. Damn thing shat through the eye of a needle for a week. Got your dose wrong, didn't you? But they were early days, hey. And I've got to give it to you, you learned fast.'

'Shut up.'

Danny's eyes narrowed. 'Your old mum came to the rescue that time, didn't she? Told your old man she'd accidentally poisoned it with some kitchen scraps.' He took a drag and blew out a puff of smoke. 'But she made sure you didn't screw up again. Your poor old man didn't know what the hell was going on that autumn. One minute his horses would be running like they'd had pepper shoved up their arses, and the next they couldn't outrun a donkey.'

'I said, shut up.'

Danny tapped his nose. 'But old Danny-boy knew. Old Danny-boy was watching.'

Aaron took a step toward him.

The smile on Danny's face dropped. 'I wouldn't,' he said. 'I can still go to the stewards.'

It was Aaron's turn to smile. He didn't give a shit any more. Danny could do his worst. He'd already lost the thing that mattered to him most.

'Go right ahead. After this morning, I'm beyond caring.'

Danny glared at him. 'You don't mean that.'

'Actually, I do.' And to Aaron's surprise it was the truth. Danny blabbing would cost him his trainer's licence, but he could always find a normal job, maybe join Josh in the forestry industry, or work as a labourer somewhere. He had to pay for his past and this, like Sophie, was the price. 'Face it, Danny. Blackmail isn't going to work any more. So why don't you just get off my property before I throw you off.' He turned towards the house.

'This is my home,' yelled Danny. 'I belong here. The old man made me a promise. I tell no one what you did and I get to stay here even when I can't ride no more. I kept my part of the deal, you can't break it!'

Aaron stood on the top step, hands on hips, regarding him. He'd always wondered why his father had kept Danny on. Now he knew.

'Well, you're shit out of luck. I'm not my father. I can break any promise I like. Now fuck off.'

For a moment, Aaron thought Danny wasn't going to leave, but then the jockey swore and stomped off to grab his motorbike. He revved and snaked it through the yard, throwing stones and dirt and frightening the horses, before skidding out of the yard and down the drive.

Only when he could no longer hear the bike did Aaron let

himself relax. He walked into the kitchen, filled a glass of water and drank it down in gulps. Still the foul taste in his mouth lingered. He refilled the glass and stared at his favourite photograph. Rodger Laidlaw grinned back at him, his arm around the little boy he'd once loved so much.

'I'm sorry, Dad,' he whispered, and then, with a leaden heart, he headed back outside to wait for Sophie.

TWENTY-FOUR

SOPHIE STARED at the leather head-collar in her hand and grazed her thumb over the shiny engraved brass nameplate fixed to its cheek strap. It seemed so long ago that she was excited by the prospect of bringing Rowdy home, thrilled by the challenge that lay ahead. But now there was no excitement, only heartache, anger and an appalling sense of self doubt.

How could she have gotten things so wrong?

All she wanted to do was hide in her room and cry, but that indulgence would have to wait until Rowdy was safe at Vanaheim. Facing Aaron again would take every drop of courage she had, and for that she needed anger, not anguish and pain.

With an effort, she blinked her tears away and let resentment, indignation, insulted pride and outrage pile up like kindling for the bonfire of her fury.

How dare Aaron accuse her of doping Rowdy? *How dare he?* She could no more hurt a horse than fly it to the moon. If there was any finger-pointing to be done it should be directed right at him. After all, he was the Laidlaw, not her. She grimaced. It was hard to admit but Tess and her father had been right all along. Loving Aaron would only lead to hurt. She could thank her lucky stars their relationship – what there was of it – was now over.

Inflamed, itching for a fight and with not a single despairing thought to hold her back, she walked out of the tack room with her back straight and her head held high. She was bringing her horse home, and no one had better try to stop her.

In the distance, someone revved a motorbike. She threw the halter in the float, and leaned against the side door, listening. As it gunned again, she whistled for Sammy and Del. Only one motorbike had that distinctive ning-ning and that was Danny's, and by the sound of it, he'd turned the bike into Vanaheim's drive and opened the throttle to flat out.

The dogs at her heels, she ran into the tack room and, from a hook high up on the wall, took down her grandfather's old stockwhip. It was heavy – over two and a half metres in length from stock to cracker – and made of fine plaited kangaroo hide. For a brief moment, she fingered the leather but then she took a deep breath and with the lash held looped, she walked back out into the yard.

Sammy and Del were by her feet and the stockwhip uncoiled when Danny pulled to a stop. Sophie watched him, legs apart, shoulders squared, tense and ready. He removed his helmet and eyed her, then dismounted. The dogs took a pace forward. Danny ignored them, exposing his teeth in an ugly grin while continuing to walk toward Sophie.

Del growled a warning. Sophie's fingers tensed around the stockwhip's handle.

He halted, shaking his head and making a tutting sound. A trickle of blood leaked from his nose, but he didn't appear to notice.

'You didn't listen to me, did you? I warned you the boss was no good, but you wouldn't believe me. Now you're all upset.' He sighed theatrically. 'Still, it had to come out sometime.'

'You set me up. You doped my horse.'

'Me? I wouldn't do such a thing. The boss though, well, he knows all about doping horses. Bit of an expert at it, if you must know.' He tutted again. 'Terrible the way he let his father take the blame. The old man was as honest as the day is long. Killed him, it did, knowing his own son had nobbled his horses.'

Sophie narrowed her eyes, her heart crashing against her ribs. 'What are you on about?'

Danny slapped his hand over his mouth. 'Oops. Didn't you know? Oh, what a shame.'

Sophie swallowed. Her throat felt raw.

'Well, I can't say I blame the boss for not telling you. I mean, it's not something you'd want to let on, is it?'

He took another step forward. Sammy and Del bared their teeth, their hackles up. Sophie shushed them. She needed to know what Danny was talking about.

'Are you trying to tell me *Aaron* drugged his father's horses? I don't believe you. If anyone was doing any doping, it'd be you.'

'Ah, ain't that nice. Love really is blind after all,' he said, his voice sickly saccharine. Then he snarled at her. 'Of course it was Aaron who doped the horses, you stupid bitch. Speedballs, stoppers, you name it. He used 'em all. Broke the old man's heart when he found out.'

Sophie didn't want to believe him, but it explained so much – Aaron's assertions that his father was innocent, his need for atonement, the terrible secret he harboured that prevented him from loving her. Danny was telling the truth.

She wanted to cry for Aaron, for herself, but most of all she wanted to know why. Why someone as kind and sensitive as Aaron had done something so terrible, so out of character.

With an effort, she kept her face blank, unwilling to give Danny the satisfaction of seeing her pain. 'You know what, Danny? You're full of it.'

He sneered at her. 'I am, am I? Just goes to show how little you know about the boss. He did it all right.'

'Okay, then. You think you know everything. Tell me why. Why would Aaron do something like that?'

As Danny considered the question, his eyes narrowing with contempt and guile, Sophie realised that whatever he admitted was unlikely to be the truth. The real story would have to come from Aaron.

'For kicks, of course. I told you, the boss ain't all he's cracked up to be. He's got a mean streak.' He wiped his nose on the back of his hand and looked at it, then focused back on Sophie. 'A real mean streak. Like his bitch of a mother.'

That was rubbish and Sophie knew it. If Aaron had drugged his father's horses, he must have had a compelling reason to do so. He loved horses as much as she did. The only animal he'd be capable of harming with callous indifference was Danny.

Suddenly, she understood. She pointed to Danny's nose. 'He knew it was you all along. That's why he wanted me out of the way, so he could give you the hiding you deserved.' She walked toward him, the whip snaking behind her. 'Looks like you got off lightly. If it were me, you wouldn't be talking through that smart mouth of yours right now.' She stopped and then brought the whip up as though she meant to crack it. Danny cringed and shuffled backwards.

'Coward,' she said, smiling. 'But then blackmailers always are.'

Danny gave her a filthy look. 'It's the truth.'

'So what? You're still a blackmailer.' She cocked her head to one side. 'What happened to loyalty, Danny, or have you forgotten about that now Aaron's kicked your skinny arse off Hakea Lodge? Where are you going to go now? From what I can gather, there aren't many trainers who'd be keen to take you on.'

She smiled, enjoying herself. She felt safe in the knowledge that Aaron had acted the way he had only out of fear for her. Even if Danny's doping allegation were true, it wouldn't matter. She loved Aaron. He loved her. She'd forgive him no matter what he'd done.

Danny eyed her and then smugly pursed his lips. 'The boss'll have me back – you'll see.'

'I wouldn't count on it, *Danny-boy*.'

'Oh yeah? You reckon the stewards wouldn't be interested in what I've got to say?'

Sophie kept her face impassive, but inside she was boiling. Poor Aaron. That's what he'd been threatened with for all these years. No wonder he hated Danny.

'Somehow,' said Sophie with all the nonchalance she could muster, 'I don't think they'd believe a word that came out of your mouth. Admit it. You've got nothing left to bargain with.' She rested the whip handle on her shoulder, and regarded him. 'The way I see it, you've got two choices. You can keep your trap shut and maybe find someone stupid enough to take you on, or you can go squealing to the stewards like the little rat you are.' She lifted the whip off her shoulder and pointed the knobbed handle end at him. 'Just remember, the moment you do, it'll all be over. No one likes a telltale. No one.'

He shrugged. 'I might do it just for the fun of seeing the boss go down.'

'But he won't. I'll make sure of it.'

Danny studied her warily. 'Oh yeah, and how d'you reckon you'll manage that?'

'Easy. You think my father would be happy about this coming out?' She smiled, knowing she had him. 'Dad might dislike Aaron, but he loves Carol, and would do anything to protect her. One phone call warning him that this could all be dragged up again and he'll be onto you. You'd want to watch yourself then. Only an idiot would cross Dad.'

'You're bullshitting.'

'Finding his loyalty hard to believe? Well, you would. Because unlike you, *you piece of human garbage,* we Dixons understand the meaning of it.'

Danny lunged at her. The dogs didn't hesitate. They attacked, clamping their teeth down hard into his flesh. Danny bellowed, but kept coming. Sophie didn't have time to think. She used the only weapon she had. She shoved the knobbed end of the whip handle into his stomach, forcing the breath from his lungs.

He collapsed to the ground, trying to clutch at his stomach with an arm held fast in Del's jaw. Sophie called the heelers off. They'd inflicted enough damage. The sleeve of Danny's shirt was torn and bloodied where Del had locked her teeth. Around his calf, a row of puncture holes neatly circled another bite, the denim of his jeans staining slowly crimson. As if in sympathy, Danny's nose started to bleed again.

Sophie looked down at him, panting, adrenaline surging through her veins, and with deliberate menace, tickled the whip's lash against his cheek. 'Get off my property.'

Like a cornered animal, Danny's top lip curled up, exposing his yellow teeth. He crawled to his knees, his eyes glittery with hatred, and then stood. His hands clenched into fists at his side.

Sophie stood her ground and drew on the anger she'd cultivated so carefully against Aaron. Sammy and Del monitored Danny with their hackles raised, baring their teeth in a savage imitation of his misshapen snarl.

His fingers twitched and curled. The dogs growled a warning.

'I wouldn't, if I were you. Next time I won't call them off.'

His eyes dropped to the heelers and then rose back to Sophie.

'Leave. Now.'

He raised a finger and pointed it at her. She waited for him to speak, but he didn't. He just glared at her with malignant eyes, his shoulders rising and falling with his heavy stinking breaths. He coughed, the sound bronchial and thick, then hoicked and spat a globule of smoker's phlegm at her feet. Sophie didn't flinch.

'You'll keep, bitch,' he said, backing up to his bike. 'You'll keep.'

She watched him leave, not allowing herself to relax until the sound of the trail bike had faded into the distance. Only then, when peace had descended on Vanaheim once more, did she fall to her knees and surrender to the fear she'd fought so hard to keep at bay.

Aaron was where Sophie expected him to be – where he always was when something momentous had happened in his life – sitting on Hakea Lodge's back step staring out over the yard. She turned off the Range Rover's engine and smiled at him. He didn't smile back. Instead, he looked achingly sad. A man who had been on the run from his past for so long that he'd shattered the moment it overtook him.

She sighed and stepped out of the car, casting a glance at Rowdy's stable. He wasn't there. She felt a flare of panic, but then she heard a whicker and knew her big horse was fine. She blew a kiss towards his yard but didn't go over to pat him. Miffed, he pointed his rump at her. She ignored him and headed for the steps.

She approached slowly, as if Aaron were a jittery horse that might flee at any moment, her heart squeezing with worry and compassion. He didn't move, just stared at her with his mouth turned down and his eyes full of that unfathomable guilt she'd grown so used to seeing. Stubble flecked his jaw and his eyes were bloodshot, while his blond hair stuck up in tufts, as though he'd tried to tear hanks of it from his head.

She knelt in front of him and took his hands. He stared at their entwined fingers for a moment, and then pulled his from her grip as though he couldn't stand her touch.

She swallowed and shifted to sit beside him, and, unable to help herself, reached for his hand again.

'Don't,' he said.

Her insides curdled with worry. She didn't know how to handle this. She didn't know if he needed her comfort or if he'd be better left alone. Either way, it didn't matter. She couldn't go. The thought of leaving him in misery, having him believe she no longer loved him, was worse than enduring his rejection.

She closed her eyes, wishing, as she had so often in the past, that her mother was alive to help her. But she had no mother, only herself;

she'd have to rely on her own strength to get her through, just as she'd done so many times before.

'You knew Danny did it all along,' she said.

He ran his hand down his face, and then nodded.

'Why didn't you just say so?'

'I needed you away from here.'

'So you could beat him up?'

His head dropped and he stared at his hands.

She touched his shoulder. 'You didn't do a very good job of it. He was still able to walk and talk when he got to Vanaheim.'

'Bastard!' He turned to her, his eyes roving over her face. 'Are you okay?'

'Yeah, I'm fine. I had Sammy and Del, and Pop's old stockwhip.'

'I'm sorry,' he said, returning his gaze to the yard.

'It's okay. I'm fine.'

He shook his head. 'I should have protected you.'

'Aaron, I'm a big girl. I can look after myself.' She smiled. 'I only wish I could have hurt him more.'

Aaron let out a bitter laugh. 'Yeah, me too.'

'But you didn't.'

'He's half my size.'

'So?'

'I hate myself enough as it is without adding that to the list.'

She grabbed his hand. 'Don't say that. I love you. I'll forgive you anything. Even horse doping.'

He stared at her. 'Danny told you?'

'A bit.' She squeezed his fingers, wanting him to look at her, wanting him to see that it was okay. 'Talk to me, Aaron. Tell me everything. Let me prove to you that it doesn't matter.'

He looked away. 'That's not the worst, Sophie.'

'I don't care.'

'I don't know where to start.'

'The beginning will do.'

He pulled his hand from hers and pressed the heel of his palm hard into his forehead. His mouth twisted, and for a moment, Sophie thought he was going to cry.

'All right,' he said eventually. Sophie saw his chest rise as he took a deep breath. 'I was fifteen the first time I nobbled a horse. I gave it Danthron. It's a stopper, a scouring agent, the same one they used on Big Philou before the '69 Melbourne Cup.' He looked at her. 'I got the dose wrong. The horse nearly died.'

Keeping her eyes locked on his, Sophie swallowed her horror, afraid that if she let it show he'd clam up. 'Why did you do it?'

'Mum asked me to.'

She frowned. His *mother* asked him to? Why would she do that? It didn't make sense.

Aaron put his head in his hands and grabbed at his hair. Her hand went to his back, a small comfort when what she really wanted to do was hold him, but the truth had to come out. He'd been burdened with it for long enough.

'Why, Aaron?'

'Mum wanted to leave but she had no money. Everything was tied up in this place. There was already a mortgage on it, not as big as it is now, but from what Mum told me, it was big enough. If she were to get anything, this place would have had to be sold and Dad would have fought tooth and nail to stop that happening. Any settlement would have been tied up in the courts for years.'

'But she still could have left. They could have come to some sort of arrangement. Your dad could have paid her drawings from the business or something.'

He shook his head. 'She told me that, given the circumstances, Dad wouldn't have paid her a cent.'

'What circumstances?'

'Come on, Soph. You can't have forgotten.'

Realisation dawned. Sophie closed her eyes. 'My father.'

'Yeah, your father. Our saintly Member of Parliament. I was fifteen and even I could see he was obsessed with her. The longer it went on, the worse he got. Any time they had together was short, so he made sure they put it to good use. I caught them at it. Several times.' He shook his head. 'They were so wrapped up in one another they never even noticed.'

The house phone rang, making them both jump. Neither of them moved, or spoke. The ringing seemed to go on forever. When it ended, the silence was just as unnerving.

'Where was your dad when all this was going on?' asked Sophie.

'At the races, in the yards, in the paddocks. Wherever the horses were.'

Sophie remembered Aaron's comment about his mother hating not being the centre of attention. She didn't condone Carol Laidlaw's behaviour, or her father's, but she did understand a little how hard it was to come second best in the heart of someone who was supposed to love you.

They were the same, Carol and her father. Carol came second to her husband's horses. Her father came second to his wife's mental illness. No wonder their need for each other became obsessive. It must have been like finding an oasis in the middle of a desert. You couldn't drink from it enough for fear you'd never find another.

'Mum came up with a plan that'd let her quietly leave Dad and move to Canberra to be with Ian,' continued Aaron. 'But Mum being Mum, she didn't want to take responsibility for what she was going to do. She told me Dad would lose the yard if I didn't help her, and I was stupid enough to believe her.'

'You were young, Aaron.'

'No. I was stupid and I was weak, just like I've always been.'

'Don't say that.'

'Why not? It's true.'

'Aaron —'

'Don't, Soph. Just let me get this over with.' He sat stiffly upright, as though she'd placed him in a dock, forcing him to give sworn testimony. 'It was a simple betting scam. I dosed the horses. Mum placed her bets. Normally, it'd be hard to get away with, but Mum was careful. She knew not to bet big and after that first stuff-up we took a lot more care.'

'But surely she knew she'd get caught.'

'Oh yeah, but by then she'd be long gone and I was there to take the fall. I was fifteen, about to turn sixteen. Young. She figured I'd just get off with a warning.'

Sophie looked at him in dismay. 'And you were willing to do that?'

'To save this place? You bet.' He gazed around the yard. 'This place is all Dad had. It's all I have.'

'No, Aaron. You also have me.'

He stood, took a few steps into the yard, and kicked at a clod of dirt. 'I wanted her out of here so much I didn't think about the consequences of what we were doing. I didn't question why she had to do it that way. If I had, I might've worked out it wasn't all about the money – it was about hurting Dad too.' He blinked rapidly, his chest heaving. 'You know what I found out later?'

Sophie shook her head.

'She didn't have to do it. Dad would've taken out another loan and paid her off just to get rid of her. He knew Mum was screwing your old man, but he never bothered doing anything about it.' His eyes shone in the bright morning sunshine. 'I'm so like him it's not funny. We never stand up for anything.'

'You stood up for me,' she said, rising from the step and holding out her hand, begging him to take it. If he'd let her, she could soothe his turmoil, give him back his pride.

He eyed her. 'You really think so? You really think giving Danny a bit of a smack is standing up for you?'

'Yes, of cour—'

'I've never stood up for you, Sophie. Not once.'

The hand she'd held out dropped to her side and she stared at him in disbelief, her mouth open. What was he on about? He'd not only protected her from Danny, he'd protected her from himself when he'd felt the truth would only hurt her.

'I made a promise to you when I was sixteen that I'd look after you, but not once have I done that. Not once.'

'What are you talking about?'

'Your mother!'

Sophie gaped at him, her insides coiling. This was going to be bad, she could see from the look on his face.

Her voice seemed to come from far away. 'What about my mother? What did you do?'

His shoulders sagged. Slowly, he walked back to the step and sat down. He wouldn't look at her.

'When the stewards finally launched an investigation, it didn't take Dad long to work out what had happened. I always assumed it was Mum who'd told him I'd done it, but now I know it was Danny all along. Dad got it into his head that a conviction would ruin my life, so the stupid bugger told the stewards he did it. He lost his licence. Then he started drinking. I don't know why he bothered protecting me. My life ended up ruined anyway.' He stared at his hands. 'I dropped out of school. Danny moved in to help. I couldn't figure out why – he was bloody hopeless – but Dad insisted on paying him to work around the farm. I found out this morning he was black-mailing Dad too. Filthy little bastard.

'I was so angry with everyone. Mum, Dad, your old man – I was furious with them all. But you know who I decided was to blame for all this? Your mother, that's who. It was her fault Ian was screwing Mum. It was her fault Dad was drinking himself to oblivion every day. Her fault my life had turned to shit. I blamed her for everything.'

A tear dribbled down Sophie's cheek.

His tone became brutal. 'One day, Dad was so drunk he couldn't even make it to the toilet. Christ, I was angry. I was sixteen years old and cleaning up my father's piss when I should've been out chasing girls or playing footy or doing whatever it was that normal teenagers did. When I tried to put him to bed, he thumped me. I left him on the floor where he fell, stuck a bandaid over the cut above my eye, then got on the bike and rode straight round to Vanaheim, crying the whole bloody way.

'Your mum comes out of the house, sees me standing at the gate snivelling like a bloody kid and runs up to me all hugs and concern, and what do I do? I tell her everything. Everything, Sophie. I take all my bitterness and frustration out on her simply because I can't take it out on my own mother. And so I blame her. I tell her it's all her fault.'

Sophie began to shake.

'And you know what she does? She tells me I'm right, it is all her fault. And then she hugs me again and tells me that she's sorry but she's going to make it better now, and I should go home and look after my dad because he needs me.'

He took a deep breath. Sophie wanted to slap her hand over his mouth, to stop him saying what she knew was coming, but her body had turned numb.

'No,' she whispered. 'No.'

'That afternoon,' said Aaron, his voice cracking, 'your mother killed herself.'

TWENTY-FIVE

IT FELT like an hour passed before her sobs quietened to shallow hiccups. Sophie pressed the side of her head against the verandah post, blinking against a morning that seemed far too vivid. Tiredness seeped through her body and her bones began to ache, the way they did whenever she came down with the flu.

Aaron sat still on the step staring blankly at the yard. She remembered him trying to hold her and her shoving him away as she succumbed to her all-encompassing grief. He glanced at her.

'I went to the funeral, you know. You were there standing between your father and your aunt. You kept looking around as if you expected your mother to turn up, and then you looked at your father and tried to take his hand.'

'He snatched it away,' said Sophie, closing her eyes at the memory.

'Yes.'

'And then I started to cry.'

'No, Sophie. You started to scream.'

She opened her eyes and stared at him. 'Did I? I don't remember.'

'I made you a promise then that I'd look after you.'

'But you didn't.'

'No. I should have been your friend, but I wasn't.' He stood and looked down at her. 'I'm so very sorry, Sophie. For everything.'

She watched him as he walked toward Rowdy. He'd warned her multiple times that she'd never forgive him for what he'd done. *You won't be able to scrub hard enough to clean yourself of me.* He'd cautioned her and she'd heard him, but not once had she believed him. She'd never comprehended it could be this bad.

This was the man she'd loved, suffered sleepless nights for, endured endless doubts over. And he'd let her, knowing he'd done this. She bowed her head and waited for the nausea she knew was coming to wash over her. It didn't arrive. Instead, all she felt was sorrow.

Aaron tied Rowdy to the side of the float and moved to the back to unlock the ramp. He glanced at her, as if checking to see he was doing the right thing. She felt swamped by inertia, unable to rise and help him, lacking the energy to tell him to stop.

Rowdy walked up the ramp without hesitating. Aaron fixed the breech door and locked the tailgate into place. He patted Rowdy's rump, and came to stand in front of her with his hands in his pockets.

'He's right to go. Will you be okay, or do you want me to drive you?'

Sophie swallowed. She didn't know if she was capable of even making it to the car.

He crouched down. 'Sophie?'

She tried to speak, but her throat closed over and it was hard to breathe. She reached out to touch his face. He took her hand, stopping her.

'Come on,' he said. 'I'll drive you.'

She let him pull her upright and lead her to the Range Rover. Words swarmed through her head, confetti pieces printed with all the things she wanted to say, but too scattered to make sense of.

She sat in the passenger seat staring out of the windscreen, wishing her brain would start working again. Aaron stepped into the driver's seat and turned the key. The car chugged into life. Music filtered through the speakers and into her head. The latest hit for a former boy-band leader turned solo artist. A love song.

She stared at the radio, wondering what the hell that idiot would know about love. The internet was full of his kiss-and-tell stories. As if reading her mind, Aaron switched it off. She returned her blank gaze to the windscreen.

They didn't speak on the short drive to Vanaheim. Sophie still didn't know what she wanted to say. She didn't even know how she felt. Except that she was tired. So very, very tired.

When they pulled into the yard, she sat in the car with the door open but didn't get out. Aaron unloaded Rowdy, and put him in his box. He circled the stable, sniffing. A horse called from the front paddock. He lifted his head, ears pricked and alert as though his ordeal had never happened. Sammy and Del sat by the open door with their heads cocked, whining for attention. She couldn't even find the energy to pat them.

'Here,' Aaron said, holding out his hand. 'Let's get you inside.'

She looked up at him. All she saw on his face was concern, not love. Maybe love had never been there. Maybe it had been an illusion projected by her need. She dropped her eyes. 'I'm okay.'

She wasn't. She wasn't okay at all, but she still couldn't find the words to express her feelings. She loved. She hated. But she didn't know where those emotions were directed. Towards him? Her mother? His mother? Her father?

He took her hand anyway. She didn't resist, following him into the house like a child.

'Do you want a cup of tea?' he said, when they reached the kitchen.

She shook her head. Her phone sat in the middle of the breakfast bar where she'd thrown it. She stared at the icon-lit screen, her back to him. She reached out a finger and pressed the button for her message bank. Ben's tinny voice echoed through the speaker.

'Sophie, it's Ben. I just wanted to wish you luck today. I know how important this race is for you. Ah, anyway, good luck and I'll talk to you next week about those soil tests we planned.'

'He really likes you, Soph.'

She deleted the message. Her hand shook. 'I'm tired,' she said. 'I want to go to bed.'

'Okay.'

She heard him move toward the door, and her stomach filled with dread. He was leaving.

'Don't go.'

'Sophie —'

She turned to him. 'Please.'

He stared at her, his eyes luminous. She held out her hand. It still shook. 'Please,' she whispered.

She led him to the bedroom. He stopped in the doorway but she pulled on his arm and forced him to follow her in. She lay on the bed. He stood by it, looking down. She stroked the space beside her and pleaded with her eyes.

'Hold me,' she whispered and he did, cradling her gently, as if she were the most precious thing on earth.

'I'm so sorry.'

She knew he was. He'd been sorry for years, weighed down by the terrible consequences of his actions. Guilt was the heaviest of emotions. She knew, because she'd carried it herself. Her mother's suicide had scarred them all.

She pressed her mouth against his throat. His pulse beat against her lips. He swallowed and tensed. She wanted to tell him it wasn't what he thought. She wasn't coming on to him. She just wanted to feel life.

He pulled away from her, his eyes travelling over her face, trying to read what she was thinking. 'I have to go now, Sophie.'

She clutched at him. 'No.'

'It's better this way.'

'No. You don't understand. I still love you.'

He pressed his head against her forehead. 'You can't.'

'I can. I do. I love you. Don't go. Please don't go.' She began to cry again. 'I don't care what you did. *I don't care.* She would have done it anyway. You were just an excuse.'

'You don't know that.'

'I do. I know what she was going through. I know what she was feeling. I've been there. Another day, another time, it doesn't matter. She would have found an excuse to do it.' Sophie held out her arms to him, showing him her scars. 'Look, look. I did that, Aaron. I know. If it hadn't been Michael, it would've been someone else, something else. You were an excuse, just like Michael was an excuse.'

He held her to his chest, soothing her as she cried. 'Shh, shh, it's okay. It's okay.'

But it wasn't okay. If he walked out of Vanaheim, she knew he'd never come back. There'd be nothing left, because he wouldn't let there be anything. The idea sent her into freefall. She pushed away from him so she could see his face.

'Don't leave me. I couldn't stand it.'

He stroked her cheek. 'You'll feel differently tomorrow.'

'I won't. I love you.'

'You're upset. In shock. You need time to think.'

She shook her head. When it came to him, she didn't need to think. She knew.

Very gently, he pressed his lips against her forehead and held them there. Then he rolled off the bed and sat at the edge. He said nothing for a moment, just sat with his back hunched and his head down.

'I can't forgive myself for what I did, Soph. It's too big.'

She kneeled and draped herself over him, pressing her mouth against his ear. 'But *I* can forgive *you*, Aaron. The past is over. We can't change it no matter how much we might want to.'

'If you still feel the same tomorrow morning, come and see me,' he said, but there was no hope in his voice. Then he prised her loose, stood and walked to the bedroom door. His hand gripped the jamb as though he was trying to stop himself stepping through. He looked at her over his shoulder. 'Will you be okay?'

She nodded, feeling numb.

'Promise me, Sophie. Promise me you won't —' His head dropped. 'I know you said you're fine now, but I worry about you. All the time.'

'If you're worried, then stay.'

'I can't.'

'Why not, Aaron? Why not?'

'Because I don't want to see the look on your face when you wake up and realise how much you hate me.'

Sophie wished she could find the words to convince him, but her head still felt groggy. 'I won't hate you. I love you,' she said, though she knew it wouldn't be enough. He needed proof. 'I'll see you tomorrow, Aaron. First thing, I promise.'

They stared at one another, and she saw it. The feeling he refused to admit, the single thing that could sustain them through this.

'Aaron, do you love me?'

He didn't answer.

'Do you?'

'I have to go.' He gave her one last look and then disappeared.

Sophie got up and ran out into the hall after him. Aaron was at the back door. She took two steps, then halted. The door closed with a quiet click. Her shoulders sagged, weighed down by a fatigue she'd never encountered before, the aftermath of her fear, adrenaline and shock-filled morning.

With dragging steps, she walked back to her bedroom. She picked up a photograph of her mother from the bedside table. Fiona Dixon smiled happily at her.

Summoning all the energy she had, Sophie threw the frame at the wall.

TWENTY-SIX

THE MORGUE HADN'T CHANGED. If anything, it was even colder and more dismal than when Aaron had last experienced its grey-walled desolation.

He sat on a creaking plastic chair staring at his hands. He didn't want to be here, he wanted to be home, at Hakea Lodge, waiting on the verandah step for someone he knew would never come. But Danny had no next of kin and so the police had called him, and now he was here, at Harrington Base Hospital, surrounded by the bleak memories of another time.

The phone call had come just after three a.m., waking him in a panic, frightening him into saying Sophie's name down the mouthpiece. No, they said. Not Sophie. Danny. He'd collapsed back onto the bed saying, 'Thank God' over and over like a mantra until the caller coughed politely and dragged him back to the matter at hand.

Motorbike accident, they told him. Head-first into a tree. Dead on impact. Too drunk to feel anything anyway. Then they asked if he knew where the hospital morgue was and he'd told them that, yeah, he knew. He would find it again. He didn't want to, but he would.

The morgue was where they had taken his father. Cerebral

aneurism, they'd told him then. No, he'd replied, Shame. The doctor and attendant had looked at one another, and then left him alone in that frigid room with the corpse of his father and his dry-eyed but gut-wrenching grief.

He'd stroked his father's hair, grey where it had once been as blond as his own. Then he'd leaned down and kissed his forehead, all the time swearing that, somehow, he'd make it up to him. He'd turn Hakea Lodge around, become a trainer his father could admire, a son he could be proud of. It wasn't a promise he had fulfilled yet, but he would. It was all he had left.

Aaron rubbed a hand over his face, trying to erase the picture of his father on the trolley, dreading seeing the same thing again. He didn't want to crack in front of these people. He didn't want them thinking he was crying over Danny.

It hadn't surprised him to get the call. Danny drank too much, smoked incessantly, made enemies. If it hadn't been a motorbike accident, it would have been a street fight or drunken walk into traffic.

He supposed he should feel sad. A man had died, after all, but he couldn't raise an ounce of feeling. If anything, fluttering in the back of his mind was a profound sense of release. Danny was dead. He couldn't hurt any of them any more.

An attendant called his name. He rose and followed him into the room. He did what he had to do quickly and walked out, his nostrils full of the antiseptic harshness of that place of death.

He drove home and though it was early, set about sorting the horses. With no Danny to help, the routine would take longer and he needed a distraction from the horror in his head, of Danny's distorted face and broken body. He worked hard and fast, distributing feeds, mucking out, lunging horses that needed exercise, all the while alert to cars in the lane or the clip-clop of an approaching horse.

Nine o'clock came and went. The next hour dashed by even faster. No matter how many times he looked, the lane remained empty, the horses restful. They dozed with half-closed eyelids, heads low and ears flopped. He wished he could be like them. At peace.

He'd always known this would be the outcome, yet somehow he'd kept a fragment of faith burning. As he stood in his kitchen and watched the clock's minute hand move another notch closer to eleven, the hope he'd nurtured began to die. Finally, it went out.

To escape what wasn't there and with the vague idea of sorting through Danny's things, he drove to the flat, slowing as he passed Vanaheim, not seeing Sophie, but all too aware of the void she'd left.

Like Danny himself, the flat reeked of cigarettes and unwashed clothes, but it was surprisingly tidy. The jockey appeared to have collected few possessions in the time he'd lived there. Aaron looked at the cheap furniture, the rattling ancient fridge and the grimy threadbare carpet, and thought what a sad indictment of a man's life it was.

He wandered toward the bed, his attention caught by an eerie incongruity. Though the rest of the flat looked impoverished, five polished and dusted silver photo frames took pride of place on Danny's chipped and stained bedside table.

And every single one of them was of Hakea Lodge.

Aaron couldn't remember Danny taking any photographs even though Aaron himself appeared in two of them. The other three featured his father. He picked up what he guessed was the oldest. Looking ridiculously boyish, Danny grinned at the camera while Rodger Laidlaw smiled down at him, his arm slung around the young jockey's shoulder.

Aaron sat down on the bed staring at it, all thought of cleaning the flat gone, and quietly mourned a man who he now realised had loved his father. A man who had loved Hakea Lodge as much as he did. They should have been friends, but instead they had ended up hating one another. And now they would never reconcile.

Carefully, he put the photo back in its place and then, for the first time since he was sixteen, he allowed himself to cry for all that he had lost.

———

By the time he made it home it was past midday. When he saw the empty yard, his breath came out in a shudder. Though he knew it was pointless, there had still been a tiny spark of hope in his heart that Sophie would be there, waiting for him.

You should have told her you loved her.

But then, he should have done a lot of things.

He felt another stupid surge of hope as he opened the back door, but there was no note from her on the kitchen table, and no message on the answering machine. He pulled his phone from his pocket. As it had appeared all morning, the screen remained blank. Desolate, he tossed it on the table.

It was time for the fool's fantasy to end. Sophie wasn't coming. Then again, he'd known that all along.

He made himself a sandwich, but found he couldn't eat it. He tried to read the paper instead, but the words kept turning backwards, as though he'd suddenly developed dyslexia. He tossed the paper aside and tipped his tea down the sink. Through the kitchen window, he spied the jaundiced lawn he'd planted to replace his mother's garden. Despite a lack of care, it had grown. He decided then he'd get the mower out and cut it.

Anything to take his mind off Sophie.

Lawn mowing only killed an hour, so he went in search of other jobs. He settled on cleaning out the feed room. It was a mess – a result of too many hours spent mooning over Sophie when he should have been paying attention to the yard.

He filled all the feed buckets with soapy water, scrubbed them out, and left them in the sun to dry. Then he laid out a tarp in the yard and hauled sacks of oats, corn and chaff onto it. He washed down the steel racks where he kept veterinary supplies, dusted the contents and replaced them neatly on the shelves. He folded empty chaff bags into stacks and tied them in bundles ready for recycling, then spent a sneeze-filled hour dusting cobwebs and sweeping the floor, swearing when Hakea Lodge's overstuffed resident carpet python frightened yet another year off his life.

When it was all done, he made up the evening feeds and distributed them to the horses. As they ate, he mucked out the yards, then, struck by a money-making idea, spent another hour shovelling horse manure into empty corn sacks. He'd advertise them for sale in the local paper. Gardeners loved that sort of stuff.

As Aaron had intended, by the time he trudged toward the house, he was exhausted. Weariness seeped through his bones, cramped his strained muscles, stung his bloodshot eyes, but it couldn't mask the ache he felt for Sophie. He grabbed a beer from the fridge and took it outside, but not to his customary verandah step. Instead, he walked to the front of the house and sat in his filthy clothes on the porch, staring at the road, waiting for a car that would never come.

Tomorrow would be another hard day. Alone, it would take all morning to muck out, feed and work the horses. Then, in preparation for the arrival of his new charges, he'd spend the afternoon clearing out the soiled sand of Pollyanna's and Costa Motza's yards and replacing it with fresh fill. Back-breaking work. Exactly what he needed.

He finished his beer and watched the sun drop slowly in the evening sky, trying not to think of Sophie. It was over. He had to be strong, like her, and let it go. She hadn't come. She wasn't going to come. He had to accept it.

But still he waited, and it was only when true darkness fell, when he couldn't see the road any more, that he finally gave up and, with slow, tired steps, walked into the house.

A hot shower made him clean, but he didn't feel any better. He stared at his stubbly reflection and thought how old he looked, as though time had carved fissures in his face when he wasn't looking. He knew it was fatigue, but he sensed there was something else too.

Heartache, he supposed. Regret.

He shaved, hoping that might make him feel more human, knowing he was kidding himself, but he found it helped a little, so he brushed his teeth as well, applied deodorant, combed his hair. He looked at himself again and smiled wryly.

Add a clean pressed shirt, some nice jeans and polished boots, and he'd be ready for a night out on the town, chasing girls with Josh. Perhaps one day, he might even be up for that again. Sometime in the distant future when he'd finally recovered from loving Sophie.

He shook his head. Who was he kidding? By the time that day arrived, he'd be stuck chatting up the old biddies in his nursing home.

He wrapped a towel round his hips and wandered out into the kitchen to where he'd left his clothes warming by the stove. Three steps in, he stopped, shocked.

Standing by the sink with that shy smile curving her mouth, and her grey eyes huge with hope and longing, was Sophie.

TWENTY-SEVEN

SOPHIE GAZED AT AARON, waiting for him to speak. He didn't. He just stared with wide eyes. Neither of them moved. As the seconds passed, the silence began to thrum.

And then it began to hurt.

Her smile slipped. She crossed her arms, lifted her thumb to her mouth intending to gnaw on the nail, but then dropped it.

'I came this morning,' she said, her voice betraying her anguish. 'But you weren't home.'

She'd wanted to come first thing, as she'd said she would, but the long, restless night convinced her she needed time to probe her feelings. Her choice affected Aaron's life as much as hers, and for his sake as well as her own, she wanted to be sure. So she'd turned to the friend she could rely on most, who'd been with her through the worst and best, whose affection and loyalty was unquestioned.

Chuck had quivered with delight at being saddled again. The moment she mounted, he broke into a jog, snatching at his bit, eager to be off. Sophie let him have his head, laughing as he put in several happy pigroots, and rode him out to Vanaheim's highest point. Sensing her need for calm, Chuck had stood quietly while she stared into the distance toward Harrington cemetery, and there she'd thought about her mother, her father, about Tess and Carol. About forgiveness and what it meant. Whether love could really bury the past.

Then, though she still had no answers, she'd turned Chuck down the hill and they'd ridden along the stock lane to the gate of the lowest paddock and gazed across at Hakea Lodge.

In the morning glow, the land looked magical. Mist lay thick in the hollows, curling around the landscape like an ethereal fleece. Stroking Chuck's neck, she explained to him all that had happened. Telling him her fears and doubts. How she wanted to be certain that in a day, a week, a month's time, she'd still be able to hold forgiveness and understanding in her heart.

As she spoke, the sun rose higher and warmed the countryside, and the mist turned cobwebby, as though a thousand spiders had cast their silk during the night. Slowly it burned away, exposing the yard and Aaron's house.

Revealing the truth of where her heart and her future lay.

Smiling, she'd gathered the reins, kicked Chuck into a canter and, ignoring the startled whinnies of Buck and Costa Motza as they passed, ridden straight to Hakea Lodge.

Only to find the place deserted and the kitchen, when she walked inside, as quiet as it was right now.

Unnerved by Aaron's silence, she raised her thumb again and gnawed at the nail. Still he said nothing. He just stared at her with eyes that expressed nothing but disbelief and something else she couldn't fathom. Something that sent fear crawling between her shoulderblades. Something terrible.

'Danny's dead,' he said.

She couldn't help the rush of relief or the sigh that emerged from her mouth. She understood now. Aaron's heart was in turmoil, torn between guilt and relief. She still had hope.

Danny's death – any death – was tragic but she had loathed the jockey as much as he had hated her. He had threatened her, attacked her on her own property. Sophie refused to feign sorrow.

'How?'

'Drunk. Lost control of his bike. Hit a tree.'

'Forgive me if I can't find any words of sympathy.'

He nodded. He stood on the other side of the kitchen staring at her, bare-chested, with only a towel hugging his hips. Once more, silence throbbed between them.

Droplets of water sparkled on Aaron's shoulders where they had fallen from his wet hair. Except for the tan that covered his forearms and ranged halfway up his biceps his skin was pale, coloured only by a dark-blond sprinkling of hair that rose up his belly and then spread lightly across his chest. Although Sophie had pressed against his body, she saw he was far more muscled that she had realised. Not body-builder six-pack muscled, but firm and fit-looking, with shoulders and arms that made her think of protection and safety and all-encompassing love.

'Why didn't you wait or come back?' he asked suddenly, and the cracked edge in his voice told her the answer was important, that his next move depended on it.

Her eyes prickled with tears. The dismay she'd felt at finding Hakea Lodge empty hadn't left her all day, no matter how many times she'd tried to convince herself Aaron's absence wasn't deliberate. Nor could she shake the memory of his leaving Vanaheim the day before. She'd thought she'd seen love in his eyes. She'd thought she knew the truth. Yet he had left without answering her question, without admitting what he felt.

Perhaps it was because he couldn't.

It was that fear that had stopped her from waiting, had kept her from returning, trapped her immobile with uncertainty until her deep, desperate need had finally driven her back to his door. Back to the man she loved but could still lose.

And now it had come down to this.

She crossed her arms over her chest and hugged herself – a pathetic shield against the rejection she still feared would come.

'I thought you were hiding from me. That you didn't want me to come.' She stared at him, willing him to understand. 'I thought I had it wrong again. That maybe you didn't care about me at all.'

'Oh, Soph. You know that's not true.'

'Isn't it?'

'No.'

She chewed at her bottom lip. This wasn't how she wanted it to go. She'd imagined some stupid romantic falling into arms and passionate kisses and declarations of love. But this was awkward and tense and she didn't know how it would end. She didn't know if he was going to accept her forgiveness, when his acceptance was the very thing her heart craved. She *loved* him and that feeling would never stop, no matter what he believed.

'I wanted you to come, Sophie,' he said quietly. 'I hoped and prayed for it, but I never thought you would. I thought you'd —' He stopped and looked at the ceiling, his eyes shining.

'You thought I'd wake up and all that love I had would have turned into hate.'

He nodded.

'It hasn't. It never will. I still love you. I can't stop.'

He ran his hand through his half-dry hair, sending it sticking up at angles.

'You don't believe me?'

'I want to, Soph. More than anything, I want to.'

Hope sent a warm flush through her breast. She had to ask. She had to find out for sure. More than ever, she needed the truth.

'Aaron, do you love me?'

He gazed at her, blue eyes fathomless but warm, and growing warmer with every beat of her buoyant heart.

She waited, her breath suspended, her mind tumbling between uncertainty and the promise she saw in his expression. The promise of a future overflowing with love.

Then he crossed the room and cupped warm hands around her face. He smiled tenderly, and her heart floated out of her chest, hovering above them like a love-filled balloon. The truth was hers at last, gifted in a single smile like a luminous pearl. A treasure just for her.

'I'm crazy about you, Soph. You're the most beautiful person I've ever known. Inside. Outside. All over.'

A teardrop swelled in her eye, fat and hot. 'Do you mean it?'

He nodded and gently kissed the corner of her eye, capturing the tear before it fell. 'Yeah. I mean it. I've always meant it.'

And then, even more slowly, copying the moves he'd made all those months ago in the feed room, he brushed his delicious lips over her eyelids, before tracking his way toward her mouth in a dozen delicate kisses.

For a brief second, she fretted he was going to stop. That he was going to pull away and rub his hands through his hair and tell her he'd made a terrible mistake. But his lips stayed where they were, moving softly against her skin as he gave voice to a sentiment that came from the very depths of his heart.

'I'm sorry, Sophie. I'm sorry I've hurt you so much. I'm sorry for everything.'

'I know you are. But it doesn't matter any more. I love you and that's all that counts.'

He pulled away slightly to look at her with eyes desperate for reassurance. 'Promise me it's okay, Soph. Promise me you want this. Promise me —' His voice choked.

'That I forgive you?'

He nodded.

'I promise you all that and more.'

Arms that spoke of strength and safety hauled her against his bare chest and she knew this was the place she belonged, in his arms, hearing his heart pound. Feeling his lips moving in her hair as he whispered the words she had once doubted she would ever hear.

'I love you, Soph. You make everything bright and beautiful and give me happiness and hope.'

'And I love you.' She pushed away from his chest and gazed up at him, her mouth twitching with a grin that wanted to beam out like the sun. 'But if you don't kiss me right now, I'm going to explode.'

He laughed and then in one swift movement his mouth was on hers, kissing her with exquisite, heart-twisting tenderness. A tenderness that soon gave way to passion as Sophie melted against him.

'I'll never fail you again, Soph. I promise,' he whispered, abandoning her mouth to kiss his way across her face and down her neck, as if he didn't want to leave a single patch of her skin unblessed. 'Never.'

But the promise was unnecessary.

It was something she knew already.

———

Sophie half-opened an eye. Aaron was propped against the pillow with his head in his hand staring at her. She smiled.

'How long have you been looking at me like that?'

'About an hour,' he replied, then leaned over and kissed her.

'Good morning.'

'And good morning to you.'

She rolled to her side. He reached out and brushed his index finger over the nub of her nipple, sending a delicious thrill to her groin. Her breath caught. Excitement flared in Aaron's eyes. He stroked again and she closed her eyes, her mouth parted as she concentrated on the rush of feeling.

'Christ, you're beautiful,' he said, before pressing his mouth against hers.

The night before, he'd made love to her like she'd always dreamed he would. With infinite desire and breathtaking care. His own pleasure had come second to hers, so much so that she'd had to ask him to stop, to let her to explore and learn and delight in his body. To allow her the thrill of giving.

And when they'd finished, drowsy, at peace and wrapped in love, he'd laid his head on her chest and listened to her heartbeat with closed eyes as she'd stroked his hair and floated on a cloud of pure bliss, knowing this would be hers forever. But most of all, knowing he was healing, one perfect kiss at a time.

He broke the kiss to say, 'I love you.'

She grinned and pulled him on top of her. 'And I adore you. You snored, by the way.'

'I was happy. That's the best night's sleep I've had in months.'

'Good. I hope it's the first of many.'

They smiled at one another and Sophie felt so full of love she could burst, but then Aaron sobered.

'Can I ask you something?'

'Anything,' she said, tickling his sides. 'I'm all yours. Mind, body and soul. Especially body.'

He didn't laugh or squirm as he had the night before when she'd discovered his hidden ticklish spots. The serious expression remained in place.

'Who's Michael?'

She frowned. Michael? Then she understood. Her eyes slid away from his. Why did he have to ask? Why did he have to spoil this moment, this first, perfect morning with that? Michael Fenton was the last person she wanted to talk about. He was part of a past she'd already left.

'No one important.'

His expression clouded. 'Soph, you're lying, and you never lie. Who is he?'

'I told you,' she said, trying to wriggle from under him, 'he's no one important.'

He grabbed her arms and turned them over until her scars showed. 'He did this, didn't he?'

'No, Aaron. I did that. No one else. Me.'

He stared at her, blinking.

She pulled her arms from his grip and reached up to hold his face between her hands. This was something he had to understand. He couldn't keep festering over it. These scars had faded. They no longer held meaning.

'I'm not doing this with you. You have to stop. I'm responsible for what I did, not Michael. Just like you're not responsible for Mum. You didn't kill her. She did that all by herself, just like I did this all by myself. Don't spoil our first morning together by raking up the past. It's over, gone forever. I love you. That's all you need to know.'

He shook his head, then picked up her hands, kissed both palms and pressed them together, holding his kisses against her skin. 'I don't deserve you.'

'Yeah, you do.' She winked. 'Now, where were we before you so rudely interrupted?'

'I think I was about to tell you how much I love you.'

'Liar,' she said, wiggling her eyebrows and tugging a hand from his to trace a fingertip down his chest. 'I think you had more on your mind than love.'

'You reckon?'

'I know.'

He tucked a loose hair behind her ear and smiled. 'You're beautiful, you know. Inside and out.'

She kissed the tip of his nose. 'So you've said, but if it's not too much trouble, can we cut the sweet-talk and get on with it? I've a lot of catching up to do.'

For a moment, he looked at her, stunned, then he laughed. 'Well,' he said, nuzzling her neck and running warm hands over her fast-rousing body, 'a good trainer always follows his owner's orders . . .'

Heart
OF THE VALLEY
CATHRYN
HEIN

A vivid, moving and passionate story of love and redemption set in the gloriously rich landscape of Australia's Hunter Valley.

Brooke Kingston is smart, capable and strong-willed, and runs her family's property with dedication and skill. More at home on horseback than in heels, her life revolves around her beloved 'boys' – showjumpers Poddy, Oddy and Sod.

Then a tragic accident leaves Brooke a mess. Newcomer Lachie Cambridge is hired to manage the farm, and Brooke finds herself out of a job and out of luck. But she won't go without a fight.

What she doesn't expect is Lachie himself – a handsome, gentle giant with a will to match her own. But with every day that Lachie stays, Brooke's future on the farm becomes more uncertain.

Will she be forced to choose between her home and the man she's falling for, or will the very things that brought them together tear them apart?

Order your copy in ebook or paperback from your favourite retailer today.

DEAR READER

Thank you so much for reading *The Horseman's Promise*. I hope you enjoyed Sophie and Aaron's journey to love and happiness. If you did, and you have a few moments, I'd be very grateful if you could leave a rating or few words in review to help others discover my books.

If you'd like to know when my next release comes available plus gain access to exclusive content, news and giveaways, please subscribe to my newsletter via my website.

More information about me and my books, including the inspiration behind *The Horseman's Promise*, along with plenty of other fun stuff, can be found at cathrynhein.com.

Web: cathrynhein.com
Facebook: facebook.com/cathrynhein
Twitter: @CathrynHein